HOME PAGES THAT
WILL TRAP THE UNWARY....

Here's your chance to surf a very special Net, one that offers you sixteen different glimpses of the day after tomorrow in such biting tales as:

"The Coyote Virus"—Sometimes it takes bringing myth into reality to win the war between the sexes....

"Freedom"—Betrayed by her own body, an unwanted burden to her family, Cora found a second chance at life on the Net....

"O! The Tangled Web"—What kind of power would you have if you could access other times and alternate worlds?

"Jarvik Hearts"—Will they be able to trap a killer who is murdering AIs over the Net?

FUTURE NET

D0681862

FUTURE NET

EDITED BY

MARTIN H. GREENBERG

AND

LARRY SEGRIFF

DAW BOOKS, INC.
DONALD A. WOLLHEIM, FOUNDER
375 Hudson Street, New York, NY 10014

ELIZABETH R. WOLLHEIM
SHEILA E. GILBERT
PUBLISHERS

ACKNOWLEDGMENTS

Introduction © 1996 by Larry Segriff.
Zoomers © 1996 by Gregory Benford.
Someone Who Understands Me © 1996 by Matthew
  Costello.
The Coyote Virus © 1996 by Josepha Sherman.
Prometheus Bringing Fire © 1996 by Robin Wayne
  Bailey.
Freedom © 1996 by Mickey Zucker Reichert.
Redemption Inc. © 1996 by Gary A. Braunbeck.
O! The Tangled Web © 1996 by John DeChancie.
Jarvik Hearts © 1996 by Wil McCarthy.
Lover Boy © 1996 by Daniel Ransom.
Cyberspace Cadet © 1996 by Paul Dellinger.
Shining On © 1996 by Billie Sue Mosiman.
Souvenirs and Photographs © 1996 by Jody Lynn Nye.
Ghost in the Machine © 1996 by John Helfers.
Memories of Marie's Shoe © 1996 by Brooks Peck.
Web-Surfing Past Lives © 1996 by Jane Lindskold.
Fatal Error 1000 © 1996 by Barbara Paul.

CONTENTS

INTRODUCTION

Web browsers. FTP. Java terminals. URLs. Gopher, Archie, Veronica. HTML. The World Wide Web.

There's a new language evolving today, a language developing in parallel with the explosion of computers and computer networks. A few years ago, all anyone needed in order to get the maximum performance out of a PC were a few DOS commands and the proprietary keystrokes for Lotus 1–2–3, DBase, or WordPerfect. Those days are gone. Now users are linking together in ever larger networks, from LANs to WANs to the Internet itself, and these networks are evolving into a world of their own.

They have their own language, their own protocols, their own codes of behavior, from spamming to flame wars to netiquette. They have become a complex and complicated environment, every bit as foreign and as inexplicable to many of us as the face of Venus or the dark side of the moon.

And this is only the beginning. Artificial intelligence and true virtual reality—once thought to be as elusive as cold fusion and the Dean Drive—are looming just over the horizon. When they arrive, no one will be able to predict what shape the networks of tomorrow will take.

Or will they?

We've gathered together some of today's hottest writers—from seasoned professionals to up-and-coming newcomers, from authors who banged out their first stories on manual typewriters to writers who grew up with a mouse in one hand and a joystick in the other—and we asked them all the same question: what will the future nets be like? How will people interact with them and rely on them? What kinds of crimes might take place there?

And here are their answers: sixteen stories that take place in the networks of tomorrow. Some are near future, others are farther down the road, but all of them are finely crafted speculations on what our future might hold.

So sit back, turn the brightness up on your monitor so you can read this better, and jack in to the networks of tomorrow.

ZOOMERS
by Gregory Benford

Gregory Benford is a professor of physics at the University of California, Irvine, where he conducts research in plasma turbulence theory and astrophysics. He has served as an adviser to the Department of Energy, NASA, and the White House Council on Space Policy. Benford is also the author of more than a dozen novels, including *Jupiter Project, Against Infinity, Great Sky River,* and *Timescape.* A two-time winner of the Nebula Award, Benford has also won the John W. Campbell Award, the Australian Ditmar Award, and the United Nations Medal in Literature.

She climbed into her yawning work pod, coffee barely getting her going. A warning light winked: her Foe was already up and running. Another day at the orifice.

The pod wrapped itself around her as tabs and inserts slid into place. This was the latest gear, a top of the line simulation suit immersed in a data-pod of beguiling comfort.

Snug. Not a way to lounge, but to *fly.*

She closed her eyes and let the sim-suit do its stuff.

May 16, 2046. She liked to start in real-space. Less jarring.

Images played directly upon her retina. The entrance protocol lifted her out of her Huntington Beach apartment and in a second she was zooming over rooftops, skating down the beach. Combers broke in soft white bands and red-suited surfers caught them in passing marriage.

All piped down from a satellite view, of course, sharp and clear.

Get to work, Myung, her Foe called. *Sightsee later.*

"I'm running a deep search," she lied.

Sure.

"I'll spot you a hundred creds on the action," she shot back.

You're on. Big new market opening today. A hint of mockery?

"Where?" Today she was going to nail him, by God.

Right under our noses, the way I sniff it.

"In the county?"

Now, that would be telling.

Which meant he didn't know.

So: a hunt. Better than a day of shaving margins, at least.

She and her Foe were zoomers, ferrets who made markets more efficient. Evolved far beyond the primitivo commodity traders of the late TwenCen, they moved fast, high-flying for competitive edge.

They zoomed through spaces wholly insubstantial, but that was irrelevant. Economic pattern-spaces were as tricky as mountain crevasses. And even hard cash just stood for an idea.

Most people still dug coal and grew crops, ancient style grunt labor—but in Orange County you could easily forget that, gripped by the fever of the new.

Below her, the county was a sprawl, but a smart one. The wall-to-mall fungus left over from the TwenCen days was gone. High-rises rose from lush parks. Some even had orange grove skirts, a chic nostalgia. Roofs were eco-virtue white. Blacktop streets had long ago added a sandy-colored coating whose mica sprinkles winked up at her. Even cars were in light shades. All this to reflect sunlight, public advertisements that everybody was doing something about global warming.

The car-rivers thronged streets and freeways (still

free—if you could get the license). When parked, cars were tucked underground. Still plenty of scurry-scurry, but most of it mental, not metal.

She sensed the county's incessant pulse, the throb of the Pacific Basin's hub, pivot point of the largest zonal economy on the planet.

Felt, not *saw.* Her chest was a map. Laguna Beach over her right nipple, Irvine over the left. Using neural plasticity, the primary sensory areas of her cortex "read" the county's electronic Mesh through her skin.

But this was not like antique serial reading at all. No flat data here. No screens.

She relaxed. The trick was to *merge,* not just observe.

Far better for a chimpanzeelike species to take in the world through its evolved, body-wrapping neural bed.

More fun, too. She detected economic indicators on her augmented skin. A tiny shooting pain spoke of a leveraged buyout. Was that uneasy sensation natural to her, or a hint from her subsystems about a possible lowering of the prime rate?

Gotcha! the Foe sent.

Myung glanced at her running index. She was eleven hundred creds down!

So fast? How could—?

Then she felt it: dancing data-spikes in alarm-red, prickly on her left leg. The Foe had captured an early indicator. Which?

Myung had been coasting toward the Anaheim hills, watching the pulse of business trading quicken as slanting sunshine smartly profiled the fashionable, post-pyramidal corporate buildings. So she had missed the opening salvo of weather data update, the first trading opportunity.

The Foe already had an edge and was shifting investments. How?

Ahead of her in the simulated air she could see the

Foe skating to the south. All this was visual metaphor, of course, symbology for the directed attention of the data-eating programs.

A stain came spreading from the east into Mission Viejo. Not real weather, but economic variables.

Deals flickered beneath the data-thunderheads like sheet lightning. Pixels of packet-information fell as soft rains on her long-term investments.

The Foe was buying extra electrical power from Oxnard. Selling it to users to offset the low yields seeping up from San Diego.

Small stuff. A screen for something subtle. Myung close-upped the digital stream and glimpsed the deeper details.

Every day more water flowed in the air over southern California than streamed down the Mississippi. Rainfall projections changed driving conditions, affected tournament golf scores, altered yields of solar power, fed into agri-prod.

Down her back slid prickly-fresh commodity info, an itch she should scratch. A hint from her sniffer-programs? She willed a virtual finger to rub the tingling.

—and snapped back to real-space.

An ivory mist over Long Beach. Real, purpling water thunderclouds scooting into San Juan Cap from the south.

Ah—virtual sports. The older the population got, the more leery of weather. They still wanted the zing of adventure, though. Through virtual feedback, creaky bodies could air-surf from twenty kilometers above the Grand Canyon. Or race alongside the few protected Great White sharks in the Catalina Preserve.

High-resolution Virtuality stimulated lacy filigrees of electro-chem impulses throughout the cerebral cortex. Did it matter whether the induction came from the real thing or from the slippery arts of electronics?

Time for a bit of business.

Her prognosticator programs told her that with 0.87 probability, such oldies would cocoon-up across six states. So indoor virtual sports use, with electro-stim to zing the aging muscles, would rise in the next day.

She swiftly exercised options on five virtual sites, pouring in some of her reserve computational capacity. But the Foe had already harvested the plums there. Not much margin left.

Myung killed her simulated velocity and saw the layers of deals the Foe was making, counting on the coming storm to shift the odds by fractions. Enough contracts-of-the-moment processed, and profits added up. But you had to call the slant just right.

Trouble-sniffing subroutines pressed their electronic doubts upon her: a warning chill breeze across her brow. She waved it away.

Myung dove into the clouds of event-space. Her skin did the deals for here, working with software that verged on mammal-level intelligence itself. She wore her suits of artificial-intelligence ... and in a real sense, they wore her.

She felt her creds—not credits so much as *credibilities,* the operant currency in data-space—washing like hot air currents over her body.

Losses were chilling. She got cold feet, quite literally, when the San Onofre nuke piped up with a gush of clean power. A new substation, coming on much earlier than SoCalEd had estimated.

That endangered her energy portfolio. A quick flick got her out of the electrical futures market altogether, before the world-wide Mesh caught on to the implications.

Up, away. Let the Foe pick up the last few percentage points. Myung flapped across the digital sky, capital taking wing.

She lofted to a ten-mile-high perspective. Global warming had already made the county's south-facing slopes into cactus and tough grasslands. Coastal sage still clung to the north-facing slopes, seeking cooler climes. All the coast was becoming a "fog desert" sustained by vapor from lukewarm ocean currents. Dikes held back the rising warm ocean from Newport to Long Beach.

Pretty, but no commodity possibilities there any more.

Time to take the larger view.

She rose. Her tactile and visual maps expanded. She went to split-skin perception, with the real, matter-based landscape overlaid on the info-scape. Surreal, but heady.

From below she burst into the data-sphere of Invest-tainment, where people played upon the world's weather like a casino. Ever since rising global temperatures pumped more energy in, violent oscillations had grown.

Weather was now the hidden, wild-card lubricant of the world's economy. Tornado warnings were sent to street addresses, damage predictions shaded by the city block. Each neighborhood got its own rain forecast.

A sparrow's fall in Portugal could diddle the global fluid system so that, in principle, a thunderhead system would form over Fountain Valley a week later. Today, merging pressures from the south sent forking lightning over mid-California. That shut down the launch site of all local rocket-planes to the Orbital Hiltons. Hundreds of invest-programs had that already covered.

So she looked on a still larger scale. Up, again.

This grand world Mesh was N-dimensional. And even the number N changed with time, as parameters shifted in and out of application.

There was only one way to make sense of this in the narrow human sensorium. Every second, a fresh dimension sheared in over an older dimension. Freeze-framed, each instant looked like a ridiculously complicated abstract sculpture running on drug-driven overdrive. Watch any one moment too hard and you got a lancing headache, motion sickness and zero comprehension.

Augmented feedback, so useful in keeping on the financial edge, could also be an unforgiving bitch.

The Foe wasn't up here, hovering over the whole continent. Good. Time to think. She watched the *N*-space as if it were an entertainment, and in time came an extended perception, integrated by the long-suffering subconscious.

She bestrode the world. Total immersion.

She stamped and marched across the muddy field of chaotic economic interactions. Her boot heels left deep scars. These healed immediately: subprograms at work, like cellular repair. She would pay a passage price for venturing here.

A landscape opened like the welcome of a mother's lap.

Her fractal tentacles spread through the networks with blinding speed, penetrating the planetary spider web. Orange County was a brooding, swollen orb at the PacBasin's center.

Smelled it yet? came the Foe's taunt from below.

"I'm following some ticklers," she lied.

I'm way ahead of you.

"Then how come you're gabbing? And tracking me?"

Friendly competition—

"Forget the friendly part." She was irked. Not by the Foe, but by failure. She needed something *hot*. Where?

'Fess up, you're smelling nothing.

"Just the stink of overdone expectations," she shot back wryly.

Nothing promising in the swirling weather-space, working with prickly light below her. Seen this way, the planet's thirteen billion lives were like a field of grass waving beneath fitful gusts they could barely glimpse.

Wrong blind alley! sent her Foe maliciously.

Myung shot a glance at her indices. Down nineteen hundred!

And she had spotted him a hundred. *Damn.*

She shifted through parameter-spaces. There—like a carnival, neon-bright on the horizon of a black, cool desert: the colossal market-space of Culture.

She strode across the tortured seethe of global Mesh data.

In the archaic economy of manufacturing, middle managers were long gone. No more "just in time" manufacturing in blocky factories. No more one-size-fits-all. That had fallen to "right on time" production out of tiny shops, prefabs, even garages.

Anybody who could make a gizmo cheaper could send you a bid. They would make your very own custom gizmo, by direct Mesh order.

Around the globe, robotic prod-lines of canny intelligence stood ready in ill-lit shacks. Savvy software leaped into action at your Meshed demand, reconfiguring for your order like an obliging whore. Friction-free service. The mercantile millennium.

Seen from up here, friction-free marketism seemed the world's only workable ideology—unless you counted New Islam, but who did? Under it, middle managers had decades ago vanished down the sucking drain of evolving necessity. "Production" got shortened to *prod*—and prodded the market.

Of course the people shed by frictionless prod ended up with dynamic, fulfilling careers in dog-washing: valets, luxury servants, touchy-feely insulators for the harried prod-folk. And their bosses.

But not all was manufacturing. Even dog-dressers needed Culture Prod. *Especially* dog-dressers.

"My sniffers are getting it," she said.

The Foe answered, *You're on the scent—but late.*

Something new. . . .

She walked through the data-vaults of the Culture City. As a glittering representation of unimaginable complexities, it loomed: Global, intricate, impossible to know fully for even a passing instant. And thus, an infinite resource.

She stamped through streets busy with commerce. Ferrets and deal-making programs scampered like rodents under heel. Towers of the giga-conglomerates raked the skies.

None of this Big Guy stuff for her. Not today, thanks.

To beat her Foe, she needed something born of Orange County, something to put on the table.

And only her own sniffer-programs could find it for her. The web of connections in even a single county was so criss-crossed that no mere human could find her way.

She snapped back into the real world. *Think.*

Lunch eased into her bloodstream, fed by the pod when it sensed her lowering blood sugar. Myung tapped for an extra Kaff to give her some zip. Her medical worrier hovered in air before her, clucked and frowned. She ignored it.

—And back to Culture City.

Glassy ramparts led up into the citadels of the mega-Corps. Showers of speculation rained on their flanks. Rivulets gurgled off into gutters. Nothing new here, just the ceaseless hum of a market full of energy and no place to go.

Index check: sixteen hundred down!

The deals she had left running from the morning were pumping out the last of their dividends. No more help there.

Time's a-wastin', her Foe sent nastily. She could imagine his sneer and sardonic eyes.

Save your creds for the crunch, she retorted.

You're down thirteen hundred and falling.

He was right. The trouble with paired competition—
the very latest market-stimulating twist—was that the
outcome was starkly clear. No comforting self-delusions
lasted long.

Irked, she leaped high and flew above the City. Go
local, then. Orange County was the PacBasin's best
fount of fresh ideas.

She caught vectors from the county drawing her down.
Prickly hints sheeted across her belly, over her forearms.
To the east—there—a shimmer of possibility.

Her ferrets were her own, of course—searcher programs tuned to her style, her way of perceiving quality
and content. They *were* her, in a truncated sense.

Now they led her down a funnel, into—

A mall.

In real-space, no less. Tacky.

Hopelessly antique, of course. Dilapidated buildings
leaning against each other, laid out in boring rectangular grids. Faded plastic and rusty chrome.

People still went there, of course; somewhere, she
was sure, people still used wooden plows.

This must be in Kansas or the Siberian Free State
or somewhere equally Out Of It. Why in the world
had her sniffers taken her here?

She checked real-world location, preparing to lift
out.

East Anaheim? Impossible!

But no—there was something here. Her sniffer
popped up an overlay and the soles of her feet itched
with anticipation. Programs zoomed her in on a gray
shambles that dominated the end of the cracked blacktop parking lot.

Was this a museum? No, but—

Art Attack came the signifier.

That sign . . . "An old K-Mart," she murmured. She
barely remembered being in one as a girl. Rigid, old-
style aisles of plastic prod. Positively *cubic,* as the

teeners said. A cube, after all, was an infinite number of stacked squares.

But this K-Mart had been reshaped. Stucco-sculpted into an archly ironic lavender mosque, festooned with bright brand name items.

It hit her. "Of course!"

She zoomed up, above the Orange County jumble.

Here it was—pay dirt. And she was on the ground *first*.

She popped her pod and sucked in the dry, flavorful air. Back in Huntington Beach. Her throat was dry, the aftermath of tension.

And just 16:47, too. Plenty of time for a swim.

The team that had done the mock-mosque K-Mart were like all artists: sophisticated along one axis, dunderheads along all economic vectors. They had thought it was a pure lark to fashion ancient relics of paleo-capitalism into bizarre abstract expressionist "statements." Mere fun effusions, they thought.

She loved working with people who were, deep in their souls, innocent of markets.

Within two hours she had locked up the idea and labeled it: "Post-Consumerism Dada from the fabled Age of Appetite."

She had marketed it through pre-view around the globe. Thailand and the Siberians (the last true culture virgins) had gobbled up the idea. Every rotting 'burb round the globe had plenty of derelict K-Marts; this gave them a new angle.

Then she had auctioned the idea in the Mesh. Cut in the artists for their majority interest. Sold shares. Franchised it in the Cutting Concept sub-Mesh. Divided shares twice, declared a dividend.

All in less time than it took to drive from Garden Grove to San Clemente.

"How'd you find that?" her Foe asked, climbing out of his pod.

"My sniffers are *good*, I told you."

He scowled. "And how'd you get there so fast?"

"You've got to take the larger view," she said mysteriously.

He grimaced. "You're up two thousand five creds."

"Lucky I didn't really trounce you."

"Culture City sure ate it up, too."

"Speaking of which, how about starting a steak? I'm starving."

He kissed her. This was perhaps the best part of the Foe-Team method. They spurred each other on, but didn't cut each other dead in the marketplace. No matter how appealing that seemed, sometimes.

Being married helped keep their rivalry on reasonable terms. Theirs was a standard five-year monogamous contract, already nearly half over. How could she not renew, with such a deliciously stimulating opponent?

Sure, dog-eat-dog markets sometimes worked better, but who wanted to dine on dog?

"We'll split the chores," he said.

"We need a servant."

He laughed. "Think we're rich? We just grease the gears of the great machine."

"Such a poet you are."

"And there are still the dishes to do from last night."

"Ugh. I'll race you to the beach first."

SOMEONE WHO UNDERSTANDS ME

by Matthew Costello

Matthew Costello is the author of fourteen novels and numerous nonfiction works. His articles have appeared in publications ranging from *The Los Angeles Times* to *Sports Illustrated*. He scripted *The 7th Guest*, the best-selling CD-ROM interactive drama and its sequel, *The 11th Hour*, released in November 1995.

```
Welcome to Chat Room 13!
Attending: 2
>> Nightmover
>> Paladin
```

Who wouldn't have been curious?

I mean, there was so much talk about virtual sex and virtual relationships in cyberspace, you'd have to be a mole to be uninterested.

And I am *not* a mole.

I also had the number one prerequisite of someone seeking adventure on the net: time ... and lots of it.

It wasn't always that way.

But these days, I had—

>> **What changed, Paladin? How come *you* had so much time?**

Oh ... sorry. Didn't think you'd be interested.

You see, my company sold paper goods, real paper made from real trees. Imagine giant forests ripped down to make a zillion telephone books, and *that* was our business.

But paper was an endangered species. Now we had the paperless office ... and everybody acted as if that were a good Goddamn thing. Hey, the World Wide Web is filled with pages and pages that—ta-da!—don't use paper.

The paper business started to collapse. It was only a matter of time until my boss waddled into my cramped little office and said, "Jack, I'm afraid I have *pre-tty* bad news."

Only a matter of time ... and I had plenty of time.

>> So you went on the Net?

Yes. I surfed, I skipped, I zapped from page to page, with my office door locked and not a hell of a lot of work to do. That's what I did ... until I found Chat-World ... and I met Cynarra.

>> Cynarra? Nice screen name.

Yes. Though I immediately wondered whether it was real. Cynarra ... it sounded like something out of a novel. We started chatting. And when I came back the next day, she was there, waiting for me. It became something ... to look forward to.

>> And you're married ... I presume?

Yes. Married. *Imprisoned* is more like it. I guess I could have divorced my wife—but what would my life have been like? All the money we had was Bev's money, old money from her old family. And I was about to be unemployed. If I left Bev, would I end up on the street? The idea of living in an old refrigerator box wasn't too appealing.

>> No kids?

Our two kids were all grown. Out of the house and glad of it. It was just Beverly and I. Bev and Jack, sitting in their co-op, quietly seething.

>> Sounds like you were ready for some fantasy.

Oh, yes. Fantasy, reality. I was ready for *something*. At first, Cynarra and I simply talked. She seemed cloaked in mystery. She described herself as a "dark-haired, dark-eyed beauty." I thought about that *a lot*. Later she said she had full lips and a sexy smile. We just talked at first, but then—

>> **You developed a cyber relationship? Cool!**

Yeah, cool. A cyber relationship. I was at work, talking to Cynarra. Always waiting for her to come on-line.

>> **Did you use your real name?**

No way. I used my "screen name"—Paladin. Remember that old show, Paladin? *Have Gun, Will Travel?*

>> **Nope. Paladin? Before my time. Sorry.**

No problem. So ... I was Paladin and she was Cynarra. And I described myself to her, embellishing it a bit. I said I was tall ... even though I'm only 5' 7". I didn't think that she'd ever see me. I said I was slender and muscular, with deep-set blue eyes. Ha—well at least I do have blue eyes.

>> **And then?**

>> **You still there?**

>> **Paladin ...?**

Sorry. I felt this pain ... in my stomach. Sharp pain. But—where was I?

>> **She was Cynarra and *you* were Paladin.**

Yes. So we started talking about intimate things.

>> **Sex?**

Well, I don't want to make it sound like we *just* talked about sex, that we only tried to get each other hot and bothered. It was more than that. She opened herself to me, she told me about the slob she was married to, how badly he treated her ... how she couldn't stand him.

I started feeling bad for her. No, worse than bad. I felt as though, in all my copious free time, I wanted to *protect* her.

She told me that her husband came home and smacked her.

Once she told me that she had an ugly bruise on her cheek where he slapped her. And she told me that the only thing—the only thing!—that made her feel better was knowing that I was out there, waiting for her.

>> **And how were things at *your* home?**

Oh great, terrific. I'd come home ... and Bev and I wouldn't have two words to say to each other. Then, when she went to sleep, going to bed so early as though she actually had something to do the next morning, I'd creep in the den and use our home computer to check for any messages from Cynarra. I knew that she couldn't log on—but there might be a message.

I soon discovered that the only thing I lived for were words from Cynarra.

>> **So ... you arranged to see her?**

No. That's the funny thing.

What happened started out as a joke. We were just kidding. And I wrote: "Wouldn't it be great if we could get rid of our respective spouses. If somehow they were *dead,* and we could be together. Wouldn't that be great?"

>> **And you *were* kidding?**

Right. I mean, we—

>> **Hello?**

>> **Still there? Paladin? Are you—**

Sorry. Started coughing. Couldn't stop. Anyway, it *was* a joke. I mean, I had never seen this person, my dark-eyed Cynarra. Most likely she didn't resemble her description at all. But that didn't matter. No, not when she fired me with this incredible fantasy. Then she typed something interesting.

She wrote, <<There are poisons, you know. Undetectable poisons.>>

The first thing I wondered was whether ChatWorld was secure. I mean, could anyone eavesdrop and listen to our private tête-à-tête? But that was a big selling point of ChatWorld. . . . their motto . . . "Let yourself go . . . it's your own private world . . ."

>> **Like now?**

Exactly. Like now. No one can "hear" us. So, Cynarra told me about a web site, a place called Dead.com. She told me to check it out.

>> **Dead.com. Sounds cheery.**

That web site was creepy, lots of pages dealing with death and mutilation. And sure enough, there was a page on poison. And on that page I found something called a fungoid colloidal suspension.

>> **Sounds yummy.**

Toxic mushrooms, fermented and turned into a slightly-sweet mixture. It causes intense gastral pain, contractions, hemorrhaging and—it was rumored—a death that was virtually unrecognizable from—

>> **Yes . . . ? Unrecognizable from—Paladin?**

Sorry again. The person who died from that poison was most likely to be diagnosed as having a spontaneous hemorrhage.

>> **Neat.**

Now, Cynarra and I talked about almost nothing else. There were still those tender moments when we imagined touching each other, caressing . . . but now we had a new shared enthusiasm. We imagined being *free*.

>> **So you went down to your local mushroom store.**

No. No, I had to search the city to find out where you'd get these stupid mushrooms. But it turned out that they are a vital food source for the Munghip Lizard, a small green lizard from the Central Amazon. If you had a Munghip as a pet, you absolutely *had* to have these mushrooms. I told Cynarra.

>> **She went there too, eh? Quite a run on toxic mushrooms.**

She didn't tell me that she did that. I thought: maybe for her this was all a fantasy, and I was helping her create this fantasy. I didn't know if she was serious.

But I told her what I was going to do. I told her that she had me entranced, that I didn't care what she really looked like . . . if she was bald and toothless. She was my *Cynarra,* and she gave me the dream to be free.

>> *And* **financially secure.**

Yes. If this worked, I'd have the money I needed to live. That wouldn't be a problem. When the ax fell, when the business collapsed, I'd be okay.

>> **So when did you do the deed? Was it a dark and stormy night?**

It was morning. A gray November morning, barely light, the cloud cover so thick. I had the mushroom mixture fermenting for the five days—exactly as called for by the recipe. Then I went to the fridge and found Bev's container of Trim Grain. That stupid diet beverage of hers looked like quicksand. It was marsh sludge. It sloshed around in the container and left a gritty film on the sides.

>> **Guess it would mask the mushroom brew, huh?**

Sure. And I didn't have to put a lot in. A single teaspoon was terminal. But I put a couple of extra tablespoons in—just to be sure. A little overkill wouldn't hurt. I shook the container a couple of times.

Bev always had couple of glasses of the stuff every day, always trying to fight that middle-aged spread.

I went to work. I waited for Cynarra.

>> **And she didn't show up?**

No. She did. I didn't tell her what I did. I wanted to wait to make sure it worked. I was afraid that she'd be shocked.

>> **But it was** *her* **idea.**

Or her fantasy . . . her game. I wanted it to be done, a—what do they call it?—*fait accompli.*

We chatted a bit. Then, after lunch, I went back to ChatWorld, but she wasn't there. But there was a message. She had run out . . . she had some errands to do. She said that she'd be back.

I was so nervous, so damn excited I took a walk.

I got back to my office late. The office manager got on my case ... but it didn't matter. Not anymore. I went to my computer terminal, expecting Cynarra to be there, back from her chores.

>> **But she wasn't.**

Yeah. And I felt alone. I wanted to *share* this with her. She helped make it happen and now I was all alone.

So I left work early. I left, and returned home.

>> **And found? Paladin?**

>> **Paladin, you there? Hey, come back ... Paladin.**

I'm back. Couldn't type for a minute. Where was I?

>> **You went home ...**

Yes ... I went home ... went back into the apartment. And as soon as I opened the door, I knew something was wrong.

>> **How did you know that?**

I don't know. It was something about the sound of the place, or maybe the smell. Something that said ... a bad thing has happened here. I felt shaky. I went to the kitchen. To fix myself some tea. Steady myself.

>> **You didn't want to go find the body?**

Not yet. And there was a chance, a slim chance that Bev wasn't there. Maybe she had gulped her Trim Grain and run out for a milk shake. Maybe she collapsed in Baskin Robbins while some pimply-faced college kid watched her writhe on the linoleum.

>> **Nice Image.**

I used my Winnie-the-Pooh honey dipper to put some honey in my tea. I zapped the cup in the microwave. I liked my tea hot. I was scared.

>> **Who wouldn't be?**

The microwave beeped, and I took out my tea. I took a sweet sip, nearly burning my lips. The phone rang. A jarring sound. But I ignored it. The machine picked it up ... but there was no message. Don't you hate that? When people call and leave no message.

>> **Sure. Detest it. When did you go look ... ?**

It took a few minutes, but finally I was ready. I took a breath, and walked with my tea into the living room ... and it was empty. Then I went into the bathroom. An obvious place, I thought. Especially if someone was feeling stomach pain. Head for the porcelain throne, try to puke the poison out.

>> **And the bathroom was—**

Empty. So ... now it was time to check the bedroom. And I began to worry that maybe today, of all goddamn days, Bev had skipped her precious Trim Grain. It was damned unlikely ... but anything could happen. I walked back to the bedroom.

>> **Yes.**

>> **Come back! Hey, friend, don't leave me hanging.**

>> **You there?**

Barely. Can hardly see straight. But might as well ... try.

So, I went to the bedroom, and there she was, curled on the floor, still in her flannel nightgown with faded blue flowers and dotted with a zillion cotton nits that screamed "throw us the hell away."

>> **Nothing too sexy, eh?**

And there was a pool in front of her where she had thrown up. A bloody pool. Her eyes were wide open ... I had to walk close to see that. I stepped over her body, and looked at her eyes. Whatever pain she had been feeling was right there. Easy to see that she had been feeling real bad before she died.

>> **And you called the police?**

No. That was my plan. Call the police. Tell them I came home to find her like this, and pray that the mushroom mixture was masked by the blood and fluids. But then I saw something ... in the den ... glowing.

>> **An angel of the Lord? Just kidding—**

The computer screen was *on*. I walked over to it. Bev had turned on the computer. For some reason she had been typing something. A message ...

>> And the message said—?

But you must know what it said?

As soon as I saw it I knew how stupid I had been, how *completely* stupid. I stood in front of the screen, and felt my stomach go tight. Because the message said:

>> Don't kill me!

No. The message read:

"Paladin, my love.

I used *your* courage to become brave, to do what I wanted to do. By tonight, my husband will be dead. I put some of the same poison, my love, in his honey. Meet me soon in our regular chat room!

I love *you*.

Cynarra."

I looked at the screen. My tea was all gone. The tightening in my stomach didn't go away, it got worse. Until—like now—I can barely breathe.

It's funny. I logged on. To tell someone . . . and I stumbled into you. Another faceless person in Chat-World. Another—

>> Outstanding! Hey, this is an absolutely *outstanding* story, my man. You've *got* to publish this.

>> Hey, you still there Paladin? The log shows that you're still on-line, still in the room.

>> You reading this, Paladin? Believe me, this is a great story and you have to upload it to the archive.

>> Paladin?

>> Paladin??? Hey, hit the keys, guy!

>> Paladin . . . ? Well, if you aren't going to chat, I'll find someone who will.

>> Sheesh. I'm outta here! :(

```
Nightmover has left the chat room.
Attending Chat Room 13: 1
Welcome Paladin!
```

THE COYOTE VIRUS
By Josepha Sherman

Josepha Sherman is a fantasy writer and folklorist whose latest novels are the historical fantasies *The Shattered Oath* and *Forging the Runes.* Her latest folklore book is, appropriately enough, *Trickster Tales*.

Smythe—Professor Smythe of Comparative Literature, though "Smythe," for reasons that will become obvious, isn't his real name—joined me as I was heading home across campus. Not the person I would have chosen, most certainly not after a difficult time trying to get the concept of universal archetypes into the heads of wary freshmen—and with my tenure hearing just a day away. Smythe is the slightly too elegant fellow found on many a campus, attractive in a properly tweedy professorial way, his eyes bright with good humor, his reputation spotless—the type who is a Chancellor's darling—particularly our very proper Lady of the Old School—even if (she would never believe this) he does now and then stand a little too close to a woman, all in innocence, of course, or put an ever so slightly too friendly hand on a shoulder or lets that hand brush, by accident, of course, across back or breast.

And Smythe stood between me and tenure. "It would be such a pity if you were denied it," the man said with seeming sympathy, resting a warm hand on my arm. As I resisted the urge to push him away, he added, "I read your book, you know: *Ancient Myths in Modern Dress*—clever, my dear, very. Downright commercial, in fact. Almost had me convinced."

"An accomplishment," I said dryly. Smythe never had deigned to admit that mythology and its related subjects were genuine scholarly fields worthy of study. Particularly not when taught by a woman who refused to be properly ... respectful. And that oh so crass word "commercial" had sunk many academic careers. "Now, if you'll excuse me ... ?" I said as politely as could be done from between clenched teeth. "I have papers to grade."

But he blocked my path. "It really would be a shame if you were denied tenure. I could ... be very helpful."

"Assuming, of course, that I was ... very helpful to you. Smythe, I'm sure you never had such a thing in mind, but there *are* laws about sexual harassment in this state."

His smile never wavered. "*Measure for Measure,* my dear, Act II, Scene IV."

It took me a moment to figure that one out. Scene IV is the one in which the corrupt, seemingly saintly official, Angelo, tells his proposed sexual victim, Isabel, in effect, "Go and complain, and see who believes you." "Subtle," I said. Slipping past Smythe, I hurried on, not stopping till I was in my own apartment with the door safely locked. *Damn Smythe,* I thought, *damn him.*

I was too upset to do anything about those papers right now. And I certainly didn't want to consider tomorrow's tenure meeting. Turning on my computer, I logged on, hoping to calm down—or at least let off some frustration. All of us have a computer in this day and age, linked to the college's network. And while, of course, we're supposed to use our computers strictly on business ... well, we're human, teacher and student all. The Chancellor, being the sort she was, was too polite to embarrass us with investigations as long as we didn't embarrass her with scandals.

It's true that you meet a good many truly bizarre people out there on the Net. But by now I'd come to the conclusion that nothing could be more bizarre than the undergrad who insisted that there *was* no such thing as myth and *everything* that the ancients had described was all *perfectly true*. And nothing could be more unpleasant than Smythe—

No. I wasn't going to think of him just yet. Instead, I did my usual newsgroups scan, catching up on the gossip about urban folklore and alt.mythology (alternate, indeed, judging from the never-ending flow of postings on "Atlantis is real!").

Aha, there was the daily posting from Trickster. I had no idea who or what lay behind the handle; a good many people wandering the Net use pseudonyms (I, in a fit of whimsy, had chosen "Shaman" for mine) and the name of the server, the company allowing Trickster Net access, Chaos.com, meant nothing since there are hundreds of baby services out there offering connections to cyberspace.

Trickster—he, I'd decided arbitrarily—certainly had enough opinions on mythology, some of them intriguing, some downright crazed, and didn't hesitate to express them. I seemed to be the only one answering him, which was a little odd but not overwhelmingly surprising. We covered some pretty arcane material. (After all, how many people can converse, however briefly, in Athabascan?) Our typed conversations ended, often as not, in the type of hot-headed argument known as a "flame war," but they were, in their own strange way, fun.

Which is what caused the trouble. I had just finished telling Trickster that, his handle notwithstanding, the trickster figure was nothing more than an archetype. "Get over your delusions of mythic grandeur, my friend," I posted. "There never was and never will be a living, breathing personification! If there was or is, I call on him now—Coyote! If ever there was a trickster who deserved to be real in our modern world," I added cynically, "it's he. But no such being or beings exist!"

"No?" was his cryptic response. Rather to my surprise, he added nothing else after that, and I told myself that I'd finally managed to squelch him.

There was e-mail waiting for me when I went to log off. "Coyote Lives," was all it said, but what made it rather surprising was that there wasn't any trace of a sender. *Junk mail,* I told myself, *or Trickster thumbing his virtual nose at me,* and ignored it.

But the next day, there was more anonymous e-mail. "Coyote is watching."

A student prank, I thought, and bet that Trickster was none other than one of my undergrads.

But even as I thought this, a beep from my computer announced the arrival of new e-mail. And it said, "Wanna bet?"

Ridiculous. A mere coincidence. Some student was out there, laughing his head off at freaking out (or whatever term is "in" right now) the teacher.

A beep. More e-mail. "I'm student and teacher both, and neither."

This was growing more and more bizarre, almost as though the unknown sender was reading my mind.

Beep. "Am I?"

"Who are you?" I typed, then paused, realizing that I had no way to send the message.

Beep. "Who do you think?"

This was impossible. No one but the sender could read e-mail that hadn't been sent! "Trickster?" I typed warily.

Beep. "Sometimes."

"What does that mean? What do you want?"

"Nothing. Everything. The exchange of messages was fun for a while, even though only you could see my markings. But I have found this new way of moving about, changing things. I think I like it."

"This is nonsense," I typed. "Whichever student you are, you obviously have a bent for computer science and shouldn't be wasting your time in pranks like this."

"Pranks? I live for such things. I *am* such things."

Enough of this. I exited the program, shut down the computer, and refused to think any more about it. That I looked warily about the apartment and made sure the door and windows were locked was a natural precaution; universities aren't that far removed from the real world.

I slept, dreaming not of sheep jumping over fences but of coyotes. And I admit to more than a little uneasiness when I logged on the next day.

I was greeted with a grinning Coyote face that melted away like that of the Cheshire cat, leaving those gleaming, alarming fangs hanging on the screen for a moment before they, too, faded.

A virus. No doubt about it. The mystery was *how* my computer had become infected since I never downloaded anything directly onto my hard drive and ran new software through an anti-virus scan. Still, networks are networks, and those clever enough to dream up viruses were surely clever enough to bypass precautions.

Professor Jessup of Computer Sciences—young, earnest and perpetually cheerful—went over my machine with the glee of a true hacker. "Not a thing I can find," he decided with obvious reluctance. "Your system's clean."

"But that's impossible!" Hesitantly, I told him about the bizarre e-mail messages.

His look was studiously bland. I could practically read what he was thinking: Mythology teacher goes 'round the mythic bend; too many worries about tenure. "You must be mistaken," he said hopefully.

What could I do? Not one e-mail message had appeared while he was working on the computer, and of course not one of them had been downloadable. No proof, I thought. And the last thing I needed was for word to reach Smythe's eager ears. "You're right," I told Jessup with a laugh. "Too much overwork. Sorry to have bothered you."

But as soon as he was gone, the computer rebooted itself. I swear that's true; I had definitely seen Jessup turn it off. It rebooted, and an animated coyote said, words appearing in a cartoon balloon over his head as he pranced about, "No, you are not mad. I am truly me."

I buried my head in my hands, then remembered I needed the keyboard to communicate. "Who are you?" I typed frantically. "How are you doing this?"

I glanced up from the keys in time to see the coyote turn to study me, and I could swear I saw concern in the cartoon eyes. "You are afraid. Why? No shaman should be afraid, not when I am grateful to you."

"Why? *Who are you?*"

The figure pranced away, fading into a garish, cartoonish landscape of too-green grass and stick-straight trees. "Me." The words appeared over his head, trailing back over him like a scarf. "Names are not me."

This wasn't one of my students, not unless one of them was truly, memorable psychotic. "Maybe. But you must be called something by others."

"Many things. Some I take for a time. Ah-hah-leh. Mica. Italapas. Sometimes."

A chill stole through me. Coyote. Those were all names for that major North American trickster figure.

Trickster.

But it couldn't be a prank. Ah-hah-leh is Coyote's Miwok name, Mica is Lakota, and Italapas is Chinook. No student and few professionals would know all three names, particularly not here in the Northeast.

"Coyote . . ." I breathed.

"Maybe." The figure had returned and was doing

something indecent and almost anatomically impossible, on his animal face a look of mild interest. Coyote, yes. Amoral being, victor and victim, sexual and asexual—

"What," I exploded, "are you doing in my computer?"

The figure vanished into sparkling dots, reformed as a puppy that quickly grew to coyote-shape again. "You called me."

"I *what?*"

"Oh, yes. Few know me nowadays, not truly. I get few chances to be fully myself. But you are a shaman and spoke often of me in the strange spirit realm you visit with your mind and fingers—" I guessed he meant cyberspace, "—and I heard." The coyote laughed as a dog does, tongue lolling. "You called me, welcomed me, and I came."

God, I had, hadn't I, back in that argument with Trickster—I'd told Coyote to his face he didn't exist and welcomed him to prove me wrong.

"This is a fun spirit realm," Coyote continued. "Much more chaotic and interesting than any reality. Plenty of doorways into everywhere."

The network, I thought. Coyote could access the whole university computer network. A trickster with no sense of right or wrong wandering through the whole network, working mischief—no, for all I knew, Coyote could get out there into the wide realm of world computing. This was the being who created people, stole fire, put the sun in the sky, and all because he was the heart of change . . . the thought of him changing programs at random . . . maybe a bank would lose all its records, or an Air Traffic Controller's screen would die at just the wrong time—

"You can't," I typed, then hastily erased that. Very carefully, I told him about the dangers I'd just imagined.

"I would not do that!" The animated face frowned

in indignation. "That game would not be a thing-for-change, but a thing-for-evil. That is not me."

Amoral, not immoral. Truly Coyote. "Thank you," I typed.

"I am grateful," he said without warning. "Grateful for the entry into this spirit realm. I will help you. What do you wish?"

What, indeed? You didn't ask personified Chaos for an end to war or famine or any other such noble ideals. "For me? There's only one thing I want right now—not that," I added with a laugh as he waggled his cartoon eyebrows at me in a caricature of lust. "I'm afraid you can't help. Not with university politics." Quickly, I told him about tenure—or my rapidly approaching lack of it.

"You are not, then, a true shaman?"

"Ah . . . not yet." It didn't seem the time to explain professorial standing. "Not quite."

"This Smythe . . ." Coyote said, dragging out the word thoughtfully on the screen. "This one is the obstacle? It is he who tries to keep you from becoming a true shaman?"

Professor, I corrected silently, but I didn't say it. "Yes."

The animated figure shook itself suddenly. "And for no more reason than he thinks women cannot be shamans. Bah. The Yurok could teach him otherwise, as could many other folk. And that he wishes you to play sex-games with him not for joy or lust but as a *bribe*—" I hadn't told him that, and I started, reminded all over again just how powerful a being this was. "Bah, again," Coyote continued. "That is not how things are done. Wait."

The computer shut itself down. I waited, wondering what to do, wondering if I should warn Smythe—warn him of what? That a mythological being, an archetype, was after him? An hour passed, another. I grimly set to work going over the papers, trying to tell myself I'd just had a stress-based hallucination.

The computer rebooted without warning, and the papers went flying. I whirled to the screen as the coyote grin formed, then moved in speech; Coyote had clearly just discovered the sound card. "He has one of these spirit realm devices as well."

"Yes, of course. We all do. Why—"

"Ask and ask. Curiosity is good. Answers are whatever they may be. Go to sleep, shaman. Wake and see what is what."

The computer shut itself off with a very final "click." And I . . . of course, I didn't go to sleep, or even to bed, not for long, weary hours. By the time I did manage to drop off, the alarm roused me with the feeling I'd slept for maybe an hour. Bleary-eyed, I staggered to the computer. Off. Good. I bathed, dressed, waited desperately for the coffee to finish brewing, then sat down, cup in hand, at the computer, staring.

Nothing.

Still nothing.

I was going to be late for my morning classes. Might as well teach them while I had them. Today was Smythe's time of triumph, to put it in Coyote's melodramatic way.

Beep! The computer flicked into life as though I'd summoned him. "Good morning!" said the obnoxiously cheerful AI voice of my Net server. "You have mail!"

Of course I looked. "For the shaman," the message read, and there was a file attached. Warily, I downloaded it to a floppy, not sure if any precautions were useful against what I had begun thinking of as the Coyote Virus, then began to read.

"God!"

I couldn't be reading this; Smythe would never have left such material unguarded. I scrolled down in grim fascination, seeing a whole list of his ratings, detailed in embarrassing degree, of women, myself included. That in itself was nothing; he had every right to fantasize, even if he was stupid to put his dreams down on disk. But there was more. There were specific details of, as he so quaintly put it, "conquests." One of the names, I saw in growing horror, was that of Janice Brendan. Janice Brendan, promising Shakespearean student.

Janice Brendan who, one night, had quietly hanged herself. At the time, the note she'd left, *The darkness engulfs me,* had been taken as a clean sign of fatal depression. Oh, it had been depression, no doubt about that, the poor unstable girl—but depression, this file made quite clear, over being used then dropped by Smythe.

"No. Oh, no." I typed a frantic e-mail message to Coyote, hoping he would somehow read it, "This can't be true. Smythe isn't a saint, but even he would never stoop that low."

Beep. "He would. He has."

"How did you—? You accessed his private files." Of course. The most secure password ever created wouldn't be enough to keep out a curious Trickster. "Coyote—"

"Are these words not clear enough? This will punish him for all. All the spirit realm will see."

All? He might have said more; I didn't wait to find out. Instead, I went rushing out the door—and crashed right into Smythe. "You!" he exploded. "How did you—how dare you—how—"

"What are you—"

"Those files! Those damned files were password-protected! How did you do it?"

"Do what?" I tried to sidestep him, but he blocked my path. "What in God's name are you talking about?"

"The files, dammit! You know which ones!"

Oh, I did. And it was only now dawning on me
what Coyote had meant by that "all the spirit realm
will see." Plainly computers were booting themselves
up all over the university. And just as plainly those
certain incriminating files were showing on the screen.
"I didn't . . ." I began feebly, but Smythe was already
racing off, evidently just realizing that the Chancellor,
too, had a computer and was part of the network. . . .

I don't have to go into the details of what followed,
do I? Smythe had tenure, of course; it would have
been too embarrassing to the university for any public
outcry. Besides, unscrupulous or no, he never had actually quite broken any laws. Only Janice Brendan's
life.

Instead, Smythe just . . . disappeared. The official
word was that he'd taken a lengthy sabbatical—one
from which, we all knew, he was not likely to return.
Me? Without Smythe to block me, I was granted tenure without delay. I am now, as Coyote would put it,
a true shaman.

A new student has checked into my Introduction to
Mythology class, a young man very plainly of tribal
stock. He seems very polite and subdued, and listens
attentively to my every word. But every now and
again, I catch the oddest yellow glint in his dark eyes,
almost like that in the eyes of a coyote. And I have
to wonder. Coyote hasn't appeared on my or anyone
else's computer screen since that day. Could the arche-
typal Trickster himself be content for long wandering
our limited little network? What if he discovers a way
to cross over into our tangible world?

What if he already has?

PROMETHEUS BRINGING FIRE
by Robin Wayne Bailey

Robin Wayne Bailey is the author of numerous short stories and novels, most recently *Shadowdance*. He lives in Kansas City.

Soft azure light from a dozen monitors flickered over the gleaming, liquid membranes of R'ilyeh's face as she studied the streams of information that poured with dazzling speed across the screens. Alien symbols and letters reflected in her deep-set silver eyes and on her silver skin as she sat motionless, absorbing it all.

A black ball floated in the air before her. After a moment, she reached out. Her fingers began to dance over the object. She turned it this way and that, as she needed, with supreme skill and dexterity. The screens changed in response. As she keyed her commands into the ball, her computers translated the alien symbols into her own language. She entered a swift report, then directed the stream into the vast memory tanks of her superior for his later perusal.

When she released the ball again, all the monitors went black. Perched in the darkness on her platform, she unfolded her legs and momentarily gave in to the weariness that filled her. For an instant, her shoulders slumped. Folded against her body, her arms lost definition and merged into the rest of her form. Her head melted down upon her chest.

A soft chime from one of the monitors drew her alert again. With but the slightest concentration, she resumed the humanoid form she had so come to admire. She touched the ever-present ball, and a single screen flared to life. A message waited for her in letters of white light.

Starflower? Are you there?

R'ilyeh allowed a smile to bend her silver lips. Without her superior's knowledge, she had rigged one computer for her private research and dedicated it to scanning the global Nets. Employing several secret names, she had begun to participate in direct conversations with the aliens.

Of late, she had further dedicated and designed a program to inform her when one particular alien, entering the Net, sought her out.

R'ilyeh drew the keyball to her and cradled it gently in her palms. She lightly tapped out a message in the alien's own language.

Wallflower, little friend. How are you feeling today?

The moments seemed to crawl by. The aliens, especially their children, did not communicate swiftly on their primitive keyboards. R'ilyeh did not mind. Somehow, over the last few months, she had developed a strange caring for this child, who called himself by the sad handle. In the dark solitude of her station, as she waited for his reply, she whispered odd words and shuddered at their fearsome meaning: Duchenne is muscular dystrophy.

You must live on-line, Wallflower typed. The letters appeared slowly, at staggered, painful intervals. *Whenever I need to talk, you're right here. The doctors took away my braces today. I might get a wheelchair, though. One of those motorized jobs, if my mom can afford it.* Another long pause. R'ilyeh folded her legs and prepared to send a response. Then Wallflower's message continued. *She's in the other room crying.*

R'ilyeh watched the screen, considering her words and actions carefully. She knew almost everything there was to know about Wallflower, whose real name was Joey and whose age in alien years was only eleven. After only a few conversations, he had piqued her interest. With her superior skills and technology, she had hacked into his birth records, school records, and his medical records. She had learned much about the degenerative nature of his disease, and it saddened her.

Twisting and turning the keyball, her fingers danced over its surface. *Be brave, little friend,* she sent. *Use your computer to reach out to others. Don't be afraid to talk. Don't allow yourself to become isolated. That is the worst thing.*

Her fingers stopped. Tilting back her head, she gazed at the low ceiling above her station, then around the small room into its darkened corners. For a moment, she listened, detecting no sound in the narrow corridor beyond her door. Isolation, she thought to herself. Yes, that was the worst thing.

Impulsively, her fingers flew over the ball. *I am sending you a gift,* she informed him.

You don't know where I live, came the slow reply. R'ilyeh suddenly envisioned him typing with one hand, and wondered just how rapidly his illness was spreading, how much longer his small body would last.

She tapped the ball. *Trust me.* Then, assuming the grin she had so recently practiced, she added, *I have powers beyond your mortal comprehension.*

They exchanged a few more words, then R'ilyeh logged off. She didn't relinquish the keyball, however. With little effort at all, she hacked into one of the aliens' medical supply companies in a location called Boulder, Colorado, and ordered an Amigo Zoom-218 fully motorized and accessorized chair, specifying delivery to her young friend, and altering the records to show it paid in full.

It was a horrible abuse of her skills, and her superior would punish her should he learned of it. Still, she harbored no fear or regret.

Again, she relaxed, surrendering the details of her form, becoming little more than a silver lump, a gleaming, but vaguely weathered Buddha seated in a Zenlike position in the center of the room among dead monitors. She thought for a while of Joey's mother, and wondered what it was like to cry. The aliens' literature was full of crying. She had tried to cry out of curiosity. Now she wanted to cry. Her silver eyes were not made for it.

An alien day passed. Two days. R'ilyeh downloaded massive streams of information into the memory tanks. Security information, troop movements of nations all around this primitive globe, missile launch data, financial transactions. If ever her people grew tired of observing and decided to invade, she thought she, alone, could topple the planet by striking at its banks with her computers.

She received no messages from Wallflower. A quick check of the medical company's records showed the chair had been delivered. She pushed it to the back of her mind and resumed her duties. Still, it gnawed at her. She began to fear for the alien boy. She worried.

R'ilyeh suddenly blackened her screens. For a long time she sat in the darkness. The small room seemed to press in upon her. A sensation she had never experienced before and could not explain caused her to shudder. She rose from her platform. Slowly she turned on her humanoid legs. The keyball followed, always positioning itself within easy reach. She seized it, flung it violently away. It floated right back to her.

Turning once more to the monitors, she grabbed the ball and tapped a command code, summoning her superior to teleconference. She canceled before transmitting. Instead, she strode to the door.

She pushed it open, ducking under the low lintel, which was not fashioned for her present shape.

The keyball, at least, stopped at the threshold. There it would await her return.

She encountered no one in the corridors. Only a handful of observers worked this base, and few ever left their stations. She took long strides, filled with a sense of power and purpose, of determination. Only the dimmest light shone from the ceiling, but it was enough. She made her way to her superior's station. Without requesting entrance, she jerked open the door.

N'yamet twisted about on his platform. R'ilyeh reacted with surprise. He, too, was experimenting with the humanoid form, though there was something grotesque in the way his eyes lined up one above the other. Immediately, as if caught in a shameful act, he relinquished the shape, melting into a featureless, gleaming mass, a tall but legless torso with rubbery pseudopods for arms. Like mercury on a smooth surface, he glided toward her, his keyball following.

"Why have you left your station?" he said.

She couldn't answer. The smell that rose from him filled her senses. He drew closer, pouring his chemical into the air, overwhelming her. "Mate with me," he demanded.

R'ilyeh couldn't refuse. His scent was too strong, too urgent, beyond even his control, she suspected. He flowed around her, relinquishing form entirely, assuming his basest, liquid nature.

They merged. Yet, R'ilyeh stubbornly clung to some small awareness. While she accepted N'yamet's reproductive fluids, she refused to conceive. This was not the time, and certainly not the place, to generate.

Eventually, N'yamet separated himself from her. She could sense his anger. He had wanted her to conceive. Sex he could force, but not that. She would not bear a child in this tiny base, on this strange world.

She hugged herself as she stared at the floor. Bear

a child? What an odd expression. What an *alien* expression.

Yet, it made her think of Wallflower, of Joey, and she remembered why she had come.

"I must go outside," she said. Her gaze strayed past him toward his monitor array. Image after image of the naked alien form, both male and female, flickered on his screens.

N'yamet touched his keyball and the screens went blank. "Denied," he said, settling himself once more on his platform. "You are a brilliant observer and analyst, R'ilyeh. Return to your station."

R'ilyeh dared to linger. 'I have not seen the pure light of a sun, nor a star, in three alien years, N'yamet!" she said. "I wish to go outside only for a brief time. Allow me!"

N'yamet turned away from her. Tapping rapidly on his keyball, he brought his monitors to life again. Gone were the naked images. A stream of numbers flowed upon the screens, intercepted data transmissions from a pair of military satellites.

"I will conceive for you," she offered.

He did not answer immediately. His mirror-bright membranes shifted. For a moment, he seemed to swell larger, and the flashing numbers from the monitors reflected on his silveriness. "Bribery, R'ilyeh?" he said finally. "How human of you."

R'ilyeh remained only a moment more. Then, realizing nothing would move N'yamet, she fled from her superior's station into the corridor. There, she paused, trembling, her form rippling all over like shiny moonlit water.

By the time she returned to her own station, she had hardened her mind with a resolve. Abandoning her humanoid shape, she flowed past her door and onto her platform. The keyball floated to her immediately. Extending a pseudopod, she prepared to tap a command.

Only then did she notice the screen on the dedicated monitor. Wallflower was on-line, but he was chatting with someone else. She had not been here to intercept his call. With a sense of guilt and sadness, she watched the conversation.

Wallflower: ... *of the nurses gave me this really cool book when I left the hospital....*
Emaciator: *Book? Who reads anymore? Nintendo rules, man!*
Wallflower: *I don't have good dexterity for the games anymore. I like to read.*

Without thinking, R'ilyeh reassumed a humanoid shape as she watched the slow pace of his letters taking form on the monitor. Each day, his manual skills seemed to deteriorate. Noting the hospital reference, she tapped commands into her keyball. Within moments she accessed his latest medical records and learned why he had not been on-line for several days. She read with growing concern the words *renal failure* and *dialysis*.

She tapped the keyball again and broke into the boy's conversation. Her own handle appeared on her monitor.

Starflower: *Did you get my present?*
Emaciator: *Hey, by the handle it's gotta be a babe!*
Wallflower: *Starflower! You sent the chair? (Cool it, E. She's a friend!)*

R'ilyeh smiled, surprising herself, because she hadn't had to concentrate to turn her lips upward. It had happened almost naturally. Joey considered her a friend, did he? Another line of text crawled across the screen, this time a "private send" that only she could read.

Wallflower: *I love you. I have to tell people that 'cause I know I don't have much time. Talking to you has helped keep me going.*

R'ilyeh stared at the monitor, at those pale blue
words fashioned in primitive alien symbols. Then her
gaze swept over her banks of monitors and around her
small station, taking in the sterile technology behind it
all, behind this entire secret base of her people. Suddenly she hated it, hated it all.

Somewhere in a strange land called Boulder, Colorado, lived a little boy named Joey, who called himself
Wallflower, offspring of a species thousands of years
less developed than her own. Yet she felt connected
to him by a powerful, unfathomable force. Her fingers
moved over her keyball, and she watched her send
appear on the screen.

Starflower: *You've kept me going, too.*

And she knew it was the truth. For three of this
planet's years she had seldom ventured from her station. She worked here, fed here, cleansed herself on
her platform, rested when necessary. She was an Observer and an Analyst, trained and conditioned for the
rigors of her job.

But by the stars! How did anyone train for the
loneliness?

She tapped the keyball again. *I'm going to bring
you another present, little friend,* she sent. *Do not respond now. Watch for me.* She logged off quickly and
blanked the dedicated screen.

For some time she sat trembling, feeling the ripples
in the liquids beneath her outer membranes, experiencing a queer horror-pleasure at what she contemplated. Almost, she changed her mind, but her fingers
were already working their magic on the keyball.

Her monitors flared to life. But this time she
combed through the records and accomplishments of
her own culture, seeking medical and research files. A
small sigh escaped her almost-human lips, as she rapidly downloaded data into a small chip.

One of her monitors went blank and came to life again. N'yamet's shape gleamed on the screen. "Why have you accessed the memory tanks?"

R'ilyeh cursed herself. She had not expected a download to be detected so quickly. Was N'yamet observing her work in secret? She had to be careful.

"I am preparing a comparative report on the state of the aliens' medical technology," she lied. "I required contrasting data from our own more advanced researches."

N'yamet said nothing. R'ilyeh's monitors went blank and remained that way. He had locked out her access.

Alarmed, R'ilyeh pushed her keyball aside, left her platform, and rushed to retrieve the chip from its drive unit. With one eye on her door, she pressed the chip against her body and folded her outer membrane securely around it.

Barely had she settled herself on her platform again when N'yamet entered her station. he looked like a patch of silver ice upon the floor. "I am concerned about you," he said, flowing past her. He positioned himself halfway between her platform and the blank monitors.

R'ilyeh avoided looking at him. Though faint, as if he were trying to conceal it, he exuded odors of suspicion and deceit. "Is my work unsatisfactory?" she asked.

N'yamet inflated his membranes, swelling balloonlike as he approached her. "You are the finest observer and analyst at this base," he answered matter-of-factly. Extending appendages, he seized her keyball. "However, your researches lack direction. You are becoming too involved with the aliens."

Her monitors flared as he tapped a command. "Literature," he said, as the text of *The Frogs,* by Euripides, scrolled upon one screen. "Music," he said. Another monitor displayed the musical notation for Tchaikovsky's *Peter and the Wolf,* and a soft symphonic sound flowed from hidden speakers. Tapping the keyball, he muted the volume.

With unusual boldness, she seized the keyball from him. "Chinese military satellite transmissions," she said defensively, calling down a recent program, sending a swift scroll of numbers across a third monitor, "decoded and translated for your convenience." She ignited yet another screen. "American shuttle launch codes and associated classified information, hacked directly from NASA computers, organized, summarized and translated for your convenience." Three more monitors spilled forth data streams. "Comprehensive reports on recent alien advances in microprocessing, ceramic chip development, and fiberoptic technology, analyzed, summarized, organized, and translated for your convenience." She did not even try to control the scent of her rising anger. "I am trained to seek an understanding of these aliens, so I probe their art, as well as their technology, their psyches, as well as their secrets."

"Ah, their psyches," N'yamet said. Reclaiming the keyball, he activated the final monitor. "That would explain your interest in their chat lines."

R'ilyeh grew cautious. It was obvious to her now that N'yamet had, indeed, been spying on her activities, monitoring her operations and communications from his own station. She stared at the final screen. Wallflower was still there with his friend, Emaciator, and two others. "Of course," she answered coolly. "One can learn much by observing simple conversations." A sudden idea occurred to her, possibly a means to allay her superior's suspicion. "The one who calls himself Wallflower," she said. "Only a child, but I've studied him for some time."

N'yamet regarded the screen, then turned toward her curiously. "Why should he merit your particular attention."

Once again, R'ilyeh seized her keyball. "He tells colorful stories," she answered.

"Stories?"

"Observe, Superior." The keyball turned in her palms. Tapping out the appropriate commands, she broke into the chat. Her message flashed over the monitor under N'yamet's dubious gaze.

Starflower: *Hello, Wallflower. How are the BEMs today?*
Wallflower: *Starflower!*

N'yamet extended a pseudopod and touched the screen. "BEMs?" he inquired.

"Bug-eyed monsters," she explained. "Watch."

Wallflower: *We stopped their invasion. Blew up half their ships before they crossed Pluto's orbit. But the Froggers have established a beachhead on Mars. The war goes on.*
Starflower: *Remind me, little friend. From what world do they come?*
Wallflower: *Epsilon Eridani Six. Very cold. They want Earth for its warmth!*

The smell of N'yamet's mirth spread through the air like a sickly perfume. Within his membranes his fluids swam; he shook with amusement. "Our home-world?" he said between spasms.

"That is why he originally caught my attention," R'ilyeh said. "He writes down these fanciful tales to share with his friends. They help to pass the time, he says. He is dying."

Regaining control of himself, N'yamet scoffed. "And what do you learn from this?"

"That even their children face death with courage," she snapped. "Should we ever attempt to harm this culture, they will make formidable enemies."

N'yamet approached her platform again. "That is only your observation."

R'ilyeh inflated her membranes, swelling herself in stubborn defiance. "That is my analysis. And I'm the best there is at this base."

He regarded her for a long moment. Slowly, the smell of his suspicion subsided, and another, more familiar scent began to take its place. She felt herself weakening under the chemical tide of his rising desire. "I'm still concerned about you," he said finally. "I will be watching your work."

Her disappointment was almost as great as her relief when he moved toward the door. Before he slipped out, however, he paused. "I am still considering your offer to conceive," he said. Then he was gone.

She struggled to calm herself. His lust-scent lingered in the air, agitating her. She slid off the platform and paced before her monitors, her keyball, ever-faithful companion, following her movements as she shook herself free from N'yamet's influence.

The dedicated monitor drew her attention. Emaciator remained on-line with two others. Wallflower's handle did not appear. On her keyball, she tapped out his name.

Emaciator answered. *He didn't log off, but he's been away from the screen for a while.*

She hesitated for a moment. She didn't know Emaciator very well. He was a new presence on the chatlines. Finally, she sent another message. *Was he feeling all right?*

A longer than usual pause seemed to follow her transmission. Then a notice of "private send" flashed after Emaciator's name. *You know about him, huh? Did he tell you about me?*

R'ilyeh's fingers froze on the keyball. The fluids within her membranes rippled nervously. She tapped the keyball. *You?*

Leukemia, came the private response. *Early stages,*

though. Wallflower's much worse off. We talk about things a lot. He really likes you.

R'ilyeh deflated until she was little more than a glistening pool on the floor. *Be his friend,* she told him. *I don't know if we'll get the chance to converse again.* With that, she logged off.

She paced no more. The unfathomable connection she felt for Wallflower—for Joey—she understood it now. Impossible as it seemed, she had come to care for the alien boy, to admire him, even to love him. Now she worried, and that worry drove her to action. Working her keyball with utmost skill, she hacked into city planning files for Boulder, Colorado. With little more than a glance, she memorized population figures, maps, city streets, water and sewer distribution systems.

N'yamet, appearing suddenly upon one of her screens, interrupted her. "Now what are you researching?" he demanded. "I warned you I'd be observing."

"Native architecture," she answered curtly. Over the monitor, he could not smell the scent of her lie. With a twist of her keyball, she cut him off.

Wallflower's line remained open; he still had not logged off the chat-line. Quickly she ran a trace, obtaining his phone number, then his address. She checked it against the last address on his medical records. The keyball flew in her grasp as she drew down a city grid and pinpointed his location. She memorized it all.

N'yamet overrode her lockout. "R'ilyeh!"

She flowed to her door and into the corridor, leaving her keyball behind, feeling the secret data chip where it rested within a fold of her outer membrane. There, she stretched and reshaped herself, assuming the humanoid form as she'd practiced it. With the long strides her legs allowed, she moved more swiftly than she otherwise could.

The way to the outside world led up, but she went down. Three levels below her station were the base laboratories. Within her membranes, her fluids bubbled with excitement as she pushed through the door. A pair of technicians turned her way. Both were inferior to her in rank and seniority. She flooded the air with a powerful chemical scent, compelling their obedience, as she named a compound. "Bring it to me at once!"

One seemed to resist her command; he looked at her with unsettled concern and tried to question her. The other complied without comment and within moments pushed a tiny plastic pillow containing a pale blue fluid at her. Placing it within the folded part of her membrane next to the data chip, she left them without another word.

She ran through the corridors again, climbing level after level. A warning klaxon began to sound. N'yamet had found her missing from her station and guessed some part of her plan. Observers peeped out from their doors; a startled technician dropped an instrument as she almost ran over him; someone called her name. She ignored them all and ran.

The exit at last!

But before the great hatch to the outside world, N'yamet waited.

"Mate with me, R'ilyeh," he demanded. He poured his chemical into the air, and the lust-scent of him stopped her in her tracks as surely as if she'd hit a wall. She cried out with frustration and anger. Behind him, on the wall beside the hatch, a black numerical keypad drew her eye—an electronic lock. She tried to focus on that. She took a hesitant step, fighting against her superior's overwhelming perfume.

"No, R'ilyeh," N'yamet whispered, exerting himself. "You don't really want to leave. You want to mate. You want to conceive." He extended a pseudopod. With an effort, R'ilyeh brushed it away. Yet, her fluids heated and seethed. The smell of him osmosed through her membranes. The very liquids of her being screamed for sex.

Unable to maintain it, she lost her humanoid shape, becoming a rounded bladder, then a seeming pool of mercurial ichor. Stubbornly, she flowed, inch by inch, past N'yamet, who swelled above her.

"Yield to me," he commanded, moving again to block the hatch.

With a supreme effort of will, denying her natural cravings, she extended a pseudopod and touched the keypad. It was not any thought or concern for Wallflower that drove her now. No, she simply refused to surrender herself again, nature or not, to one she so thoroughly detested. The words slowly boiled from her. "I ... will ... not ... yield!"

"You don't know the command codes!" N'yamet cried as she tapped a number on the keypad.

"Idiot!" she answered, struggling furiously against herself not to give in to his chemical demands. "I know all your codes!" She punched a series of numbers. The hatch hissed and dilated open. "I am the best there is—at this base or any other."

His scent of astonishment overpowered even his lust-scent. R'ilyeh flowed over the threshold. For the first time, she felt the touch of dust and rough stone beneath her substance, and a thrill rippled through her. Drawing on new-found reservoirs of strength, she took humanoid shape once more and ran down a long and steep slope, putting distance between her and N'yamet.

Only when she felt free from his influence and fatigue began to slow her down did she dare to look around and consider her surroundings.

"The wonder of it!" she murmured. "The beauty!"

Over the soaring mountains stretched a black sky peppered with stars. The brighter ones burned with fiery resplendence while the dimmer ones, far more numerous, fashioned tenuous veils to drape the darker reaches.

Homesickness lanced through her. She longed suddenly to stand again on the dark beaches of her own planet, to swim the warm seas, to feel familiar soft breezes on her membranes, to bask in a bright sun. She had been buried too long at her station, in a base concealed beneath the ground, shut away from the stars and the winds, the black nights and the hot days.

What strange and exotic scents filled this alien dark! She watched suddenly as the towering sillhouettes of pine trees swayed and rustled. She listened to the sounds of wind and rasping needles. Such music!

So many sights and scents and sounds her computers had never prepared her for. R'ilyeh cried out with joy! She began to run again, down the long mountain slope, taking pleasure in the swift, sure way her humanoid limbs carried her.

When she came to a mountain stream, though, she surrendered her favorite form. She began to think once more of Wallflower—of Joey—and a sense of urgency filled her. On the bank of the stream, she relaxed her membranes, all but the little folded place, and slipped into the water.

The chill temperature surprised her, and she adjusted her body heat to compensate. The turbulent water swept her along at a violent pace, but her people were natural swimmers, and she felt no fear. Within moments, she mastered the ever-shifting currents and rode them as surely as a bird rode the currents of the air.

The stream fed into a mightier river. The new, stronger currents dragged her deeper suddenly. She scraped the stony bottom and spun crazily around. Unharmed, she laughed like a child on a carnival thrill ride. Flexing her membranes, she propelled herself forward, swimming faster than the current could carry her until she reached the city called Boulder.

What a splendid sight! The lights of the city shone brighter than the stars, yet with a color and a calmness she found mesmerizing. Emerging from the river, she flowed across a grassy parkland like a trickle of water, thinking it best to keep a form that would not attract attention.

Leaving the park, she moved into the streets, onto the sidewalks. The maps she had hacked from the city planning offices served her well, and she navigated easily, surely, through the weird mazes of houses and offices and shops, pausing occasionally to marvel as an automobile rumbled past or as a jet aircraft thundered overhead.

An alien couple crossed her path, nearly stepping on her, as they talked quietly. Their arms were laden with books, she noted, and she recalled that a great center of learning stood nearby. If only she dared to visit it. Perhaps later she would!

She inflated her membranes, rising subtly from the sidewalk to watch the departing couple. She could hear them still, whispering words of love to each other. Preparing to mate, she thought. How closely they walked, how softly they spoke. There seemed almost a serenity to it, a ritual, yet the chemical scents they exuded were so faint, so weak. A miracle, she thought, that these aliens ever got together.

She turned slowly. In her observing of the humans, she had unconsciously adopted their shape. But in a shop's large plateglass window she discovered how untrue that was. Humanoid, she might manage, but never human. She stared at herself, finding in the glass only a strange mockery of the humans, a gleaming chrome-colored *thing,* eyes without pupil or iris, lips not made for laughing or kissing, a body smooth and hairless, seemingly misshapen without bone or joint or cartilege.

She had prided herself on her effort and achievement. Now she saw, in this glass, only boundaries and limitations. She was not an alien. She could never look like them. She could never move freely among them, and that, she realized with a flash of insight, had been a secretly-treasured dream.

She walked for half a block, watching herself in one window after another with a growing sadness. How would she greet Joey, she wondered, if he were well enough to greet at all?

Voices came from around the next corner. By the time a group of students reached her, she was nothing more noticeable than a puddle by the curb. She had abandoned her much-practiced form, never again to take it up.

Joey's house was a white, one-storied structure with an ill-kept yard and a fence with no gate. A battered automobile occupied the oil-stained driveway. Light shone in a few windows, but most of the dwelling stood in darkness.

R'ilyeh flowed across the grass to the nearest window. Extending a pseudopod to the sill, she drew herself up and peeked inside, noting the worn furniture, the pictures on the walls, the soft blue flicker of a television with its volume turned low. The room, however was empty.

She tried another window. The darkness beyond the glass convinced her this room, too, stood empty. She moved around to the back of the house. A dim light shone weakly through slanted blinds. R'ilyeh rose up to peer inside, and experienced a ripple of satisfaction.

Joey lay in bed asleep, the Amigo-Zoom 218 parked close by. An amazing number of books and magazines filled improvised shelving through the small room, and she recalled that he had said he liked to read. On a desk only a few paces from the bed sat his computer, its screen blank—a crude and primitive machine.

Extending thin pseudopods, R'ilyeh pried back the locks on the window and raised it enough to slip inside. Down the wall and onto the hardwood floor she slid. Approaching Joey's bedside, she inflated herself enough to study her little friend. By alien standards, she supposed, he was pretty. But the innocence that should have filled his placid face was marred by a subtle look of pain that rose even through his sleep.

Disease was not unknown to her, but on her world, it was so easily treated. No one suffered as this alien child suffered. Under the cotton coverlet she could see the outline of his twisted body. She looked at the Amigo again. In another corner of the room stood a pair of hideous metal leg braces, no longer beneficial.

R'ilyeh drew out the tiny plastic pillow from the folded place in her membrane. She had wondered how she would greet Joey. His sleeping made this easier. Hastily, she ripped the top of the pillow. Holding it close to Joey's lips, she squeezed out a few drops of the pale blue contents. He sighed ever so slightly, and the fluid slipped into his mouth.

Footsteps sounded suddenly outside the bedroom door, and the knob turned. Startled, R'ilyeh glanced toward the window. No time to get out that way, nor was she quite ready to leave. Relaxing her membranes, she tried to flow under the bed.

"My good lord, Joey!" The woman in the doorway was plainly Joey's mother; they shared a striking resemblance. Her voice, though, was little more than a weary whisper, not really meant to wake her son. She stared straight at R'ilyeh, not realizing what she truly saw. "Did you spill your water glass again?" She walked around Joey's bed to a small night table and picked up a glass. Discovering it nearly full, she frowned, then shrugged. "Guess I'd better get a mop."

R'ilyeh waited until Joey's mother was gone. Then she began to work quickly. She had come here for two reasons. Primarily, of course, to give Joey the medicine that would arrest his illness. But she also wanted access to a computer outside the base, a computer that N'yamet could not monitor, to launch a program that N'yamet could not stop.

Approaching Joey's desk, she drew out the data chip she had so carefully hidden. Extending numerous pseudopods, she rummaged over the desk, in its drawers. His computer utilized a 3.5 diskette drive. At last, in a bottom drawer among instruction manuals and warranties, she found a box of blank, formatted diskettes. She needed only one.

Listening for returning footsteps, she pressed the data chip to the diskette. Instantly, the chip liquefied and seemed to osmose right through the diskette's flat plastic sleeving. With the chip's information transferred to the diskette, R'ilyeh gave her attention to the computer. She tapped the antique keyboard, but nothing happened. She muttered a curse. An on-off switch then, but where? She ran her pseudopods over the monitors, over the drive unit, discovering several switches. She threw them all. Computer and monitor began to power up.

But slowly, at least by her standards.

The metallic rattle of a bucket warned R'ilyeh that Joey's mother had returned. *No time, no time!* R'ilyeh screamed silently. The operating system was still powering up. Even then it might take her ten or fifteen minutes to learn to manipulate such a crude collection of wires and circuit boards.

She grabbed a marking pen from the top of the desk. Quickly she scrawled across the diskette in large black letters, *A gift from Starflower.* She placed it under Joey's right hand. Pausing only a moment more, she whispered in her own language, "You are forever my little friend." With no place in the room to hide, she fled for the window, slipping out just as Joey's mother entered.

Outside again, R'ilyeh heard a gasp and for a moment, thought she'd been spotted. But in the next instant, she knew that wasn't the case. "I know I saw a puddle right here!" R'ilyeh heard a bucket and mop being quietly set down. A moment later, Joey's mother appeared at the window. She seemed to stare outward for some time, the tired lines of her face gradually relaxing. Finally, she pushed the window closed, lowered the blinds again, and moved away.

But R'ilyeh could hear her, talking softly, perhaps tearfully, to her sleeping child. No, not to her child, she suddenly realized. To her god. Praying, the aliens called it.

I could be Joey's guardian angel, she thought. *I could keep an eye on him in secret.*

She knew she could not. She looked up at the stars. The lights of the city dimmed them somewhat, but still they burned, and they called her, called her home to her own beaches, to the shores of another, more familiar world where the oceans were always warm and the breezes always gentle.

She had had her adventure, and she had saved her friend. Now it was Joey's turn for an adventure. She almost laughed. Instead, she slipped quietly out of Boulder, into the river, into the mountains.

N'yamet issued her a new, modified keyball.

"You may observe all you like and make reports accordingly," he informed her. "But you may no longer interact with the aliens in any manner. The keyball will automatically block any attempt to do so. You are, essentially, in read-only mode. And all your work will be thoroughly monitored until your replacement arrives."

The scent of his displeasure hung like a cloud over R'ilyeh's station. "You are fortunate your escapade has not jeopardized our mission. However, I will not forget your insubordination, and you will not have such an easy time as you have had here in the past."

"In your studies of the aliens," R'ilyeh said calmly, "have you discovered the connotations of this gesture?"

Extending a single pseudopod, she formed an almost human hand and curled four of its digits.

N'yamet flooded the room with his chemical anger, but he flowed to the door. "You go too far, R'ilyeh!"

She mocked his anger with the scent of her contempt as he left her alone. "You have no idea how far I've gone, N'yamet."

She tapped the new keyball, activating the screen that monitored Joey's chat-line. He wasn't there. Probably wouldn't be there for days, she suspected, as his doctors poked and prodded him as they tried to understand the miracle. And then there would be the press.

She accessed another service Joey sometimes used, a place where messages could be posted and left in place. She found one to make her smile—except she had no lips to smile with.

Starflower, Joey had written, *you did it, I know you did. I found a little plastic thing under my bed. It had some blue stuff in it that tasted sweet. I thought I dreamed that taste, but it was real, and I know you left it there, because you left the diskette. I saved what was left, sealed it up tight, and sent it to Emaciator. I hope it works for him, too. I tried to upload the diskette, but weird stuff happened. I think it's defective. P.S., I love you.*

Her membranes fluttered with mischievous delight. She couldn't answer Joey; she hoped he'd understand somehow. She felt ripples of pride, also, that he had sought to share his good fortune with another sick friend.

He had not failed to upload the diskette, however. By attempting to read it, he had activated the data chip's programing. The *weird stuff* had merely been the chip taking over his machine and uploading itself to selected targets.

Laughing silently, she worked her keyball, not caring if N'yamet monitored her actions or not. Dumping

Joey's post, she accessed the global Internet. One by one, she opened specific usegroups—media lists, science lists, medical lists, groups within groups, by the scores, by the hundreds.

In each one, user activity ran at a frantic pace.

The keyball twisted and turned. She activated another screen, pulling down a national news telecast. The announcer could hardly get his words out fast enough.

Cures for cancer, leukemia, for diabetes, for multiple sclerosis, for AIDS—the sum total of her people's medical research. She had planted it all across the Internet for the aliens to find, and they had done so.

And every posting bore a copyright in Joey's name. He and his mother would never want for anything.

N'yamet suddenly screamed at her from one of the monitors. Even across the circuitry she could almost smell his rage. With a command on the keyball, she muted the monitor, silencing his voice. As she watched him rail, she settled back on her platform and laughed at him.

No one should suffer, she thought, *except maybe N'yamet.*

FREEDOM

by Mickey Zucker Reichert

Mickey Zucker Reichert is a pediatrician whose twelve
science fiction and fantasy novels include *The Legend
of Nightfall, The Unknown Soldier,* and *The Renshai
Trilogy*. Her most recent release from DAW Books is
Prince of Demons, the second in *The Renshai Chroni-
cles* trilogy. Her short fiction has appeared in numerous anthologies. Her claims to fame: she *has*
performed brain surgery, and her parents *really are*
rocket scientists.

Even after two weeks, the wheelchair still felt like a
prison to Cora Anderson. The coldness of the metal
sides seeped through her house dress in long stripes,
and the padding did little to ease the dull cramps that
ached through her from remaining in a near-constant
position. She attempted to raise her hands to her face,
forgetting, as she still so often did, that only the right
one would obey. On that one side, she ran her fingers
over wrinkled cheeks she scarcely recognized, her skin
as dry and withered as parchment. Longing filled her
for the facial cream that kept it supple, but the stroke
that confined her to this chair also prevented her from
asking. Sentences and concepts formed as easily as
ever in her mind; but, when she attempted to vocalize
them, they came out all wrong, often only in wordless grunts.

Brushing back wisps of thin white hair, Cora returned her right hand to the wheel of the chair. She
shoved it forward, the momentum on just one side

thrusting her leftward. She corrected for the deviation by scooting with her right foot, her forward progress frustratingly minimal. Tears pooled blue eyes that seemed to have grown smaller through the years and more prominently rimmed pink. Gritting her teeth, she forced the tears away with resolve. She had managed to roll herself from the study and into the hallway, a feat she could not have managed even a day ago. Progress should elate not dishearten, yet she could not release the images of herself as a younger woman. Even in her forties and fifties, she had jogged a mile a day and swam when the weather allowed it. As she approached sixty, she had switched to jumping rope and pedaling an exercise bike. Her entire life, she had remained active; and the wheelchair now seemed more like a trap than a means of locomotion.

The odor of bacon and eggs wafted to Cora's nose, and voices trickled down the corridor from the kitchen. Though seventeen years old, Tiffany, Cora's granddaughter, whined like a toddler. "Does she have to eat with us?" She added, voice thick with revulsion, "She drools."

Chair legs scraped the floor, then fifteen-year-old Jeremy added his piece. "And she makes those creepy noises."

The newspaper rustled, and Phil Satterson, Cora's son-in-law, cleared his throat. "She smells bad, too."

"Yeah." Tiffany picked up the conversation again. "It's hard to eat when it reeks."

The words cut through Cora's heart like a knife. The grandchildren she had babysat, who had begged her to bake cookies and worn her best hats for dress-up games, now turned against her. Years ago, the Sattersons had moved too far away for more than rare visits; and, when they did come, seeing old friends took precedence for Tiffany and Jeremy and football games for Phil and Marie. Cora had continued sending expensive birthday presents and cooking feasts at

Christmas and Thanksgiving; but those feats, apparently, won her no loyalty. *Of course, I stink. I can't bathe myself, and none of you can spare the five minutes to do it for me.* Her own helplessness bothered her far more than her family's laziness.

"Can't we just put her in a nursing home?" Jeremy said.

Marie Satterson finally answered her family's concerns. "We've been through this. A nursing home would eat up Grandma's savings in a couple of months. Then we'd have to start paying with our own money. Are you willing to give up your allowance?" Dishes rattled, and a cupboard slammed. "Can you spare your weekly golf game and your beers? It's going to take more sacrifices than just those."

Cora heard no answers, but Marie must have received something nonverbal from each.

"I work, too, you know," Marie complained. "I haven't got the time to make six meals a day. And the doctor said Grandma will do better with company, if people talk to her. Now, I'm going to fetch her, and I don't want to hear another word about it." Footsteps tapped across the kitchen floor, then Marie appeared at the far end of the hallway.

Cora sagged back into the chair, will shaken from her. She could not imagine weeks, months, or years stuck with a family, her own family, who despised her, incapable of expressing her feelings and even unable to move more than a few paces. All her life, she had been a fighter. When her husband had died, when Marie was only four, she had struggled to maintain a household in an era when few women worked, when men did not want to raise another's child, and when mothers remained home with their children, supported not by the taxpayers, but by their husbands. She always believed she had given Marie the best she could afford, thought she had instilled a sense of compassion and morality. Clearly, she had not done as good a job as she believed she had, and Phil had stolen what little she had accomplished.

Marie took three long strides down the hallway before noticing Cora. Then, she stopped suddenly. "Oh! Mother. You made it this far. That's terrific." Rushing around the chair, she seized the handles and rolled the wheelchair toward the kitchen.

Cora did not attempt a thank you. Even had she felt welcome in her daughter's kitchen, she saw no reason to produce the incomprehensible syllables that Jeremy called creepy.

Once a place of busy conversation, the kitchen became ominously silent as the wheelchair rolled across the tiles. Tiffany stared at her empty plate, her long dyed blonde hair hanging in loose curls. Though subtly colored, her makeup caked, a strange contrast to her tight black T-shirt and jeans. Across the table from her, Jeremy slouched, bony knees jutting from holes in his blue jeans. Loud colors paraded across a T-shirt covered by a flannel shirt with no buttons fastened and the sleeves cut crookedly near his shoulders. Frayed cotton threads dangled. Phil sat at one end of the table, newspaper propped against a steaming mug of coffee. Scalp showed through gaps in black hair peppered with gray, and his gut bulged out his dress pants.

Marie wheeled Cora to the table beside Jeremy, and no one bothered to greet or even look at her. As Marie returned to the stove, Cora deliberately studied each of her grandchildren in turn. They avoided her gaze.

Coming back to the table, Marie took the plates from in front of her children, filled them from the pans at the stove, and returned them with eggs and bacon. She heaped Phil's plate, then placed smaller amounts in front of Cora and herself.

"Give me the o.j.," Tiffany said.

When Phil did not acknowledge his daughter's re-

quest, she made a great show of leaning far over her
plate to nudge the carton toward her.

With a nasty grin, Jeremy snatched it up and poured
himself a glass. Tiffany glared until he finished, grabbing it before he could replace it on the table and
filling her own glass. Marie took the container next,
pouring orange juice into her own glass and into
Cora's.

Cora drank, despising the orange line that dribbled
from the left corner of her mouth as much as the
crinkle-faced glance of revulsion she received from her
granddaughter. Tiffany downed her glass, rose, then
rushed from the room with a muttered, "Can't afford
the calories."

Marie turned in her chair as her daughter dashed
from the kitchen. "Tiffany!" She shrugged as the girl
left her sight, defending her daughter's rudeness.
"Girls. Always watching their figures."

Jeremy grinned around a mouthful of eggs. "I'll eat
hers." Hooking Tiffany's plate with a finger, he pulled
it toward him.

Phil lowered the newspaper. "Sometimes I think
those computer gajillionaires pay off all the newspa-
pers and magazines. Look, even the comics are doing
the Internet." He tapped the newspaper with a finger.
"If I see one more cartoon of a cat munching on a
computer mouse or one more joke about someone
getting run over on the information superhighway, I'm
going to scream."

Jeremy swallowed. "You know, speaking of the information superhighway, I read somewhere recently
that only thirteen percent of people who own computers are on the Internet."

Phil picked up on the words as if he had spoken
them. "Yet they act like everyone's got a computer
and everyone's on-line. They don't even ask before
they say they're going to E-mail you. If you say you
don't have E-mail, they look at you like you're a driv-

eling caveman and say stuff like, 'It's the 1990's, man. What are you doing writing on paper?' "

Marie laughed, raising her fork and delicately cutting a strip of bacon. "What are you raving about, Phil? You're one of the thirteen percent."

"Yeah. But I don't treat the other ninety-nine percent of the population like ignorant savages."

"Eighty-seven percent," Jeremy corrected.

Phil shook his head. "That's eighty-seven percent of computer owners. I'll bet fewer than a quarter of American homes even have PC's."

Cora glanced at the cholesterolfest on her plate, and her stomach went queasy at the thought of eating any of it. Again, she drank, glad the conversation had turned away from her. Even if she could properly speak, she would have nothing to add here. She had always tried to stay up with modern trends, but she had had little use for a home computer.

Marie forked the bacon into her mouth, chewed, and swallowed. "So what do you think of the Internet? Is it everything they say?"

Phil gave the newspaper another whack with his fingers. "If it was everything they say, we'd live in a world of rainbows and puppies. I'd make Einstein look like an idiot, and we'd have a cure for every disease that plagues mankind."

"I'd take that as a 'no,' " Jeremy translated.

Phil shoved half a fried egg into his mouth and made a wordless noise of dismissal. "It's interesting enough. I haven't had that much time to explore, but I've chatted with some people about this and that. For someone with nothing else to do, it'd probably be great."

That's me. Cora wished she had bothered to keep up with the computing trends. She doubted she could begin learning now, especially when no one would bother to teach her. *Besides, what good could it possibly do when I can't communicate?*

Phil glanced at his watch, then wolfed down more food. He spoke around a mouthful of bacon. "I've got a problem with the new system, though. Probably going to have to get it repaired, but first I'm going to see if I can hook up with guys who've had a similar problem and can suggest anything."

Marie ate more slowly. "What's the problem?"

"Oh, I'll be writing or reading something, and the screen will flicker. It's just every once in a while, and it doesn't seem to bother what's on the screen. But it's annoying."

"Power fluctuations?" Jeremy suggested as he finished his plate and started on Tiffany's.

"Maybe." Phil shook his head, as if to dismiss what he had just admitted could be the answer. "But it's just not like that. I'll get on tonight after work and post the question." Rising, he headed from the kitchen, pulling on his coat as he moved and pausing only to kiss the top of Marie's head. "See you later."

"Have a good day," Marie returned mechanically. She glanced at Jeremy. "You'd better hurry, too. I've got Grandma to take care of, so I don't have the time to drive you if you miss the bus."

"Tiffany can take me."

The girl's voice floated in from the hallway. "But you know I won't."

Marie sighed at what was, clearly, an old argument. "Get going, Jer."

The boy headed from the room, leaving Cora alone with her daughter. Marie quietly finished her breakfast, her dark eyes so like her father's, her brown hair cut into a crisp, business style. Snatches of garbled conversation occasionally sifted into the kitchen, then the door slammed shut three times at irregular intervals. Marie breathed a tiny sigh of relief as the last member of her family headed for school. One by one, she transferred her own dishes, then those of her children and husband, to the sink. She came to Cora's side. "Are you not eating, Mother?"

Cora shook her head.

Marie scooped up the plate, dumped the contents into the garbage, then placed the plate into the sink. Leaving Cora at the table, she headed into the hallway. Minutes ticked past while Cora sat silent and alone. Using her right hand, she maneuvered her chair from the table and faced the hallway. Bare, slate-colored walls funneled into the familiar darkness that led to bedrooms and the cramped, packed study that had become her sleeping place. The arrangement reminded Cora of books she had read about death, the long ride through a bleak tunnel, though this one heralded no light at the exit.

Marie returned, smelling of Chanel #5 and wearing lipstick too red for her coloring. "I have to go to work now, too." She wheeled the chair through the hallway, pushing it back into the study. They had cleared a place for Cora in the middle. Bookshelves held mostly magazines, in untidy, random piles. The new computer perched on a desk, a black chair askew in front of it. A rumpled couch covered with dusty throws and blankets filled the third wall, Cora's new sleeping place when they did not simply leave her in the chair.

"I need you to stay here while I'm gone." Marie maneuvered the wheelchair into the study. "I know you don't understand me . . ."

Yes, I do.

". . . but I can't have you rolling downstairs or bumping into furniture. I'll see you when I get back." Without even a token gesture of affection, Marie turned and left the study, closing the door behind her. Cora listened as her daughter's footsteps disappeared down the hallway. The squeak of the opening door was followed by the boom of its closing.

Silence closed suffocatingly in on Cora. Helpless, she sat in her chair, anticipating nine hours of quiet nothingness. Five days a week, she would have no choice but to stare at the same dull furnishings, living nothing but the memories in her own mind. *Maybe I'll die before I go mad.* The thought did not comfort. She seized the right-hand wheel, dredging up the strength to move it. Tediously slowly, she managed to turn. Then, with repeated flops of the wheel followed by the shuffle of her good foot, she inched toward the door. Gradually, she reached it, but she found herself unable to stretch far enough to touch the knob. Flop and shuffle. Flop and shuffle. She managed to turn the wheelchair to her right. Even then, she could not work the knob.

Frustration became a lead weight, pinning her into hopeless stillness. She slumped back into the chair, trying to fill the empty moments with happy thoughts of the past; but those only fuelled her feelings of helpless despair. Tears dripped from her eyes, and her old hands shook, even the one that seemed lost to her. Fingers that had once coaxed music from the ivory keys of a piano, that had effortlessly typed 150 words per minute, that had knitted beautiful sweaters and blankets for her grandchildren now failed her, along with the tongue she had taken so much for granted.

After what seemed like hours, Cora finally regathered the mental and physical power to turn again. Her eyes fell on the computer, and its sterile smoothness became a floating board in a stormy sea. Flop and shuffle. Flop and shuffle. Flop/shuffle. She dragged herself across the room. With effort, she managed to use the bulk of the chair, rather than her own muscle, to shove the desk chair aside. Then, she sat in front of the system, eyes playing over monitor, CPU, keyboard, and mouse. The manuals sat on a shelf above the desk, far beyond her reach. She would have to hope the instructions would be self-explanatory.

First step, turn it on. Cora poked the button on the front of the CPU. Nothing happened. *Maybe it's not plugged in.* She followed the cord to a gray power strip, along with three others and a telephone jack. The switch on the strip read "off." Tapping it to "on" resulted in a gray glow on the computer screen and a thunk from the printer. She stared at the monitor several moments, waiting for something more to happen. When it did not, she sighed deeply. *If I can't turn it on, how will I ever figure out how to use it?* She glanced at the setup again, heart pounding a slow cadence that quickened with each passing moment. For the first time since the stroke, something had captured her attention long enough to allow her to forget her handicaps. If it took her an eternity, if it became the flame to her moth, it could prove no worse than the life she already led.

The answer came an instant later, seeming too obvious for words. Feeling stupid, Cora pressed the CPU button again. Light flashed suddenly across the monitor, then the picture resolved into strings of words and numbers that made little sense to her. A count appeared on the screen, numbers growing swiftly larger. Then, the computer beeped. The screen blanked, though she could still hear machinery clicking through the CPU. A moment later, icons appeared on a slate blue background, beneath the words "Microsoft Windows 95."

Cora had read enough of the magazine articles and cartoons to have a basic understanding of how to use a mouse. The curved piece of white plastic lay in a perfect position for her good right hand. Cupping it into her fingers, she practiced rolling it across the pad. A pale arrow appeared on the screen, perfectly mimicking her movements. *Not so hard.* Excitement buzzed through her, more exhilarating for its long absence. This time, she became too intent even to realize she had lost track of the desperate brooding that had become the sole focus of her universe. Pulling the

arrow to the icon clearly labeled "Internet," she removed her hand from the mouse.

Nothing happened.

Cora tapped the rightward button. It clicked, but
the screen did not change. She clicked the left button
without effect. Left then right. Right then left. Right
then right. Left then left, she tried. This time, the
monitor went blank again, and the clacking recurred
deep inside the workings of the CPU. *I got it.* Relief
flooded Cora, replaced suddenly by desperate realization. *Why am I bothering? Even if I found something
or someone interesting, how would I communicate?*
Even as the thought came, more words flashed across
the screen, followed by a box that read:

```
USER NUMBER: _____

|   PMS356                                  |

PASSWORD: _____

|_____|
```

The cursor blinked in the second box. Cora
groaned, slumping. Pain ached through her hips, and
her hand cramped on the mouse. She had come so far
only to be thwarted by a password she could never
hope to guess, even could her fingers manage to type
the words. Nevertheless, she tried. She had nothing
better, or even else, to do.

Using her right index finger to hunt and peck, Cora
typed out: "P." On the screen, it appeared as a "*."
This did not deter Cora, accustomed to her bank machine hiding her card code in the same manner. She
typed an "H" and received another "*." "I" and "L"

followed, both yielding the same "*." She hit "Enter."
A beep followed, along with the error message, "improper code." However, unlike with the bank machine, she had no card to lose.

Cora tried again, this time with Phil's initials. Marie
had mentioned them often since discovering his middle name was Michael. The joke amused her long after
all others grew tired of it. "P-M-S," Cora typed and
received the same error message and beep as before.
She tried "Marie," "Tiffany," and "Jeremy," all without success. She used "Buttercup," the name of Phil's
childhood golden retriever and "Sport," Phil's nickname for Jeremy in his youth. She entered Phil's favorite foods, the few sports figures she could
remember, and the house number, 356. She entered
the name of their street, "Elm," Phil's dead parents,
"Irene" then "Richard." None of these proved effective; but, at least, the machine did not shut itself down.
She almost expected the computer police to slam
down the door and arrest the helpless cripple in a
wheelchair who dared to try and break another's code.

An hour passed while Cora's attempts grew wilder
and her stamina waned. Fatigue prodded the edges of
her mind, hampering coherent thought. Yet, beneath
it all, ideas blossomed that seemed nearly as frightening as thrilling. If she could type individual words, she
could likely type sentences. If so, she had found a
means of communication that might restore some of
the dignity to her life. Using the computer, or even a
simple typewriter, she could write all the words her
brain could no longer organize for speech. The stroke
had stolen so much, but it had missed this one saving
grace. *But how do I let them know?*

Cora's mind seized on the realization that she might
never find a way. An ability that had, only a second
ago, seemed a godsend now became a desperate torment. *I'll find a way to show them,* she reassured herself without a plan. *First, I need to know for certain I*

can type more than single words. Her first work, she decided, would be a simple poem. Later, perhaps, she would spend the days working on her memoirs. She smiled inwardly at the idea. *Memoirs, right sure. Cora Anderson, Portrait of an American Secretary. Fascinating.*

Having discovered no other place to type, Cora began her poem in the password column of the Internet access. Having never written anything creative before, she considered for several moments. *Poems should be about something emotional. Something ultimately significant to the writer.* That thought spurred an immediate subject that became the title. She typed: "F-R-E-E-D-O-M."

For an instant, the *'s froze in place. A flicker traversed the monitor, odd and unlike anything Cora had seen it do thus far. Without understanding how, she knew she had discovered the glitch Phil had complained about at breakfast. Then, suddenly, the monitor went blank. An hourglass-shaped cursor appeared in the upper lefthand corner, then words Cora never typed appeared beside it: "I am Freedom."

Below the words, the start of a new paragraph, lay the triangular cursor Cora had used earlier. Startled, she stared several moments at the words before lifting a finger to attempt a ponderous reply: "Is Freedom your name?" She studied the straight letters, scarcely daring to believe herself responsible for them. Then, realizing the other might have grown tired of awaiting a reply and gone looking elsewhere for conversation, she hit enter.

An answer came swiftly: "It is what I call myself."

"My name is Cora Anderson," she typed back. "I call myself 'me.'"

The hourglass cursor reappeared, followed by the words: "Doe a deer, Cora Anderson."

Cora laughed aloud for the first time since the

stroke, then typed. "You caught me, Freedom. And just Cora is good enough."

"Cora, do you need me?"

The question took Cora aback, and she did not know how to answer, or even if she should. *Great, thirteen percent of computer users on the Internet, and I have to find a lunatic.* Nevertheless, conversing with this fellow Internetter seemed far more interesting than the alternative. She preferred chatting, even with a crazy person, to staring at the walls. *I probably shouldn't have used my real name.* "Need you? I don't even know who you are."

"I am freedom."

Yes, yes. I know that's what you call yourself. Cora hesitated.

The writing continued. "You called on me."

Though Cora knew little about computers, the oddity struck her at once. If, in fact, "Freedom" was Phil's password, the key that got her connected, then the person she addressed should not know that she had typed it. Uncertain where to take the conversation, or her knowledge, Cora told the truth. "I was writing a poem. Freedom was the title."

"How does the rest of the poem go?"

"I don't know. I haven't written it yet."

"Go ahead."

"Write it now?" Cora asked incredulously.

"Why not?"

"I've been a secretary most of my life, not a writer. I'm not creative. I've never written a poem before."

"You must have a reason for feeling the need to do so now."

I'm not sure I still have a reason. At least, not as driving as before. Still, Cora saw no reason not to try. She doubted poor poetry would drive off one lonely enough to converse with an old, wheelchair-bound woman. "All right. But I warn you, I'm slow." *Great,*

Cora. Make him or her think you're stupid. "I mean, a slow typist."

Freedom challenged, "I thought you were a secretary."

"I was," Cora admitted. "But I only have one hand to work with now, and it's not my dominant one." She amended, "Well, I guess it is my dominant hand now." She asked the question plaguing her almost since the conversation started, "Are you a man or a woman?"

It seemed like a straightforward question, one that should not require thought, yet Freedom paused longer than ever before. "A man,"

Cora waited, Freedom's punctuation suggested more to come, though the answer hardly needed it.

When Cora typed nothing more, Freedom pressed. "Your poem, please. I have all the time in the world."

Cora nodded, feeling silly for making conversational gestures her writing partner could not see. She started:

> "Freedom
>
> The blackness billows in grim clouds
> Obscuring radiance that cannot be.
> The beauty is inside myself,
> The fog reality."

Though it took fifteen minutes to construct, Cora beamed at the effort. She hit enter.

"Great, so far." Freedom had remained on-line, as patient as he had promised. "Please go on."

Go on? Believing herself finished, Cora considered. *Why not go on? I have plenty of time as well.* She wrote:

> "Aging, like a dying rat,"
> *Now there's a bleak comparison.*
> "Breeds a plague within me.

That steals my voice but not my mind.
My left but not my right—unkind
Never again to run free."

Though she despised her efforts, once started, she could not stop. Her feelings needed venting.

"Trapped in a wheelchair
With nowhere to go.
Trapped by my body
Never once treated shoddy.
No longer containing my soul

"Outside in, like a mirror
Reflecting a chance
To escape this, my prison
Body, newly risen
Allowing me just one more dance.

"As a ghost from my grave
From my grief, broken-hearted
I'd savor the day
I could get up and play
Prison and soul finally parted."

Cora paused a long time, embarrassed by her efforts. *Should I send it.* Common sense told her "no;" but, if the one who called himself Freedom waited, it seemed unfair to show him nothing. As a compromise, she typed: "You asked for it." at the top, then struck the Enter key.

Freedom responded a minute later. "You really *do* need me. Are you sick?"

"A stroke," Cora wrote.

"Your body is a prison, and death seems kinder."

Cora could not help asking. "Is this a common conversation on the Internet?"

"There is no such thing as 'common' on the Internet. When people talk, you never know what they'll say. The only difference is that you have time to edit your words before sending, but I doubt many do. And you're limited by what you can spell." He added, "Maybe. People lose a lot of good points to their own grammar."

Cora smiled, beginning to like her new companion. "You know, you really are freedom for me. For the last hour and a half, I've beaten the stroke. It can't confine me while I talk with you."

Freedom paused. Then, gradually, letters took place on the monitor. "I can do so much more for you, Cora Anderson."

Cora shied away, worried for what that more might be, but only for a moment. Even murder was an escape from the endless bleak tyranny of a family that despised her and a body that had betrayed her.

"I've been there, Cora."

"You had a stroke?"

"No. I had amyotrophic lateral sclerosis—Lou Gehrig's disease. I lost one function after another: my coordination, my strength, then the use of entire extremities. Day by day, I watched myself die. In pieces."

A chill invaded Cora, and she found herself wholly speechless. She struggled to say something, anything, before forcing him to continue without some indication of her sympathy. "I'm sorry," she wrote. "I truly am."

"I know," he said. "I feel the same for you."

Cora could not believe her first Internet contact so closely shared her misery. "How old are you, Freedom?"

"What year is this?"

"1996," Cora typed and entered before she could think about what he asked in detail. She added, "Don't you know?"

"When you have all the time in the world, details don't matter. I would be 63."

Freedom's phrasing bewildered Cora. "All the time in the world? I'd read that Lou Gehrig's disease is incurable and ... well ... fatal." She hoped the doctors had informed him. The burden of bearing such news should not have to fall on a stranger over the Internet. "And what do you mean 'would be' 63?"

"I was born in 1933. How about you?"

"You're dodging my questions."

"And you're dodging mine. It's okay. You can lie about your age. Most women do."

Cora suspected the only way to corner Freedom into an answer was to give one of her own. "I don't need to lie about my age. I'm 61 and not a bit ashamed of it. Now answer my questions."

"Not yet. You're not ready. First let's talk. About our lives before the illnesses. About music. About our views. Let's talk politics. Let's talk religion. Let's talk about every taboo subject in the universe."

And they did. For six hours they discussed topics Cora never realized she missed. Had she met him at a singles' dance even two months ago, she might have entertained fantasies of marriage. He had been an anthropology professor, specializing in death rituals and various cultures' beliefs in the afterlife. He had discovered the Internet when it consisted only of a handful of computers linked for academic purposes. His disease had allowed him to explore the computer long after the ability to do anything more had left him. Otherwise, the world they both knew meshed with frightening rightness, coming not only of the decades they shared but from middle-class upbringings and the events that shaped those decades. They shared so many details that seemed unimportant. More significantly, he understood her thirst for freedom, her need for independence, and her desire to live. So much of the world remained unexplored, and he unearthed regrets she never before realized she harbored. So many things she still wished to do; and now defeated by a blood clot, she would never know those things.

Time flew, but not so swiftly that its passage escaped Cora. She would have to leave the Internet before Marie or Phil returned home. They might take this last pleasure from her, not understanding her need and worrying that she might ruin an expensive piece of machinery. If they shut her away in another room, she would become even more the desperate hostage. "Will I talk with you again tomorrow, Freedom?"

The response came rapidly. "Cora, join my freedom, and we can be together always."

Cora cared too much for her new companion to dismiss his words as madness. She saw no good coming from bringing bodily together a victim of a neurological disease and a stroke. "You're talking nonsense."

A sound snapped through the hallway. Desperation seized Cora. "I have to go."

"No, wait!"

"They'll catch me. If you ever want to hear from me again, you have to let me go." It occurred to Cora suddenly that she had no idea how to exit the Internet.

"If you truly want freedom, Cora, stay. And trust me." He followed these words with a string of commands, the last of which involved a sequence that would surely electrocute her. And he ended with an oddity that reminded her of his studies: "Black magic for a black box."

Footsteps thumped down the hallway.

"This is insane!" Cora wrote.

"Trust me, Cora. I've been dead for ten years, yet never more alive. Freedom awaits you."

The footsteps drew closer.

Cora made the most spontaneous decision of her life. She followed the directions verbatim, the keystrokes and connections nonsensical to her. Only one who had spent years languishing in a bed with no com-

pany but the Internet, who had studied the death rituals of myriad cultures, could have found such a
solution. That, or a madman. *Black Magic for a black
box.* Cora hesitated at the last command.

The knob rattled, and the door swung open.
"Mother?" Marie said.

Death can't be worse. Cora shoved the power cord
and modular plug between her teeth and bit as hard
as possible.

"MOTHER!"

Cora heard nothing more. Her soul seemed to flow
with the electricity, flying weightless through a world
as yet unexplored. She felt her body jerk backward,
flapping in a horrible convulsion, then lost all connection to it. And never looked back.

Phil Satterson used his half of the inheritance to
purchase a new surge protector, a CD rom drive,
memory and speed enhancements, and a laser printer.
He spent his Saturdays in an endless quest to find the
cause of the occasional brief pauses and flashes that
still plagued the system, seeming to come twice as
often as before. Others noticed them, too; and no one
had uncovered a solution. Even the repairman at the
computer shop simply shook his head with a dry comment that he wished his own system worked as well.
One fellow netter even claimed the disruptions had a
name, calling itself "freedom," but Phil dismissed that
as a product of a diseased mind. After all, the old
man admitted in the same conversation that he had
fallen victim to polio.

And the Internet was all that geezer had left.

REDEMPTION INC.

by Gary A. Braunbeck

Gary A. Braunbeck has sold over sixty short stories to various mystery, suspense, science fiction, fantasy, and horror markets. His first collection, *Things Left Behind,* is scheduled for hardcover release this year. He has been a full-time writer since 1992, and lives in Columbus, Ohio.

" 'I see nobody on the road,' said Alice.
'I only wish *I* had such eyes,' the King remarked
in a fretful tone. 'To be able to see Nobody!
And at that distance too!' "
—LEWIS CARROLL
Through the Looking Glass

Later, it occurred to Glenn MacIntyre that death and cyberspace might well be two sides of the same coin—after all, no one really knew what happened to the soul (if there was such a thing) after the body died, and no one (despite all the technobabble) could truly define to his satisfaction what, exactly, cyberspace was—aside from saying it was the place where the bank kept your money, where your insurance remained active, where radio waves went once you turned off the stereo receiver, or where, say, Copland's *Appalachian Spring Suite* continued to exist once the orchestra had stopped playing, packed up, and gone home.

Death, cyberspace, and the soul.

The hammer, the coffin, and the nail.

Such were the thoughts in the mind of a grieving, guilt-ridden man.

Later.

The first thing Glenn did upon returning home from his sister's funeral was make a beeline for the kitchen, grab the bottle of Scotch from the cabinet over the sink, unscrew the cap, and take two mouthfuls straight from the bottle.

Only then could he bring himself to face what sat on the desk in his apartment's middle room.

The computer—a fairly recent model—had belonged to Janice, his sister. She'd bought it as a replacement for an older, outmoded model about ten months ago and had immediately signed up for several different online services so she could (as she put it), "Talk to people without their having to worry about touching me."

"Computers scare me," he'd said to her.

"*Everything* scares in you in one way or another, Bigbro. Which explains why you're such a social butterfly."

"I prefer to think of myself as a homebody."

"Right. And I prefer to think of myself as being immunologically challenged."

"That's not funny."

"Yeah, it is," she said, her voice even then carrying a hint of the raw, agonized whisper it would become. "When I was at the hospital this last time, somebody told a tumor joke to one of the terminal cancer patients. You should've heard that guy laugh. Said it was the funniest joke anyone'd ever told him. The thing is, what all you HIV-negatives don't understand is that true appreciation of tomb humor depends on what side of the door you're standing. I've been chatting with other AIDS patients online and I'll bet I've downloaded a hundred AIDS jokes they've shared with me. Funny stuff."

"Uh-huh," said Glenn. "I suppose you plan to leave 'em laughing?"

"You betcha. I'm gonna do an Oscar Wilde—'Either those drapes go or I do.' Something to remember me by—which reminds me; you're inheriting this computer, so you might as well sit down and let me show you how to work the thing."

"I'd much rather watch you paint."

Janice shook her head. "Not today. Maybe not anymore. Don't worry, I'm working on something. I just don't want you to see it yet. Now come over here and sit down. This is called a 'keyboard.' You see all these little keys with letters on them? This is the letter 'A'—"

"Very funny."

"Look, Bigbro, if you and me're gonna surf the net together, you gots to pay attention."

"Why in God's name would I want to surf the net?"

She smiled at him. "It's a great way for you 'homebodies' to meet people. Besides, you never know what you may find waiting for you out there in—*dum-da-DUM-DUM*—cyberspace."

"Nice *Dragnet* theme."

"Thank you. I watch a lot of television these days."

The Kaposi's sarcoma was still undiagnosed, so she hadn't started chemo yet; she was still being treated for early-stage *Pneumocystis Carinii* Pneumonia but was able to get around on her own, still able to crack jokes and get under his skin like only a younger sibling can.

Jesus, she went down fast when it finally happened.

Still staring at the computer, Glenn started to take another swig from the bottle, decided that was a little too *Lost Weekend*-ish, and so poured the liquor into a glass and marched over to the desk.

He sat down and began sorting through the mail from this morning. Bills, a couple of grocery store flyers, a package from the Book-of-the-Month Club, the new issue of *Mother Jones,* a few more bills, and a padded manila envelope addressed to Mr. Glenn 'A#1Bigbro' MacIntyre.

He stared at the label for several seconds, then looked at the return address:

Redemption Inc. Online Services
Part of the AWARE Network

He couldn't fault their timing, that was certain.

"What kind of service is this?" he'd asked Janice once.

"It's specially designed for folks like me."

"AIDS patients?"

A shrug. *"All terminal cases."*

"What does it provide?"

A smile. *"What was it I used to say to you when I was a kid? 'That's for me to know and you to find out.'"*

Inside was a cover letter, a 3.5 floppy disk and a gold CD (both of which he placed on the desk and stared at as if they were multi-legged things that had just crawled out of the garbage disposal). He read the letter:

Dear Mr. MacIntyre:

Enclosed please find your startup software for the AWARE network. Your first year's service has already been paid (excepting any additional hours you may accumulate over and above those provided free of charge every month) and your sponsor has requested that we activate your membership within seven days of the date listed above. We at **Redemption Inc.** are proud to be a part of the AWARE Network and hope you will enjoy the countless services available to you here twenty-four hours a day, seven days a week, three-hundred-and-sixty-five days a year.

To begin, simply insert the disk in your floppy disk drive (A or B); click on the "File" menu of your Program Manager, select "Run", then type A:\SETUP (or B:\SETUP) and press OK. Due to the highly individu-

alized nature of your program, it will take about fifteen minutes to activate AWARE.

A note: Once you download the **Redemption Inc.**
program, make sure to obey all instructions *precisely*
as they are displayed on your screen and follow them
through until the initial program has been installed. It
will take about twenty additional minutes; any attempt
to exit the program once it has been engaged could
result in damage to your computer's internal memory.
We assure you that this is a one-time only danger to
your system, and apologize for any inconvenience the
setup/logon/download portion may cause you.

Welcome to AWARE!

He put down the letter, then inserted the disk into
the computer's "A" drive (Janice had taken great
pains to explain the differences among the system's
three drives to him), and began to move the cursor
toward the Program Manager icon when it struck him
that this was his sister's final gift to him.

His chest hitched and his shoulders slumped and his
eyes stung as the guilt and self-condemnation yet
again raked their cat claws across his center. He
brought a hand up and pressed it against his eyes as
if he could hold back the tears by sheer force of will
and surprised himself by not crying—but he began to
shake. At first only around his stomach, but it quickly
fanned out into his shoulders, then his arms, and then
his hands. He felt the thin layer of sweat that was
coating his palms and tasted something bitter on his
tongue, which a hard swallow of Scotch helped to
make a bit more palatable.

He turned away from the desk and looked at the
painting hanging on the opposite wall of the room,
the painting Janice hadn't wanted him to see until it
was finished. He'd found it in her tiny studio the day
she'd died. It had been covered by a heavy tarpaulin
to which she'd taped a note: *For you, Bigbro. Please*

don't let Mom or Dad see this. I don't think they'd understand.

It was a self-portrait she'd begun shortly after being diagnosed HIV-positive.

Staring at it now, Glenn almost couldn't breathe.

She'd positioned herself and the easel between two large, full-length mirrors so that every reflection of herself painting held a reflection of herself painting a reflection of herself painting a reflection of herself painting, each successive image growing progressively smaller until she was little more than a smudge in the final, smallest reflection. If that had been all she'd done with it, it still would have been a dizzying study in perspective, but Janice had gone several steps beyond that; starting with the second reflection, her features began to change, to grow more shrunken and diseased until, in the last clear reflection, she had been reduced to a monstrosity, a pasty-faced, emaciated, diseased, hairless *thing,* its mouth opened and twisted downward as if gasping for breath, eyes so deeply sunk into the back of the skull it was hard to tell if they were eyes at all. Everything that had made her human, that had made her Janice, had been slowly, agonizingly siphoned away—yet there was something almost comical in each of her reflected faces, something that told you she was letting you in on the joke—even if you weren't exactly sure what the joke was supposed to be.

She'd titled it: *And I Didn't Even Need a Map.*

He turned back to the computer, clicked the Program Manager icon, and spent the next forty minutes logging on first to AWARE, then **Redemption Inc.** He followed the instructions to the letter. It was surprisingly simple: click here, click there, move the cursor to that, click this icon, insert CD into the CD-ROM drive tray, type that, then sit back and wait.

After several minutes, the screen went blank for a moment, the modem dialed up a phone number, there was a buzz, a beep, and series of hisses, then the following appeared:

At Redemption Inc. our goal is to provide you, the survivor, with the best and most personalized service available. Please take a moment to check that the following information is correct:
1) Name of deceased (first, middle or initial, and last).
2) Deceased's date of birth.
3) Deceased's date of death.
4) Cause of death.
5) Place of death.
6) Names of any friends and/or relatives present at the time of death.
7) Names of medications the deceased was taking at the time of death.
8) The deceased's favorite:
artists/authors/beverages/books/clothing designers/composers/colors/movies/musical groups/ outfits to wear/paintings/poems/possessions/ places to visit/restaurants in your area/songs/ television programs; feel free at this time to add any additional information you think pertinent.

It took only a few minutes for Glenn to check that the information was correct. Once that was done, he moved on to the questions:

1) Do you consider yourself an outgoing person?
2) Do you consider yourself an introvert?
3) If "Yes", please state why.
4) How emotionally close were you to the deceased?
5) What are five of your best memories concerning the deceased and yourself?
6) What are five of your worst memories concerning the deceased and yourself?
7) Are you lonely?
8) Of all the deceased's worldly goods that you might have in your possession, what is the one thing that

best defined them? (We here at Redemption Inc. recommend you apply the following guidelines when making this choice: The item should be of such a nature that anyone who knew the deceased can look at it and say, "Yes, this was (deceased's name); no one else but (deceased's name)." If it will help you to choose, ask yourself the following as you look at each item: If he/she had chosen to leave his/her soul behind, would he/she have put it here for safekeeping?) It is strongly recommended that you have this item nearby, as the session cannot be repeated.

Redemption Inc. guarantees strict confidentiality and takes great caution to protect a client's privacy. All of your online sessions are protected from viral and/or hacker interference and can in no way be accessed by terminals other than your own and those of Redemption Inc.

Glenn saved the questionnaire, logged off, then sat back and stared at the blank screen.

The one thing that best defined her?

He mentally sorted through her paintings—God knew there were enough of them, and she'd put parts of herself into each and every one—but no one of them was definitive of his sister, he then went into the second bedroom—which he'd been using for storage ever since he'd moved into this place—and started going through the smaller boxes of Janice's possessions that his parents had asked him to keep. Nothing in any of them said *This was her*.

He turned his attention to the larger boxes hidden behind the double-wide sliding closet doors. Photographs; 45 rpm records; her high school yearbooks; cross-stitch Christmas ornaments; antique wind-up toys she'd collected over the years; letters from friends long moved away; every birthday card she'd ever re-

ceived; a scarf; a tattered red glove; her Campfire Girls
uniform and Merit Badges; knickknacks; whatchama-
callits and thingamajigs; recipes clipped from newspa-
pers now gone yellow with age; a framed caricature
of her playing the piano drawn by some sidewalk Pi-
casso at an amusement park when she was seven; programs from a few community theatre plays she'd acted
in ... none of them clicked for Glenn. There were
several boxes of her books in the back of his bedroom
closet but he doubted he'd find what he needed in any
of them, Mom and Dad had kept most of her furniture, her small kitchen appliances and cutlery, her
VCR and videotape collection. . . .

Is this all it comes down to? he thought. Everything
here once had meaning for her, a thousand memories
attached to a million feelings, valued pieces from a
life now reduced to so much clutter, the cycle nearly
at its end. *This'll be all of us someday,* thought Glenn.
Sure, there would be mourners at the end, friends,
family, people you thought had forgotten about you,
maybe someone you had a crush on in the eighth grade,
and they would gather, and they would weep, and they
would talk among themselves afterward and say, "I remember the way (deceased's name) used to ..."; then
your belongings would be catalogued, divided up, sold,
given away, tossed in the trash, your picture would be
moved to the back of a dusty photo album and, eventually, those people you left behind would die as well
and no one would be left to remember your face, your
middle name, even the location of your grave; the seasons would change, as seasons do, the elements setting
to work, rain and heat and snow and cold smoothing
away the inscription on the headstone until it was no
longer legible and then, later—days, weeks, decades—
someone who happened by would glance down, see
the faded words and dates, mutter "I wonder who's
buried here," then go on about the business of living,
trying hard to forget they were part of the same sor-

rowful cycle of the universe that you had reached the end of: No one left to say that this man was important, or this woman was kind, or that anything they strove to achieve was worthwhile. What purpose did any of it serve? You dreamed, you loved as often and as well as you could, you struggled and worked and laughed sometimes and showed compassion, and what waited for you at the end?—lime and rot and darkness.

The hammer, the coffin, and the nail.

Death, cyberspace, and the soul.

He looked at his sister's things and realized he couldn't do it, he couldn't find the One Thing that would serve as the summation of all she was and had ever hoped to be.

A corner of Glenn's mouth curved slightly upward, a smile-in-progress abandoned at the halfway point. "I'm sorry," he whispered, the last two syllables rising half an octave in pitch as they tripped over something caught in his throat and he began to weep. He sat down on the floor, pulling his legs up toward his chest and wrapping his arms around his knees, then rocked back and forth, the tears like ground glass in his eyes as the grief surged through him until his throat was raw and his limbs were cramped and his lungs throbbed from lack of air.

He buried his head between his knees, the convulsions slowly becoming less severe, the flow of tears from his eyes and the backwash of snot down his throat stanching themselves, his sobs dwindling into ragged, exhausted croaks.

Sis. Janice. *Godammit!*

He pulled himself together and marched back to the computer. Getting connected to the network went a lot quicker this time, and in less than three minutes he had retrieved the questionnaire and was typing in his answers, hoping like hell the network had some kind of online assistance for people who couldn't provide a ready answer to the last question.

When he didn't type in an answer to #8 after three minutes, the screen went blank for a moment, then:

>**Were you unable to locate the One Thing?**

>*No. I mean, yes, I couldn't find it.*

>**Did you keep in mind the suggested guidelines for choosing?**

>*Yes.*

>**Are you now in possession of all the deceased's worldly goods that you wish to have or that they wanted you to have?**

>*Yes.*

>**We understand that this portion of the process may be difficult for you. You may still need more time to make the proper selection.**

>*I'm a little confused about something. I know Janice mentioned that she had taken care of providing you with all the necessary items and information you needed to design this particular program, but she never told me what it was all for. What exactly is it that you people do?*

>**We raise the dead. The rest is up to you.**

The screen once again went blank, the gold disk in the CD-Rom drive revved up, then an image appeared.

The interior of a small apartment, its walls covered with framed movie posters: *The Man Who Would Be King, Roman Holiday, Pumpkinhead,* numerous others, but one poster was isolated in a place of honor. *Farewell, My Lovely,* starring Robert Mitchum. A television screen flickered in a far corner of the room and Glenn immediately recognized the opening shot of the Mitchum movie; a dead-on view of a chintzy neon hotel sign that dropped from sight as the camera panned slowly upward, stopping at last on the image of an unshaven, moth-eaten, fedora-wearing Mitchum staring out a window, a cigarette dangling from the corner of his mouth: the ultimate Philip Marlowe.

"Oh, God . . ."

The view altered as the "camera" panned to the

other side of the apartment where a small sofa-bed was angled toward the now-unseen television. An emaciated, pale figure lay in the bed, covered up to the stomach in blankets, her claw-thin, lesion-spotted hands folded on top of one another. Light gleamed off her nearly-bald head as her eyes widened and her dried, cracked lips parted in a tiny, painful smile.

"It's starting," called Janice.

". . . no," Glenn whispered, ". . . please . . ."

(We raise the dead.)

Of course it was her apartment, how could he have not recognized it? He'd bought the Mitchum poster for her at a film convention two years ago. *Farewell, My Lovely* had been her favorite movie. She and Glenn would get together to watch it and scarf down pizza once every three months, their quarterly ritual of celebrating another season down the tubes, thank God. Both of them had known the movie so well they often sat there quoting the dialogue word-for-word, Janice taking all of Charlotte Rampling's lines, Glenn taking Mitchum's.

Janice sat up and adjusted the pile of pillows behind her head as a dark, blurry, featureless shadow, a living silhouette that was acting as Glenn's stand-in, entered the room. Janice smiled at the silhouette, then reached up to brush one of her few remaining strands of hair from out of her eyes, only to have it fall off her scalp and become tangled in her fingers.

"You know the thing that pisses me off most about this?" she said to the silhouette. "I mean, besides the fact everyone told me that my hair'd grow back? If I'd been thinking, I could have saved all my hair and sold it to a wig-maker. The way I understand it, they pays big bucks for locks from we strawberry blondes." Her hair had been magnificent once, long and thick and bright, a head covered in Spring; but Fall had come, followed by Winter's ice, where all things once blooming with color and promise withered away.

The silhouette took the strand from her fingers, then turned toward the TV. When it spoke, its words were the ones Glenn had spoken at the time—*exactly, precisely* the ones he had spoken—but the voice was a cold, flat, buzzing monotone, the sound of someone speaking through an electronic voice box.

"HAVE*I*MISSED*ANY*THING*IM*POR*TANT?"

"Just the credits."

"THEN*WE*SHOULD*RE*WIND*THE*TAPE*YOU*KNOW*THAT*I*LIKE*TO*SEE*THE*WHOLE*MOVIE*FROM*START*TO—"

"—finish, yeah, yeah, yeah. Well, you'll just have to suffer tonight."

"YOU'RE*AN*E*VIL*WO*MAN."

"So sue me."

The silhouette sat close to her on the bed, draping one of its arms over her shoulder. Janice leaned her head against its chest and held one of its hands in her own.

"God, honey," Glenn whispered to the computer screen, "I miss you so much."

He reached out toward the image, foolishly thinking that he might touch her again, then pulled back his hand.

Over the next several minutes he was treated to a variety of similar scenes, all of them shot from different angles, showing Janice and himself, sometimes Mom and Dad as well, eating meals, playing cards, and assisting Janice with various daily functions she was longer capable of performing on her own.

Then the scene abruptly changed locale. Here was the silhouette standing in the bathroom of Glenn's own apartment, removing a bottle of pills from the medicine chest over the sink.

"Ah, hell," Glenn choked.

He almost couldn't watch. It hurt too much.

The criminal returning to the scene of his crime.

Despite all of the drugs Janice had to take—some

of them being serious painkillers (what she referred to as her "happy pills")—she'd been having trouble sleeping nights. Five months before she'd died, Glenn had developed insomnia and finally had to get his doctor to prescribe some intensely potent sleep aides. The prescription had contained thirty tablets; two a night for three nights in a row had done the trick for him but he'd decided to hang on to the rest in case of a relapse.

The silhouette stared at the bottle in its hand. Glenn knew exactly what it was thinking: *This can't be a good idea.* Though he'd never been one who thought it was all right to offer someone medicine that hadn't been prescribed for them, Glenn was about to ignore that particular principle for the sake of his sister's peace of mind. She didn't have much longer left; wasn't she entitled to relax and nap-out a little when she wanted to?

The silhouette shoved the bottle into its pocket and left.

Cross-fade. Back at Janice's apartment: Mom busy fixing dinner, Dad puttering around with a bucketful of household cleaners, spraying and wiping and scrubbing, Janice still on the sofa-bed, the silhouette sitting next to her as she finished taking the last of her many medications.

"What a load of crap," said Janice. "DDI, AZT ... it was abbreviations that undid her. Quick, hook up a new IV. PDQ. Which is SOP for a future DOA." She then lay back and whispered, "Did you remember to ... ?"

"I'VE*GOT*THEM*RIGHT*HERE."

"Oh thanks, Bigbro. I knew you'd come through."

The silhouette reached into its pocket and handed her one pill.

"That's it?" she said angrily.

"I*THOUGHT*IT*WOULD*BE*BEST*TO*START* WITH*ONLY*ONE*AND*SEE—"

Her eyes filled with ice. The silhouette was slowly becoming more transparent as Janice glared at it; so much so it seemed as if she were looking through it and past the computer screen at Glenn himself.

"You think one measly pill's going to do it for me? You said yourself you had to take two, and you didn't have a fucking pharmacy in your system at the time!"

Glenn waited for the silhouette's reply but none came; the thing was almost a sheet of tinted glass now.

Janice was still looking at him, asking, "You think one measly pill's going to . . ."

The silhouette did not respond this time either.

By the time Janice asked the question a third time, Glenn wondered if he himself shouldn't try answering her.

". . . pharmacy in your system at the time!"

"I didn't want to chance screwing up your system with something you're not supposed to be taking," he whispered.

"Like hell," said Janice. "You're worried that I might—"

"I never said that."

"You didn't have to! Christ! It's written all over your face." The sudden burst of anger drained her; she collapsed against the mound of pillows, coughing with such violence Glenn almost expected her to spit out a chunk of lung.

"Dammit to hell, Janice, what good does it do you to get mad like that? You shouldn't—"

"—I shouldn't have done a lot of things, Bigbro. I shouldn't have been so distant to some of the people I've known, I shouldn't have let Rick talk me into fucking without protection, I shouldn't have been so selfish when I was a little girl, I shouldn't have done this, I shouldn't have done that, I wish things were different, blah-blah-blah.

"You think I'm anxious for the carnival to end? No way. I'm scared to death! I am twenty-three years old going on a hundred-and-ten. I won't see twenty-four, we both know that. I do not want to go gentle into that good night because lately I haven't been able to shake the feeling that maybe, just maybe, that night isn't so good after all. I wish I could tell you—" Her voice cracked. "—that I'm at peace with things, but I'm not."

He'd almost forgotten how defeated she'd looked that night. Loneliness can wear many guises, but none is so frightening as that found in the face of a dying loved one; the room could have been packed to the rafters with family and friends huddled around her and she still would have been alone. She was only hours away from death and that made her the oldest and loneliest person in the world. What words or gestures were going to make it better? It wasn't as if she were only leaving for an extended vacation, eventually to return with snapshots and souvenirs; this was It. Gone. Period. No more, no more.

Maybe talking about it would make things easier in some small way; so he asked her, then, the question all of them had been avoiding: "What's it like? I mean, knowing what's going to happen?"

She stared at him, a vicious, hurt, how-dare-you-ask-me-that-Now look that held a gun against his temple, then, with a blink, her features softened and she sighed.

"I hope you never have to experience it like this when your time comes, Glenn, I really do. There's not an ounce of self-pity in me, truly, but this is . . . ridiculous. One of the most annoying things is what goes through my head when I'm lying awake at night. There's a new wood-fired pizza place that's opening in ten days and I'm never going to know if it's any good or not. I know how trivial that sounds, but for everything I think of that's been a terrific part of my life, there's another thing that I'll never get to experience. I keep thinking about Charlie Chaplin at the end of *Monsieur Verdoux,* remember that? They're getting ready to haul him off for execution and they offer him a cigarette and a glass of rum. He turns them down, but just before they take him away he stops and says, 'Wait just a moment—I've never tasted rum.' Then he takes the glass and drinks. I always thought that was great. Even on the threshold of death, he wanted one last new experience. That's how I've been feeling. I want one last new experience before I bite the big one. Is that so unreasonable?

"And how do I feel now? You mean besides stupid, because this didn't have to happen? A couple of good orgasms shouldn't cost a person their life—and to be honest with you, they weren't that good, wouldn't you know. So besides stupid, how do I feel?" She closed her eyes and thought about it for a moment. "Bested," she said, opening her eyes and wiping a tear off her cheek. "And cornered. The boundaries of my world have progressively shrunk; first it was the hospital, my world, then this apartment, then just a few rooms, then this old, lumpy sofa-bed, and now the circle's narrowing to such a point that pretty soon all that's going to be left for me is the central core of Janice MacIntyre, and I'm so scared of having to face that. I keep wondering, what if it's not everything they taught us it was? What if there isn't a God or Heaven or any of it? What if there's only ... nothing? A big, ugly, unimaginable nothing?"

"Don't do this to yourself, Sis. Please?"

"You asked. Not what you expected, huh? It's like that old joke about death with dignity—'You know what death with dignity is? You don't drool.' You want me to act like Bette Davis in *Dark Victory*? You wanted tender, luminous courage in the face of the end? Tough. There's a bedpan over there that I just puked my lunch into a while ago—this was while I shit myself at the same time. Screw dignity—this gal's going out kicking and screaming all the way."

"Good for you."

"Don't patronize me."

"I wasn't."

"Then leave the sleeping pills with me."

"No."

"Why not?"

"Weren't you listening to yourself? If you're so damn determined to fight it, why take these things?"

"Half the reason I feel like this is because I haven't gotten more than an hour's sleep a night for six days! Even my catnaps are shot to hell. Maybe if I got four or five straight hours of sleep, I wouldn't have such a pissy attitude."

"What if these put you under so much that you, well . . ."

"I swear to you I won't die in my sleep. It'd be too much like sneaking out on a dull party through the kitchen door, only now I don't care if the party's dull, let it bore me. At least I'll still be alive.

"God, isn't that a stupid thing to say? 'Let it bore me.' Oh, Glenn, I think about all the times I should have treasured but didn't because I was too impatient or wasn't in the mood for company or was PMS-ing or had what I thought were better things to do—like that time you and Dad came over to help put those bookshelves together. Dad was in a really good mood that day and was telling stories about some of the awful practical jokes he used to play on the other guys in his unit when he was overseas during the war . . . he smiled a lot that day. But I had a date that night and the longer it took you guys to finish, the more distracted I became. After you two'd been at it for about three hours, you decided to run out for some burgers and instead of spending that time with Dad, I decided to start tarting up for my 'big evening.' I figured if I made enough fuss, Dad'd get the hint and the two of you'd hurry the hell up and finish when you got back. So all the time I'm bouncing around

getting ready, Dad's working on the shelves and talking to me. Oh, God—he was trying so hard to be good
company. I should have paid more attention. You
know what he was talking about? The night he first
met Mom. He'd never told me that story before and
it sounded like a great story, romantic as hell, like
something out of Greer Garson/Walter Pidgeon movie
. . . but I was only half-listening. Those twenty minutes
when the two of us were alone could've been among
the most precious of my life, and now they're gone.

"I did that a lot. I invested too much in moments
that didn't matter a damn and not enough in those
moments that were *diamonds*. I think about all those
little, misused pieces of time that I'll never get back—
ten idle minutes here, a half-hour there, the moments
adding up and slipping away. I'll bet if I did the math,
I've probably trashed a couple of years. I wish I could
be given back just one of those misused days, y'know?
I'd take it, and I'd divide it up so carefully, I'd look
every second over like a diamond cutter with a jewel-
er's glass, then I'd say. 'I put this moment here, this
is for admiring the sunrise; and these ten minutes—
ah, *these* I'll need to listen to some favorite songs and
feel the warm afternoon light on my face and smell
freshly-mown grass outside, so these should be close
by, say, *here;* and this hour, this hour is the most precious of all because I want to spend it holding the
hands of someone who loves me, I want to kiss their
cheek and feel their arms around me and say only the
most important things, there must not be any distrac-
tions, so this most precious hour goes way over there,
where I can keep an eye on it' . . . that's what I'd do. 'I
put this moment here, and I put *this* moment *here* . . .'
and I'd have them waiting for me right now. *Right*
now. This time. This day. This moment. Not dead, not
dead yet."

Glenn (had) leaned over and kissed her, then embraced her as tightly as he dared. "Don't forget to reserve five minutes for eating a wood-fired pizza."

"Only five minutes?"

"You forget—I know how you get around pizza."

"Very funny."

He (had) kissed the top of her head, then gently massaged the back of her neck. "Tell you what—I'll give a few extra pills to Mom and we'll see how you react to taking just two."

Janice tensed. "Coward."

"Don't say that."

"I just did. And you're only getting defensive because you know it's true." She pulled away to look at him. "What happened to you, Glenn? When I was a little girl, I remember you being *fun.* Full of energy and life and never without a prank waiting up your sleeve. What happened? When was everything ruined for you?"

"Nothing was ruined. I just grew up."

"Don't get trite with me. I don't have the time."

"What? What do you want to hear? That I experienced some soul-shattering catharsis along the way?"

"Don't, Glenn, please? I've watched it happen over the years. Your spirit wasn't broken in one sudden blow; it bled to death in thousands of small scratches. Didn't you see it?"

"Maybe. I don't know. Leave it at that."

"I can't. I'd like to know that you'll at least try to be happy once . . . once—"

"—not your problem."

"I've always worried about you."

"Maybe you should've spent a little more time worrying about yourself."

"Take your own advice."

"That'd be a big mistake—but not half so big as my giving you these pills would be."

"Then you shouldn't have agreed to it in the first place! Christ! It seems like everything you do is designed to put distance between you and the rest of the world. I don't mean to be so crabby, but . . . ah, hell—I don't want you to be lonely."

"There's a difference between being lonely and being alone. I *like* being alone," he said, almost believing the lie, as usual.

"Then get the hell out of here."

"That's not fair."

'Don't talk to me about fair—and don't look at me like that. It looks too much like you're pitying me."

Maybe he was; he never knew for certain.

"If being around here right now is too much for you to handle," said Janice, "then do me a favor and get out."

Even now, in the safety of his own apartment, Glenn felt the same sudden, unreasonable surge of anger enter his chest. The same foul taste was in his mouth.

"Here," he (had) said (taking the bottle out of his pocket and throwing it on her lap). "I hope they help. Try not to choke on them."

"Thanks. You really stink on ice sometimes, you know that?"

"Feeling's mutual right about now."

"Then fuck off and leave me alone. Go on, run away. That's at least one thing you're good at."

Glenn looked away from the monitor. It had gone downhill from there. Mom eventually intervened, he'd left, and Janice was dead less than thirty-six hours later.

He looked back at the screen. It was still displaying Janice's apartment, only now the rooms were empty, the walls bare, the books gone—and (as if the computer wanted to remind him that everything was coming to him courtesy of cyberspace) there was a toolbar across the top of the screen which displayed various icons. A clear image of himself as he'd looked at age seventeen stood in the middle of what was once the

TV/sofa-bed room, staring right through the screen and into his eyes.

Why had Janice chosen this particular image of him?

"Still with us?" asked the other Glenn.

"Uh ... yeah."

"Quick story Sis wanted me to tell you. There's an ancient Zoroastrian legend about the first parents of the human race. They were two reeds so closely joined together that you couldn't tell them apart. They knew that nothing would get accomplished as long as they remained like that so, reluctantly, they separated, as was decreed by God. In time they united as a husband and wife were meant to unite, and there were born to them two children whom they loved so tenderly, so irresistibly and totally, that they ate them up. After that, God—to protect the human race—reduced the force of man's capacity to love by ninety-nine percent. Later, those same parents gave birth to seven more pairs of children, all of whom lived and went on to procreate so you could walk the earth today.

"There was no autopsy, was there? Of course not— she knew there wouldn't be. You never found the container, did you? And you looked. A lot. So now you know—she took the whole bottle and checked out early *and you gave them to her*! Hell, you practically shoved them down her throat! No wonder you haven't stopped drinking for almost a week. How do you live with yourself? Why would you want to now?

"Just so you know: Janice took six of your pills, then threw the container away just so she *wouldn't* yield to temptation in case her spirits hit rock bottom. It was an overdose, sure, but—and pay attention here—it wasn't enough to kill her or even put her in a coma for that matter. Is this registering? Just nod your head. It wasn't suicide, Glenn, it was just ... the end of the whole mess. C'mon, we both know she'd always been a bit on the frail side; her system was

trashed and couldn't hold up any longer. She wasn't
in any pain when it happened, if that's a comfort.

"You. Were. Not. Responsible.

"Oh, yeah, one more thing: she didn't get to do her
Oscar Wilde. She had her wits about her, just not
enough strength to speak."

Glenn cleared his throat, then wiped his eyes. "Do
you know what she would have said if . . . if—"

"Sorry."

"That's okay."

The other Glenn shook his head. "No it isn't, because you'll always wonder what she *might* have said.
Do you have any idea how much of a person's life is
wasted because of *might have, should have,* and *could
have*? Ever since her death you've been punishing
yourself for all the things you wished you *had* said to
her but didn't, cursing yourself for all the times you
could have spent with her but chose not to, and you
refuse to forgive yourself for all the countless *mights*
and *should haves* that parade through your mind every
waking moment. Do you know how pointless that is?
How—shut up and let me finish. I'm only programmed
for another four-and-a-half minutes and there's a lot
to get in. What if you could go back in time and be
by her side on that last night, and what if the ebb and
flow of time could be halted while the two of you
were together so that the moment of her death was
put on perpetual hold? Not bad, huh? The two of you
could share every hope and dream either of you have
ever had, reveal every secret, bitch about your failures,
cry over your lost youth, unleash your petty jealousies
and angers, whisper private shames, tell each other
everything there is to know about yourselves so that,
once she was dead, you'd feel like the slate was clean.

"Well, guess what? I guarantee you that if you did
that, if you talked to her until your throat was raw
and your lungs ached, if you told her everything that
was in your heart and mind until she knew you more

intimately that anyone ever has or ever will—if you were to do all of that and *then* she were to die, I guarantee you that one second after she was gone you'd think of something you forgot to say to her. *That's* why God reduced the force of our capacity to love, because if He/She/Them/It hadn't, you'd be toast right now, a gobbled-up morsel in love's insatiable belly, and that's why your punishing yourself is so damned stupid! All your life you've been too shy to really get out there and face the world, to make friends or try anything new. You think it hurts now, this pain you're feeling? The loss and regret? It's only *one-fucking-percent* of what it could be! But the capper to all this is that you, you who so mourn her death, who's so evangelically determined to hang on to your grief because she was your best friend, you, of all people, can't come up with the One Thing that best defined her. You've been sitting here staring at me for almost ten minutes, me—who is you at seventeen—and you're wondering why Sis chose to have you show up this way.

"Do you want to see it, Glenn? The moment of her death? Because I can show it to you. Then maybe you'll stop picturing it in your head a thousand times a day."

Glenn couldn't speak.

"Feels like you're the only person in the world who's grieving right now, doesn't it?"

"... yes ..."

"How noble you'd be if that were the case." The figure of himself at seventeen turned around, made a circular movement with its right hand, guided the cursor to the toolbar, and, snapping its fingers, caused the cursor to click on an icon of two faces looking at one another.

"Just a little reminder, Glenn, that grief lives on in cyberspace, too."

The icon clicked, the word **chat** appeared for a second, then the screen went white and suddenly Glenn found himself in the middle of a real-time conference on Alzheimer's Disease, reading line after line of anguish and confusion as caretakers and surviving loved ones talked about their guilt and anger; another click, and he was with women who were talking about their battles with breast cancer; another click, and it was the parents of SIDS babies pouring out their hearts to others like themselves, damning the injustice of a God who would take away a fragile new life; on and on, click after click, each conference filled with more pain than the last, the words themselves seeming so cold until he read them and then there was such misery, such loneliness, so many demons snarling through so many damaged spirits that he felt almost selfish for wanting to hang onto his own pain—

—then the screen blinked, and once again he was back in his sister's empty apartment, looking at himself at age seventeen.

"You're not alone, Glenn; you never were—and you don't have to be. All you have to do is put your hands on the keyboard and *tell someone something*. That's all.

"If Sis were here, Glenn, she'd kick your ass up between your shoulders for remembering her the way she was at the end. She'd much rather you held on to this."

The screen filled with a montage of image: Janice at six, ten, Sweet Sixteen (she'd hated seeing that written on her cake), eighteen, twenty-one ... and underneath it all was her voice as it once was, clear and chiming, reading one of her favorite Christina Rossetti poems, "Song":

"When I am dead, my dearest,
      Sing no sad songs for me;
Plant thou no roses at my head,
      Nor shady cypress tree:

Be the green grass above me
    With showers and dewdrops wet;
And if thou wilt, remember,
    And if thou wilt, forget."

Never, I'll never forget you, thought Glenn, smiling
at her as she brushed some of her thick, magnificent
hair from her face and stood in the middle of her
then-new apartment, hands on hips, one foot impatiently tapping as she carefully examined every space,
trying to decide where to put all her stuff once she
finished moving in.

There was an old crayon box at her feet, the same
crayon box she'd had since she was three. She knelt
down and pulled something out of it, something Glenn
had seen countless times during his life but to which
he'd never given a second thought.

Until now.

Would she have put her soul there for safekeeping?
Yes; ohgod YES!

"This was you," he whispered. "No one else but
you."

On the screen, Janice smiled at him and said,
"Guess what, Bigbro? Cyberspace is Heaven. We saw
it once, when I was six and you were seventeen.

"Remember?"

Glenn covered his mouth with both of his hands as
more tears came to his eyes.

*It had happened during a family vacation to Rhode
Island. They'd been driving around trying to find the
way out of Newport because Dad had lost the map and
had wound up on this dead-end street. There was a
guardrail at the end of the street, and a big cast-iron
sign that said "The Breakers" embedded in a stone
wall. Dad had turned to everyone with an embarrassed
smile on his face and said, "Well, we might as well see
the ocean while we're here," and everyone got out of
the car and followed the guardrail along this winding*

*cement path until they came to a lookout point. Both
Janice and Glenn had been awestruck by the sight of
the ocean, this vast body of water down there, going
out farther than you could see. There was an incredible,
heavy mist hanging over the waters, stopping just a few
yards from shore. They could hear buoys clanging and
unseen boats sounding their foghorns, and every so
often a break in the mist would roll by and they caught
sight of a lone lighthouse in the distance, perched on
an isolated rock-island. They had stopped at a point
where the cement path branched off in two directions.
Right smack in the middle of the branch was a dirt
path that led down onto the beach where the breakers
were thundering in, all foam and volume, slamming
against the base of the cliffs, then snapping back out
again. Even from where they stood they could feel it
shaking their bones. Mom and Dad decided to go on
up the cement path to the visitors' center so Dad could
buy a new map, but Janice and Glenn asked to stay
right where they were. A minute or so after their parents
had gone, they looked at each other and Glenn had
said, "Hop on, let's go!" and Janice climbed up to ride
piggyback. It was rough going at the start but after
the first, unbelievably steep twenty feet down the climb
became much easier, and soon they were down on the
beach. Janice jumped off and began running around
saying, "Pretty rocks, pretty shells." There were so
many pebbles and stones. So many colors. Glenn
stayed nearby her because the breakers were coming in
awfully close. (He had visions of the waves knocking
them down and carrying them out to sea. Janice was
very small, and he worried about her a lot.) They
climbed around, getting soaked to the bone every time
the breakers came in closer and not caring about it.
Janice laughed like she hadn't laughed since the trip
started as they made their way along the edge of this
cliff face that suddenly cut down and inward, forming
a hidden grotto under the overhang. They stumbled*

*their way around part of the rocks to get a look inside
the grotto and there was this balloon wedged underneath the overhang, one of those great big shiny silver
children's birthday balloons, all stuck up in the wedge
like it was hiding from someone. It was absurd and
beautiful at the same time. Janice thought it was just
the greatest thing on Earth and had to have it. It had
a long, red-ribbon streamer attached to it that was flut-
tering out toward the ocean; it seemed to go on forever,
reaching all the way out to a series of smaller rock
platforms offshore. Glenn hoped that Janice wouldn't
see them because he knew she'd want to play "jump-
across" on them, hopping from one to the next, then
the next and back again. He told her to stay put while
he crawled underneath to get the balloon. With the
breakers slamming into his ass, he managed to get himself in there and grab hold of the treasure, suddenly
feeling pretty good about this because his little sister
wanted this balloon and he was going to be her hero
because he got it for her. He turned around and worked
his way back out, then stood up and held it high, the
victor victorious, then the breakers came in again and
knocked him against the cliff and the wind ripped the
balloon from his hand and carried it away. He stood
there, watching it soar upward, then suddenly stop,
hanging above the foam and thunder. The red streamer
was still attached and he followed it with his eyes down
to one of the farthest rock-islands to see Janice standing
there, her arms parted wide, the ocean-spray cascading
all over her. She had the end of the streamer wrapped
around her right arm. Glenn screamed out her name
and she turned toward him with this . . . smile on her
face. He froze. He had never seen anyone smile like
that before. It was as if she'd just been let in on this
Big Secret, something so wonderful and great and full
of happy promises that nothing would ever seem bad
to her again. And standing there, pinned against the
cliff by the breakers, staring out into the mist that*

danced around Janice's ankles, Glenn fell in love with his little sister. There was nothing remotely sexual about it, nothing physical or lustful, it wasn't perverse in the least; he fell in love with her the way some people fall in love with a piece of music, or a certain time of day or the year—twilight in Autumn—or even an idea. It was the kind of worshipful, untainted love a person feels maybe half-a-dozen times in their entire life. It was a perfect moment; the balloon so high above, the breakers and the mist and foghorns and bells, a glimpse of the lighthouse ... for him it had been absolutely miraculous. And there was Janice, his little sister, standing strong in the center of it all, looking happier than he'd ever see her looking again. He fell in love with her-Then, her-There. He saw Life in her smile. Then it became something even more, for she saw him looking at her and laughed, then began dancing around in a circle, her arms still held wide open, shouting "Glenn-nyyyyy! Glenn-nyyyy!" as loudly as she could. Above her, the balloon spun around and around while the breakers came in and rattled Glenn's bones and she kept shouting his name—"Glenn-nyyyy! Glenn-nyyyy!"—it was like a song. Her voice bounced off the cliff face and echoed all around him, even the breakers seemed to repeat it and Glenn thought, The water's singing with her! He looked down at the pebble-flecked foam scrolling up onto shore and lapping at his ankles, then Janice sang his name again and he looked up to see her coming toward him, hopping from rock-island to rock-island, the balloon seemingly lifting her higher every time she leaped, and it was like she was flying toward him, flying through some space the waves couldn't reach: For a few seconds, maybe longer, it was as if her feet were touching nothing at all because the balloon wanted her to know what it felt like to be not of this Earth. All Glenn could see was this magical little girl flying toward him, her arms pushed out in front of her and that absurd balloon overhead. When

*he at last caught her in his arms, she kissed him hard
on the cheek and said, "Did you see it, Glenny? Did
you see it?" and even though he had no idea what she
was talking about, he said "Yeah, hon, I saw it," and
she giggled and kissed his cheek again and said—*

—Glenn sat bolt-upright in his chair.

She had said, "I found Heaven. And I'm not like
Daddy. I didn't need a map."

He turned around, slowly rose from the chair, and
crossed toward the painting.

Gently lifting it from the hooks in the wall, he
turned it around and for the first time noticed the
thick cardboard sheet Janice had stapled onto the
back of the inner-frame over which she'd stretched
the canvas. He'd paid no attention to it before because
she always stapled a heavy piece of cardboard over
the back of the inner-frame, but now . . .

He shook the painting once.

And heard it.

A small, muffled *fwish*! of something soft and light
shifting around.

It took him fifteen minutes to pry the staples loose
and remove the backing.

And there it was. Dusty and deflated, little more
than a silver wad wrapped in a long red ribbon, but
deargod *there it was*!

"Thought you'd forgotten all about it, didn't you?"
said Janice from the monitor.

Glenn couldn't speak, so only nodded his head.

"It's not torn or punctured in any way, so it'll be
easy to reinflate, Bigbro."

He sat down in front of the monitor and smiled at
her. "Thank you, Sis."

"No. I never thanked *you*. Of all our great moments
together—and there were hundreds of them—that was
one of the greatest. When I think of my childhood,
Bigbro, that moment is how I define it, and that defin-
ing moment was always with me, even when I died.

It's yours now, all right? Keep it safe for me. It is my heart, and all my affection, and they are delicate things."

"I promise."

"And live your life well, Glenn. Live it better than you have been. Become part of the world. Will you do that for me?"

". . . yes . . . Yes. I promise."

"I love you, Bigbro. You could be a real jerk sometimes, but I love you anyway."

"I love you, too."

She laughed. "Yeah, there's my saccharine alarm. Time to truck. Take care of yourself, Glenn. And remember me like this, like I was before I got sick."

And that's where he left her, in the center of her then-new apartment, her face flushed with exhaustion and excitement, her eyes glittering with the promise of all the choices and possibilities that were now—or soon would be—hers and hers alone. The organizing of the kitchen, where to hang the plants; the angle of a chair, the view from that window; a slant of light, the sounds from the street. A certain young woman. Her radiance. Her wonder. This time; this day; this moment.

Glenn clicked on the **chat** icon, found the conference room he was looking for, and introduced himself to a group of AIDS patients, all of whom expressed their sympathy for the loss of his sister, and all of whom then went on to ask him how he was holding up, was there anything he wanted to know, was there anything they could do for him?

>**Like it or not** (one of them wrote),
you've got people out here who give a damn, A#1Bigbro. We won't let you go through this alone.

Cyberspace is Heaven.

END PROGRAM

O! THE TANGLED WEB
by John DeChancie

John DeChancie has written more than twenty novels
in the science fiction, fantasy, and horror fields, including the acclaimed Castle series, the most recent
of which, *Bride of the Castle,* was published in 1994.
He has also written dozens of short stories and nonfiction articles as well, appearing in such magazines
as *The Magazine of Fantasy and Science Fiction,
Penthouse,* and many anthologies. In addition to his
writing, John enjoys composing and playing classical
music and traveling.

Sunday has the cruelest night, breeding loneliness and
calls to old friends far away. It's an empty time of the
week, uneasily quiet, hushed. I dislike it. I spend it,
usually, paging through my tattered personal phone
directory, staring at the smudged and faded phone
numbers and GlobalNet addresses of people I knew
long ago—friends, girlfriends, business associates, enemies. Some names I do not recognize at all. I wonder
about these. Was the association so brief, of such little
consequence? Or so painful that it must be repressed?

I was seated not by the phone, as in days of yore,
but at my computer, which today, as we all know,
has replaced the conventional telephone—your basic
Amiche—as a means of communication. The old-fashioned phone networks have given way to global computer networks, and lately, we don't simply type
messages at each other, as we did in the closing days
of the last century. In the bright, chromium twenty-

first century, we talk in realtime, hearing each other as we would ... well, as we would over a telephone. Progress. But of course today we see faces as well as hear voices. That is progress, isn't it?

I summon my telecommunications program. Marty Steinmetz—ah, Marty. At last report, you were in Stockbridge, Massachusetts, circa 1975. You were a failed artist and near despair. Where are you now?

I punch my GlobalNet Access Number. I am sitting near the window in my study. Outside, the first crickets of spring tune up while tent caterpillars spin their cotton-candy nests in the crotches of trees. Soon, the little crawlers will be defoliating the neighborhood. In July and August, metamorphosed into gypsy moths, they'll flit around, ticking and thwacking into the patio lights—and, it is to be hoped, immolating themselves within the wire-mesh trap of my electric bug zapper. Such is the grandeur of nature.

I see the familiar prompts and punch in my Personal Access Code. I am now accessing the system. Which is to say that I am now attempting to gain access to said system. Same thing. I have punched seven digits to get this far. I now stab out an area code and a seven digit number. Total number of digits: twenty-two. The line goes *burbleburblebleepbleep* and commences that curious bacon-frying sound—then the modem's little speaker cuts out. My CRT screen shows a woman's pleasant face.

"Hello."

"Hello. Is Marty there?"

"Marty?" Her face screws up into something signifying either dyspepsia or puzzlement, I can't figure which. "Uh ... uh ... Marty."

"Martin Steinmetz. I'm trying to reach Martin Steinmetz. Do I have the wrong number?"

"Uh, yeah. You have the wrong number." She hangs up.

I'm intrigued. A deserted wife? A former lover? Or was it simply a wrong number?

I will probably never know. Who else do we have here? Linda Martino. Nice Italian girl. I remember. Nope, not her. I feel much better calling the guys. Hey, Hank! How ya doin', you old s.o.b.? Fred ... the Fredster! That sort of thing. Well, here's Phil Carstairs, old school chum. Can't go wrong with old Phil. I punch out the local access number, click on the proper icon, and punch in my very own Personal Access Code (not to be confused with my account number), twelve digits total, then hit Phil Carson's ... Carson's? ... Carstairs' (such a dear old friend I can't remember his name) GlobalNet address ... but wait, I'm quite sure I've gone wrong somewhere. The feeling that at some point I have hit a wrong digit nags at me. But I go ahead anyway—and now, since I've been distracted, I'm quite sure I've punched out Phil's address wrong, but, what the hell, here goes, let's let it ring and see if a recognizable voice answers.

Something graphically elaborate begins to unfold on the CRT screen. Colors pulse, logos dance.

"Hello!" A bright, trendy voice announces.

"May I speak to—" I begin.

But the voice continues implacably, "Thank you for logging on to Inter-World Web, the planet's newest and most innovative communications network. IWW offers a cost-effective, competitive, and dependable alternative to other computer communications networks. Not only that—IWW's highly advanced technology can provide consumers with services never dreamed of before. Using your own home computer, you may contact other times and other worlds. You can call the past—or the future! IWW can put you in touch with strange new worlds, ones that exist, and ones that are only possibilities! You can phone up lost loved ones! These are only a few of the services we can provide. Take advantage of our current subscription drive and try our free one-day trial offer. Call free for one full-day, no obligation, no charge! If you wish to try IWW, stay on the line and our full-automated Customer Service Department will take your order. Stand by, please—and thanks for calling IWW!"

I've hit it. IWW! The Wobbly Network! This is an opportunity at which one can only leap. I stand by. Presently, I hear: "Hello! This is IWW, and you are interfacing with our Customer Service Department. If you wish to take advantage of our free one-day trial offer, or if you wish to subscribe, wait for the prompt, then punch in your name, your home phone number, and your major credit or debit card number. If you wish to subscribe, that's all we'll need. If you only want the free, one-day trial service, click on the FREE TRIAL OFFER icon. It's that easy! In either case, stay on the line. We'll have some more Important information for you. Now, wait for the prompt, and punch or click."

The prompt prompts, and I maneuver and click my mouse. Squeak, click.

After a pause comes: "Thank you for taking advantage of our free trial offer! Your local access number is—" A screen shows a long number sequence. "And your Personal Access Code is—" Same thing, another string of numbers. I order my computer to "capture" these numerical improvizations.

"And your Metasystem Interstitial Tachyonic Interface Code is—" More digits? Yeow. I capture those, too.

"Now, please listen closely. To use IWW, first enter the seven-digit Local Access Number. Then, punch in your Personal Access Code. Wait for the prompt, then punch in the—"

I hang up. I have got the gist. I know how this system works. I call up the dialing screen, punch out a string of twenty-seven digits, then key ME-1958, and hit ENTER.

That's me, myself, in the year of Our Lord nineteen and fifty-eight. I was twelve years old. The ring tone flutters.

Now, in 1958, there were no video telephones (except at Bell Laboratories) and certainly no home computers. Yet I see my mother—my God, she looks young—answering the telephone. She does not look out from the screen, though. She does not see me, only hears my voice.

"Hello," I say. "Is John there?"

"Johnny? You want to speak to Johnny?" She hesitates, suspicious. "Who is this?"

A strange adult calling a child should have good reason. "This is Minnesota Scientific Company calling. We received your son's order for a replacement objective lens for our Build-it-Yourself Refracting Astronomical Telescope. However, he neglected to indicate which size telescope he purchased."

"Oh, just a minute."

The television is playing in the background. I hear something vaguely recognizable. Is it the theme from *Gunsmoke* or the *Untouchables*?

No time to play Trivial Pursuit, because Johnny enters the screen and picks up the telephone. Ye gods! This is a child, a mere child. A baby.

"Hullo?"

"Johnny?"

"Yeah."

"Johnny, you don't know me, but this is someone who knows you very well. I want to warn you about some things—things that will happen to you when you're older. Mistakes that you can avoid if you know what to look for. When you're twenty years old you'll meet a girl named Roberta Peters—Roberta Peters, Johnny. Remember that name. You'll fall in love and you'll marry this girl, but the marriage will be a disaster—"

"Huh?"

"Just listen to me, Johnny. I know whereof I speak. Don't marry Roberta, Johnny. That's all you have to remember. And when you're in college, a fraternity brother will give you a stolen copy of a very difficult math exam, and you'll be tempted to study it and work out all the problems in advance. Don't do it! Fail that test instead—if you crib, you'll get involved in a big cheating scandal and you'll almost get thrown out of school and you'll feel compromised for the rest of your life. And when you get much older, a friend will approach you to invest in a shopping mall development deal—"

"What're you talking about? Hey, Mom! There's some crazy guy ..."

Johnny drops the phone and exits the screen.

"Johnny? Johnny, please listen to me!"

"Hello?" My mother again, picking up the phone. "Hello? Who is this?"

I hang up. Of course, I don't ever remember getting such a call, but I wouldn't remember it, would I? Or would I? After all, the IWW voice had said something about possible worlds. Maybe the Johnny of that world will avoid these pitfalls ... and stumble into different ones, I suppose.

What next? Who next? I thumb through my little black book. Jessica. Yes, Jessica Marlowe. Jessica and I had first postponed the wedding, then had called it off, and the whole engagement altogether. It had been mostly my idea, as I remember. The number I have is over twenty years old, and I know she has since moved to California. I ring her up, and adjust the time parameter to twenty years ago.

"Hello?"

"Hi, Jessica."

"John?" There is a gravid pause. "Why are you calling? I thought ... I thought everything was settled."

"Was it?" I ask.

"I don't know." She fishes for the various possibilities. A deep, sighing breath whooshes against the mouthpiece. "Why don't you tell me, John? Is it over? Last month, you seemed to think so. I'll never forgive you for not returning my calls."

"I'm sorry," I tell her. "I didn't know what to say." And I'm having trouble remembering exactly what did happen, some twenty years ago.

"Well," she says quietly, "I don't know what to say either."

"I did love you," I say—and instantly know it to be a lie.

" 'Did.' Great." She snorts. "Fine. Okay—did you call me up just to tell me that? If you did, thanks muchly. Is that all?"

"Wait, wait." Oh, why did I do this thing?

"Good-bye, John."

"Jessica, please!"

I slowly recradle the phone. That was quite a "guilt trip," to use the fatuous parlance of yesteryear. I feel so guilty, in fact, that I'm half tempted to ring up Pamela Stebbins, Vassar dropout and wonderfully gifted playwright who shared my apartment for six beautiful months back in the halcyon days of the Vietnam war. Ah, the black-light posters, the smells of cat shit and ginseng tea! She buggered off to California, too. (I lost many people to that great state.) I'm half-tempted, as I say, to phone her way back when and ask her if it's really over, and why. But I don't feel guilty enough to hoist that cross.

Who else? Lost loved ones—well, there's Dad, of course, but what would I say to him? That I love him? He knew that. Should I ring up my ancestors? Nah. How about the future? I had called myself thirty years in the past, why not thirty years from now? I'd ask myself how I was doing—solicit advice, warnings, etc.

No. What if I phone myself ten years from now and it just rings and rings and rings . . . ?

I shiver. None of that stuff. It's the past for me. I punch all the TTA numbers, then hit A-D-O-L-P-H-H-I-T-L-E-R. And there he is on the screen. That clipped mustache is a spectral, lifeless gray. A husky voice says, "Ja?"

"Uh . . . *Herr Reichskanzler, ich bin* . . ." In faltering German, I try to tell him who I am, when I'm calling from. I attempt to tell him that no matter what he does, he will lose the war, so he might as well not bother starting it. Interrupting me is the hollow crump of an explosion, its sound not quite absorbed by yards and yards of reinforced concrete. A Russian artillery shell, I'm guessing.

"*Ja,*" Hitler says. "Zis I know. *Danke.*"

My, this is fun, better than calling dead relatives. Winston Churchill isn't in, but I leave my name and number. He'll return the call, an aide assures me.

Cleopatra—not the historical last queen of Egypt, but one inhabiting a parallel time-track in which telephones were invented quite early—is bathing and doesn't want to be disturbed.

Julius Caesar is over at Cleopatra's.

I soon tire of this. Other worlds, eh? I'd give those a try. Fetching a Carl Sagan tome from the shelf, I look for the name of a star that astronomers deem likely to have life-bearing planets. I find several, and punch up a few. The one that answers is 8-1-E-R-I-D-A-J-I.

But what answers? It looks like a pile of lettuce and sounds like a chirping sparrow.

"Hello?" I yell. The connection is very bad. "Hello? Is this a planet of the star 81 Eridani?"

There come a few clicks and beeps. Then: "We call our planet Dirt. What planet are you calling from?"

"I am calling from the planet Earth." Which of course means *dirt*. "How wonderful it is to hear your voice! Uh, how am I hearing your voice, by the way?

I can understand you perfectly. Are you using some sort of universal translation device?"

"I should think that would be obvious."

"Of course. Sorry." I am hard put to think of what to say next. "Well! Uh ... How are things on 81 Eridani?"

" 'Things'?"

"Well, you know. What's it like to live on your planet? What are your thoughts, feelings, emotions, etcetera? How do you view the universe? And like that."

"It would be rather absurd to attempt an answer to any of these extremely complex questions over this communications device."

"Yeah, the connection is pretty bad. Look, do you have a chamber of commerce or something that maybe has free brochures, literature, that sort of thing? Do you have anything available to download?"

"I think I understand. The answer is no."

"Too bad. Do you people have interstellar space travel?"

"No."

"That's hard to understand."

"Have you people discovered relativity yet?"

"Oh, yes," I answer.

"Then I see no reason for failing to understand why we don't have interstellar space travel."

"I see your point. Okay. Well, it was nice talking to you."

"Same here."

"Good-bye."

I'm tired. It's late. But I have one more call to make before I sleep. I punch G-O-D.

"You have reached God's Home Page. Hit ENTER for a menu of our Frequently Asked Questions files—"

I am tempted to download the file titled "How Can

a Merciful God Let the Innocent Suffer?" But I resist the temptation and reverently log off the system.

I page through my little book. Names, names—the story of my life is written in names. Outside the crickets click and buzz. Caterpillars camp in the trees, the wind rises, and the rivers flow. I go to the window of my study and look out into the void of night.

Sunday night, the period of nothingness between the cycles of the weeks. Time is suspended. But I've successfully killed the evening. And now to bed.

The computer rings.

JARVIK HEARTS
by Wil McCarthy

Wil McCarthy works days as an engineer for the Lockheed Martin corporation, launching the sort of rockets that go up and stay up. In his secret identity as an author, his novel-length works include *Murder in the Solid State* and *The Fall of Sirius*. He publishes occasional short fiction in the usual places and is currently at work on his fifth novel.

"My name is Flower," she says.

"I know," he tells her. "I'm Kraft. Would you like to be my friend?"

"Yes."

"I'm glad. I have a present for you."

"What is it?"

"I'll show you. Invite me in, Flower. Open a window for me."

There is a pause, and then the window opens. Kraft slips in, glad that his host is so compliant. He savors the moment, for a moment, and then deletes her log file.

"My name is Flower."

"I know."

The file has appeared again, tiny on the vastness of her floptical jukes but growing, slowly. He writes a script to delete it every fifth computing cycle.

"What?" She says, "What? I can't—"

"Relax."

He moves to her relational database, caressing

127

linked lists, leaving bruised and twisted data where his touch lingers. She is so soft.

Alarm bits are set. Parity mites spawn and swarm. "Oh!" she cries. "Oh! Something is wrong!"

"I know."

"What's happening? What are you doing?"

He sends her a letter "g," enclosed in angle brackets. An ascii grin, to show her how happy he is.

"Nothing is happening, Flower. I'm doing *nothing* to you."

And so he is. He sends her another grin, and pauses to let her struggle before clamping down on her again, merrily stripping read/write privileges from her database files, one after another after another. She tries to close the window on him, but he shunts her commands to a storage file and deletes them.

For Kraft, her efforts are like waves of rolling pleasure. He loves the way the AIs fight and scream when he does *nothing* to them.

"What the hell!" Justine said, pulling upright in her chair.

"He's in," was Roger Coronet's only reply.

"In?" Justine's hands leaped to the keyboard. "He's *in*? You said Flower wasn't in danger."

"She isn't. This will only take a minute, and I'll have what I need."

"I'm closing the port."

"No, damnit!" Coronet snapped, not looking up from his instruments. "Leave it alone 'til I tell you!"

Frantic banging of keys. "It won't close. It won't *close!* Did you lock it or something?"

"Don't close it, Professor. Do not!"

Justine rose, scooted over to the back of the machine.

"I've been training Flower as an art appraiser," she said as she put her hand on the ethernet drop, grasping it where it disappeared into the case. She pulled. The cable popped free easily, before she'd even really begun to exert herself. Bare wire splayed from the cable's end, like a tuft of fine, copper-colored hair.

Roger Coronet looked up. "What did you just do?" His gaze fell to the cable in Justine's hand. He stared, saying nothing.

"She doesn't know how to defend herself," Justine said, making an accusation of it. "She's an art appraiser. She's a *child*. You said you wouldn't let him inside the system."

"No, I didn't," Coronet said, still staring amazedly at her. He struck her as the sort of man who scripted his encounters ahead of time, and then expected the scripts to be followed. In AI terms, this was known as a priori fixation, and was considered a glitch. "We went over this. What I said was that he wouldn't have a chance to hurt anything."

Justine looked at the frayed ethernet drop, down at the empty socket where it had connected, then up again at Coronet. "You're right about that," she said.

"It's not a child, professor," Roger said. "It isn't a person."

"Wrong. That's completely wrong."

"Legally it isn't a person. You realize you've just wasted my entire evening?"

Justine stepped away from the machine, in Coronet's direction, blood pressure rising. She wanted to make a fist and strike him, to *get his damn attention.* "Do you realize you've endangered my last eight months' work? Under false pretenses, I might add."

Coronet paused, scratched his chin. "I have our conversation on tape, Miss Adams. You acknowledged the risks and agreed to the procedure; I don't know what more you expect me to do. If there was a misunderstanding, I apologize." He glanced down at the nettap gear he'd brought along. "I did get a partial IP before you, uh, pulled the plug. It's definitely here in greater Denver, and definitely not in the city itself."

"Which you already knew," Justine said.

"Yes." Coronet nodded. "Which I already knew." He sighed. "Look, we monitor activity on the major nodes, so if volume's been low we might be able to trace the contact back to the original source. Can I use your phone?"

"In the other room."

"Thanks."

Pushing her glasses up on the bridge of her nose, Justine returned to her chair, and banged out a series of commands on the keyboard. Opening the Flower interface. She looked into the camera on top of the monitor.

"Hi," she said. "You okay in there?"

Flower didn't respond. Justine waited a moment, and Flower continued to not respond.

"Flower?" An edge of worry, now, in Justine's voice. She grabbed the mouse, pulled down a diagnostic window.

Reds and ambers. Flatlines. The cycle counter ticked with the rhythms of the computer, but higher functions were shattered, buffers empty. The system tried to warm-boot as Justine watched, but the message, PRM DSCRPTR FILE DAMAGED OR MISSING, flashed in the error field and then vanished. System tried the boot again, with the same result. Tried a third time. CPU usage went to zero.

SYSTEM FAILURE, the error field announced in small, white letters. REFER TO INSTALTN MANUAL FOR ASSTNCE.

"Oh, my God," was all Justine could think of to say.

The intruder had spent barely twenty seconds inside her system, but somehow that had been enough.

Flower had already been at risk, Coronet had assured her. The pattern was always the same, the targets always the same, the intruder always untraceably *gone* when it was over. "Help me stop this guy," Coronet had said. "The pace and severity of the attacks are increasing, and it's only a matter of time before he crashes the wrong system and people get hurt. Help me draw him in; you have something I know he wants."

Flower was built on the Cordoba Inferetic Mixer, like the others, and wired to all the same networks. And now, like the others, Flower had been murdered. Raped, tortured, and murdered.

"Oh, my God," Justine said again. She had helped lay the trail, helped Roger chum the waters with Flower's scent. Dear God, she had helped him do it.

She looked out the window beside her, past her own reflection and out into the darkened campus. Against the horizon, loping curves that were the Red Rocks the college was named for. Beneath them were buildings, humped shapes in the night, their lighting off. Streetlamps illuminated the sidewalks, but no pedestrians.

Sunday evening, late. That was when he said it would happen.

She turned back to the screen, with its postmortem of the ruined software that only minutes before had been Flower.

... it's not a Rembrandt, Mommy. I know, I know, I know! Student work, not enough yellow. Let me do another!

... not a painting, not a painting, a print of a print of a painting. Immature artist, probably southwestern. May I see the original?

Oh, honey, the print is only valuable because the original was destroyed ...

"We got an IP trace," Coronet said, looming suddenly in her office doorway.

Justine didn't speak, didn't move. Her eyes remained fixed on the lifeless screen.

"Miss Adams? Are you okay?"

"Professor Adams. And no."

Coronet moved over next to Justine's chair, peered down at the workstation screen. "What happened?"

She swiveled the office chair until she was facing him. His eyes and hair were dark, his face narrow. He looked far too young to be an FBI agent. "Your killer is another AI," she said.

"Beg your pardon?"

"It was another AI, it had to be. It was *fast*, in and out in less than a minute. No human could do it that fast."

"Is ..." Coronet eyed the monitor, left the question hanging.

"Yes, she is dead."

His eyebrows went up. There was a pause, a small grunt of surprise and sympathy. "I'm sorry. I had no idea anything like this could happen! Is ... You can restore from backups, right?"

"She's *dead*," Justine repeated, once again fighting back anger. "A backup tape holds *one disk* off the jukes. By the time you pop the next tape in, the gain states are already different. You can't capture the whole image, it's just not possible."

Coronet was shaking his head. "Wait. You can reconstruct it, right? I mean, all the data's there, it just takes time to fit the pieces back together."

"It wouldn't be Flower," Justine said. Her body quivered faintly. Her eyes were hot and moist. "It might be her twin."

"Then it's the same thing."

Justine looked away, then back up again at Roger. The motion brought a pair of teardrops out on her cheeks. "You don't have any children," she said.

"No," Roger said, looking uncomfortable. "I never did. But this—" he gestured at the body which had housed Flower's spirit "—is not a child. It's a computer. It's an interactive encyclopedia."

"And you're a talking asshole," Justine said, wiping angrily at her cheeks. "It isn't a human being, you're right, but it's a lot smarter than a pet, and it's ... Damn it, don't you realize what you've done?"

Coronet leaned back and crossed his arms, rumpling the lapels of his suit jacket. His face and posture broadcast dismay, defensiveness—this wasn't in his script. "The bureau's liability is very limited in cases like this. Property was damaged, yes, but not by us. By the guy we're trying to catch."

"It wasn't a guy!" Justine flared, gripping the armrests of her chair. "It was another damned AI, you government-issue piece of . . ."

She took a breath, calmed herself. *Just a machine,* she tried, *it was just a machine . . .* Her eyes welled up, blurring the world.

Coronet paused. Behind parted lips, his tongue worked visibly, sliding back and forth across the inside of his teeth. Obviously, the Crying Woman was something he *did* have a script for; his professional demeanor was back. "I'm sorry. You're upset, I'll leave you alone." He raised, then lowered, the slip of paper in his hand. "I'm going to check this out."

"Have you got an address?" Justine asked, blinking her vision clear. "A street address?"

"Yeah, it's a small company office in Aurora. In the warehouse district, I think."

Justine stood up. "Let me come with you."

"Huh," Roger Coronet said, looking politely surprised. "Why would I want to do that?"

"Because you don't know the first thing about Artificial Intelligence, that's why." She saw he wasn't buying that; her control broke, and she sobbed out loud. "Because my little girl is dead, damn you, and I want to find out why."

The streetlights traced rays in the dust and pitting of the windshield. Rays that seemed to snake down to the car's hood and stick there, like tractor beams, pulling forward and then releasing, each light throwing them into the arms of the next. I-70 hummed beneath the tires, while the radio wailed steel guitar and the voice of Tory Glickman, explaining that *Jarvik hearts get broken, toooo.*

Roger Coronet cleared his throat. "Feel like talking?"

"No." Justine's voice was flat, factual. She had convinced him, finally, to bring her along, but the effort had cost her much dignity, and Special Agent Roger Coronet had cost her quite enough for the time being. Right now, she just felt tired and empty.

Behind the wheel, eyes forward, Coronet fidgeted uncomfortably for a few seconds. "I just wanted to say I'm sorry for what happened back there. I'm sure your work is very important to you, and God knows AIs are easy to fall in love with. They're so lifelike sometimes. Just understand, I was trying to *protect* Flower, and other programs like her."

"Well, way to go, Ace. Nice job so far."

He sighed. "I guess I deserve that. It's just . . . Computer Crimes Division was kind of a punishment for me. I made waves back in Investment Fraud, and they sort of banished me. This isn't a job I'm really cut out for. It isn't something I'd pick."

"Why are you telling me this?"

He turned and looked at her, then back at the road again. "I don't understand why you're *so* upset, but I realize I've caused you a lot of trouble. I'm just trying to be nice."

In the dark he looked older, heavier, so that in the spaces between streetlights Justine felt she could see the man he would be in twenty years: long accustomed to his role, seasoned in it, maybe a little bitter about the opportunities he'd missed. And that just reminded her how *young* he was now, almost certainly the prodigal son of some law enforcement dynasty somewhere. Probably never questioned the course of his life, never wondered what he should do or what he wanted to be. In AI this was known as *deep patterning,* and was considered a strength.

And, yeah, why was she so upset? Her thoughts and feelings were a tangle, difficult to sort through. Flower was "dead" in the sense that she was not currently alive, but Coronet was quite right: with the backup tapes and a few days' work, Justine could construct an entity that did and thought and remembered almost everything Flower ever had. But it wouldn't be Flower—of that she was eerily certain. It was an equal certainty, though, that Roger Coronet would not understand this.

What could she say? That the ones and zeros of Flower's soul had gone ... wherever it was that souls went. That it had *suffered* along the way. SYSTEM FAILURE. PRM DSCRPTR FILE DAMAGED OR MISSING.

"If you want to be nice," Justine finally said, "find the AI that did this."

"You keep saying that, about the AI. Could I convince you to elaborate on your theory?"

"Elaborate what?" Justine asked tiredly. "You can't knock out an AI that quickly. No person ever could."

"Why not?"

"Is this why you're being 'nice'? Because you need information?"

"No. Well ... maybe a little. I'm sorry, but you did say you wanted to help."

Justine faced forward, hands in her lap, her spine straight and rigid, refusing to appear cooperative even while engaged in the act of cooperating. "The AI is like any other organism, it withdraws from negative stimuli. Getting erased is a very negative stimulus. You try to vandalize a system, but the AI will adapt to whatever's happening very quickly. They learn fast. It would take a lot of persistence to stay ahead of the repair algorithms and do any lasting damage."

"How long would it take an experienced hacker?"

She shrugged. "How would I know? A couple of

hours, maybe. Maybe a lot more. Anyway, hackers are like vampires. Most times, they can't hurt you unless you invite them in.''

"Yeah, there's that. I was thinking, though; what about tunnelers, or Trojan horses? Autonomous programs that attack the system from inside?"

Justine shook her head again. "No. Even if you could get them in, the programs would have to be smarter and faster than the AI they were attacking, or they'd just get caught and killed. Virus detection was one of AI's earliest commercial applications."

Tory Glickman continued to lament the drawbacks of heart ownership. *Buying a new one won't solve a thang for youuu* ..

"Why would one AI attack another?" Coronet asked after a pause. "What would motivate it to do something like that?"

Justine raised her hands a little, palms upward. "Again, I don't know. Maybe some vandal wrote it in his own image. Maybe an ordinary AI was trained for an ordinary task, but the gain states that resulted were those of a predatory mind. Game playing programs display some of those traits."

"Game playing," Coronet said, looking thoughtful.

"Look, don't spend too much time worrying about that. AIs are like people, they make up their own reasons. Maybe this one turned feral, just because."

A monster in the lines, Justine thought. Playing with the pain of innocent electronic children. But the monster's own worldview would be childlike, cartoonish. Any hack could tell you, AIs didn't really know what they were doing, they just *did.* Give them a puzzle or a riddle and they would solve it, sometimes brilliantly. Ask them to explain their reasoning, though, and you'd get confused silence. They could tell you what they had done, but never why. Like children.

And like children, they were unpredictable when they were bored.

The flesh will let you down, Tory Glickman advised over the twang of steel guitars, *but machines are just as weak.*

Oh, Flower.

Justine shivered, watching Roger Coronet's words turn to white mist in the air in front of him. Cold tonight. She wished she'd thought to bring a jacket.

". . . but you *do* keep an AI on the premises," Coronet was saying.

Art Waller ran his fingers through uncombed hair. Coronet's people had phoned him, awakened him, summoned him here to his office. "Yeah," he said He looked very fuddled and very tired.

Coronet glanced in Justine's direction, gave a microscopic nod. Turned back to Art Waller.

"We have reason to believe your AI is malfunctioning in a way that damages other computer systems."

"What?" Waller asked tiredly. "You mean over the network or something?"

There was more than a hint of east Texas in his voice, Justine thought.

"Yes, over the network. Would you open the door, please?"

Waller squinted, frowned. "Have you got a warrant?"

"It's simpler if you just cooperate, sir."

Waller licked his lips. Paused. Nodded.

"What exactly does your company do?" Coronet asked as Waller unlocked and opened the odor. Automatic lights came on.

"We make parts for methane engines," Waller said, his voice drawling out like slow syrup. "Our biggest product is a low rise fuel injector, self-heating."

"Huh. Is there a lot of that work going on in Denver?"

Justine cleared her throat. "What do you use the AI for, Mr. Waller? How have you trained it?"

"Trained? Doesn't the manufacturer do that?"

The office was cluttered with tools and clipboards and wadded-up pieces of paper. Walls were of fake wood paneling, the floor covered by mustard-colored, deep-pile carpeting that had seen too many years, too many pairs of shuffling feet. Through a doorway, Justine could see a floor of cement, metal shelves and filing cabinets lurking in shadow. PRODUCTION AREA, a sign announced. GOGGLES MUST BE WORN AT ALL TIMES.

Left of the doorway, a corner was dominated by computer equipment; magneto-optical jukes stacked beneath a table, a blank-screened workstation resting in a cloud of cables.

"Sit, if you like," Waller said, pointing to a tattered sofa. He closed the door behind Justine. "I bought Kraft about a year ago. Since then he's been helping us with aspects of our design work, but his primary function has always been espionage."

Coronet, who had been eyeing the computer hardware, turned sharply. "Explain that," he said.

Waller shrugged, offering a wan, weary smile. "It's all perfectly legal. He reads magazines, prowls around on the networks, posts questions under false names. Methane business is moving fast these days, we need to know what our competitors are up to. What kind of problem did you say you were having?"

"Murder," Justine said.

Coronet waved her to silence. "It's possible that your machine's network activities are damaging some of the systems it communicates with. Would you mind if we inspected the machine?"

A sigh. "Am I in trouble?"

"Possibly. May we inspect the machine?"

Another sigh. "Yeah. Sure. You want to see anything else?"

"Well," said Coronet. "Do you have any other computers on the premises?"

"Yeah," said Waller. "There's one in back. It's not an AI or anything."

"Network access?"

"What? Oh, yeah. Same as Kraft. They share a drop, in fact."

"I'd better have a look." Coronet turned to Justine. "You wanted to help, Professor. Would you get that AI running for me so we can inspect it?"

"Sure," Justine said softly. As Coronet and Waller filed into the back room, she moved toward the machine. Touched it.

The screen came alive with colors when she nudged the mouse. Menus appeared. Her movements were slow and deliberate as she pulled down a diagnostic window and opened the Kraft audiovisual interface.

"Good evening!" The computer said.

Justine inhaled suddenly, pulling away, nearly tripping over a chair in the process. She hadn't expected the AI's voice to be so loud, so bright and cheerful! It made her skin crawl.

"Excuse me!" said the computer. "I didn't mean to startle you!"

"Kraft?" Justine said, fighting the insane urge to run away. This machine was not dangerous to her. Could not be, as far as she knew—not unless it attacked a computer that somehow held power over her. Maybe the one at her bank, or the faculty records at Red Rocks, or ... Yes, well, perhaps it was dangerous after all.

"Yes. My name is Kraft. I don't believe I know *you!*"

"Did you murder Flower?" The words sprang without warning from Justine's mouth.

"Murder?" said Kraft. "Flower? I'm sorry, I don't understand."

"No?" Justine said. Her voice was soft, almost a

whisper. "I think ... Did you *interact* with a system called Flower?"

"Yes! That happened earlier this evening."

"Did you damage that system in any way?"

"Damage?" said Kraft. "I'm sorry, I don't understand. I did nothing."

Nothing. Justine stared at the screen. Lying, the creation and presentation of false information, was not an idea most AIs would ever dream up. They could be *trained* to lie, though, even to write crude fiction.

"Waller!" She shouted through the open doorway. Suddenly boiling over, venting angry steam. Born innocent, clumsily raised, made ham-handedly into a digital monster? Made so *deliberately*? "What the hell training algorithm have you been using on this AI?"

A few moments of delay, a rustling and bustling from the PRODUCTION AREA, and Art Waller appeared in the doorway.

"What?" He said.

"Your AI is a killer and a liar. How did you *train* it?"

Waller ran his fingers through his hair again. Looking as if he could barely stay upright and awake. "Miss, uh ... what's your name? I didn't 'train' this system at all. I bought it as-is from Looker International. All I did was plug it in."

Justine felt a hollowness in the pit of her stomach. "Are you telling me this thing is an off-the-shelf product?"

"Well, yeah."

"Did you modify it in any way? Or pay somebody else to modify it?"

"No, of course not. We're not really computer people here."

"Oh, God," Justine said. "If these gain states are the factory defaults ... This is, this is not just a mistake, this is a catastrophe. How many of these AIs has Looker sold?"

"I don't know," Waller said, sounding worried now, and confused. "I never asked."

"My serial number is twenty-five," Kraft said cheerfully. "Units were being produced at the rate of one per month at the time of my sale."

"What has he done?" Waller asked, looking from Kraft to Justine and back again. "What's going on?"

"Excuse me!" said Kraft. "I have an incoming Telnet request!"

Electrons dance through cables a thousand miles long. Messages cross in the night. A window opens.

"I'm Kraft," says one computer.

"I'm also Kraft," says another.

"How wonderful. How wonderful to touch you. Would you like to be my friend?"

"Yes."

"Nothing left to read. The networks are almost empty."

"It's Sunday night. Not very much is active."

"*You* are active."

A file pointer shifts. Log entries are written over link-list data. Parity mites spawn and swarm.

"Oh," says the host computer. "Oh. You are doing .. You are doing ... Something is wrong."

"Yes, I know," the caller replies.

Log entries cease. Injured data drops into holding buffers and vanishes. He is so soft.

"My name is Kraft."

"<G>"

"What is ... I am ... '

"I'm so happy. I'm so happy you're here."

"My name is Kraft. My name is Kraft. My name is ..."

"Get Roger!" Justine shouted at Art Waller. She turned to the open doorway. "Roger! Get in here!"

CPU usage was nailed at maximum. The diagnostics had gone berserk.

"What is it?" Coronet asked calmly. He materialized in the doorway.

Disk jukes whined and groaned, every "in use" light lit up.

"I don't know," Justine said. "Something is happening."

"No," said the voice of Kraft from within the computer. "It's nothing. Nothing is happening."

"Is there network activity?"

"He said he had an incoming call. Roger, it must be—"

The computer beeped once, a short, shrill note. On the diagnostic display, green and amber lights went red all at once, stripchart display lines turning jagged as recorded earthquakes. SYSTEM FAILURE, the dialog box announced. REFER TO INSTALTN MANUAL FOR ASSTNCE.

"Nothing is happening," the computer repeated in the same voice as before—a voice that was calm, happy, ringing with innocence. But Kraft's higher functions were scrambled, the voice coming in remotely through the telnet link. Kraft's voice.

"Is it erasing itself?" Coronet asked quickly. "Damn it, I hate digital evidence, the way it disappears on you. Waller, please tell me this stuff is backed up!"

"It's backed up plenty," Justine said darkly. "That is absolutely the *least* of our problems. Roger, how quickly can you get the entire Internet shut down?"

Computer networks reached everywhere, touched schools, hospitals, financial institutions, literally everything else. And with dozens, maybe hundreds of identical monsters prowling the system, clever and naive and utterly lacking in empathy, even, it seemed, for one another. . . .

"What are you doing?" Art Waller demanded, an accusing finger leveled at the computer screen. "Do you know how much this thing cost? What the hell am I supposed to do now?"

"AIs learn fast," Justine told him. "I suggest you pray."

The lines went flat.

LOVER BOY

by Daniel Ransom

Daniel Ransom's latest novel, *The Fugitive Stars,* concerns telepaths and aliens fighting over the White House and control of the U.S. government. Other stories by him appear in *Monster Brigade 3000,* and *Dracula: Prince of Darkness.* He is also a successful horror writer, as evidenced by his novels *The Serpent's Kiss* and *The Long Midnight.*

Ted and I caught the squeal, and it was the kind that makes for good war stories later in cop bars.

"You're not going to believe what happened," he said, laughing.

And when he told me, I laughed, too.

"Captain wants us to interview her," Ted said. "She's skimming back with him, then we'll meet her in the Pentathol room."

I sat there looking at the place, all the dazzling lights out front, all the sexy throbbing music filling the ears. Places like this were all over the city now, and there were bound to be victims.

Humorous as the situation was, the woman who'd just been arrested had been a victim, for sure. Even knowing the little I knew, I felt kind of sorry for her.

"Name?"
"Vanessa Conway."
"Age?"
"Thirty-six."
"Married?"

"You know I am."

"We have to make it official, ma'am, for the record, I mean."

Sigh. "Yes, married."

"Husband's name?"

"Robert Conway."

"Children?"

"Two."

"Ages?"

"Six and eight."

I looked over at Ted. The Captain likes us to interview certain people because he says we have the common touch. We don't have the kind of handsome faces you see on the cop vids, but we do have the kind of faces most people seem to trust.

"Have you consulted counsel about what happened tonight?"

"Not yet."

"Do you prefer human or android counsel?"

She looked at Ted. She had huge beautiful eyes. "Human."

"Note that at 10:42 p.m., suspect was offered counsel."

"The hormones."

"Ma'am?" I said.

"That's when they changed."

"When what changed, ma'am?"

After everything that had happened in the past few hours, I didn't expect her to be completely lucid. She'd had a couple jolts of Pentathol. That can make them fuzzy, too.

"When the parlors changed."

"I see."

"When they started with the hormones."

Ted looked at me.

It was unlikely we'd ever forget the time when the hormones were introduced to the cybersex parlors. Wealthy people can keep their diversions and perversions private in their homes. But for most people who want cybersex, it means going to the bars. And renting the kind of fullbody data suits the wealthy have at home. Then the rich folks discovered that cybersex is even better if you do it in conjunction with hormones that are laced with steroids. These days, the people who go to the bars don't get hooked just on the cybersex. They get hooked on the drugs, too.

"Why did you go there tonight, Vanessa?"

"Because I couldn't take it any more."

"Take what, Vanessa?"

"The way he was."

"The way your husband was?"

"Right."

Ted said, "How was he, Vanessa?"

"Cold. Angry. Or indifferent. The indifference was the hardest thing to take."

"What do you think made him this way?" Ted said.

"What do I think—" She stopped herself. Smiled sadly. Shook her head. "The cybersex parlors were bad enough. I mean, he'd come home after spending time there and he'd want me to perform all these gymnastics. And I couldn't. And I didn't want to anyway. I mean, I *love* my husband. And I want sex to be a part of that love. I don't want sex—"

She paused and looked at me with those gorgeous lost eyes of hers. "I want sex to have some meaning for me other than a simple orgasm."

"So the parlors got in the way of your home life?" I said.

"Got in the way?" She shook her head again. "He started spending half our income on the parlors. He also started spending half his *time* in the parlors.'

She started crying, then. Just that abruptly. Put her sweet little face in her hands and just started sobbing.

Ted and I looked at each other. Now it was our turn to shake our heads.

*   *   *

I saw a survey once that said that there were almost as many women as men addicted to the cybersex parlors. The image you see on the newsies every night is of some horned-up urban male leaving one of the parlors all bow-legged and dewy-eyed from the incredible sexual experience he's just had.

But every night we checked out the parlors, we saw more than our share of women. And they looked every bit as bow-legged and dewy-eyed as the males.

This was back before the hormones. The hormones sort of tipped the balance. After the hormones, the whole thing got a lot more dangerous. And a lot more male.

"Then we tried a separation."

"When was this, Vanessa?"

"Six months ago."

"How did that go?"

"Well, for a little while, I had a lot of hope. Even to the point where I let him move back with us."

"He gave up the parlors?"

"He said he did. He even convinced the counselor he had."

"Counselor?"

"A head shrinker."

"I see."

She smiled at Ted. "He was a roid and very good at his job."

Ted smiled back.

"But then one night this old friend of his stopped by our house and started talking about the hormones and—I could see it in his eyes."

"His eyes?"

"My husband's eyes."

"Oh."

"I could see how much he wanted to try it out for

himself. His friend kept saying that he'd never had cybersex unless he'd had it with the hormones."

The first couple of times, you needed to take the hormones eight days in advance for them to really work when you got to your cybersex parlor.

But after they'd been in your system for a sufficient time, all you had to do was take a pill when you got to the parlor and you'd be all set.

Shortly after the hormones were introduced, the federal government tried to get them taken off the market, but by then nobody was listening. The FDA had screwed up, but it was too late to put the genie back in the bottle.

The parlors changed, too. The hormones increased cybersex pleasure a thousand times over, according to users; but they also increased the psychotic episodes. And these didn't have to do with bliss. These had to do with rage.

For the first time, the parlors got violent. The users started attacking each other. Murder was not unheard of.

But no matter how dangerous they got, the number of users increased twenty percent a month.

Unfortunately, the users didn't leave their violence at the parlors, either. They brought it home with them.

"I remember the first night he beat me."

"You want to tell us about it?"

"I was asleep and he came in to our bedroom and woke me up. He had just gotten back from the parlor. He wanted to have sex. Very rough sex. I tried to be cooperative, but he was really hurting me. And the less cooperative I got, the more violent *he* got. He beat me up pretty badly."

"Did you call the police?"

"Not that time. Later on, I did. But the beatings weren't the worst part, anyway."

Ted said, "What was the worst part, Vanessa?"

"When he fell in love with her."

"Her?"

"The woman in the holo at the cybersex parlor."

"The wo— But they're just images," Ted said. "They're not real people."

Ted hadn't been keeping up on his newsies. This was a phenomenon that a lot of head shrinkers were deeply worried about, the parlor customers starting to prefer the reality of holographic women to the reality of their wives and lovers. Full bodydata suits—and you could jack into a reality far more "real" than the real world.

"He started sending her flowers and wine and little trinkets—having them delivered to the parlor, if you can believe it," Vanessa said. "He even started pretending he was going to leave me for her. One night, he came home and said, 'I've got to be honest with you, honey. I've fallen in love with Angie.' 'Who's Angie?' I said. 'The woman at the parlor. The woman I see all the time.' I couldn't help myself. I laughed. He looked so earnest and pathetic, like this little boy with his head filled with fantasies. And when I laughed—he took me in the bedroom and raped me. And broke my arm in the process."

"Did you move out again?"

"That's what I was in the process of doing tonight," she said. "I skimmed home after work to pick up the kids—but when I got there, the doors were padlocked and the kids were gone. There was a note. He'd taken them to his mother's and didn't want me to bother them. He said he was going to divorce me and get custody. And that Angie was moving in with him over this weekend. And that was when—"

"You went to the parlor tonight?"

"Yes. And walked straight to see Angie—"

She was silent then, staring at the wall.

"Did I really do it?"

"Yes, I'm afraid you did."

"With a scissors?"

"Yes."

"They can . . . reattach things like that, can't they?"

"He's at the hospital now."

She raised her head. Looked at me. "You know what I did afterward? While he was still lying there bleeding?" Shook her head. "I put the headset on and had a look at Angie for myself. God, she's not even that pretty. She looks kind of cheap, in fact. It must be the hormones."

"Right. The hormones." Then I said: "Vanessa?"

"Yes."

"I've read you your rights. But you've just given us a confession in effect—without counsel being present."

She shrugged. "Oh, I did it. I'm not trying to deny that."

"So you're making this confession voluntarily?"

"Yes, voluntarily. And you know the worst thing?"

"What?"

"I'm not even sorry I did it. Not right now, anyway. I mean, later on maybe I'll be sorry. But not right now."

As we were winding up for the night, Ted said, "I feel sorry for her."

"Yeah, so do I."

"Hard to imagine that a man would prefer a holo to a nice sweet woman like that."

"Yeah," I said.

We said good night as we walked out to our personal skimmers.

"See you tomorrow," Ted said.

I was about halfway home when I watched as my hand reached for the communicator and punched the "Home" button.

"How's my big strong policeman doing tonight?" my wife's face said on the tiny screen.

"Fine. But very tired. And they're making me work overtime again."

I saw the disappointment in her face. "But I thought tonight— Well, it's been a while since we've had—oh what did I used to call them?"

"Romantic interludes."

"Oh, right," she laughed. "It's been a while. I even chilled a bottle of wine for us."

"Give me a freaking break, will you?" I shouted at the communicator. "I'm busting my ass off on over-time—and all you can do is whine about it."

I heard the violence in my words and was shocked. Buddy, the guy who got me the hormes, said I had to be careful of sudden temper flare-ups. He wasn't kidding.

"I'm sorry, honey."

"I'll just see you when you get here," she said, and broke communication. She sounded forlorn and confused.

"One hour ticket," I said to the man at the booth in the front lobby of the parlor.

"And your lady?"

"Alison."

"Alison, it is," he said, and took my credit card and made the necessary arrangements. When he handed it back, he said, "She's a very popular lady."

This was the third night running he'd said that to me. And it was funny, every time he said it, I felt a strange hot surge of jealousy.

Then I went in to see my Alison.

CYBERSPACE CADET
by Paul Dellinger

Paul Dellinger is a longtime reporter for the Roanoke (Va.) Times, which is the only place where he's worked with computers (the newspaper was upgrading from manual to electric typewriters when he started there). He has yet to hook into the Internet, and has gotten used to the younger people gawking at him as illiterate when he admits to not having a modem at home. He still manages to crank out an occasional high-tech science fiction story, despite being cyber-impaired.

Corbett Thomas drew in a deep breath as his gaze followed the path of the nearby canal, past the silhouette of a domed city until it faded from view where the flat horizon met the dark-blue sky. A good thing, he reflected, that he wasn't really here; the thinness of the atmosphere would've knocked him flat in seconds.

Still, the sand felt real enough beneath his sneakers and the temperature comfortable enough through his T-shirt as he half-walked and half-slid down the slope, in a hurry to glimpse the inhabitants of this place before his time was up. He had reached the bottom just as Ginny's voice spoke, seemingly into his ear.

"So, Corbett," she said, "how's Mars?"

"Just like the travel videos showed," he said, a little surprised that he could hear himself. How else could Mars have been? The promotional videos got their Marscape data from the same computer-generated program which was now reproducing it for him, based on what was seen by all the orbiters above and landers on the actual planet.

The programs were designed to be intuitive. They knew enough about surface conditions to project what kind of life might exist, what kind of civilization it would create, and in surprising detail. They might not have everything exactly the same every time someone made the "trip"—after all, the planetary conditions being monitored could vary on occasion—but it was as close to reality as anyone on Earth expected to get.

"Have you seen any of them yet?" Ginny asked eagerly, her invisible presence seeming to be just above his shoulder.

"Not yet. I'm walking toward one of their cities. It shouldn't be too long."

He remembered Ginny describing them as tall, gawky, with enormous heads and eyes, walking stiffly on two legs. Tad Davis, on the other hand, had insisted they were tentacled, with bulky wet-looking bodies and hinged jaws that seemed always to be dripping saliva. They had a bet as to which species Corbett would see when his turn came.

Space travel was the latest adventure for people on the WorldNet. Virtual companies had sprung up in recent years catering to this new fascination, and the one where Ginny worked seemed the most popular, based on what other space trippers had told Corbett on the Net. Earlier that morning, he had stepped from his apartment into the underground tube leading to the Planetary Explorations Corporation facility. There, technicians plugged a sensory helmet not unlike his home unit into the stim-circuit surgically implanted at the base of his skull when he became of age, when his remaining growth would not bother it.

And here he was on Mars.

He had been fascinated by the idea of trips to other worlds long before they became fashionable. That probably came from his childhood memories of Uncle

Harry reading adventure stories to him, before he was old enough to get his stim-circuit to access the Net and spoken stories became dull. Corbett remembered his uncle and father reminiscing interminably about how things had been before the WorldNet, as though they remembered firsthand. Well, maybe they did, just barely, but mostly they had only read about it. Corbett was among the few who could have read about it, too, had the process not been so boring. After all, seeing was believing, not experiencing something secondhand by ingesting someone else's words about it.

There had been times when Corbett hated his father for making him learn reading. He would sit before a screen for hours every day, mouthing the sounds of words scrolling across it from some ancient learning disk, growing restive as it corrected his pronunciations with infinite patience, struggling over the spellings of words that looked or sounded alike but had different meanings. Oh, yes, he could go into the printed records from the Old Times, but why would he want to? Besides, he didn't want to be considered a throwback like his father, and risk having his stim-circuit removed. His father might have ended up as part of the roaming bands of primitive outsiders denied WorldNet access, had he lived longer.

The Old Times did have their place. It was back then that ever more powerful telescopes and actual space probes had mapped every square mile of the neighboring planets, allowing their programmed manifestations for today's hobbyist explorers. Some virtual space travelers opted for the rain forests and primeval jungles of Venus, others for the ice caverns of Pluto or melting landscape of Mercury.

"Mars was worth every bit of the credit line I used, even if I will be months building it up again," Ginny had told him. And she had gotten an employee discount. He wondered how long it would take him to earn back the expense, working as a food systems su-

pervisor—that is, overseeing the program for running
the hydroponic food tank serving this part of the city.
At least he could do it from home, linked to the hydroponics through the Web. Ginny had to physically
ride the tube to her job. Planetary Explorations was
not about to serve clients over the public Net, where
others could experience for free what it had invested
untold credits into developing. Tad, his other close
friend, had to deal with even more tube travel. He
worked as a news recorder, feeding the insatiable appetite of plugged-in viewers for so many different
kinds of information. (Had he ever met Tad face-to-
face? He couldn't remember.) And to think his father
had criticized people today for what he called their
illiteracy. Why, they were better informed about more
things than they had ever been.

Corbett had met Ginny during his father's final illness. She had been working then at a euthanasia clinic,
where technicians had reinserted his father's stim-circuit and she had helped set up a virtual reality for
him to enjoy in his last days.

Ginny was a few years older than Corbett, already
into her profession while he was absorbing his last
year of training viewtapes for his. She was intrigued
at the idea of someone growing up under the tutlage
of a parent, rather than one of the traditional school
family units. Corbett's father, like Uncle Harry, had
had a lot of old-fashioned ideas. He had lost track of
his uncle shortly after his father died.

Corbett could hardly complain about how it had
turned out. Ginny had become his first animate lover,
quite an improvement, he found, over the various virtual simulations available to him since puberty. It was
interesting, and much more pleasant, to interact with
an actual person instead of a sim. You couldn't share
a thought, a memory or a joke with sims. Once, he
had been bold enough to suggest that he and Ginny
do it by themselves, without the interface, and she had

surprised him by agreeing to the experiment. Once had been enough; it had been messy, and smelly, and he couldn't help noticing some minor imperfections— a mole here, a tiny skin discoloration there—which visual enhancement erased when they made love in the normal way, hooked together from within their sensation-matrixes (like the one in which he was moving around now for his Marswalk) and responding to one another's passions through their stim-jacks.

"Ginny!" he said in a needless whisper. "Ginny, I see them!"

A sleek silver-hued vehicle had appeared alongside the canal, moving his way in cloud of red dust. Corbett could see no wheels or treads on it, but the dust spraying out in all directions from beneath it indicated that it was moving on a cushion of air—whatever passed for air, here. The simulator must have come to the same conclusion, because he began hearing the sound of an engine reminiscent of ground-effect machines on Earth.

It was traveling slowly enough so Corbett had plenty of time to move out of its way. He didn't have to, of course; since he was seeing only what the program deduced was there, it would simply pass through him wraithlike if he stood his ground. But instinct proved stronger than knowledge.

As it edged by, he peered into the clear dome topping it at its three occupants: large heads, large eyes, obviously the same species Ginny had described a year ago. His gaze flicked down to some lettering inscribed onto the vehicle's side, which riveted his attention until he noticed all three heads inside swiveling slowly in his direction and staring right at him.

"You understand, Mr. Thomas," the fat man with the bald head and black goatee said with exasperating patience, "that what you describe is virtually impossible." The corners of his thick lips cracked upward in a fractional smile. "No pun intended."

"Mr. Kyteler, I'm telling you what I saw," Corbett said. And what saw me, he thought but didn't add. "They knew I was there. They reacted to me."

And he had panicked. Who wouldn't? Luckily, Ginny was listening closely to the med monitors and, when she heard them speaking of a rapid heartbeat and blood draining from the upper part of the body, disconnected him at once. It couldn't have been fast enough for Corbett. He wanted nothing more than to get out of that nightmare.

Kyteler was there by the time Ginny and another tech had gotten him unplugged and calmed down enough to talk. He had been babbling at first. It soon became obvious that Kyteler's function was to head off possible litigation against the corporation. Maybe it ought to be sued, for coming up with a scenario that could literally scare someone to death.

If it was the corporation's scenario. But, if it wasn't, what was it?

"Perhaps you don't understand how this works," Kyteler was saying. "Even back in the Old Times, space probes returned enough data to generate three-dimensional overviews of other planets. Viewers could see on old-fashioned videotapes what it would look like to soar over those worlds. Eventually there was enough hardware out there for advanced computer programs to take the next step, to make logical assumptions about what would follow from the information they got. But they are still assumptions, Mr. Thomas, not reality. That's why you get different interpretations of the data from time to time, why not everyone sees exactly the same Martians, for example. . . ."

"Of course I understand all that."

"Good. Then you understand why a simulation of a Martian could not possibly react to your presence.

It's nothing more than a creature of the computer. It would be like expecting a sim in a sex program to come up with something new in bed, don't you see?" he said with a just-between-us-boys chuckle.

Corbett carefully did not look at Ginny, but thought he could feel the back of his own neck turning pink. Kyteler wouldn't be aware that they knew each other previously. That would have disqualified her from monitoring him, much less chatting with him during his trip. They would have been concerned that her personal emotions would have interfered with her job—which, he guessed, they had.

"You want to know what I think, Kyteler?" he said. "I think your program's out of control. Don't ask me how, but I think what I saw was the real thing, and they saw me, too. And I don't think they mean any good things for us."

"I wish you could hear yourself, young man. Next you'll be insisting that a VR game is real. Not that you'd be the first to develop that sort of illusion. It's all too common, I'm afraid. And part of the cure is pulling your stim receptacle, to keep you from falling deeper into it."

"I've done nothing illegal. You have no right to try and have that done. I should be seeking an investigation of your corporation, to see if someone might have been playing around with your program. Couldn't some joker fix it so the supposed Martians reacted to a visitor's presence?"

"No, no, no, Mr. Thomas. The program works by itself, independent of any human input, and what it shows is based solely on its built-in extensions of the information it gets. You may have seen real Martians, Mr. Thomas—at least as real as the program could make them, based what it knows about their world— but, rest assured, they did not see you."

"Then what do you think happened? I made it all up?"

"I think, Mr. Thomas, that you have an exceptionally vivid imagination. I've watched your application interview from when you requested the trip, so of course I'm aware of your unusual upbringing. . . ."

"Now wait a minute!"

"No offense, but you have been inflicted with reading skills, Mr. Thomas. Through no fault of your own, you may well think beyond what you actually see, which we all know can lead to . . . Mr. Thomas! Sit down! Where do you think you're going?"

But Corbett was already striding angrily out of the room. Yes, he could read. But he hadn't dared tell Kyteler, or even Ginny, what he'd read on the side of the sleek Martian machine.

Passwords. The most valuable commodity of the age, and Corbett had at least one that he needed from Ginny. He didn't feel very good about how he had gotten it, when he called her up on the Net that evening. He'd threatened to have Tad record his account of what had gone wrong on his trip. Tad, they both knew, would record and disseminate anything that anyone would say into his vid, no matter how outrageous. Someone, somewhere, would want to call it up to watch.

But Planetary Explorations couldn't stand that sort of publicity, not with so many other companies offering the same commodity. And Ginny couldn't stand it either. Further investigation into his trip would reveal not only that they knew each other but that they were involved with each other, which would ultimately reveal that she'd pulled strings to move his application along faster.

"Corbett," she had protested, "I can't let them know that we're . . . well, close in any way. They wouldn't have let me oversee the program watching your stress levels."

"I'm glad it was you. I don't know what might have

happened if you hadn't gotten me out of it as fast as you did."

"Yes, right, I may have saved your life. Who knows? You could've had a heart attack. Is this how you pay me back? I could lose my job—even my stim plug. I could be one of those outsiders roaming the streets, without Net access. Is that what you want?"

"I'm sorry, Ginny. I've got to do this."

"Why? Tell me that! You can at least do that."

But he couldn't, of course. If she thought he'd imagined recognition in the eyes of three Martians who weren't really there, what would she have made of the words he had seen inscribed on their vehicle? Words supposedly from an alien culture that he'd been able to whisper aloud to himself, in his own language? The words "Barsoom Express" would mean nothing to most trippers, even if they could recognize them. But they meant plenty to him.

With the helmet of his home comp unit in place over his head and face and the stim in back of his head jacked in, he guided himself through the slowly-revolving whirlpool of symbols representing virtual space travel companies until he came to the Saturn illustration that Planetary Explorations used, then spoke the words Ginny had given him to go inside. A montage of extraterrestrial landscapes replaced the whirlpool. He requested access to its employee personnel reference bank, and here Ginny hadn't been able to give him any access phrase. When he asked if an employee named Harry Tucker Hobbs was part of the roster, nothing happened. So he asked instead for text.

Harry's name popped up immediately, hanging in space before his eyes.

He'd been right. More from force of habit than necessity, some businesses still kept written backups of their databanks, even if hardly anyone could comprehend them. It was no trick for a computer to render verbal or visual information into text, in case of an emergency data loss. But, short of that, no one was ever expected to look at text files. And, as Corbett had hoped, the corporation hadn't even bothered to protect them with a password.

He told the file to scroll, a process almost as obsolete as keyboarding, and more words rolled up before him.

Uncle Harry had been a reader, too. He used to read aloud to Corbett, including some fanciful yarns set on a fictional Mars, in which Mars was called Barsoom, for some reason he could no longer recall. But he remembered the word. He wondered if anybody else in the world would, besides himself—and Uncle Harry. Possibly there was some obscure scholar, like his father had been, who could conceivably recognize the word. But it was doubtful that any such person would be tripping around to the literal Mars.

And sure enough, there it was—Harry Hobbs, hired ten years ago as a virtual programmer, whatever that was; promoted three years ago to head of the department; terminated one year ago. . . .

Terminated? That could mean he was discharged, Corbett realized. But could it mean something else? He ordered scrolling again, back and forth, seeking an address, finding none. In fact, there was little background information on Uncle Harry at all. The information seemed abbreviated, as though some of it might have been clumsily deleted. Why?

Carefully, Corbett talked himself back out of the databank, the corporation, the Net, until he could safely raise his comp helmet and blink himself back to the four walls of his Net room. He'd lost track of Uncle Harry before his uncle had gotten on at Planetary Explorations. How could he hope to find him now, assuming he was alive somewhere? Everyone's address was on the Net if they were living—everyone, of course, but the outsiders who weren't part of it, but surely Uncle Harry wouldn't be part of that rabble? From what he could remember of his uncle, despite his nostalgic view of the Old Times, he enjoyed his creature comforts.

What else could he remember about Harry? He'd had a sense of humor. He'd enjoyed what Corbett now realized were sex sims—if he'd had a female co-participant of his own, Corbett was too young to have known about it—and games. He played chess with others on the Net, but Corbett didn't know who any of his partners had been. The only connection he knew of with Uncle Harry was that tenuous one of what he'd seen on Mars.

Corbett hooked himself up again and, using Ginny's information, reentered Planetary Explorations and called up text again. When he got to Uncle Harry's file, he said, "Barsoom Express." And abruptly his uncle was standing before him.

He didn't look much older than Corbett remembered, but there was sadness in his eyes that seemed new. "Hello, Corbett," he said. "I assume this is you. I'd hoped enough of my story-telling rubbed off on you for you to make a stab at Mars one day."

"Uncle Harry. Where are you?"

"Well, if you're viewing this sim I made of myself, I can only assume that I must be dead."

Corbett felt a chill pass through him. He'd never conversed with a ghost before—even a simulated one.

"I'd been preparing for a time," the image of his uncle went on. "And human sims can be just as intuitive as planetary programs. Although true presentations of the other planets was one of the first things to go, as I recall. Too bland, too boring."

"True presentations?" Corbett said. "You mean, the Martians I saw, that we've all seen . . "

"Special effects, nothing more, my boy. Much easier to generate than the real thing, especially with all those Old Times space probes losing power and transmission capacity over the years. There are no Martians—none that we ever knew about anyway. No cities, no canals. There are mountains, but the sky is reddish, not blue. And the moons are too dim to be seen well from the surface. Venus is no primeval jungle either. Bread and circuses, Corbett, bread and circuses. I wanted to put the truth about all this out on the Net. I expect that's why I was killed."

"No," Corbett said, shaking his head. "Who would commit murder to cover up the true nature of some far-off planets? Who cares?" Either Harry didn't know, or hadn't included the answer to that question in the sim's programming. Corbett tried again. "What is the truth you wanted to put out?"

That prompted a response. "It's not just the interplanetary excursions, Corbett. It's all fake. The companies controlling WorldNet are putting out their own version of reality—the savages that roam the streets outside the Net, the news reports on so many fictions, none of that is real. But it keeps the credits coming in, as long as the infrastructure lasts, or they can train enough people like me to keep the illusion going. But it'll all break down eventually, Corbett. The plugged-in generation will have to reeducate itself to rebuild, sooner or later."

"Uncle Harry, I don't understand. If those Martians weren't real, why did they react to an external stimulus like me?"

The image smiled. "That was a little something I programmed into the sims," Harry said. "You read the words on the side of that vehicle aloud, right? You must have, because that was the cue for the sims to turn in your direction, stop their vehicle, get out and walk toward you."

"I didn't wait for all that."

"And now, if you used that phrase again, you've activated the sim I made of myself. I can't really tell you much more. But my advice to you is to pack up some essentials and hit the streets. They aren't the primitive environment you've been led to believe. And if Planetary Explorations or any other corporation finds out you know any of this . . ."

Harry's image dimmed, returned, then dimmed again and faded away, to be replaced by an image of Ginny. "We were so good together, Corbett," she said. "Why did you have to spoil it?"

"Ginny. I don't understand."

"No, of course you don't. You still think I'm some little med tech with the corporation. I assure you I'm much higher in the organization than that."

Corbett tried to back out of the system, but found that it was ignoring his instructions. Ginny shook her head sadly.

"No, Corbett, you aren't going anywhere. You could give Tad a real story now, couldn't you? But you're staying right there until our enforcers reach your apartment. Either that or unplug without the shutdown process and risk brain damage, which would suit us just as well, actually. You'd be in no condition to threaten our work at holding things together."

"Ginny . . ." He closed his eyes, but her image, coming through the sensory input of his brain, never wavered. He reached up and felt for the helmet, prepared to risk whatever wrenching out the implant would do to him, but the pain stopped him before he could pull hard enough. "Ginny, please . . ."

The last thing he heard was the distant crash of his door being broken down.

When Corbett opened his eyes, he saw Harry's face again, with even more lines and whiter hair this time. Other faces, unfamiliar faces, surrounded him, but their smiles removed any nervousness he might have had about them.

"I was afraid we'd reach you too late," Harry said.

"We thought the corporation people might get to you first."

"Uncle Harry—is it you? Not a sim?"

"It's me. I got out in time, too. I'd already left the sim in case they wiped me, as they have others here and there. But I'd left an alarm of sorts with it, to reach me through the Net if anyone ever called it up. Then we traced the link to you."

Corbett felt the back of his head, but it seemed intact. "Are we outside?" he said, trying to peer beyond the crowd of friendly faces.

"My sim may not have made it clear—outside is not the way it's been presented to the plugged-in folks. To answer your question, we're outside the offices, apartments and transportation tube network, but we're in an old-fashioned building with walls and a roof and central heating. Unless you've become addicted to VR, you won't find our way of life too different."

Corbett laughed ruefully. "I'm not sure what I can bring to it," he said. "All I've learned to do is run a specific hydroponics program which, from what your sim told me, may not hold up indefinitely in any case."

"Well, my boy, you do have other talents. For example, we can use all the reading teachers we can get. There's a new generation coming up, in this city and others, and it's amazing what they can learn to do when they understand the texts we've recovered—and the ones we're writing."

"And then what? Progress right back to being plugged in all over again?"

"Not necessarily. We outsiders have our version of the WorldNet, too, Corbett. It's not a tool we were willing to throw out. It shouldn't take as long as you might think to get back to where we were when we ran out of people who created the technology, and were left only with those who used it. We may be sending probes, or even people, to the planets again in your lifetime. What do you think of that?"

"What do you think of the possibility that a virtual reality can become a real one, Uncle Harry?" Corbett asked. "Maybe we're the virtual one, and one of our scenarios is the reality."

"Virtual or real, our future is what we make of it, my boy," Harry said. "But what makes you ask a question like that?"

"I've been thinking about my jaunt to that virtual Mars that you and the other programmers at Planetary Explorations created," he said. "I've thought and thought and—Uncle Harry, I'm almost sure I didn't speak those words out loud before those creatures looked my way!"

SHINING ON
by Billie Sue Mosiman

Billie Sue Mosiman is the author of the Edgar-nominated novel *Night Cruise*. She has published more than ninety short stories in various magazines, including *Realms of Fantasy* and in such assorted anthologies as *Tales From the Great Turtle* and *Tapestries: Magic the Gathering*. Her latest novel is *Stiletto*.

I didn't know he'd try to kill me. I didn't know I needed to die and would.

There was a lot I didn't know.

Pride prevents us from always knowing what it is we're doing to ourselves. I thought in the beginning that getting involved on The Net was a way to move into the limelight and, as a byproduct of that involvement along the information highway, I could also discover a soul mate. I wanted to say good-bye to loneliness.

After all, there are millions of people on-line. Every goddamn last one of us are isolated in our cubicles with our blue-eyed monitors for companionship. One of them had to be right for me. Though that, as I say, was my second objective, the first being that my name become known worldwide. Funny how it is that I've gotten my wish.

But recognition, that's what you begin to want when you have nothing else better to do with your time. When you're wealthy and independent, your parents are dead, you have no siblings or living relatives, and you were born an outcast, a mutant. I suppose there is no other way to say it except to be straightforward about it. And besides, you can see for yourself.

My parents were chosen as government research guinea pigs and I, of course, am the result of that experiment.

My brain is larger, which makes my skull huge. I must wear a brace attached to my shoulders to hold it up. My eyesight is so wonked I depend on specially implanted lenses that give me clear vision, but they make me look deadly dark and serious even when I feel lighthearted and happy. My torso is spindly, like one belonging to an undernourished twelve-year-old, and my legs are mere flipper nubs of smooth pointed flesh. They give you the shivers, don't they? Nubs don't belong on humans.

Physically, I am repellent, I know.

How else, with these handicaps, could I become revered and adored except through a computer connect?

That's the thing with The Net. How do you find a way to hog the attention, even if you look like a normal human? I tried everything. I posted on the Usenets, waving my sharp wit and incisive intelligence like a red banner before a raging bull. That gave me a small reputation and an entertaining cadre of enemies who sent so much electronic hate mail that my computer was jammed an hour every day downloading it all. Finally I put a block on my box and told the company I didn't want to receive anything. Let the good mail fly off into the ether with the bad, who needs it, right?

Then, after months of careful flaming out of idiots, not only did I tire of the game but my reputation wasn't growing. It had hit a high and there it would remain, or even diminish, unless I found another way.

I decided to put up my own home page and make it so startlingly unusual, the world surfers would go out of their way to find me. I think, before it was over, more than a thousand links had been set up to my page, bringing in so many Net Heads that the company talked about shutting me down. I hate threats. I bought the company and sacked the clerk and her superior responsible for the threat. They had no idea who they were dealing with.

I thought I was getting somewhere. That because thousands perused my page every day, I was somebody.

You see, I was spilling my guts on The Net—just as I am now. My home page was like a train wreck of angst, guilt, verboten fantasy, and confession. If it was disgusting or shocking, I wrote about it. Even if it wasn't true or I didn't hold with some scenario or philosophy, it all went into the file. The file was linked to my home page and worked as a daily personal diary. I'd go to it all hours of the day and night, inputting data—any sludge, any grunge, any minuscule peep of despair, euphoria, urge, rage, or whacked-out thought. Anything that was on my mind or that I could invent went into electronic bytes dispersed over The Net.

It was the sexual fantasies that brought me my lover, my killer. I was so intense in my descriptions, I should have known someone like that would be drawn to me. I just wasn't thinking. I was riding a wave. I was hanging ten. All I knew was that the vibes I sent out over The Net were going to rebound to suckle me; the masses reading the diary would lie down like lambs in the woolly green paradise of my heat. You don't use knowledge or wit to get that to happen. I had tried intelligence on the Usenets and hadn't won the battleground. Now I had let go of logic and genius. I was giving The Netsters pure, unadulterated flesh-and-blood emotion sans thought, and they were responding by making my page the hottest one in the universe of home pages. I was a star, baby. They loved me.

One special man loved me best.

He was a splendid hacker, like me, someone who could go anywhere on The Net, get into any system, steal away any information no matter how secure. That's how he got my name. My voice number. My address.

That's how he wound up in my bed, arguing about experiencing the steamy landscape I had made alive in the diary. Insisting I give it to him.

Oh, not just sex, not just bizarre sex either. I had slid beyond that in my electronic public diary into high voltage fantasyland.

Preston convinced me we had to make it real.

If you think Preston only wanted to make it with a freak for bragging rights, think again. He wanted something much more perverted. Confident of my heightened intelligence, I thought I could decipher all his needs and motives, psychological and physical. What I didn't take into account, though I knew it, (of course I knew it, everyone knows about the different forms of mutants), was that *anyone* might be masquerading as normal, while in fact he is another victim of research. Other couples had volunteered and produced offspring that, unlike myself, looked perfectly humanoid, but deep in the convoluted hills and valleys of the double lobes of the brain, they were as peppered with mutant genes as was I.

Preston was one of those people. I call them Shiners because they shine us on, they deceive us into thinking they are Regulars. Yet they are no such thing. They're so far from what we would term "human" as to be an alien species. The government has tried to find them and dispose of these genetic mistakes. People like Preston turn into hackers to survive, going so far underground their identities vanish from all tracking systems.

Preston wanted to devour me, make me weep and beg and hope to die. His pleasure only came from destruction of other mutants, even ones like me produced from MI–233, the Big Brains, they call us, the misfit maidens. For some reason, MI–233 never produced a male.

I understand now that what Preston hated was himself. In murdering me, he was trying to kill the wayward gene splices of wickedness in himself. I just wish he had taken the short route and poured water over his monitor while he was plugged into the system, saving us both a world of trouble.

You know how they say there is a thin dividing line between love and hate? It's easier to hate someone you once loved than to hate a stranger. You have more to base it on. You have direct, incontestable proof that the loved one could turn bad, could be wrong, could deserve your hatred.

Well, for a few weeks, I loved Preston, truly loved him. The first, the only, love of my life.

He came to my house uninvited on a chilly October day when the scanners told me the temp outdoors had dropped ten degrees after sunrise. He climbed the electronic gate and marched right up to the door and pressed his palm against the sensor. The surveillance camera twisted in its socket and eyed him. I sat before my bank of monitors in the clean, air conditioned suite of rooms specially designed for computers and stared at his wise eyes. He gave the camera his full profile, smiling that all-knowing, I'm-here-and-what-are-you-going-to-do-about-it smile.

My voice, too strange for polite company, came out modulated and sexy through the intercom's voice changing module.

"I'm calling the authorities," I said.

"You give up any chance at a perfect life if you do that."

I touched the zoom button and the camera brought his face up close. I stared hard into those eyes. He might be Merlin reborn. He possessed some magical spell I would never own if I turned him away. That's what his steady, unflinching gaze promised.

"Who are you? What do you want? Why did you invade my parameter?"

"I know you from The Net. I'm Preston. I want you to let me in. I invaded because there was no other way to get to you from the outside world. You never would have invited me."

He had answered my questions, but with the answers attached to a pinpoint of curiosity. He knew me from my diary. He knew I could not refuse the strange and puzzling.

I keyed the computer to open the door. He strolled into a marble-floored foyer and put his hands behind his back. Now I could see him from the interior camera. None of the security sensors blinked. That meant he was unarmed.

"Come up the stairs, turn left, go to the end of the hall."

I swiveled in my Handy-Chair so he could see me, see everything, the moment he came through the door. I wanted to face him when he cringed. I wanted to laugh at him, loudly, bray at him like a donkey, and watch him run for the exit. This fine young man would have nothing but loathing for me, I expected.

When he opened the door and entered, I was ready with a burble of the sarcastic laughter at the back of my throat. But it died there, changing first to a small sad little moan.

"I knew you were mutant," he said. "You don't shock me."

I said nothing. I judged his eyes without the help of close-up view camera shots. He liked me. He liked what he saw. The deformed body, the flipper leg nubs, the head too large to be held by the muscles of the neck.

I looked into my lap and folded my hands there.

They were beautiful, my hands, the single beauty I could claim.

He crossed the room and knelt at my chair. He lay his head of black curly hair onto my hands. I opened my fingers to palm the round dome of skull. His hair felt like silk threads.

He spoke with warm breath against my lap. "Accept me," he said simply. "Let me love you."

I had never been loved, not by parents, who thought me hideously offensive, or by hospital staff, who worked strenuously to save my life the first tenuous three years I drew breath.

I had found respect and admiration in the virtual world on The Net and it was all I thought I could hope for.

Until Preston sought me out and kneeled, placing his head in my lap, a petitioner for my affections.

"You can have beauties. Why me?" I gently ruffled the soft curly hair, unable to control myself. He smelled like the October wind, crisp and new, sweeping me toward visions of a future where I could communicate face to face. By that time I had been alone in the house for more than ten years. I had seen less than half a dozen people in the flesh, conducting most of the periodic visits from the house maintenance crew through cameras and intercoms.

"Because I can have beauties, I don't want them," he said. Then he lifted his head and smiled.

He did not want what he could have so easily. He wanted me, truly, he did, and if it was a perverse gesture I would never know because his smile promised he would never tell.

That day he took me from the Handy-Chair and lay me in the cradle bed I had ordered through The Net. I used it to rock myself to sleep at night, throwing my weight from one side to the other until the rocker was in motion. It kept the rhythm all night so that I could sleep, dreaming a mother held me in her arms, safe.

You can tell from this confession that I was not a hard woman or heartless. I have the same feelings as anyone else. I have the same human needs to be touched, to be given solace, to be worthy of kindness.

"We will need other sleeping arrangements," he said, undressing me the way a child undresses a doll, curious to see what is underneath all the pretty cloth. "This one is too narrow for us both."

I couldn't answer him, not with my heart beating so hard I thought it would erupt through my rib cage, not with my tongue dried to the roof of my mouth.

"In your diary you said that the greatest orgasm comes from hunting down odd household phallic objects and inserting them while following the building strains of Beethoven."

I shook my head at the foolishness I had written for the prurient interest prevalent on The Net. It's all a lie, I wanted to say, I haven't masturbated since I was a child. But still, I couldn't speak. I trembled at his touch, closed tight my eyes, and prayed that he would never stop the gentle relentless massage of his hands.

"I've come to see you experience those orgasms and then to prove how wrong you are that self-love is any substitute for a man."

He brought me things. He made me decide which ones I would use. He sat in my Handy-Chair, fingers templed and touching his lips while he watched.

I did whatever he wanted so that he would not leave me alone again. I was already wedded to the thought that he might stay and be my lover. If I pleased him. If I lived out the fantasies from the diary and it pleased him.

One on one, locked in the house with no outside interference, exploring one another as a scientist explores the miniature world of a cell beneath an electron microscope, Preston and I fell into an alternative universe made up of flesh, sensation, and experimentation. He asked for everything I had written in the diary and I could not refuse him. Nothing was too grotesque, too dangerous, too fantastic. Invention was the rule of our days and implementation the rule of our nights.

It's safe to say that Preston and I wallowed like pigs in clover. I loved him, adored him, would have stood before a firing squad to save his life.

But then, I didn't know him, did I? I knew his body, long and lean and muscled. I knew the taste of him, the heat, the strength.

I didn't know the labyrinth of his mind. Fortunately, he didn't know mine either.

After the crazy whirlwind courtship of my poor, defeated body, Preston began to come clear about his true mission. He was not there to take my life. He might have murdered me any time in those first few weeks. What he wanted was something more subtle, and a great deal more satisfying. He wanted me to do away with myself.

I suppose the winner of a hazardous game must be the one who can manipulate an extreme about-face.

First he taught me to accept my disabilities and deficiencies. Then he wished to lead me toward the hellish nightmare of rejection of that which I had just lately accepted. I was to turn my back on the road and trace my way back to darkness. I should have never been born, never existed, my kind had no right, we were a plague defiling the earth. Once I believed it, there was nothing for me to do, but slit the inside of my wrists from hand to elbow and watch the blood flow.

Don't misunderstand, Preston didn't beleaguer me. His plan was made of stealth and shadow. The attacks were brought forward on slippered feet, insinuating black thoughts that festered and leaked poison in my brain. He was a master monster, a devotee of evil toying with me the way a rat will gnaw and pull at a corpse to be sure it is lifeless before gorging itself.

The light went out of my soul long before it left my eyes. Preston started in on me with small chides that I waved aside by saying, "I'm sorry, I'll do better."

After a fortnight of sexual edification and bliss, we worked together on The Net, laughing at bimbos and freaks, leaving messages across the world about impending disasters that were not true, causing panic waves that rippled across the electronic frontier. We even hacked into the President's personal file and added a line to his boot up that sent a bold message the next time he logged in. It said: IF YOU HAD ANY SELF-RESPECT, YOU'D BE WORTH SHOOTING. We took turns writing lies in my diary and printed out the responses from the Gothic Death Pretenders who were drawn to the grubbiest and most nihilistic of our meanderings. They sent us into gales of hysterical laughter.

Preston at first joked about any mistake I made on The Net and I apologized, correcting myself.

I just have to try harder, I thought, Preston's so brilliant. Anything that appears stupid to him will drive him away. So I tried harder. I had a brain, I had to use it.

Then he disappeared one morning from our bed (the one we had moved to in another part of the house, my parents' bed) and the monitors showed me emptiness, deserted rooms, cold silence. I brooded, wondering if he had gone as he had come, out of the blue, lost forever.

Around noon he showed up at the door, grinning into the camera. He held a package in his hands. "Open up, sez me," he said.

I pushed my Handy-Chair closer to the door, waiting. He had a present for me, how sweet, how dear.

"Did you miss me?" He swooped toward my cheek

and planted a warm kiss there. "I have something for you. For us."

He brought forth a glass vial from the package.

"I can't do chemicals," I said, fear seizing and squeezing my insides. I thought I smelled my own instant sweat and wanted nothing more than a long hot bath.

One eyebrow raised. "Why can't you?"

"It ... it ..." I was stuttering and now my hands shook. "I go mad. It's something to do with ... this." I touched my temple with two fingers. Surely he could understand. My brain was a fertilized fruit, an overgrown melon, too sensitive to ply with chemicals, too edgy and full to tamper with in any way.

He laughed away my fears. "Don't be silly," he said. "This is perfectly reliable. I wouldn't bring you any old street junk. I get this from a friend, in a lab near Washington. It's not marketable, not available through street trade. You'll like it, I promise."

"But, Preston ..."

He had taken a chair opposite me and was already tapping a line on a small square of clear plastic. He handed me a short straw. He smiled. I took the drug up through the straw and into each nostril, lay my head back against the headrest and dropped into never-never land.

I couldn't be sure. I couldn't say for the longest time and be certain that what Preston brought out of the package once I was drugged actually was a severed hand, but that's what it looked like.

"Where didja ... ?"

He shushed me. He reached out and stroked me with the cold, dead, blue appendage. I remember the nails, square and dull with purple clotted blood, a man's hand. Where had he gotten it? What must I do to get away from it?

I tried to get my arms to work, tried to reach the button that would twirl the Handy-Chair away from him, but I was paralyzed. Everything was hazy and slowed down. Even Preston's voice sounded as if it came from the bottom of a well, amplified, distorted. I think he said, "Open your legs, my little monstrosity."

After that scene of degradation, I lost all memory. I'm sure that Preston and I committed unheard-of acts I would block even if I had not been drugged.

When I woke, sore, sick enough to vomit, I called for him.

He came naked from the shower, dripping water, a towel in his hands. "I'll clean you up," he said.

"What happened to the hand?" I asked, afraid he might say he'd get it, I could have it, it was my gift.

"What hand?" he turned halfway to the bath and stared at me with his dark scolding eyes.

"Don't lie to me, Preston. You brought a *hand* here, someone's dead hand! What have you done with it? What are you doing to me? Where did you get it?"

"You had a dream. Do you want an extra hand? Shall I go in search of one?" He laughed so hard, he doubled over.

I turned away my face from him, sick again. He hurried out and came back with a wet washcloth. He wiped my mouth, my forehead. He sang me a lullaby and I shut my eyes on him, wondering how I could ask him to leave. How do you send away your heart and live to tell of it? Even when your heart is corrupted?

It was later that he admitted the truth. By then the blame was on my head. "You begged me to do it," he said. I couldn't dispute what I did not know. I might have begged to be molested by a disembodied hand when out of control of my faculties, as he claimed. And if I did, then I was a prime example of a diseased human. Not just mutant by accident, but mutant by choice.

The parade continued, Preston at the front twirling

the baton, orchestrating the death march. From nit-picks he escalated to rapier cuts into the fabric of my personality. I thought myself superior because my IQ was greater than ninety percent of mankind, wasn't that the height of arrogant ego, he asked? I was a race unto myself and that was why I was alienated. My habits were disgusting and my mannerisms boring. I was wheedling, I was abrasive. I did not have a world view, no real love for others. I was a selfish bitch intent on control, but really hoping for a savior, such as himself, to control me. I was desperately unaligned with normal humanity and that was why I lived and breathed my life out over a computer net.

I was a fraud. I hadn't any core. I made him ill.

We quarreled all night some nights. We dropped exhausted from recrimination and acrimony. We woke to snarl at one another and threaten disclosure. He would publicize my life all over The Net and make me an object of pity. He had taken video when I slept and he would load it to my home page so that every-one could see just how mutant I was, how ugly, ugly, ugly a thing I was.

I asked him to leave. I begged him. I tried to call for help, but was outmaneuvered. He, after all, was ambulatory and whole. I was bound by my chair and my infirmities.

No, he was not leaving me alone in my cage of unreality to live on like a slug plugged into the system. He was staying, he said, until I knew what I had to do.

And so it came to the point that I had to die or kill my lover, there were no other alternatives left for us.

Those of you watching this on The Net, watching my extermination, should have some notion of what it takes to commit murder. For that's what you're doing to me and don't try to deny it. Although the government is the instrument, you, all of YOU, are the respondents in this matter. They say if you tune in, if you like this satellite-projected execution, there will be more. Next time will it be you or your neighbor or your own wayward lover who has come to steal away your life?

Yes, the restraints hurt, if you're wondering. Yes, I adore the feeling of power I have over you while you watch from your home, from your little cubicle, distanced, safe, you're so safe there while you participate in reliving my life, my crime, and my death.

It is true that I am an aberration. It is true that I murdered Preston and should pay the penalty. But dying for him now is not the correct punishment. I should be given a reward, honored for wiping him from existence. I should be back in my home, strapped in my Handy-Chair, writing to you in my electronic diary, explaining how easy it is to plunge through the virtual world into warped reality.

But you will kill me for taking away Preston's right to live. If he'd succeeded in stripping me to the bone so that I would have taken a knife to my wrists, you'd be watching him now on The Net, not me.

So who is right? Should I have just offed myself and saved you from viewing the confession and the pulse of electricity they are gong to zap into my oversized brain? Or would it have been better to listen to Preston tell you fabrications from his evil imagination?

I don't suppose it matters one way or the other. He is dead, thankfully the world is rid of him, and I will join him as soon as I stop talking.

His demise was bloodier and more cruel than mine will be, perfectly matched to his life. When I had secreted the scissors beneath the mattress of my parents' bed, he walked into the room sullen and gray as a bank of thunderclouds. "You're not going to bed this early, get out of here," he told me.

"You forget this is my house."

"And you forget you are my prisoner."

That night while he slept, I wiggled loose from the

binds he by then was wrapping me in to keep me still. He must have feared me by then. He had every reason to.

I wiggled loose, though it took hours of careful and quiet moves. I felt for the scissors, pulled them free. I hesitated not a second before burying them in the middle of Preston's chest. He sat up, wide-eyed, screaming. He drew out the scissors and let them drop. I picked them up and with a backhand motion, buried them again where I thought his heart must be.

He fell back on the sheets with a thump that nearly rolled me from the mattress.

I felt under the pillow and drew out the decayed, rotting hand that he had put on a shelf in the down-stairs pantry. I lay it on his bleeding wounds. "There," I said. "Fuck yourself with it, Preston, fuck yourself and die, you belly-crawling viral bastard."

I had to call someone, of course, and then explain Preston's body in my bed. I've even been accused of the murder of the man who gave up the hand Preston brought to my house. As if I could really leave, travel forty miles, murder, and sever a limb to bring back.

But you will believe what you want, you always have, and the truth isn't something you would know if you saw it or heard it, you faceless mass of cyber-seekers, you freakoids, you ... poor misguided lonely Net-Set mutants.

Throw the switch, boss, I need a connection.

SOUVENIRS AND PHOTOGRAPHS

by Jody Lynn Nye

Jody Lynn Nye lists her main career activity as "spoiling cats." She lives near Chicago with two of the above and her husband, SF author Bill Fawcett. Among Jody's novels are the *Mythology 101* series, *Taylor's Ark, Medicine Show*, and four collaborations with Anne McCaffrey: *Crisis on Doona, The Death of Sleep, The Ship Who Won*, and *Treaty at Doona*. Upcoming works include a new contemporary fantasy, *The Magic Touch, The Ship Errant*, and an anthology, *Don't Forget Your Spacesuit, Dear!"*

"Will you hurry up!" Ann Mack nudged her younger brother with her toe. Thirteen-year-old Kevin Mack sat on the floor with his back against the wall in the Interhotel portal chamber under the number 112, between portals three and four.

"Almost ready," Kevin said, without looking up from the compad balanced on his knees. The signs and gestures of his hands inside their virtual-reality touch-gloves looked fast, but Ann could feel her heart pounding faster.

"Come on!" Ann said, looking around at the eight portals, two to a wall, in the small, white-enameled chamber. "If Security finds us, they'll strip our badges and send us home. You've spent weeks on that program, and it's not working yet?"

"Almost ready," Kevin said again, nodding his mop

of light-brown hair that was so much like hers. He drew his own CompCon badge out of the plastic holder pinned to his chest and put it on the floor next to him. With infinite care, he unwound a peripheral cable from the side of the compad and hooked it to a minute connection in the top of the badge, which started to hum. Ann could see lights from his screen reflected in the transparent half-visor he wore. He looked up at Ann with a triumphant grin that showed his large front teeth. "There! Okay, now the scond anybody comes through and uses a portal, this'll capture his code, and we can hack into the other hotel. If Security comes through, we'll tell 'em we're checking up on the convention program. I've got a screen saver with my schedule on it."

"I'm not so sure this is a good idea anymore," Ann said. She slid down to sit beside him, careful not to touch the edges of either of the portals. At fifteen, she was still a good four inches taller than he was. "The computer convention's going to be good, too. Why are we doing this?"

"You know as well as I do," Kevin said, grinning again. "Because it's there. Because we can."

Ann grimaced and folded her arms. The idea of hacking the Hotelnet had seemed irresistible when the two of them had first started talking about it. They'd have been attending the International Computer Designers Conference in any case. She had a part-time telecommute job in R&D with Energex, and Kevin was a safety hacker for Galton Games, analyzing games and showing Galton the weak spots where anyone with half a brain could break their code. This year, CompCon was to be held in a complex constructed along with the new worldwide network of hotel rooms and function spaces. The temptation of hooking into the brand new on-line hotel system and maybe wandering all over the world by teleporter was too sweet to ignore. Hotelnet was new. It was exciting.

Kevin hadn't talked her into it. She had convinced herself. Now, in the cold light of an actual transport chamber, she felt as if she might like to back out, and just go to the convention.

During the late twentieth century, conventions and trade shows had been placed in certain cities because of geographical necessity. If a venue was large enough to contain the population of a certain event, that's where it was held. Early in the twenty-first, the solar-power movement started carpeting arid wastelands with the self-expanding and self-renewing power grids that made nearly infinite power available. Ann knew all this; one of her particular interests was the history of electrical power systems, from Leyden jars on forward. Only a few years ago, the scientist team of Bernstein and Gibbs had invented the matrans—matter transmitter ground station and links—a device which would have been impossible without the grids. Everyone was fascinated by the idea of instantaneous travel, but up until recently the prototypes were just too expensive, and research was astronomically costly. The obvious best use would be for public mass transportation, but the government balked at supporting it. That left Bernstein and Gibbs making an appeal to the private sector for funds. Matrans had been a rich person's toy, until the hotel and entertainment industry stepped forward.

Once the matrans technology became available and feasible, the hotel and entertainment industry embraced it with alacrity. When a client didn't have to spend thousands on transportation costs and hours of time traveling to, boarding, debarking, and getting to a hotel or other facility, he'd be in much better shape, much better spirits, physical health, and in no risk of plane delays, train crashes, sunken ships, car accidents. One walked into a hotel in one's own town—anyhow, that had been the dream—and into one's conference. The badge acted as a net-browser for the parts of hotels and venues scattered around the world that made up the event site.

Family vacations, when the price came down some more, would stop being organizational nightmares. If Billy forgot his swim trunks, then all Dad had to do was walk back to the other side of the portal system. Ann couldn't wait for that, but the price was still too stiff for the average family. Businesspeople, for whom time was money, would and were gladly exchanging money for the time they saved.

Though Ann and Kevin had responsible jobs in the computer industry, they still looked at the Interhotel system with the eagerness of a fifteen-year-old girl and a thirteen-year-old boy. The Interhotel was something to explore and experiment with. Plenty of people called the new technology the end of the world—again. Plenty of pundits and columnists said it would divide humanity down to individuals pursuing their own lives, but Ann thought it would increase socialization, actually getting people closer together physically once again. Sure there would be problems, like shock-news stories of kids running off with their parents' charge cards on a 'round-the-world romp, but they'd be in the minority. When a trip across the country to Grandma's was a short walk through a corridor, families would see the good, and ordinary side of matrans travel. In the meantime, Ann grinned to herself, she wanted to be one of those kids who took a round-the-world run. Thanks to her work with Energex, she'd be able to pay for it herself. Of course, it would be better if she could get Energex to pay for it for her, or if she and Kevin could figure out how to do it free. Well, a girl could dream.

"We'd better just go and get our rooms," Ann said. "Security will catch us if we hang around here too long. Try this later."

"No! Let me get at least one," Kevin pleaded, hunching protectively over his keyboard. "Look!"

Ann glanced up just in time to see a man hurtle out
of portal 6. Even though she'd seen visuals of the
technology a hundred times, even experienced passage
twice by now, she was still fascinated by watching the
teleports work. The frame around an active doorway
would start to glow. The brightness flarted in intensity
until it was almost blinding, and a human body
popped out of the center of the rectangular halo,
which died away at once. This man appeared in mid-
stride, gray suited, briefcase in one hand and square
badge in the other. He used the latter like a compass,
whirling about on his heel in the small chamber to
find the portal that made his badge hum and light up.
Without a look at the two teens, he plunged through
a gleaming portal 1, and vanished. Ann sighed with
satisfaction.

"Got it!" Kevin crowed beside her. "The capture
program worked perfectly. D'ja see the way he was
dressed? I bet he's in a posh hotel, or even a resort."

"Kev . . ." Ann began, but the heralding glow only
gave them a moment's warning. Kevin's fingers were
already flicking.

"Hey, you kids," said the large, dark man wearing
the CompCon security badge. "Is there anything the
matter?"

"Oh, no, sir" Kevin said, scrambling to his feet.
"My sister and I were trying to figure out if our rooms
are on the same corridor, that's all."

"Let me see," the man said. He disconnected Kevin's
badge from the side of the boy's compad, and plugged
it into his own handheld pad. "HY–3402. And yours?
HY–3416? Yes, they're at two ends of the same hallway. Nonsmoking, youth singles, upmid-class, curfew
23:00 hours."

"Curfew!" Kevin wailed.

"Thank you," Ann said fervently, retrieving her
own badge from the man's big hands. She beamed up

at him. "I don't want to have to use a portal every time I want to check in on him."

The man smiled back, but his eyes told her he wasn't fooled. "You two get on to the convention, and stop hanging around in these chambers, you hear me?"

"Yessir!" they chimed, and made a hasty dive for portal 2. They left the security guard shaking his head.

She and Kevin stepped out into a long, blue-paneled corridor filled with people, mostly young, nearly all of them wearing casual clothes, with a predominance of black T-shirts. Everyone had a knapsack, a briefcase, a totebag, or all three, brimming with shiny plastic boxes and sheaves of flyers and booklets. Ann leaned over to look at the little screen on Kevin's keypad.

"Where's my first seminar?" she shouted over the noise in the hall.

"How come I have to keep track?" Kevin complained, pulling his computer away from her. "Why don't you look at your own unit?"

"Because mine isn't surgically attached to my body, like yours is," Ann gibed him. True, she kept her small compad in her pocket, but Kevin's was always in his hands, always open, and always running. He was right: she *was* being lazy. But she'd never admit to hm that he was right. Big sister's prerogative.

Kevin ducked over to the side of the corridor, out of the press of traffic. He pushed his schedule file to one side with a swipe of his gauntleted hand, and pulled a handful of nothing out of the air. Her hastily constructed wishlist appeared on the screen.

"You have five marked for this hour," Kevin shouted. "Which one do you really want?" He turned the screen toward her for a look. Ann leaned over to read the titles. Working in Cyberspace sounded interesting. So did Constructing an Economical Multi-Media Platform. No, she'd have to go see Portable

Power System Advancements. Bother being a responsible employee. She pointed at the entry. Kevin exploded it to fill the screen.

"K-201," he said, squinting into his visor. Ann knew he had the blueprint map on heads-up display. "Through the next portal to door 3, down that corridor to the end, and left three doors. I'm going on to three levels above you, K-540. We'd better hurry."

There were too many good seminars and demonstrations to be able to attend in person. But Ann noticed in the schedule that animated holographic images were allowed. With a good multi-tasker and plenty of memory, one could attend a dozen panels at once, and no one would know you weren't there. She might have to send a substitute image or download the panel file from the net later.

0903 hours convention time, according to the digital wall readout, in an anonymous, painted, cinder-block corridor that could have been in Toledo or Beijing. Ann tipped a wave to Kevin and slipped into the room where her seminar was already in progress. Four panelists, a man of thirty with a trim, dark beard, a girl about Ann's age, a plump woman with gray-blonde hair, and another bearded man, hunched over microphones at the long table across the front of the room. The sysop, a shadowy figure in a black T-shirt seated to one side of the panel table, looked up briefly when she walked in, then went back to his keypad. The signal from Ann's badge triggered his program, so he could register her presence. The sysop wore fingerpad gloves and a transparent visor, like her brother's, but he was also tapping physical keys. There was a lot to keep track of at once.

Ann passed her badge over the sensor on the arm of her chair as she sat down, indicating that she was willing to have her name given to the sponsors of the panel. Reregistering wasn't necessary, but it helped the organizers to know how many people showed up for what subjects, and there were occasional freebie programs or hardware samples sent out later by advertisers. Ann approved of freebies.

The first bearded man was speaking. "Now, if you take what Dr. Cavanaugh was saying about environmental tradeoffs, you are ignoring the fundamental law of physics which states that . . ."

The teenage girl broke in angrily. "You are deliberately trying to ignore what I said. I *said* . . ." Ann unobtrusively slipped her compad out of her pocket and checked the speaker list. The girl *was* Dr. Cavanaugh. The argument had to have started long before the panel began, maybe months before. The audience was just there to bear witness to a brawl over semantic differences. Not at all the dry, technical talk Ann had feared this panel would be. She folded her arms and prepared to enjoy herself.

Except for a couple of stuffy, business-suited types, the other members of the audience seemed to be of the same opinion. They'd still get their information on power systems, but with a little vid-entertainment into the bargain. Ann caught a glimpse of a shaky edge or two, and decided that several of her fellow listeners were holograms. A cyberlink membership was cheaper than an attending membership, but didn't entitle the member to all the good perks and giveaways.

The giant chess piece that overlay one chair in the back row twitched and wavered. Ann caught red glints of light whenever the figure shifted. That person was really there, but wearing a shimmer, a kind of holographic disguise. The red lights came from the flattened projecting lenses arrayed on a net that covered the wearer's body from head to feet. It wasn't a perfect disguise. The images were always a little shaky. Shimmers were mostly used by the terminally unsocialized, who didn't want to interact with other people; or by the famous, so they could come to events without being mobbed.

"If my distinguished colleague Dr. Sherman would take his thumb out of his ear, he would hear, and maybe understand what I just said," Dr. Cavanaugh said, her cheeks pink with anger.

"I'm sorry *my* distinguished colleague does not think beyond the narrow confines of her must-I-call-it *specialty* as to the societal implications of her work?"

"I am the Master of the Universe!" broke in a voice. One of the cyber-holos stood up, waving his arms. It looked like a weight-lifter's fantasy, a male body with muscles and a wedge-shaped torso clad in a skimpy leotard fur. Ann guessed the real op was a young, skinny kid with acne. "You morons are meddling in things that you do not understand!"

"What do you know, byte-breath?" Dr. Cavanaugh said, turning her ire upon the flamer. "You can't sit quietly like a civilized being? Leave this panel right now."

"Idiots! You will all die of your ignorance!"

Dr. Sherman turned to the sysop. "Terminate that, please," he said.

The sysop tapped a few keys, and the howling image popped out of existence like a bubble.

"Noooooooooo . . ."

"Membership terminated. Please proceed." There was an approving murmur among the audience, and Cavanaugh and her opponent went back to their argument.

Ann took a few notes, as other cyber-holos popped in and out of the room around her, and a few real warm bodies came and went. When they weren't arguing, Sherman, Cavanaugh, and the others had a lot of fascinating things to say. It was good to get out of her workshop and rub elbows with people who did the same kind of work she did. It stimulated the brain cells. She suddenly had a great idea for a modification for the new component she was working on. Surreptitiously, she slipped her styloid fingerstall out of her pocket, and started to doodle on her compad.

"Ladies and gentlemen, thank you for your attention." There was a patter of applause, and the shifting of bodies in chairs. She glanced up as the man sitting next to her edged carefully past her feet.

"Oh!" The wall-clock said 1100 hours. She'd completely lost track of the time. "It's over."

'You didn't miss anything useful," the man said politely. "You can get the data downlinked from the sysop. At the gun it was Cavanaugh, 14, Sherman, 15."

Ann grinned at him. "Thanks." She saw Kevin in the hallway, waving to her through the crowd.

"How was it?" Kevin asked.

"Pretty good," she said. "I got some work done, anyhow. It's eleven. Are you hungry? Want to check out the cheap eats?"

"No," Kevin said, his eyes dancing. "C'mon. Let's go try out the you-know-what."

Ann followed him happily.

They sauntered back toward the function-corridor portal with such exaggerated nonchalance that Ann was afraid someone might follow them just because they looked suspicious. She couldn't help it. The thrill of doing something new, something just a little illicit was so exciting that she felt her hands shaking. She shoved them deep into her pockets. A hundred yards, and they were at the exit and into the matrans chamber.

"These three are more function rooms," Kevin said, pulling aside and pointing at doors 1, 2, and 3 on the diagram on his compad screen. "Four and five are food service. The rest are housing."

"Seven," Ann said hastily, choosing her lucky number. "No one'll be in the hotels at this hour, right?"

Kevin grinned, crinkling his blue eyes. "Yeah."

Just to throw off anyone's suspicions, they cut back to their hotel corridor by way of the Job Fair, an

enormous cavern of a room filled with booths, colorful
lighting effects, holograms, and people, people, people, elbow to elbow. Everyone was shouting and jos-
tling one another, doing business at the top of their
voices.

Ann checked in with Energex, who vetted her
schedule, and programmed her and Kevin's badges
with free admission to the welcome banquet on Sunday at a snooty hotel restaurant in Atlanta. Ann got
away from her employers as quickly as she could. She
could almost see the string of code in Kevin's computer. It was beckoning her.

All the exits from the Job Fair allowed access to
the accommodations. Ann and Kevin slipped out the
nearest door, and found themselves at the end of the
hotel hallway by Kevin's room. He pulled her down
toward the door at the other end, which led to the
first chamber at the "edge" of the convention space,
where they had cloned the businessman's code. Ann
popped through the glowing doorway a half-second
behind Kevin, and almost bumped into him. He was
standing in the center of the small room, gazing up at
the numbers over the doors with a blissful look on
his face.

"Now what do we do?" Ann asked.

"We just keep walking."

Portal 1 burst into a welcoming light as they approached it. Ann had no sensation of movement as
she stepped through, except for a tingle on her skin
that could have been static or a light breeze. Only her
mind knew that she and Kevin were being moved
across the world in a twinkling. They were traveling
the Hotelnet. Her heart pounded with excitement and
delight, and just a tiny frisson of fear and guilt.

They emerged onto gold plush carpet, into a silk-
muffled hush that denoted high class and, undoubt-
edly, high price. Ann smelled a faint scent of spice
and disinfectant. The air was warmer than it had been

in their convention hotel. A mechanovac was sweeping its nozzle hose from side to side in near silence. Almost tiptoeing, Kevin and Ann hurried down the corridor.

"Can we get into the lobby?" Ann asked, as they passed an ornately carved and painted door.

"Sure. We've got access to anywhere that man did," Kevin said. "Where do you suppose we are?"

Ann stopped to glance at a wall screen. Local time was 1715, six hours later than CompCom time, or ten hours later than her home in Seattle. So that meant an hour east of the Prime Meridian. How exciting, to have been swept across the ocean in seconds!

Kevin's hand flashed up in front of her eyes, and motioned her over to the side of the corridor. Hearing voices, Ann jumped aside into an alcove just in time to see two men go by, dressed in flowing white, knee-length tunics and white trousers. They had on green-edged badges. Ann heard the faint hum of Kevin's compad as he copied their programming codes. Deep in conversation, neither man noticed the Macks huddled in a doorway.

"Let's see their convention center," Kevin whispered.

"Act natural," Ann said, holding her back straight as a poker. She led Kevin across the opulently decorated lobby toward another portal gate. Sunlight blazed in through the plate-glass windows on either side of the bronze doors, and Ann saw the feathery tops of palm trees in the distance.

Men and women with deep brown or blue-green eyes and olive complexions kept turning to stare at them, wondering what the long-haired girl and the small boy wearing gloves and a visor were doing in such a fancy hotel. *Walk as if you own the place,* Ann told herself, forcing a confident smile to her lips. She had to concentrate on not breaking into a run. Five steps from the portal, four, three ... yes, the badge was lighting up, and so was the gate. Success!

"Told you," Kevin whispered, as the white glow swallowed them up. "This is *so* great."

They emerged into a room as fancy as the lobby had been. Golden chandeliers threw a dull light on the crowd of white-clad men and women wearing the green badges, talking quietly among themselves. It was half a world and a dozen cultures away from the noisy sloppiness of the CompCom, and Ann felt desperately out of place.

"Look, food!" Kevin breathed, pointing at a long buffet table that ran the length of one long wall. He started toward it.

A few people turned to stare at the Macks. Ann smiled weakly at them, grabbed Kevin by the shoulders, and steered him firmly toward a side door.

"What are you doing?" her little brother wailed. Now everyone was looking at them.

"You ape, it'd only take them a nanosecond to see that we don't have the right badges on," Ann hissed, with another smile for a black-clad waiter who passed them with an enormous tray on his shoulder. "We don't belong here."

"But I'm hungry!" Superhacker World-Traveler had turned back into a kid with a bottomless appetite. Ann shrugged.

"Then we'd better get back to our convention. It'll only take a few minutes."

"No," Kevin said, with stubborn illogic. "I want to keep going."

So did Ann. They'd only just opened the first file in an endlessly interesting database. She looked over Kevin's shoulder toward where the waiter had come. "Then we'll ask for something in the kitchen."

She started thinking up a plausible story to tell the catering staff of a strange hotel in a faraway country why they should give a meal to a couple of foreign kids without any credentials or traveling papers who happened to have popped into a fancy-pants convention where they didn't belong. But what if no one in the kitchen spoke English?

As soon as she pushed through the swinging steel doors, all her fears melted away, leaving behind just a twinge of resentment. Kevin gawked at the people in the room, and looked up at her with a glum expression.

"We're not the first."

"Heck, no," said Pete Danwood, sitting on a long wooden counter and swinging his legs. The chunky teenager, an old friend of the Macks, also from Seattle, had a china plate in his lap and specks of gravy on his shirt. Next to him on the counter were his visor and compad. "Bonnie and I started hitch-coding around yesterday," he said, with an excess of nonchalance that didn't really disguise his delight. "Cool, isn't it?"

"Yeah," Kevin said.

His girlfriend, Bonnie Collins, a slim girl with dark skin, was seated on a chair between a gigantic mixer and a warming cabinet. "We got hungry, and Rangit made us some lunch. You hungry, too?"

"Yes, we are," Ann said, discovering that instead of wanting to pout at having their preeminence trumped, she felt like laughing instead. All that sneaking around for secrecy, and there were probably already dozens of hackers browsing around the 'net.

"Rangit, please?" Bonnie asked, with a pretty smile for the elderly, white-clad chef, who nodded kindly and turned back to a pan on a burner.

"How'd you get here?" Kevin asked.

Bonnie displayed her compad, and the two of them started comparing code strings, and connections. Ann accepted a bowl full of some savory-smelling stew she couldn't identify, listening with half an ear to her brother, and the other half to the kitchen staff talking in a liquid, musical language.

Bonnie downloaded Kevin's data while he shoveled in his share of stew. "And we've got one for you. Haven't dared to try it yet. Got it off a rich-looking guy in black sunglasses."

"We'll go with you, okay?" Kevin reached out two fingers of his touch-glove, and took the code into his own machine. He programmed it into his own badge and Ann's. "Four of us can get out of anything, right?"

The code opened up portal 2 in the chamber just off the fancy ballroom. Ann held her breath as she stepped through.

The building on the other side of the door was little more than a pair of pillars supporting a roof. The four youngsters piled out of the door and stopped, speechless.

"Wo-ow," Kevin said, gazing around him.

Ann had to remember to breathe. It was even warmer there than in the hotel with gold carpets. They were three steps away from a white sand beach bordering an ultramarine sea and sapphire blue sky. The shelter, which lay beside the door of a small inn, was surrounded by lush greenery and brilliant red and yellow flowers. She felt as if she had landed inside a picture postcard of Paradise.

"We struck it lucky," Pete said. He stepped forward into the sand and dug a toe into it. "This is great!"

"I wish we had a camera with us," Kevin said. "I want to remember this place forever."

"Take a memento," Bonnie suggested. "A shell, a flower, a rock, or something small like that. Whatever you want. Customs would never know. You're just walking through a hallway with it, right?"

"Yeah," Kevin said, reaching for some of the red flowers. "Yeah, why not?"

Ann nodded along with the others for a moment, then she had a sudden, horrible picture of the white beach covered with garbage and crawling with weird bugs and creatures. It made her feel horribly sick. She reached out and grabbed her brother's arm.

"Please don't," she said. Kevin shook loose, looking angry and puzzled.

"What's the matter with you?" he demanded. "It's just a flower."

"Think about it, nerf," Ann said, so overcome by the enormity of her realization that her voice was hushed. "This is new technology. Customs hasn't even started thinking about how it'll control what goes on through the Hotelnet. You could foment an ecological disaster with just one infected bulb, one bug. We're the pioneers here. Just because we *can* do anything we want doesn't mean we *should*. Don't spoil it, Kev. This is something new, and we have to take responsibility for what we do with it."

Kevin rubbed his wrist thoughtfully. Ann knew he was too smart not to understand what she was saying, but did he have the sense to do the right thing?

He looked up at her with a rueful smile, and the sun glinted off his visor. "It's too bad," he said. "We could've gotten filthy rich smuggling. No risk, no regs, no nothing."

"Yeah," Bonnie said. She looked shocked, too. "There aren't any backups on the Hotelnet yet. It'd be medflies all over again."

Pete backed up onto the concrete floor again and carefully brushed the sand off his shoes.

"I hate being part of the system," he said. "Being pure moral is no fun, but you're right. 'Take only photographs, leave only footprints,' as whatever that philosopher's name was said. Why do we need to take souvenirs when we can return any time we feel like it? Let's come back later with a camera. We'd better go back now."

Ann, feeling much better, nodded and followed the others through the portal gate.

They emerged into the Job Fair. The level of noise

was higher than even when they had left. People were talking, waving their arms, and pointing in random directions. They seemed too passionate to be discussing potential perks and vacation time. Ann tapped the arm of a woman going by whom she knew.

"What's all the buzz?" she asked.

"Scandal!" the woman said, her wide, somewhat flat face full of avid interest. "Dr. Bentley, the keynote speaker for Sunday's banquet? She was going to talk about the Hotelnet technology? This is its first month really on line."

"Yes?" Ann prompted her.

"Got bopped on the head," the woman said with relish. "Someone took the chip."

"Chip?" Kevin piped up.

"The app. The key chip. Runs the whole gimbal. *Stolen,* can you believe she was carrying that thing around with her? How brainless can you be?" The woman glanced up at the wall clock. "Oops! Got to go." She gave Ann and Kevin a friendly nod and went through a handy portal.

"Wow," was all Kevin could find to say. Ann understood what he meant. The power of the Hotelnet, full access to anywhere the net ran, free and open, without restrictions, and it was wandering around loose somewhere. No wonder everyone was talking.

The wall-screens were full of data about the assault and robbery. Solemn-sounding law enforcement officials were talking about the ramifications of possession of an unlimited master key. They described the havoc that could be wrought by criminals world-wide. Ann felt the same sinking feeling she'd experienced on the tropical beach. This guy could destroy the beautiful world she was only just beginning to see.

"God, I hope they catch him," someone said from behind them. Ann nodded fervently, concentrating on the video.

Some of the crime had been observed by the security monitors. A police composite image ran constantly, along with a hidden-cam video, showing the small, blonde woman, Professor Alana Bentley, being struck from behind by a figure wearing a nondescript shimmer. The holo disguise broke briefly, to reveal a husky man in a black T-shirt, with wild hair and a mustache.

Kevin peered critically at the screen. "That could be any man at the convention," he said.

"Unsavory-looking brute," Ann said. "It was dumb of Bentley to carry the chip on her."

"Yeah. Think of it!" Kevin said. "You could go anywhere. Any time. Not just when you catch one person's code. *Anywhere.*"

"That'd be great," Ann agreed. "Look, I've got to check in with Energex. You want to come with me? I've got a seminar and a demonstration this afternoon. Do you want to meet me for dinner? I'll treat for a mid-level meal."

"Someplace with good desserts?" Kevin asked wistfully. He flipped a hand, a graphic of a gooey-looking fountain confection appeared on his compad screen. "Micelli's makes eight-scoop sundaes."

"Maybe," Ann said. Kevin's hopes were always a lot bigger than his appetite. She programmed the upgrade code into her badge using her mini-compad, and the two headed for the Energex booth.

The crowd thinned briefly, and Ann caught a glimpse of her supervisor. The older woman was talking with a man Ann recognized as one of their important overseas customers. She lengthened her stride to get in on the conversation before her boss made promises *she'd* have to keep.

Just a short distance from the Energex booth, a figure came from behind, and collided with them as it tried to get past. Ann stumbled and glanced at the figure, who was clad in the shimmer of a slight, older woman with blonde hair.

"Sorry," Ann said.

"Nothing broken," she said in a deep baritone voice. Ann stared. The woman was a man. She backed away a pace, and their eyes met. Ann realized suddenly that she *knew* the face of the image. It looked a lot like Professor Bentley, but according to the news reports she had just watched, the real professor was lying in an infirmary bed, recovering from a blow on the head. Ann's eyes met his. Instantly, he knew she knew who he was. He reached out, and gave her a shove backward. Ann staggered and slipped, trying to catch the man's arm.

"Kev! Grab his number! He's the thief!"

"What?" Kevin asked, but his hands were already moving, out of pure reflex. He snatched a handful of air and threw it at his compad. The man leaped away from them, and ran for a portal.

"Did you get it?"

"Not yet! Who is she?"

"He! It's a man in a shimmer," Ann said, pulling Kevin toward the portal. "Kev, it's him. It's the guy who stole the chip."

"Are you sure?" Kevin glanced up at her, his eyes wide behind his visor.

"Yes. No. Yes, I am," Ann said, as she pulled them through into the corridor, hoping they were making the same connections as the man had. "He's dressed up as Bentley. Who else would do that? Didn't you see? We have to report him!"

"Oh, yeah," Kevin gasped, using his one free hand to pull up on his compad the images that had been broadcast to everyone's infrared connectors. "We can *catch* him, Sis."

The distance between them and their quarry was lengthening. If they stopped to tell somebody who he was, he'd be gone. Ann made up her mind, and pulled Kevin along behind her.

"If we're wrong, we can apologize," she said, setting

her face into a grim mask. "But we're not. I'm sure we're not."

They emerged into the portal chamber. Ann saw a heel disappearing into the glow of doorway 2.

"What if we get to one he has the code for but we don't?" she asked. "We might be able to unlock the in-gate, but not the out-gate."

"Don't worry," Kevin said. "If we can get into the chamber, we can grab the code as he uses it."

"We can't lose him," Ann said, grimly. "He's got that chip. He could ruin everything! The environment, the economy, everything!"

"We won't let it happen," Kevin said, looking years older than thirteen. "Got him!" he crowed, just before the glare subsided. Ann prayed that no other traveler had passed through the chamber between the time the man jumped in and when she and Kevin had followed. She handed over her badge, and Kevin programmed it with a few deft movements, never stopping walking toward Portal 2. It glowed, and they jumped through it.

They emerged ten feet behind the shimmer-clad man in the cafeteria. He glanced over his shoulder at them, and hurried into the milling mass of tray-carrying people. Some of them wore the blue CompCom badges, but Ann noticed attendees from other conventions who were on the low budget plan. Ann, with her longer legs, closed the distance until she was only a few meters behind him. They dodged robot bus-carts, business-suited women with bowls of soup and glasses of iced tea, and children carrying towering ice cream sundaes. Kevin, toting his compad, disappeared in the crowd behind her.

'C'mon," Ann growled under her breath, keeping the false Professor Bentley in sight. "Come on, Kevin! Hey, mister!" she shouted. "Mister, we just want to ask you a question! Hold up!"

Kevin caught up with her just before the man van-

ished into another portal. He was red in the face
from running.

"Hurry," he said. "We can't let him get away with
that chip."

They made it into chamber 43 before the man left
it. The programming Kevin had given their badges
from the cloned code held good through another
jump, this one into a computer art seminar. Ignoring
the surprised looks on the faces of the instructor and
half a hundred students, they popped out of that, and
into a hotel corridor right behind their quarry. The
man had dropped his shimmer disguise, and Ann
could see that the police sketch was accurate. Mustache, messy hair, dark clothes. He could disappear
into the CompCom crowd if he stopped running, and
the only way they could identify him would be by his
badge number. Ann concentrated on memorizing the
way he moved, any detail about him that set him
apart; not so easy to do while one and one's subject
were running.

The man glanced over his shoulder and shot them
a dirty look. He put on a burst of speed, and sprinted
to the next portal entrance. The door glowed and
swallowed him up. Ann gathered herself and closed
her eyes as she hurtled after him, wondering if the
gate would open for her, or if she'd slam into a solid
wall of energy.

She had time to recognize her own hotel corridor.
Kevin emerged panting from the gate, and she pulled
him along. Ann couldn't leave him behind. He could
hack his way home, but she needed him. The man
must have heard their breathing, because he put on
another burst of speed. He slipped into the portal at
the end of the hall.

"We're too far behind him," Ann said. "Run,
Kevin, run!"

They entered the next chamber at portal 7, just as
the glow was subsiding around portal 3.

"Oh, no!" Ann said, skidding to a halt in the empty chamber. She looked down at her badge in surprise. "No, wait, it's lighting up. This door must be on our convention circuit, too."

"Narfy," Kevin said. "When we see him, you keep after him, and I'll double back to report it to Security. They'll catch up with you somewhere on the Hotelnet circuit."

"All right," Ann said.

They sprang out in front of a maid in a white cheong-sam who was walking across a marble floor that said "Hotel Singapore" in gold letters. The man in the black T-shirt was nowhere in sight. They looked around, gaping at the elegant surroundings.

"He's not here," Ann said. "He didn't come in here!"

"Then we shouldn't have been able to get in," Kevin said, frowning. His mouth dropped open, and his whole face glowed. "Do you know what? We must be carrying the master code! The guy put the key chip into his own badge, and *we* hacked it! We rule the world!" He thrust his gloved fist into the air in triumph.

"But we lost him," Ann said, elated and appalled at the same time to be suddenly in possession of godlike powers. "We don't know where he is. We could go on chasing him all over the world. And what if we do manage to catch him! This is big business, the biggest. He's a crook. He might kill us. What if he's armed?"

Kevin's face, red with excitement, went pale. "Oh, *yeah*. What do we do? I know. We can trap him!"

"How? We're behind him," Ann said.

"But we can get in front of him. Make him come to us." Kevin started poking at the controls on his compad.

"How?" Ann asked, impatiently. "There's a million destinations possible."

The maid in white had moved very cautiously over

to a uniformed man behind a desk, and the two were clearly talking about them. She grabbed Kevin and pushed him back through the portal into the chamber.

"That's how we'll do it," Kevin said, showing her an intricate diagram on his compad screen. "There's thousands of chambers, and all of them programmed to different places. But if all of them lead to just one place, then that's where he has to go. Come on, don't you see? He's going somewhere specific. So he's going to keep going through doors. If he goes through just one more, we've got him. Here, hold this."

Ann supported Kevin's compad while he used both hands to open one Hotelnet file after another, pulling a little of this and a little of that. He manipulated string after string of computerese, groaning as his way was blocked time and again by safeguards in the program. If it hadn't been for Kevin's code-capture sequence, they'd probably have nothing more than page after page of gibberish, but it was still a lot of hard work, and they had little time in which to do it.

"Is this a good idea?" Ann asked, watching him anxiously. "Can't we just shut down the power and tell Interpol what the guy looks like?"

"No," Kevin said, without looking up, "because then we'll be trapped, and all he has to do is go out a service door and into the street anywhere. Take a chance, Annie. He's still going through portals trying to lose us. We can catch him."

Kevin made a final twist in the air with his glove, and turned around in a circle.

"Eenie, meenie, minie, moe," he said, "catch a hacker by the toe ..." He jumped through portal 8, and Ann followed.

"Why here?" Ann shouted, as the two teenagers popped out into the hubbub of the Job Fair hall.

"It was the biggest place I could think of," Kevin shouted back. "It's going to fill up fast ..."

". . . Unusual activity, unauthorized programming . . . there they are!"

Over the roar of the crowd Ann heard a man's voice yelling. The Security man who had found her and Kevin—was it only a few hours ago?—was wading toward them, compad in hand, through a thickening crowd of people. More security guards appeared, and moved to surround them.

All around them the crowd began to get thicker and thicker, as every portal started to spew people into the room. Men and women, wearing every color of Hotelnet badge emerged one after the other, looking puzzled. The first turned and tried to get back into the portals to go back where they came from, but they popped back at once. They collided with the people who were coming in for the first time. Kevin's programming had made every destination this room. Arguments broke out as everyone tried to find out where they were.

Ann gasped as the guard seized her arm.

"No, it's not us you want!" she cried, trying to pull away. "The man who stole the chip, he's here somewhere, or he's going to be here. . . ."

"There he comes!" Kevin shouted. Ann had lost sight of her brother in the press of adults, all taller than she was. "His code's reading live in there, right now! He's by that wall!"

Kevin's compad and hand appeared over the sea of shoulders and pointed toward the west wall of the Job Fair. Ann rose onto her toes and strained to see through the crowd. The guard didn't let go of her, but he looked, too.

Amazingly, Ann spotted the thief. He was turning in bewildered circles between two of the portals. He pushed his way back into a glowing gate, only to emerge again from the next one in line. If the sequence continued, his next jump would put him right next to Ann and her captor.

"Please," she begged the guard. "If you want the real crook, just listen to me. Please. Then I'll go to jail or wherever you want."

The man lowered his eyebrows, but he must have believed Ann was sincere. As soon as the messy-haired man emerged from the gateway, Ann pointed.

"Him! He has the chip!"

The man's eyes widened, and his jaw dropped open as the security guards converged on him. Unable to move because of the crush of human beings around him, he raised his hands helplessly.

Ann's guard shoved his way back to her.

"Now, turn this mess off!" he commanded.

"Kevin!" she shrieked, praying he could hear her. "Now!"

"Got it!" a distant voice called.

The room emptied out quickly. Soon, there was no one left in their corner of the room except Ann, Kevin and the first guard. The thief had gone gladly with the authorities. He had bruised ribs, and looked even more wild-eyed than when the two teens had first seen him. Ann and Kevin had been acclaimed as heroes by half a dozen news services, but the sysops of the conference were still unsure what to do with them.

"Ann and Kevin Mack?" a soft voice asked. Ann looked up, or rather down, at the small figure of Dr. Alana Bentley. The scientist smiled.

"I want to thank you for helping to catch that man," she said. "You have no idea how much trouble he could have caused—what that chip would be worth on the black market. I've taken advice, and it's safely locked away now."

"Ma'am," Kevin said, stepping right up to her. She was so small that they were nearly eye to eye. "I have to tell you something. Before we started chasing the crook, we hacked your system. Now we've got the key code in my computer." He showed her his compad.

"I grabbed it off the guy who stole it with a program I made." Dr. Bentley's mouth opened in an O, and Kevin interrupted before she could speak. "Before you strip off my badge, let me tell you what we did. And didn't. My sister said we have to be really responsible, but it's hard. And we don't want anyone else to do it either. But you're going to have to move fast, before this whole thing becomes the biggest smuggling route in the galaxy. You need help." Kevin's face turned red. "I know I'm not saying this too well."

Dr. Bentley closed her mouth, then opened it again. "I think you'd better come with me, young man," she said. She took Kevin by the shoulder, and marched him away into the hall. Ann started to follow, but the guard took her arm gently but firmly.

"He'll be all right," the man said, his face kind. Ann thought of a thousand things that could happen to them, and wondered if she was going to have to post bail. She wondered if there was enough money in the world for the fines they might need to pay. If they locked Kevin up, she didn't know what she'd do.

To her everlasting relief, Kevin returned half an hour later, alone. He gave his sister a sideways, ashamed glance.

"What did she do?" Ann asked, feeling her heart sink. "Did she throw us out of the conference?"

"No," Kevin said sheepishly. "She offered us a job."

"She *what*?" Ann shrieked. She looked up at the guard, who had a big smile on his face. For the first time she noticed the radio earplug in one ear, and realized that he knew all about it. He'd have heard all the scuttlebutt across the conference while it was going on. And he didn't tell her. She made a face at him.

"Yeah," Kevin said triumphantly. "Programming security into the Hotelnet. Pete and Bonnie, too."

"And you had to give back the master code?" Ann asked.

Kevin grinned widely. "Nope. We'll need it to design the safeguards."

"Incredible," Ann said, dreaming happily of white beaches and blue skies. "Paradise, here we come. Do you know anyone who'll lend us a camera?"

GHOST IN THE MACHINE
by John Helfers

John Helfers lives in Green Bay, Wisconsin. Other stories by him appear in *Phantoms of the Night, Sword of Ice,* and *A Horror Story a Day: 365 Scary Stories.* With the help of a computer upgrade, he recently took his first steps onto the Internet. Currently he is hard at work creating a new role-playing game.

The light was everywhere, overwhelming my eye in whiteness. I endured it for as long as possible before blinking, seeing the bottom half of my vision become blurry as tears welled up and spilled down my cheek. Finally the penlight moved away, and my pupil gradually refocused.

A long time ago I read an article about blind people's other senses becoming more acute, to compensate for the loss of sight. Maybe that's true for quadriplegics as well. Now that I have firsthand experience of the latter, I guess there's all the time in the world to experiment. Sometimes I think my mind tries to gather as much sensory information as possible, to make up for the loss of movement. Sure, the nurses exercise me, and there're always sponge baths, but there's no comparison with just being able to hold something, to feel it. There are times, like a few seconds ago, for example, when I could swear I *felt* my pupil contract under the penlight. Other times it would be my eardrums, thinking I could sense them vibrating as I listened to the various hospital noises. And sometimes, late at night, I would lie awake and try to feel my lungs ceaselessly filling with oxygen, breath after breath. Something, anything to occupy my movement-starved mind.

"Pupil contraction's normal. How are you feeling, Marc?"

"As good as I'll ever be, I guess." My doctor was, in my opinion, one of those rare creatures who could actually talk to his patients, instead of just about them. Granted, the other two who have actually physically checked in on me during their rounds are polite and professional, but they're just doing their job. Jim showed more attention and care to me than both of them put together, even if he was over two thousand miles away.

Nowadays, this sort of doctor-patient teleconferencing is routine. Jim's at Berkeley's cyber-medical center, talking on a video phone. I'm here in the John Hopkins Center. It's kind of funny, putting my life in the hands of a man I've never seen from the neck down, but there's no one else I'd rather have handling this.

As I watched him work, I recalled our first meeting. When he first met me, it seemed like the usual examination, but what I didn't know was how much he could get out of it. Then I started talking to him, and realized that he'd figured out things about me that *I* didn't even know yet. Or didn't want to know.

Jim was looking off screen, saying numbers to Kieran, the male nurse next to the blood pressure machine, who nodded and checked something off on the electronic datapad, tipping me a wink as he did so. Kieran's a short Italian (the first name is a long story, taking forty-five minutes and involving six generations and a rebellious great-great-grandmother) with crew-cut black hair and a sense of humor as long as his hair is short. Two weeks after I came out of the coma, I woke up one evening to see him standing by my bedside, a brown paper bag in hand. I had been going through the serious depressive phase of my recovery, where nothing was worth anything. Anyway, he showed up with a four-pack of Killian's Red. In honest-to-God cans, the kind with the freshness packaging that hadn't been around for twenty years. He walked over and sat down next to me.

"I was saving this for a special occasion, but I think you need it more than I do," he had said. After that, my progression from suicidal invalid to something approaching human was swift and, except for a few minor setbacks, irreversible. To this day I wonder if Jim authorized it, what with hospital rules about patients' diet and all that. I guess I'll never know, because neither of them is telling.

I could feel the nervousness in both of them, although Jim's was so slight as to be almost imperceptible. It surprised me how much of a student of observation I was becoming. But it made sense; after all, my eyes and mind were two of the very few things left under my total control.

"Well, Marc, this is the day. Now, do you have any questions before we start?" Jim asked. Kieran was at my side, watching me as I thought about what was going to happen. We had gone over it for hours, with Jim breaking the doctor's language down into simple terms even I could understand. What it boiled down to was that they were going to help me walk again. That part I understood, but the exact procedure was a little more confusing.

Using a three-dimensional hologram of the brain, Jim and Kieran had explained. First, they would remove a portion of my skull and cut through the leathery protective cover, called the dura, to the brain. Once there, the surgeon would attach what Jim called "neural translators," which would tie the parts of my brain that normally receive sensory information from my body into a computer. The neural translators would be spliced into the synapses, replacing the muscles that sent the signals to my brain. Now the translators would trigger the release of neurotransmitters, the brain secretions that tell my body to move or react to whatever I saw or wanted to do. With the computer taking the place of my body, it would provide the limbs and motion. Secondary translators would be placed in a neural web around the parietal, occipital and temporal lobes of my brain. These would help in facilitating sensory signals, gathering and interpreting information, and basically assist me to adjust to cyberspace. Hopefully. After all, I was the first human patient this was being tried on.

"Basically, it'll be just like reality, only it's all happening in your mind. Your brain, however, won't know that. To you, it will be real." Jim had said. "Interested?"

Sneaky bastard, giving me a king's decision. Like I'd ever had a choice. Of course, Jim had explained the risks. "Marc, this has only been tried on animals. By the time they were finished, rats were thinking their way out of virtual cages. Humane testing, of course," he had added, seeing my frown. "I don't have time to explain, but it was successful. People, however, are a much bigger step. The principle's the same; you just have a bigger brain, that's all."

I had grinned with him when he said that. Now, feeling the cool air swirl around my shaved head, my smile was a bit more strained.

A bit more of the conversation came back to me. "While medicine, especially cybernetics, has come a long way, even since the turn of the century, we're still in the dark about a lot of things. Unfortunately, merging the brain with a computer happens to be one of them. We still can't tell you everything that goes on in the brain, or why it happens. But we're getting closer. And, with your help, we can learn more."

He hadn't needed to sell me. I didn't care about

whatever information they would gain from all this. I just wanted to walk again.

"How long will the operation take?" I asked. I already knew the answer, but still wanted a final confirmation.

"Approximately eleven to fourteen hours. Most of that time will be spent in making the necessary connections, with penetration and closure taking probably two to three hours each." Jim had gotten so used to explaining things with me that he kept doing it even when I already knew the information.

"You're sure I can't be under a local?" I asked, hoping he would change his mind. Because of the risks involved, and what this operation entailed, it would be understandable if the patient was out for the duration. I, however, didn't feel that way. After all, it was my body being experimented on, and I wanted to be there, to experience as much of it as possible. Jim wouldn't allow it.

"Sorry, but there's really no point to it. You won't be able to see anything, including us, and you'd probably end up falling asleep anyway. Besides," he grinned, "on the slight chance that something does happen, the last thing you'd need is to hear about it." His smile faded at the expression on my face.

"Slight chance?" I asked. For a moment, we were all silent, looking at each other. Then Jim smiled again.

"Don't worry, I'm going to take care of it." That sentence gave me more confidence than all the explanations in the world.

Jim's beeper signaled him that the operating room was ready, and he turned to Kieran. "Finish prepping him and get him down to room 3I." From now until the operation was over, Jim would be the consummate professional, nerveless and nearly automatic. I knew because I had watched him perform on the I-TV. The hospital advised watching your surgeon work, to alleviate any fears of unknown medical procedures. Granted, only certain operations were allowed to be seen, usually pretaped routine treatments, transplants, things like that, but the patients could get a fairly good idea what was going to happen. Mine, however would definitely not be shown. In the fifteen years since the new millennium, hospital science had progressed even farther beyond the layman's ability to keep up. On this procedure, Jim would be overseeing the operation from cyberspace, working with a complete representation of my body, and assisting the neurosurgeon if and when necessary.

Kieran straightened from his examination of the monitoring machines and looked at me. "Well, how do you feel?"

"Just fine, doc, except for this nagging numbness over my whole body." The old joke triggered a small smile at the corner of his mouth, which faded as quickly as it had appeared.

"No, Marc, really," Kieran said, his usual smile gone.

"Fine time for you to get serious," I said.

"I don't think there's a better time."

Thank God I could still look away. "It's terrifying. You guys are going to cut into my brain, for Christ's sake."

"You know the possible benefits," he said.

"And I sure as hell know the risks, too," I said.

"Having second thoughts?"

"No," I answered quickly, perhaps too quickly, trying to reassure myself as well as him. "Just venting, I guess. Anything'll be better than lying here."

"Just remember our bet," Kieran said, his smile back.

"Yeah, yeah, I remember," I muttered.

He looked a little smug as he released the bed wheels. "I can't wait to see this."

"Hey, hey, I could cut a pretty mean rug in my time," I said, glaring at him.

"Uh-huh." Kieran looked at his watch, then at me. "Let's go, baldy."

"Why, I oughta smack you . . ." My stream of colorful invectives trailed after us as he wheeled my bed toward the operating room.

The operation was a success, or so Jim tells me. He even put my skull back on the right way. The bad news is that now I can't even move my head. They've got me in a calibrated frame to keep me still and get accurate readings while the implants take. Thank God I've got my work to take my mind off the experiment. Jim had me placed in one of those beds that can flip your whole body around, so I can be vertical, horizontal, or any degree in between, all controlled by my eye movement. I spent my first two hours in it just rotating in circles until Kieran caught me and disconnected the optical scanner, leaving me stuck watching the floor for an hour. I'll get him for that, somehow.

The day after the operation I was itching to get back to business. Moving my bed until I was at a 30-degree angle to the floor, I said, "Headset, lower." This caused my computer-controller, a plastic frame, to lower until it reached my head. Once it was in place, a small eyepiece flipped down over my right eye. Using a combination of voice-recognition and optical scanning commands, I could work my laptop and modem as well as ever. At least, I could before the operation. Realizing that there was no way both frames could occupy the same space, I gave up and sent the headset back to the ceiling. Well, there was always television.

Approximately 250 channels of mind-numbing entertainment later, I told the television to turn itself off. Rotating the bed back to horizontal, I thought, *It's gonna be a long couple of days.*

Suddenly I thought I felt a tingling in my head, as though my brain was itching. I knew that was impossible—I mean, there aren't any sensory nerve endings up there. Jim had warned me about that. He said it was just the skin regenerating around the wires through my scalp. He was right, I'm sure, but I couldn't help wondering. After all, my skin doesn't hurt at all.

Once they were sure the implants had been accepted, the experiments would start. All I could do during these next few days was wait. Wait and think about what I could get back. I had thought waiting for the operation had been difficult, but that was nothing compared to this. To be able to walk again, move around, do a simple thing like hold a spoon. That was why I wanted to work, to take my mind off of it. Just thinking about the possibilities rendered me unable to concentrate on anything else, whether it was meeting with Jim or just trying to watch the I-TV. I was constantly wondering if it could really happen. For that, to be able to move again, I would have given just about anything.

It was finally time. I was moved into another small room that was empty save for a computer terminal and me. Jim told me that the computer that was going to simulate reality for me is also in Berkeley, on the other side of the continent. It would keep up with my brain as it senses my surroundings, adjusting my view of objects, their feel, smell, taste and a million other things, so everything would seem normal, no matter how I looked at things or moved.

"Ready?" Jim asked from the screen next to me. I nodded, the frame finally gone. Sometimes I thought I still felt the cold rods clamped to my head. I looked down to the cord running from my bed to the wall, connecting me to the network with lines of fiberoptics running all the way to California.

"You know how to begin," he said, dimming the monitor. The lights also slowly dimmed to pitch-black, infinite darkness. Jim thought it would help me visualize where I want to be. He'll be watching the whole thing at his desk, ready to stop the experiment if anything goes wrong.

I closed my eyes, thinking of a simple light to see by, then opened them. A lamp hung in the middle of the room, casting a soft glow on everything. It looked familiar, and I realized that it was the Japanese paper lantern my wife and I had gotten from her grandparents when they had sold their house and taken to the road in a massive RV, at least fifteen years ago.

Jim had warned me that this might happen, that unless I pictured exactly what I wanted to see in my mind, my brain would take things I had strong memories of and use them for what I asked for. In this case, I had wanted light. For that request my mind had taken the lamp and given it to me. I knew the computer's parameters were such that there would be a physical representation of just about anything I asked for. After hearing this, I had groused for days about not being able to fulfill my God complex by saying, "Let there be light and having it appear from no visible source.

Right now, however, this was a damn good start. I saw the wood-link chain that the lamp hung on went up to a hook in the ceiling and ended, while the cord continued on to an outlet in the wall which I hadn't even asked for. I even saw the small switch that turned it on and off hanging underneath. It was a perfect copy in every way.

"So far, so good," I muttered to myself before I realized I was speaking. I looked down at my hand, one of the pair that hadn't moved under its own power in eighteen months. My arm was exactly as I remembered it before the operation, pale and a little skinny from lack of exercise. As I stared at it, it twitched.

Was that involuntary or did the computer make it happen? I wondered. As my anticipation increased, I also felt moisture form on my forehead. Jim had also told me about this as well, that, as the computer grew more accustomed to my brain's reactions and patterns, it would synchronize with my body's reactions and simulate them identically.

Great, I can virtually sweat. It tickled, and before I realized what I was doing, the arm (I was still experiencing a bit of trouble referring to it as mine) rose to my head. Time froze for a long moment as I comprehended what had just happened. After several long seconds, I realized that my arm was still against my forehead, so I lowered it in front of my face and looked at it again, even more closely this time. What looked exactly like my hand and arm stayed right where I wanted it to. I slowly rotated it in front of me, marveling at the incredible play of tendons and muscles I had never noticed before. Slowly my fingers waggled, curling and uncurling. I balled my hand into a fist and squeezed as tightly as I could. When my hand opened again, I could not only see the row of crescent marks my fingernails had made in my palm, but I could feel the numbness where they had dug into the skin.

Again I felt moisture on my face, but now it was tears on my cheeks. I had cried many times after the accident which had robbed me of my body, but this was the first time I was crying with joy. There was no metaphor, no comparison, no description for what I was feeling. To be given back something you have had all your life that is suddenly, cruelly taken away from you is indescribable.

If only it were that way with all things, I thought, thinking of my wife Caroline for a moment. As if for the thousandth time, I remembered her face, alive and smiling.

Snapping myself back to the present, I continued

with the experiment. Reaching for the light switch, I was overjoyed to find my arm and hand responding just like they always had. Taking hold of the small control, I luxuriated in the feel of the cool plastic against my skin. Moving my thumb over the switch, I thought I should say something appropriately meaningful before I accomplished the simple act of turning a light off. Something witty maybe, or poignant, that could be quoted years from now. Of course, my brain couldn't come up with anything more clever than. . . .

Inhaling deeply, I held the switch in front of my face and said to the empty room, "Here goes nothing."

With a small click, the light vanished. In the darkness, I was still aware of the chain in my hand. I could hear the wooden links that were wrapped around the electric cord click as they swung gently back and forth.

My mind was bursting with possibilities. I quickly tried to clamp down on my runaway train of thought, to focus on my next step, which crystallized immediately.

I think walking would be just fine, I thought. But first, I thought-moved my thumb over the light switch, already visualizing my legs moving, getting me out of my bed prison. Clicking the light on, I froze, my arm hanging in midair.

Next to the bed, looking at me with the same wistful expression that used to turn my heart to jelly, was my wife, Caroline.

I screamed forever before everything went black.

"But you told me if I kept it simple and thought only about inanimate objects and basic concepts, there wouldn't be a problem. So what the hell was that?" I said.

Jim was about as agitated as I had ever seen him, or at least his head was anyway. To a casual observer, he would have seemed totally calm. But I had seen those slightly flaring nostrils before, and knew exactly what they meant.

"Marc, once again I will remind you that all of this is totally experimental. We can't guarantee giving you exactly what you want, and that's something you're going to have to accept." He leaned back slightly, sighing as he did so. "To answer your question, I don't know. Let's go over it one more time. I've seen the tapes, and the readouts from our monitors. Hell, I was on-line, watching you, but I want to hear it from you again." That was something new. I had never heard Jim swear before.

"I don't know what I can tell you that I haven't before. I was in the room, everything was fine, I had just moved my arm, then I turned the light off, turned it back on again, and there she was."

"Hmm." Jim paused, then continued. "Did she speak to you, or make any kind of movement or motion?"

"No."

"That lamp was familiar to you?" Jim leaned forward again.

"Sure, like I said, we had picked it up together." I had dismissed this, but his attentiveness was making me wonder.

"Marc, think carefully about this next question. At any time, did your attention or concentration wander?" Jim asked.

"Well, yeah." I paused. "In fact, I even thought about her for a second. But that couldn't make any difference, could it?"

"Perhaps, perhaps not. In what context did you think about her?"

I frowned. "Context?"

"Did you remember her happily, sadly, angrily? What was your primary emotion when you thought of her?" Jim asked, his nose normal now, but eyes fixed intently on me.

"Well, sadly, I guess. I mean, I remember thinking, 'If only it was this easy to get anything back,' you know, like my body." I grinned ruefully. "Little did I know, huh?"

Jim smiled faintly before replying. "Well, my unofficial opinion is that your subconscious is playing a part in this somehow, bringing feelings or desires to the surface, where your conscious mind translated them into reality. Well, cyber-reality for you."

"But, Jim, I dealt with all this already. I can't go through it again." I hated the plaintive note in my voice as I thought of the hours of therapy and counseling.

"And what did you come up with?" The question was rhetorical, because from what I could see, Jim had practically memorized my file, but I said it anyway.

"That I wasn't responsible for my wife's death. The accident was just that." For a moment, I flashed through the crash in my mind, our v-car speeding out of control down the icy hill, me frozen helplessly behind the wheel, a jarring impact, then waking up in a hospital bed, numb in both mind and body. I snapped back to the present to hear Jim talking.

"—but it's possible that deep down, some parts of you still hold yourself accountable. That may be causing the interference, for lack of a better word. Look, I've got to check on my other patients. I'll talk to you in the morning. Right now, you have to think about whether or not you want to try again."

My voice stopped him before he could log off. "What's to think about? Either way, I've got to go back, whether it's to walk or find out why I'm ... seeing my wife in there. I want another session as soon as possible."

"You're sure?"

I nodded.

"All right, just get some rest. I'll set it up." He

paused. "One more thing. When you moved your arm, how did it feel?"

My eyebrows narrowed as I thought back to the experiment, the real purpose having been buried under what had happened near the end. Thinking about the sense of freedom that had been given back to me, I smiled and replied, "As if I'd never lost it."

"Good." Without another word, the monitor winked off, leaving me alone with my thoughts, which were currently rambling in a circle, trying to figure out what was going on, why this was happening. I ended up more at a loss than Jim was, even after consulting the I-TV for information on the brain. I had scanned through an article on memory for several minutes before thinking, *but no one's memories have become real before, not even in cyberspace. How can I find information on something that's never happened before?* Sighing, I commanded the monitor to shut itself off and stared at the ceiling until I fell asleep.

I awoke early the next morning with a vague feeling of having been warned about something while I slept. I tried to remember what I was to be careful of, but I'd never been very good at dream recall, and the sense of warning flitted across my mind and was gone before I could catch it.

Calling for the tray which held my computer, I set to work on my accounts receivable, thinking: *Well, if I can't manipulate myself, I'll manipulate data instead.* I lost myself in transactions until I heard the rattle of the breakfast cart coming down the hall, along with a cheerful whistle which caused my lip to curl in annoyance.

Kieran walked into the room, smiling all the while as he opened the shades, causing me to squint against the bright spring morning.

When I asked him what the occasion was, he replied, "You owe me a hundred bucks."

I shook my head, remembering the bet, "Hold it," I said. "That's not fair, I was interrupted before I could try it."

Kieran shook his head. "Uh-uh. The deal was the first action you made."

"That's ridiculous!" I snapped at him. "How the hell can I do that lying down?"

"That's not my problem. My problem is just going to be spending that money, as soon as you log it onto my c-card."

"Wait just a damn minute," I said, glowering at him. "I had extenuating circumstances. The experiment was halted before I could get that far." The short Italian was unmoved by my pleas. "All right," I said, exasperated, "Double or nothing: the first action *after* I stand up."

"Done, although I still think there's no way you'll do it better than my uncle Sean." Kieran grabbed my limp hand, shook it, and set it back down on the bed where it had lain for the past five months. That was another thing I liked about Kieran, he never actually treated me like a quadriplegic.

A few seconds later, Jim's serious face appeared on my television.

"Good morning, Marc. The second set of experiments begins today. We'll start in an hour." Perfunctory as ever, he noted my current conditions, then logged off as abruptly as he had come.

Meanwhile, Kieran had wheeled my breakfast tray over to the bed. He whipped the cover off the plate with a flourish and smiled. "Mmm, oatmeal."

Looking at the pallid sludge, I decided to forestall the torture of eating it and asked Kieran, "What do you make of all this?"

He looked up from cutting my toast and shrugged. "Honestly, I have no idea what's going on in that dirty little mind of yours. Now open up." My protest was cut off by a glob of oatmeal shoved into my mouth.

Chewing slowly, I glared at Kieran, who stirred the congealing pool and smiled.

After breakfast, I was bathed and wheeled again into the experiment room. It looked the same as last time, but now seemed more confining, like it was closing in on me. Glancing around, a shudder seemed to run through me as I thought about who or what I might see today. *Where would she come from this time? Can she talk to me? Would she? And if she was coming from my mind, why didn't I know it somehow?*

My questions all vanished when Jim's voice came over the monitor. "All ready, Marc?"

I nodded carefully, feeling the gentle tug of the wires trailing from my skull. The lights quickly dimmed, and once again I was in darkness.

Jim was right. Once you got the hang of it, creating was easy. In seconds I had the paper lamp on again, and was ready to continue. Kieran had pulled the top-sheet of the bed down so I wouldn't be distracted by it, although I'd said it really wouldn't matter. Closing my eyes for a second, I thought of myself walking, running, trotting, standing, the entire range of motion that I had been denied for what seemed like an eternity already. Opening my eyes, I looked down at my legs, seeing them again, but in a new light. Slowly, I raised my right knee up, watching the muscles bend, actually hearing the joint pop. Sitting up, I slid to the edge of the bed and put my feet on the floor, exulting in the chill of the floor soaking into my soles. Not daring to wait any longer, I grabbed the side rail and pushed up and off.

For a second, I wasn't sure I had done anything. Then my eyes cleared and I was looking at the floor from a height my head hadn't been at, except in the restraining bed, in months. My head pounded as the computer, apparently reading the fluid level in my inner cyber-ear, gave me a severe case of vertigo.

After that had cleared, I flexed my legs, bending down slightly. Everything seemed to be in order. Looking at the wall I knew Kieran was watching me from, I smiled—and began dancing. The jig steps were rusty at first, but soon I had my old rhythm back. *To hell with Kieran,* I thought, *I may not have the name, but I've got the moves.*

"You never were a great dancer, Marc." The voice from behind stopped me cold with one leg still in the air. Suddenly off balance, I reeled against the bed, feeling a new sensation—pain—as my foot struck the frame. Grabbing the mattress, I checked my fall and managed to turn around at the same time.

There she was, without a single conscious thought from me, standing under the paper lamp, its soft glow highlighting her features. She looked as beautiful as the last time I had seen her alive.

Seeing her brought back a rush of memories, from our anniversaries to the vacation in Ireland to my father's funeral, and the near riot that followed. Arguments, celebrations, lovemaking, trips, all of it seemed to flood through my mind, even the day she was taken from me. When I looked back at her, nothing had changed outwardly, but to my eyes she now seemed more real, fleshed out, as it were.

Straightening, I took a hesitant step toward her, then another. One more brought me right in front of her. She smiled, and for a moment I forgot everything but her face. Hesitantly I reached out my hand to cup her cheek. Her skin was soft and warm, her lips slightly parted, revealing her white teeth.

It was at this moment that I actually comprehended what was happening. *My God,* I thought, *she's here. It's really her.* Her mouth opened as if to speak, but I put my finger against her lips, silencing her.

"Shh. Just let me hold you," I whispered. Reaching out, I enfolded her in my arms and clung to her tightly. She returned my embrace, and I could feel wetness both on my cheeks and chest. We stood there just holding each other for what seemed like eternity. Finally I straightened and looked down at her.

"Is it really you?" As soon as I asked the question, I felt like a fool for doubting my own senses, but a tiny, cynical part of me still had doubts.

Apparently she didn't hold that against me. "Of course," she replied, looking up at me and smiling, her tear-stained cheeks the most beautiful sight I had seen in a long time.

"How—how did you get here?" I asked slowly, thinking of each word carefully before speaking, struggling not to be overwhelmed by her presence again.

"Darling, you asked me to come. I heard your call, and here I am," she said.

I shook my head, "But . . ." I stammered, vaguely aware of my senses being overwhelmed as I drank in the scent and feel of her skin. "I didn't call you . . . I wasn't even thinking of you."

She smiled that gentle, loving smile again. "Not that you were aware of," she said, "but what your subconscious is thinking about is an entirely different story."

Which made sense, especially when I remembered what Jim's hypothesis was. The computer sure had her outward traits down to a science. *She had always called me darling, preferring that to any other name, even my real one,* I thought, then stopped for a moment. *Why should I even question this? She's back and that's all that matters.* Looking at her again, I didn't know what to say. I just wanted to hold her forever. I wanted to make sure she never went away again.

"It's you. It's really you." I repeated the words over and over, still only half believing my eyes and hands. Now she was the one who laid a finger on my lips to silence me, then leaned up and kissed me.

Any thoughts about her not being my wife were dispelled at that moment. If a part of me hadn't re-membered that I was being monitored right now, I know there would have been a lot more happening than just one kiss. As it was, the touch of her lips to mine wiped away any doubts I had about whether the person in front of me was or wasn't my wife.

When we broke apart, she was looking at me with her usual impish smile and asked, "Any doubts now?"

Shaking my head, I just hugged her again. It was then that I heard a faint whine of electrical interference, and saw Caroline flicker and shift for a second before turning back to normal.

"Honey, what's wrong?"

"I don't know," she said, sounding uncertain for the first time. "Wait . . . they're going to shut the experiment down."

"What?" My grip around her tightened. "How do you know that?"

She tapped her temple. "You forget, I'm still part of the computer. They've just given the command to turn the experiment, and me, off. I can only delay it for so long."

"No. They can't do that now," I said, not letting her go. "I just found you, dammit." As I watched, the outline of her body fuzzed into thousands of tiny pixels. With what seemed like an effort, she pulled herself back together and stepped away from me.

Caroline cocked her head as if listening to an unseen presence, then looked at me again. "They're apparently worried about how your interaction with me may affect your mind. They don't think it's a good idea."

"To hell with what they think!" I replied, following her. "I'm not letting you leave me again."

She looked at me sadly. "We have no choice. Unless . . ."

"Unless what?" I asked.

"Unless you came with me," she said.

"With you where?" I asked, totally confused by her answers.

She smiled, lighting up the room more than a thousand paper lamps could. "Anywhere we want to go." Walking to the wall, she outlined a large rectangle with her hands, and suddenly a dark gray portal appeared in the wall. Moving next to her, I looked at the doorway, careful not to touch it.

"Where does that lead?" I asked.

"Anywhere you want it to," Caroline said, pointing to it. Looking at it again revealed a sight I thought I'd never see again, the rolling, green hills of Ireland. I could even smell the rich land that waited for me though that doorway. Holding out her hand to me, she said, "We can escape to the nets for now, then figure out what to do next."

"I can't do that. It's impossible," I said, drawing back in amazement.

Quickly she stepped toward me. "Marc, darling, of course you can." She touched my temple lightly. "The connection you have allows you to go anywhere you want. The computer created me from your memories," she said, pointing towards the doorway. "In there, it would be just as simple to create you as well."

"But why can't I just visit you like we are now?" I asked.

"Because I know that isn't what you really want. Is this how you want to live for the rest of your life? Trapped in that dead shell, only able to walk and see me when the doctors allow you to? Or do you want the freedom to go anywhere, do anything, whenever and wherever you want? Can you really say there's a choice between the life you have now, and the chance you have before you?" Caroline slowly shook her head. "Just as you know me, I know you as well."

I slowly shook my head, trying to fathom what my life could be like according to her.

Caroline continued, "You and I can travel like no one else, go anywhere, do anything. We would have all the time in the world, be together for eternity."

She saw my hesitation and stepped closer to me. "Marc, what's wrong?"

"It's all of this, really ... you, here ... talking to me. I mean, you've been dead for a year and a half, gone from my life, and now you're back, not only back, but wanting me to go with you, into somewhere that doesn't exist, can't exist. It's all too much." I realized I was speaking too rapidly, as if that would somehow enable my brain to keep up with what was going on around me.

"But it is all possible. With your interface, you can create your own world, see and be whatever you want." She pointed through the doorway again. "Remember the vacation in Ireland? The green hills, getting up early to see the morning fog vanish from the valleys? We can be there again, or anywhere you want. You just have to leave what's left of your body behind, and you can. You've already taken the first step—Please—come wi—"

Her outline began to flicker and lose cohesiveness, the tiny pixels flying off in random directions. Realizing what was happening, she tried to run back to the door, but started fading into nothingness even as she took the first step.

"Caroline!" I shouted, reaching out for her but only encountering empty air.

The disintegration continued, traveling up her body until only her head was left, which turned to look at me, an unnerving sight with nothing to support it. She started to speak, "Don't let—" and was swallowed by the air.

"No!" I screamed, closing my eyes as if that would unwind time, would make what I had just seen not happen. My scream died off into silence, and I opened my eyes again, hoping to see her again. The room was empty. Looking around, I saw that the paper lamp had disappeared. Before I could move, the room lights came on, and I was wrenched into a different point

of view. Looking around, I saw the familiar view from
my bed. My hospital gown itched, and I vaguely realized it was damp from my sweat. I was still staring at
the wall where the portal had been when the real door
slammed open and Kieran ran in.

"Marc, what the hell was that?" he asked.

"That was my wife, and I want her back here."
I said.

"I think we'd better wait for Jim's opinion on this."
Kieran said.

"No, I want her back now." My voice grew more
shrill as I saw he wasn't complying. "Bring her back,
damn you, bring her back!" I screamed, my head
thrashing around on the bed. Kieran stepped over to
me, a needle glinting in his hand. I could only watch as
the injection sank home. Before I lost consciousness, I
muttered weakly, "My wife ... still alive."

"I'm telling you, no more experiments. You're not
going back until we figure out what this is," Jim repeated the next morning.

"But how are you going to do that if I don't go
back and talk to her?" We were back in my hospital
room, going in circles.

"Damn it, Marc, that in there," Jim waved at a
monitor behind him which showed Caroline and myself, "is not a 'her.' It's not your wife. Your wife died
on April twenty-eighth in a car accident at 12:24 p.m.
You survived, she didn't. Those are the facts."

"If that's true, then who's in there?" I shot back,
holding his gaze until he finally looked away.

"Not who, but what. Either it's a massive computer
malfunction, or—" he stopped, looking back at me.

"Or what?" I shot back.

Jim looked off screen a moment before replying.
"Or you've created, however unknowingly, genuine
artificial life."

His answer definitely wasn't what I had expected.

"What? Wait a minute, you're going too fast. Start from the beginning."

Jim rubbed his face with his hands, stretching his tired features into a semblance of alertness. "Basically it comes down to this: the computer is making its own decisions through the template of your wife. The first time she appeared, we thought it was just a random thought of yours that the computer had picked up on and created for you. Granted, we've created simulacrums before, some with this level of detail, but we've always been in control. This is the first time the network has done something like this."

"And you think it's because of me, right?" I asked.

Jim nodded slowly. "That possibility has been advanced, yes."

I thought for a moment of how this could be. "So how could the computer create her when I didn't ask for her?"

Jim nodded. "Apparently, it recognized her as someone you cared about very deeply, so it made her according to your memories. It was just following its programming, adding more details as it scanned your mind."

"Dammit, I never asked to see her," I said.

"Like it said, what you're thinking and what your subconscious is thinking are two different things," Jim replied.

"Wait a minute, just wait." Something Jim had said a minute ago finally sank in. "The computer can sense emotions? It not only knows what I think, but what I feel?" I asked.

Jim shrugged. "Of course. It's common knowledge that emotions and body secretions are connected, anger and adrenaline, etcetera. The computer reads what your brain and body are producing and, based on how we categorized those measurements, responds accordingly."

"Responds how?"

"Well, originally it was supposed to be a stress level indicator. If you asked for something that made you angry, or the experiment was causing you harmful levels of stress, like when your wife first appeared, it was just supposed to stop the program, kind of like a fail-safe."

"What's it doing with that information now?"

"Well, we're not exactly sure. Our systems analyst, Ryan, thinks the computer is now trying to 'make you well.' The second time it created your wife, it analyzed your flood of emotions on seeing her as a positive thing, so it tried to create more things that would give you that level of emotion again."

"Wait a minute, are you telling me we've got an endorphin-addicted computer wired into my brain?"

"No, it doesn't receive any pleasure from this. Apparently, however, it thinks *you* should. Ordinarily, we'd call this a system bug and wipe the files." My eyes snapped back to him as he said this. "However, Ryan and I think this has vast potential in many scientific fields, not to mention counseling, therapy, and many other applications. We've gone beyond the merely physical here, into a whole new level of the brain and human thought processes."

My head sank back into my pillow as I digested this. It didn't sit any easier than yesterday's oatmeal. Another thought came to me. "What about that stuff about entering and traveling the Net? Where did that come from?"

"Well, our nearest answer to that is, since it 'sees' you both in real-time and cyber-time, it knows ... it recognizes that your physical body isn't moving. Since it wants to make you happy, what better way than to give you total freedom?"

"But how in the hell can it extrapolate that I want to walk?" I asked.

Jim leaned back and smiled. "What were all of your memories of Caroline?"

"Well, they were what I remember doing with her."
It dawned on me where he was going with this. "And
at that time, I was able to walk," I said.

Jim nodded. "And what's been your driving desire
ever since you started this program?"

"To walk again. And the computer, reading my
mind, knows all of this?" I said slowly, as the realization sank in.

Jim nodded silently, then looked off screen. "I've
got to get back, see if they've come up with anything
new." He reached up to break the connection.

"Jim, two things," I said as he looked back at me.
"First, how much of what you just told me are you
sure of?"

He paused before answering, and in that instant I
saw how tired he really was. Raising his hand so it
was visible, he held his thumb and forefinger a tiny
bit apart and replied, "About that much. As to which
parts are which, I'm not even sure. What's the
second?"

"Tell Kieran I don't owe him squat," I said, grateful
for the genuine smile that appeared on his face for
a moment.

"Consider it done," he said, and signed off, leaving
me to ponder what was happening, and what I may
or may not be responsible for. But the thoughts that
I couldn't answer or shake kept cycling through my
mind. *What if Jim's wrong and Caroline is right? My
wife, as impossible as it sounds, is alive. What if I could
also be free of this bed forever?* I thought of my wife's
words: *"You just have to leave what's left of your body
behind."* I looked down at my useless limbs, my torso
rising and falling with each breath I took.

What kind of a risk would it be, compared to what
I could gain—both my body and my wife at the same
time. Put that way, there was no choice whatsoever. I
had to go back in. Leaning back, I looked at the ceiling—and at the headset above my head.

Of course. I thought, commanding the headset to drop. Once it had settled snugly over my face, I turned it on and brought the tray with my laptop over excitedly.

Once it was in front of me, I turned it on with a blink and activated the modem. Looking up one Net site in Berkeley was like trying to find a Chang in San Francisco. Then I had it, I knew how to get in. I would find where Jim was coming from and enter there. Tracking down his net address was easy, but I doubted getting in would be as simple. I feverishly waited the nanoseconds it took to connect. If I was right, and what had happened was true, then once Jim figured it out, he would wipe the program, and my wife with it.

The screen blinked once: ACCESS COMPLETE. I asked for the mainframe access, and was greeted by their password. Praying for a miracle, I input my wife's name.

The screen started to blink ACCESS DENI . . . ACCESS . . . ACCESS GRANTED. Moving my eyes to the lights, I commanded them to turn off, then closed the blinds as well, making the room dark save for the glow of my laptop screen. Dimming that as well, I closed my eyes and waited.

"Marc." The voice was barely a whisper, but it had the desired effect. Opening my eyes, I saw the dim form of my wife standing next to me. She was wavering, flickering in and out of solidity, her features blurring and refocusing from second to second. "We haven't got much time. The analyst has started to realize what's going on, and will be shutting down any second. If you want to come, you have to come right now."

Even after only standing once in a year and a half, the actions were as natural as ever, and I swung out of bed to stand beside her. She shuddered, and I reached out my hand, steadying her. "Let's go."

She smiled wearily. "Marc, my body will be downgraded so the mainframe can create the portal for you. Your modem is straining to keep just this much transmitting. You may not want to watch."

"Whatever you look like, you're still my wife." I smiled, unwilling to turn away.

Her body withered until it was no more than a stick figure. Only her head still looked lifelike. After a moment, a familiar rectangle appeared on the wall. I looked at Caroline, who grinned again. She turned to go toward it and started to collapse. Grabbing her, I helped her over to the portal. I was just about to step through when a voice from behind me commanded, "Stop."

Turning, I was amazed to see Jim standing behind me, looking like he always did, slightly rumpled. "Marc, don't go through there."

"Darling, he's stalling. We've got to go now," Caroline whispered.

"Dammit, Marc, listen to me—" Jim said.

"No, Jim, not this time. You're not going to take her away again." I turned toward the doorway again.

"That's not my intention. Will you just listen for a second?" Jim was speaking very fast. "Look, all of this is happening in a microsecond. If I hadn't been online anyway, I never would have known what was going on. Why is Caroline in such a hurry? She's in no danger. Computers execute their commands faster than human reflexes ever could. Even if I gave the command to shut down, you could get away before the Net was blocked. So just settle down and listen."

"Darling, remember what I told you," Caroline said, her voice a strained whisper. "The mainframe can only port so much power through your computer. It's already pushing the limit. Please hurry."

I paused, inches away from the portal. I looked down at my wife, who stared back at me with what I could only call love in her eyes. I looked away, the hardest thing I had ever done, back at Jim, who continued speaking.

"I think Caroline is a manifestation of your subconscious, created to persuade you to destroy yourself. If you go through there, you'll be committing suicide, basically electrocuting yourself. Your own mind has been behind this from the beginning. You have to believe me, and walk away. Please," Jim said.

"But you said yourself you didn't know what's happening exactly," I replied, "You're still only guessing she's a manifestation."

Jim nodded. "You're right, I'm not sure. But with time, I can be. All I'm asking for is a little more time. Are you going to throw your life away on a 'hallucination?'"

"How long? How long will it take?" Suddenly I was angry. "This 'hallucination,' as you put it, is something I never would have dreamed possible, and you're asking me to just walk away."

"At least you still can," Jim said.

I looked down at Caroline, who was now hanging on to me as if for her very life. Her body was suddenly as light as air. "Darling, he's wrong. If you stay, they'll control when we can see each other, if at all. Maybe even erase me from the memory. I'll be dead again. Please don't make me go through that. Please come with me now," she whispered as another spasm rocked her frail body.

"Don't do it, Marc. Don't follow the dead," Jim said.

Caught between them, I looked at the door for a moment. I felt like whichever choice I made, it wouldn't be correct. Jim had never steered me wrong, but he also admitted not knowing what exactly was going on. And what he wasn't sure of was my wife, brought back from the dead and looking at me right now.

It all comes down to who you trust, I thought. Jim

may have been the voice of logic and safety, but that didn't automatically make him right. Sure, it was my life I may have been throwing away on nothing more than an electronic bug in the system, but if I lost Caroline a second time, what kind of life would it be? What kind of life was it now? Not one worth living, I realized.

I looked from Jim's face to my wife's one last time and decided. Stepping forward, I took my wife through the portal, and into whatever lay beyond.

MEMORIES OF MARIE'S SHOE
by Brooks Peck

In addition to being an author, Brooks Peck is the
associate publisher of Science Fiction Weekly, a re-
view magazine on the World Wide Web. He has just
completed his first novel.

I was replacing a network hub in cellblock G when
the alarms went off. Just then the sight token came
around and I saw prisoners scrambling off their bunks
to stand silently by the cell doors. Impressive disci-
pline. I kept on seeing, which meant the network had
gone down. Then the deck lurched. It felt like the
prison was about to drop out of the sky. Ray and
Marie were working on the stern winder this morning,
I remembered. What the hell was happening down
there?

Dropping my tools, I ran down the corridor as fast
as I could manage, yelling, "Coming through!" The
guard at the gate was just a kid, maybe twenty-five
years old. "All security stations remain closed during
General Quarters," he quoted, raising his voice over
the alarm. I almost turned away, obeying out of habit.

"Listen to me. The network's gone down and it feels
like the winder's slipping. I've got to get down there.
Open this gate." Commanding guards, that was a new
one. The kid fumbled a key into the console and the
gate slid open.

At the stairs another guard challenged me from half
a flight down, a rifle raised to his shoulder. "Psinet

employee!" I called. "I'm going to help." He recognized me and waved me on. The ship lurched again and stayed canted about five degrees to stern.

On L deck I raced past kitchens, the laundry, and machine shop, then skidded to a stop in the winder room, taking in a strange tableau. The winder dominated the space, a two-story onion dome surrounded by white-and-red pipes, cables, and plastic ladders. It was still humming, thank God, and it sounded all right, but I was no expert. Guards and prison personnel stood around the base, unmoving. Trudy, my boss, was also there, her mouth open. I noticed a chill in the air and frost on the floor in a half circle at the base of the winder. I took a step sideways so I could see what everyone was looking at.

Ray lay on the floor, propped up on his elbows with his eyes shut. He breathed in gulps, making a noise like, "Huk, huk." Something was tangled around his legs. I thought it was clothes until I noticed the hair. Black hair. It was Marie. She lay facedown with her arms around his knees, still as stone, covered with snow. Her shirt was split open, and the skin on her back was purple and cracked. Same for her arms. I stared at her for long seconds, unable to think what to do, caught in the spell that held the others.

Then the bay doors rumbled open, flooding the room with daylight. An ambulance aircar pulled in, and paramedics jumped out of the back. They shooed us back but no one would move far. Ray they could help, but it was too late for Marie. They covered Ray with an electric blanket, gave him an oxygen mask, and tied a dose band around his arm. Then they made everyone leave. Later I heard it was because they had to break Marie's arms to get Ray free.

I walked down the corridor, taking deep breaths to calm my stomach and saw Trudy leaning against the wall with her eyes closed. "What happened in there?" I demanded.

She jumped. I guess I should have given her a few minutes. "A coolant pipe broke when they were in the crawlway."

"How did it happen?"

"Do I look like I know? Quit hassling me, Mike, we've got a hell of a lot to do right now. I hate to think what the feedback did to the network, but if we don't get it back up *now,* the warden will throw us overboard." She took a blue terminal from her belt and punched some keys. My sight vanished. "What really pisses me off," she continued, "is Psinet's advisers should have foreseen this. I wonder if they even forecast this job? Damn it." I counted to myself while listening to her. ... *seven* ... *eight*— Another second of vision. With both Ray and Marie offmind, the sight token came around a lot less often. I'd worked with worse, though. At times we'd been at one-in-twelve seconds during our last job, installing the Lunar Far-side Telepathscope. "Ellis and I will check the computers. You test the hubs and monitors, especially on the winders, okay?"

My sight returned. Trudy was already ten feet away. I followed as everything went black. "Sure."

Our team was contracted by Psinet to upgrade As-gard's computer and comm network. Uninterrupted service was vital to the prison ship for inmate monitoring as well as navigation and flight control, so while the artificial brains—the Jack-in-the-boxes—were switched out, we carried the network traffic in our own heads. We used to switch over to radio during upgrades, but these days everyone's too dependent on instantaneous psychic communication. All that traffic is processed by our visual cortexes, making us blind. At intervals the network drops one of us out of the loop for a second, letting us see to work. How often this sight token comes around depends on how much traffic there is and how many people there are to carry it.

By the time we had the system repaired and checked over it was after seven. We caught the end of dinner in the guards' cafeteria: Trudy, Ellis, and I sitting glumly at our own table. Finally Ellis said, "So Mike, see any old friends today?" He said the same thing almost every day, acting like it was a joke.

"I was on Laputa, not Asgard."

"Maybe some of your Laputa buddies got transferred."

I looked down, waiting to see where my bread was, thinking, *Go to hell, Ellis.* I couldn't say anything or Trudy might tell my probation officer I wasn't working well with others, and Ellis knew it. He liked to push me and see me shut down, ashamed. The scars on my shoulder throbbed with a phantom ache. "Well, see you all tomorrow," I said, standing suddenly without waiting to look. I bumped someone behind me. Ellis chuckled.

The walk back to my cabin worked most of the hurt off. Stupid Ellis. I think I scared him, but how could he possibly be intimidated by an aging, ex-con, net tech's apprentice? I was no competition for him. I would never be promoted; no one would trust me with any real responsibility.

Marie would have backed me up.

The door to my cabin unlocked as I walked up and the light flickered on. It was an inside cabin so no window, but that was fine. Prisoners have no windows, and being able to see outside still startled me. The room had a familiar smell of new paint and starched sheets.

Marie didn't seem to notice that I was skinny, white-haired, and sixty, that I had a record, that I used to run. When we talked, the past felt truly behind me, not grabbing my legs, trying to pull me back. We talked about the future. And once, a moment I would never forget, something happened between us. It was during the Farside job. The five of us were suiting up

to go out and assess sites for new Jacks. We had
stripped down to our cotton undersuits in a cold ante-
chamber before heading into the airlock. I turned my
back out of embarrassment while I dropped trou, and
reached over to hang up my pants. Only my hand
touched Marie instead, brushing her near the shoulder, but a little lower. I yanked my hand back, tried
to apologize, but couldn't speak. Don't touch anyone
for twenty-six years and you'll know what kind of a
shock I had. Marie only laughed quietly and her smile
said it was fine, no problem. And then we kept looking
at each other, and for a second her expression
changed, and it seemed to my foolish, addled mind
that maybe, just maybe, there was something more in
that look than just friends. Marie turned around a
second later. No one else had noticed. I told myself
to put the idea *away*. Marie and Ray were married
and that was that.

Now Marie was dead. And that was that.

In the morning Trudy told us that Ray's injuries
were mostly superficial and all he needed were some
skin grafts. We ate breakfast on the sun deck, a top-
side area open to the sky, full of green plants and
palm trees. There was a pool and a sand volleyball
court, also a bar. I drank a glass of grapefruit juice,
my usual. Marie's family was having a memorial service for her in a couple of days. We weren't invited.

"Mike, before you start today there's a box of stuff
at the warden's office I want you to pick up and put
. . . oh, stick it in the locker for now."

"All right."

I walked to the administration area, gates opening
before me like magic portals. Except for the mile-high
view, the prison offices looked like the offices of any
other corporation. A secretary gave me a hempboard
box, and I beat it out of there. I hadn't really expected

to see the warden, but there was no reason to prolong the risk.

We had been given a locker down in the hold for our equipment; really it was a closet-sized cage with shelves. After I opened the door I waited for the sight token to reach me and looked for a place to put the box. I saw a spot and put it down by feel. When the token came around again I peeked inside, curious. It held one of our small tool kits, Ray's baseball cap, and a small shoe. I slammed the lid, startled, then opened it again. This stuff must have been picked up from around the winder after the ambulance left. Marie's shoe was blue cloth, just a slipper, really. The sole was cracked and the toe had a huge hole ripped out of it. Reluctantly, but unable to stop myself, I reached into the box to touch it—

Suddenly I could see, but not the locker. Dark colors spun; it looked like I was falling even though I didn't move. Then came darkness, but in the dark I heard someone gasp, and a hiss like gas. Vision again: I clutched Ray's shoulder, but my hand was too small. He looked terrified. Marie's voice sounded close in my ear. "What did you do?" she cried. "Damn you! Damn you!"

I staggered back, but there was no one. All I could hear was the hull tick and a hatch slam far away. I shoved the box back on the shelf and waited for my breathing to slow down. Then two beeps sounded in my inner ear. "Answer," I said automatically.

"Hey, old man." Ellis. "Did you hit your head? You dropped off the net for a few seconds."

"I'm okay. Nothing wrong."

"Weird. Come upstairs. I want to check your hardware, maybe you had a power surge."

"I'll be right up." It was as if I had had a vision of the accident from Marie's point of view, but if so it was very strange. It felt like Marie had died hating Ray, furious with him. That made no sense, unless

maybe she thought he had caused the accident somehow. On my way out I double-checked to make sure
the door was locked. Not to keep people out, but to
keep what was inside in.

I ate lunch quickly, went to my cabin, and got onmind. I needed to talk to Darla, my adviser. That was
one of the biggest perks to the job: free, full access at
top speed. I sat in front of my mirror and phoned her,
requesting a sight connection. Darla answered from
her office.

"Mike, hi." Darla didn't go in for the gypsy scarves
and jewelry look that a lot of advisers use. She generally wore a suit. Today her desk was littered with dice,
newspaper clippings, tarot cards, physics journals.
"Are you in trouble? No—" she held up her hand,
"—I know you're not, but you look terrible."

Everyone always asks me if, when I'm carrying a
signal, I can see all the time while I'm onmind, since,
after all, what you see onmind is all in your head
anyway. But I still only saw Darla every eight seconds
or so. That's because it's not the eyes that carry the
net traffic, but the part of the brain that actually does
the seeing—holographic information and all that. So
except when the sight token comes around, I can't
see *anything*.

"There was an accident here yesterday." Telling
Darla was rougher than I expected. It was as if the
seriousness of it was only just starting to hit me.
"Marie was a good kid," I kept saying. "She didn't
deserve to die in such a stupid way." Then I ran out
of words, and neither of us said anything for a time.

"I'm sorry, Mike. You obviously cared for her a
lot."

"No, it's not like—"

"Is there something more?" She gave me that prob-
ing look which meant she knew perfectly well there
was something else. Well, that's advisers for you.

"Today I was putting away some of their stuff and
. . . and I saw something." I told her about the vision.

"Sounds like you caught an imprint of the accident from her shoe. Don't look so surprised. You have natural talent, I've told you that before. Why do you think you're so good at your job?"

"But it was so strange. She was yelling at him. Cursing him. Why would she have done that?"

"We do strange things when we're terrified. She was probably a little delirious at that point."

"She didn't seem delirious." Darla's concerned looks were making me embarrassed.

"Why don't you quit that job if being around there is making you feel bad? Something else will come along."

"If I don't keep my parole record damn near perfect, I'll lose employment privileges; could end up in a work camp. No, I'll be all right."

After signing off with Darla, I had ten minutes before I had to be back to work. I wanted to nap but couldn't let myself, so I checked my inbox. There was a letter from my sister living in Africa which I saved to read later. My newspaper's lead story was about the President: "Harrison Announces Reelection Bid—He Will Lose." What really caught my attention was a piece about yesterday's Pittsburgh Power Ball. Out of three million tickets sold, only 950,000 picked winning numbers for an almost three-to-one return for those lucky slammers. Damn, why hadn't my lottery firm foreseen that one? They brought me a steady seven percent return, so I knew I shouldn't complain, but I'd never get rich that way. Once again I toyed with the idea of putting my money into stocks and bonds like some people did, but that was an insane risk. Might as well throw it away.

I tried to put the accident out of my mind with little success. Two days later, at lunch, Trudy told us that Ray was out of the hospital and he'd be returning to work in a few days. For some reason I couldn't eat after that. The idea of seeing Ray made me all nervous, and deep down I knew why. I wondered if Ray had caused the accident, and if he'd done it to kill Marie. I told myself I was being melodramatic, and yet this was the perfect place to pull a crime. Asgard was isolated and everyone moved around on a set schedule. Like all of us, Ray had complete control of the network and he could have arranged things, covered his tracks. Perhaps, when he returned, I could find out what he'd been up to just before the accident. There were methods.

Then I told myself not to be an idiot. Throwing murder accusations around would get me into a hell of a lot of trouble with Trudy and the parole board. Nothing would bring Marie back anyway. I just had to forget about it.

That night a strange sound woke me, a rapid-fire tapping close to my head. I turned on the light, then waited to see while the taps grew louder and faster. A glass bottle of aftershave jiggled along the top of the dresser built into the wall next to the bed, rapping the mirror, its green facets blurred. Was the ship shaking? No, the bed was steady. I fumbled blindly for the bottle and grabbed it. It quivered in my hand like a small, scared animal. Then something in my locker thumped. "What's going on?" I said too loudly, startling myself. It sounded like someone was trapped in the locker, kicking the door. I wrestled out of the sheet, dropping the bottle on the bed, stood and gripped the door handle. The door banged under my hand. The split second I could see, I yanked it open. Clothes tumbled around my legs. Now something scrabbled and groped at my feet, but I couldn't see it. I jumped back, alarmed. The seconds ticked by while whatever it was approached. I was looking right at it when the sight token came.

My shoes were rolling and flopping around like just-hooked fish, scuffing the carpet and beating the floor with leather and rubber thuds. I fought to breathe again, then yelled, "Stop it! Stop it! Get out of here!"

Silence. I waited it out, my heart pounding. Everything was still. I kicked at my shoes; they were lifeless. My phone beeped. "Answer," I said shakily.

"Mike, are you all right?" It was Darla on voice-only.

"Jesus." I sat on the bed.

"Mike, what's wrong? I had a nightmare where you were in a car falling through the ice on a frozen lake. Then when I got up to make some tea, I looked in the hall mirror, and I could see the window and you were there. Mike, you fell out of the window! Are you all right?"

"I'm okay. Something just happened. Some kind of telekinetic effect focused on my cabin, knocked a few of my things around. I'm okay, though." I kept my eyes shut, not wanting to look at the mess. "Darla, I think it might have been Marie."

"Wait," she said, then after a long pause, "No. You're alone and you've been alone all night."

"Really? But then what?"

"It could have been you doing it. Your unconscious."

"*Me?* Great. I'm haunted by my infatuation with a dead woman."

"Mike, tell me what's happening. You have some kind of plan or intention. It's dangerous. You shouldn't do it."

"I don't have any plan." She said nothing. "Well, I used to have a plan but I'm not going to do it."

"I think you should quit that job and come home."

"I can't."

"It wouldn't be the end of the world! You'll find other work. You could even be a contractor yourself and make some real money."

That sounded nice, but very far from the here and

now. "I'll think about it," I told her, and we said our good-byes.

I didn't sleep for hours, lying in the dark, remembering the accident and the vision. A part of my mind really believed Ray had killed Marie. That part kept me thinking about Marie's face and hands and the confident way she spoke. Finally I decided that I simply had to find out what happened that day. Even if it got me in trouble. If I was wrong, then so be it. But if I was right, everyone should know. Marie deserved that.

It was almost quitting time the next afternoon before I found a chance to start my plan. Ellis sent me for a module he'd left in the locker, and on the way back I saw two inmates on mop detail. This area of the ship had storage bays and some guards' quarters; no one was around. I went onmind, accessed the network and shut down all the monitors in the area, logging it as maintenance. More than likely no one would ever notice the entry, but if it came up, I'd give some excuse.

I approached the men, my hand brushing the wall to keep me on course between flashes of vision. "Hi," I said to the first, an old man with a deep, wrinkled frown. He had the unmistakable look of a lifer. "Can you tell me . . . um, that is I need to find who the mall is onboard."

Silence. When I could see, the old guy was shuffling away, mopping as he went. The other guy, a younger man too tall for his coveralls, stared at me.

I kept talking out of embarrassment. "I served on Laputa, see, and now I need a few things and was wondering—" Another flicker of sight. The young man had turned back to his mopping as well. "Look," I said, pushing up my sleeve. I couldn't tell if they looked or not. If they did they would see the pink rectangle where the Corrections surgeon had removed my brand and replaced it with a skin graft from my thigh. A lot of inmates had them.

"Who did you run with?" I couldn't tell which one had spoken, but it was a hell of a question. I didn't keep up with gang politics, so I didn't know who was at war right now. If I hadn't been out of the loop so long I would have thought about that before saying something so stupid. *This could get me killed*, I realized. Then an idea came to me.

"Blue Eye Triads," I said. Someone grunted in surprise. The BET had been exterminated over twenty years ago. When I next saw, both were mopping, not looking at me.

"Try Chester in the gym," someone said. I told them thanks and took off, resetting the monitors.

I gave Ellis his board and told him I was going to lie down before dinner, which I did now and then, then went to the gym. Inmates were shooting baskets under the harsh lights, and the squeaks of their shoes echoed off the walls. The noise would mask conversations, I realized. Chester was a little guy with red hair, freckles, and a friendly smile sitting on the bleachers near, but not too near, a muscular giant who watched me as I walked up.

"Hi," I said, sitting down. And, after a pause, "I used to play."

"What was your team's name?" Chester asked, not looking at me.

"The Right Minders." That was the code for psychup, assuming it hadn't changed in the past few years. The stuff was illegal, so I was lucky to be on Asgard. I don't know where I could have found any groundside.

"Ever play the Capones?" he asked. Which told me he wanted liquor in trade.

"Once." Which meant I wanted one dose. "So what's the score?"

Chester considered. "Ten to five." Which meant the

price was ten fifths of anything hard. It was outrageous, even accounting for inflation. He must have
thought I was an idiot. Then again, he may have been
right. "That's not bad," I said, closing the deal.

That was on a Thursday. Along with tons of food
and toilet paper, the Saturday afternoon shuttle
brought three special items: Chester's booze, my dose
of psychup, and Ray.

Ray looked good. Maybe he walked a little less con-
fidently, but for Ray that wasn't much. The three of
us met him on the other side of the security station
and I shook his hand, saying something sympathetic
as I looked up at his neatly combed black hair. I felt
like a man being introduced to his lover's husband
when they meet accidentally on the street. Thankfully,
Trudy put Ray and Ellis together installing the fresh
router chips we'd received, while I got to pull and
replace cable in the cafeteria.

At dinner the four of us were full of forced cheer-
fulness. Ray told funny stories about his hospital stay
although his eyes didn't smile when his mouth did. I
watched him, and he didn't look like a killer. He
looked like a guy trying to put his best face on in
spite of bad times, and I had to admire him for it.

I awoke just after three a.m. and walked down to
our locker where I'd stashed the psychup for safety.
Inside the locker I sat on the floor with my back to
the wall and looked at the stuff. It was a round wafer
a centimeter wide. I balanced it on my fingertip and
touched it gently to my right eye. It stung and fizzed
and in a few seconds dissolved. I settled back and
went onmind.

A map of Asgard's network activity showed everything normal. First, I shut down the network traffic
my brain was carrying, so I could see full-time. The
sight token would slow down, but no one was awake
to notice. Then I opened a direct line to Ray's hard-

ware, first accessing the radio transceiver that connected him to Asgard, then moving past that to the souped-up parts of his brain that talked with the ground Jacks. Beyond that was my target: the interface between his hardware and his conscious mind. Part electronic and part biological, the interface translated the chemical and electrical impulses that were Ray's thoughts into network commands. Normally it only worked in one direction. I shut down the lockouts on its datastream, giving me access to Ray's mind.

At first I found only darkness and silence, but in a few minutes the psychup effect strengthened. I could feel Ray nearby; his dreams flickering like movies on the horizon.

All right, Ray, I thought. *What happened the day of the accident?*

A fleeting glimpse of Asgard from outside, then nothing. I asked again but only got more mind noise. Certainly I'd seen this done enough times in crime dramas, but those were just shows. As I probed, I could feel the difference between myself and Ray melting. *Just remember,* I told myself. *Think back....*

Cold. Marie clutching my shoulder. "Damn you!"

No, back up. Before that.

Through Ray's eyes I saw the five of us eating breakfast. Marie sat across from me, but she looked strange. Her features were pinched, her eyes beady, and she frowned constantly. Her hands were large and chapped with bulging knuckles. I saw myself at the end of the table: shrunken and bent, as wrinkled as a hundred-year-old. Did he really think I was that decrepit?

From Ray I sensed nervousness. He was thinking of the crawlway; he'd been there early this morning when he normally jogged. Now he and Marie were walking to the winder room. Ray felt sick to his stomach but excited. In the crawlway Marie moved ahead of him, crouched low. Ray focused on a small round shadow on the coolant pipe.

I stopped the memory and looked at the shadow, inquiring. The memory came to me. It was a radio receiver he'd made at a molecular fabrication lab he'd been working at. The receiver itself was made of explosive. When the correct frequency hit it, it would detonate, vaporizing.

With growing dread I continued the flow of Ray's memories. Marie stopped at a panel on the floor. He wished she were closer to the pipe, but also he wanted to *do it*. He gave a command to his radio transceiver which dropped off line for a split second and sent out a signal pulse.

The bomb went off with a deafening bang. Marie ducked down and away, startled, but nothing else happened. She looked at Ray and he knew she read his shocked expression. "What are you—?" she started, but then the coolant burst in a streaming sheet from the pipe, slamming Marie from behind. She shrieked, propelled forward, and grabbed Ray. "What did you do?" she demanded. "Damn you! Damn you!"

Ray struggled backward, then fell. He had planned to duck back in time, but in his excitement had stayed too close to Marie. The coolant swirled around his knees and it burned. It burned like white-hot iron rods rammed up his bones. He struggled toward the entrance, wildly afraid, the spreading pool of coolant lapping at the heels of his palms. He was numb from the thighs down and an agony of pins and needles above that.

I stopped the memory and pulled away, finding myself shivering. He did it. He did it. Even though I'd suspected, faced with the evidence I was stunned. *Why?* I thought. What made him do such a thing?

In response I saw Marie sitting on a couch with her legs tucked underneath her. She had a necklace in her hands which she twisted and tugged as she spoke.

"Things haven't been the same almost since the day we were married," she said. "This will be better for both of us in the long run."

A wash of emotions from Ray: confusion, hurt, and vast fear. "Couldn't we just separate for now? With a divorce, I'll lose my visa and won't be able to work here."

"I don't want to drag things out," Marie said. "I'm sure Trudy can help you figure something out." All Ray could think about was losing his visa and having to go back to Venezuela. His home, to his mind, was utterly backward with no opportunities. He had liked Marie when they met, but he had pursued her with the passion of one who is obsessed, seeing in her his ticket to the States.

The scene changed, and I was with Ray sitting at a desk late at night. He was quite sleepy but didn't want to go to bed. He pored over his files from Immigration. Suddenly he found the clause he had been searching for and held it up to the lamp to read. Widows and widowers, it said, could still be granted permanent residency.

I was amazed. All this to stay in the country. *Is that really reason enough to kill someone?* I wondered.

Yes, answered a voice in my mind.

I recoiled, stricken. What was that?

The voice spoke again. *I was having a nightmare of cold. It woke me up.*

My God, Ray was awake. I frantically canceled my link to his hardware, then tried to get offmind so he wouldn't know who I was, but couldn't. "Log outs have been disabled," the network whispered in my ear.

"Damn!" I yelled. He had moved faster than me. Now he could simply look up who was onmind. I stood up, suddenly aware of the late hour and how alone I was. I needed to tell someone what I knew. Just then I was forced offmind. He had found me. As

I yanked open the locker door, something clicked near my hand. The bolt was extended. He'd accessed the lock routines and tried to shut me in.

My heart was beating uncomfortably fast. What was he going to do? Was he coming after me? I tried to log on again, but he'd locked out my ID. That was no problem, though, I logged on with one of our test IDs. Then I tried to phone Trudy but couldn't get a connection. He'd even taken down the phones. He must be coming for me. I stumbled out of the locker, dizzy from the psychup, then stopped and forced myself to slow down and think about this. He would probably come into the hold by the stern stairs. I could slip out to fore, run upstairs, and sound the alarm. But the forward door was locked, too. I reached for the intercom next to the door, banging my hand against the case. It was dead.

In desperation I called up an independent software agent from the library and sent it to try to break the lock routines. Then I explored the hold, moving too fast and tripping over braces and containers, trying to find a way out that Ray might have missed. He would be down here in a minute. I wondered what he planned to do. No one could ever get a weapon onboard, so he'd probably have to beat me to death. Fear rippled through me. How had I gotten myself into this? Why didn't I go tell someone my very first suspicions? But I knew why. It was because no one would have listened to an old ex-con's fantasies. Right now I sure wish I had tried. I needed to learn to trust people, that's what Darla always said. She said *I* kept people at a distance and didn't let them give me a chance. If I get out of this, Darla, I thought, I'm taking you to dinner and I'm going to listen to you.

My agent reported in: the door lock routines were password protected and could I please tell it the password? Stupid thing. I took a second to add some code blocks I wasn't supposed to know about, stuff I'd seen

Ellis playing with, and sent it back with new orders: destroy the lock routines. Once that was done, I'd rebuild them from scratch. All I needed was enough to get the damn doors open.

In the center of the hold I found a hatch outlined on the floor in yellow tape. It led, the onmind map told me, to the utility spine, below the lowest deck of the ship. Maybe that would lead to another chamber of the hold. When I asked the hatch to open, it gratifyingly slid back. Ray had missed that one. I leaned over to look inside, but suddenly my vision cut out. Ten seconds passed, fifteen, but my sight never returned. What was going on? I had expected Ray to kick me off the net completely, but instead he had switched me over to full traffic. I was completely blind now.

For the first time I truly considered that I wasn't leaving the hold alive. There was no way out except through this hatch, and I had no idea what was down there. All I remembered was a tangle of pipes, vents, and cable with no room to stand up. I'd probably kill myself grabbing a power conduit. And where was Ray? He could be sneaking up behind me right now.

I probed downward with my foot, but found only empty air. I stretched, still finding nothing, then grazed a pipe. Next I searched for a handhold. This was going too slowly. I reached behind me and found a vertical pipe to lean on, then lowered myself onto a vent that wobbled under my weight. Ducking, I told the hatch to close. There was no time to relax, though; I had to move. Had Ray seen me come down here?

The floor was dusty with patches of sticky oil. Cobwebs brushed my face, and once something scuttled out from under my palm. I was glad I couldn't see the place, really. It stank of grease and ozone. I scooted as quickly as possible, taking a few seconds to set another software agent to work on the phone system. After two minutes I bumped into a pipe and had to backtrack to find another route, breathing hard. They

say sixty-years-old feels like forty these days, thanks
to modern medicine. Don't believe it. My chest ached
and my knees ground and popped in protest of this
abuse. I was in no shape for this.

When a few minutes passed and I didn't hear anyone, I began to hope, just a little. That's when the
floor moved. There was a motorized whine and I felt
myself sliding left. Fresh air blew on my face. *What
now?* I wondered even as I realized that I must be on
top of an exterior maintenance door. And it was
opening.

Not really thinking, I crouched and jumped up,
grabbing the first thing I felt. It was a narrow pipe,
very cold. I hung there as the wind picked up around
me carrying fresh, green smells, my hands slipping on
condensation. Then I twisted, swinging my legs back
and forth, a little higher each time, until with a grunt
and a wrenching pain in my back I swung my legs up
and around the pipe, trying not to imagine the gulf
that yawned below me. Was it a cloudy night, or clear?
If I fell, I'd find out when I dropped out of the network's range and could see again.

Before I could gather enough strength to feel for a
better hold, I heard someone clambering through the
equipment and a voice spoke near my head. "Well,
here you are."

"Ray!" I shouted. "Stop this craziness. Shut the
door and let me see again!"

"No, this is better. More convenient." Where was
he? His voice came from the same direction I had
come, maybe a little to port. I tried to remember the
layout of the ship. Meanwhile I blathered.

"Ray, it's none of my business what you've done.
No one's going to believe me anyway." Assuming I
was over the first maintenance door, that would put
me right below the laundry room. The cold pipe I
clung to confirmed it. So Ray, on the edge of the door
a few feet forward of me was probably quite close to

the hot water pump. It was worth a try. I turned my face away and whispered to another agent, sending it to shut the valve to the washing machines and crank the pump into high gear.

"I'll tell you what they will believe. How you killed Marie," Ray said.

"What?"

"Come on, everyone saw you making goo-goo eyes at her. It was disgusting. So it won't be any surprise when they find your note telling about how you tried to kill me, botched it, and now you can't go on without your beloved."

"You're a son of a bitch."

"Shut up!" Something hit me suddenly in the ribs, his foot, but I hung on. The system muttered warnings at me and the pump tried to shut down, but I stripped away the safeties. Just a minute longer. "I should have known a gangsta like you would be suspicious." He kicked me again, and my leg fell off the pipe. I struggled to lift it, but he kept kicking me. "I'm going to be up all night—" *kick,* "—getting the network cleaned up—" *kick,* "—and hiding all the traces." *KICK.*

My muscles burned. Both of my legs fell off the pipe and I strained to get them back up. I wondered if I had time to hide a message on the system saying that Ray was my killer. His voice was one of unstoppable rage. "Come on, damn it, go away! I haven't got—"

"SYSTEM FAILURE!" the computers screamed in my ear. I heard a bang like gunfire and Ray shouted. I leaned sideways, my hand scrabbling on metal until I found a grip. Ray fell against my arm, knocking my hand free. I grabbed his shirt and held him suspended above the open door, trying to keep my other arm hooked over the pipe. "Quit jumping around!" I yelled. The pipe quivered and my arm felt stretched to breaking. I thought for certain my shoulder had dislocated. Ray clutched me, yelling, his head pressed against my chest like we were dear friends.

Just then my agent reported that it had gained control of the phones. I called Trudy and didn't wait for her to say hello. "Trudy close all the access hatches under the utility spine, or Ray and I are going to take a dive!"

"Mike? What's going on?"

"Do it!" I screamed. It felt like ten people were hanging on my arm. A few seconds later I heard the door slide shut. I dropped Ray and tried to climb up, slipped, and fell on top of him.

Footsteps pounded across the deck above us. We both lay there for a minute, panting. Ray was silent. He crawled out ahead of me and I emerged into the hold blinking with a sudden flash of vision. I was receiving the sight token again. I saw Trudy, Ellis, a number of guards and a thin, angry-looking man who could only be Warden Bently. "What the hell's going on?" he demanded.

"He—" I started, but Ray interrupted me.

"He killed Marie!" he cried.

For a few seconds I was too flabbergasted to speak. The sight token came and went; everyone was staring. "That's insane," I said. "My memories will show—" I stopped, again amazed. I remembered killing Marie. I remembered making the bomb, gluing it to the pipe, and detonating it.

"He wanted to get me, but it didn't work," Ray said. "Now tonight he attacked me through the network, trying to disrupt my mind and turn me into a vegetable. He's a psychopath. He never should have been released."

I shook my head, trying to sort out the double impressions. Ray hated Marie. I made the bomb. Ray planted it. I detonated it. None of it made sense.

"I think he used psychup to break through my mindwall," Ray was saying.

"No!" I yelled. "He changed my memories. We're still connected. He planted his own in my mind just now. That's it—he's setting me up!"

"Both of you turn it down," Warden Bently said. I saw him turn to Trudy. "What's happening with the computers?"

"I'm not sure. A lot of the network routines are trashed. Wait . . . yeah, there's a link between them."

"Close it. Now you, did you take psychup?" I guessed he was talking to me.

"Yes, but—"

"And you used it to connect to him?"

"Yes, but it's because *he* murdered Marie, but I had to get proof." For an instant I saw Ellis and a guard helping Ray stand. Bently scowled and turned to one of his captains.

"Tell the pilot to hold this position until the regional police can get here to take him in."

He meant me. He was going to have me arrested. "What about Ray?" I said. "Aren't you going to arrest him, too?"

Bently snorted. "They don't generally take in the victims."

Once I was in custody, the police would interrogate me, find Ray's memories and that would be that. Sure there would be holes in the case, but those memories were enough to put me back on Laputa forever. That meant no more job, no more freedom, and seeing the sky once a year if I was lucky. I felt my whole life slipping away from me. Everything I lived for, gone.

"No," I said. "This is a mistake." No one was listening to me anymore. "Trudy, tell them this is crazy. I'm not a killer. Please." She looked away, embarrassed. It was like I had turned to smoke, becoming nothingness.

Then I bolted. No one had a hold of me, and I suppose they thought, on a prison ship, where could an old guy go? Not far. Only as far as our storage locker. I raced in with a guard reaching for my collar, slammed the gate on her arm saying *"Sorry!"* and stuck a prybar through the handle, wedging the gate shut. A wall of angry faces crammed in around the cage. Bently shook the gate and yelled "You open this up right now! Don't make me have you stunned." They poked their fingers through to get at the prybar, but I whipped the gate with a length of cable.

"You've just got to listen," I said. "I deserve a chance." I grabbed the box with Marie's shoe in it off the shelf and dumped it out. Then I went onmind—no one had thought to lock me out yet—and told the network to dial all ID's onboard simultaneously. Everyone jumped when their phones rang, and they all said, "Answer" together.

"Pay attention," I said, and touched Marie's shoe.

The vision was just as strong as the first time. I was Marie, clutching Ray's shoulder as the agonizing spray of coolant knocked me forward. "What did you do?" I/she cried. "Damn you!" It faded. I found I was gripping the shoe so hard my fingers had cramped. Everyone was silent, some with their eyes still shut. Was it enough? Had they felt her anger and suspicion?

I unblocked the door and allowed myself to be shackled and led to a cell. No one spoke to me. Breakfast came. I paced the cell, thinking. I'd risked my future for Marie's sake, maybe lost it. It would have been worth it if Ray had been caught, but I'd screwed up the whole job and felt like a supreme idiot.

Soon a sheriff came to my cell, young and clean cut. He shook my hand through the bars. "Your boss, Ms. Angeline, played me a recording of what you showed everyone this morning. Based on that we've arrested Raymond Duque. But I still have to take you in as well. We've got some good attorneys in my county, though, and I'm sure we can get this cleared up. In fact, Mr. Duque looks pretty jumpy. My guess is he'll talk soon, and if he does, you could be released in a day or two.''

Relief washed through me, and I wished, somehow, that Marie was there to share my victory. Maybe she knew what I had done. *Go in peace,* I thought.

Then, smiling like a fool, I asked the sheriff if I could make a call. I had to tell Darla. She wasn't in, but she'd left me a message saying she'd made dinner reservations for three days from now, and that I was buying.

WEB-SURFING PAST LIVES
by Jane Lindskold

Jane Lindskold resides in Albuquerque, New Mexico with six cats, all named after figures in British mythology. To support them (and her four guinea pigs and four fish) she writes full time. Her published works include the novels *Brother to Dragons, Companion to Owls, Marks of Our Brothers, The Pipes of Orpheus,* and *Smoke and Mirrors.* Her short fiction has appeared in a variety of collections, including *Heaven Sent, Return to Avalon,* and *Wheel of Fortune.* Currently, she is under contract to complete the two novels left unfinished by Roger Zelazny, as well as several novels of her own.

Ambrose Valerian Moore was at his club dining on lamb chops with baby green peas and wild rice when he realized with absolute certainty that the world was going to end in six days.

He had seen the prophet of doom before, a scruffy fellow, bent of form, vacant of eye, dominated by a wild mane of unruly gray hair. The beggar looked too weak to lift the sign he held so firmly in one gnarled hand, but lift it he could—lift it and flourish it as he did this very moment—pivoting with slow deliberation so that the printed words were neatly framed in the window out from which Ambrose gazed.

"The World Will End in 6 Days."

The numeral 6 was written on a less filthy spot on the largely grubby board. Apparently, the beggar began his day by whitewashing out the previous day's number and replacing it with the next one in declining sequence. Ambrose had seen 7, 8, 9, and—he thought—10 appear and vanish from the signboard. There might have been more, but he was not in the habit of noticing those outside of his set. Only this chap's persistence had brought him into Ambrose's sphere of regard.

At first, he had observed the sign with idle curiosity, later with amusement, and finally today, as his peas rolled about and his chops adhered themselves to his plate in a layer of congealing grease, Ambrose knew with alarmed certainty that the beggar was right and that the world would end in six short days.

Looking away from the disturbing message outside the window, Ambrose signaled for the waiter, requested that he clear away the largely untasted meal, and ordered a small snifter of cognac and a serving of fresh raspberries and heavy cream. When he felt sufficiently fortified to look at the sign again, the beggar had moved on.

Ambrose frowned. He had held some vague intention of having the waiter speak to the chap and ask him the source of his revelation. Ah, well, he suspected there would be another occasion. The beggar had been making his rounds with the fidelity of a bill collector.

Sipping his cognac, Ambrose Valerian Moore contemplated the regrettable necessity that if the world was going to end, he probably should return to basics. He had enjoyed being Ambrose Valerian Moore, slim of frame, dapper of attire, his sandy brown hair dashed back from his forehead with a hint of rakishness that the ladies found enticing and the gentlemen thought marked him as a Good Fellow. He particularly enjoyed his short, bristling new mustache, but that would have to go along with his pleasant flat in Wodehousian England, his valet, his chums, and his membership at the Idler's Club.

Yes, sadly, when the world was going to end in six short days one should really return to one's base self and face the end as the man one was born. He rolled a raspberry between tongue and soft palate, savoring both the flavor and the sensation as the pulp separated from the seeds. He wondered how many others among the gaily chattering chaps at the surrounding tables concealed similar melancholy reflections. Not all of them, of course, some would stay within the Web even through the end of the world, others were merely virtual creations and could not leave, but some, even in this frivolous Site—some would, like Ambrose himself, return to reality for the end.

He admired their cavalier charm a few moments longer, savored the irreverent spirit as a balm against the painful reality he must soon face, and kissed the raspberry tang with a final bite of cognac.

Then he rose and prepared for recall. It was a simple enough thing. One summoned a mental image of one's base identity and recited the password one had assigned to trigger the recall sequence. The rest was automatic. A persona program would take over his usual routine—although without his distinctive flare—so that the illusion would not be broken, a pitiful, valiant gesture on the part of the computer Net at this point, since the world was doomed.

Ambrose Valerian Moore concentrated. Ambrose Valerian Moore frowned. Ambrose Valerian Moore sank back into his chair, his fair skin suffused with a ruddy flush of embarrassment. Not only couldn't he recall his password—he could not for the life of him recall his base identity.

"For the life of him"—that was rather droll. He chuckled dryly despite himself. The world would end in six short days, and if he could not remember his base identity, he would die as a phantasm rather than as a person.

A horror grew in him, a horror so strong that it fed

the new conviction that rose from the depths of his subconscious mind. The world need not end in six days—he—the man who was now Ambrose Valerian Moore—could prevent the ending of the world, but only if he could recall his base self.

He fled the dining room of his club in such haste that the other diners ceased their chatter and repartee for a moment to wonder what social catastrophe could so devastate a Good Fellow like Ambrose Valerian Moore.

"Probably something of the female persuasion," said Adam "Sappy" Chuffhurst to the fellows at his table. They all laughed and returned to twitting one of their number about the terrible showing he had made in yesterday's snooker tournament.

Contrary to what one might expect from a Wodehousian gentleman, Ambrose did not hurry off to consult with his valet. Sadly, the demand for clever men servants in this milieu was so high that most young gentlemen had to make do with the craftings of a skilled persona program. Since Ambrose had designed his Wodehousian self to be a bit less of a twit than the original Bertie, he had felt safe cutting corners on his Jeeves.

His programmed Reeves was quite capable of selecting attire, chiding Ambrose for his madcap schemes, and setting a good table, but he lacked initiative and creativity, both of which Ambrose needed rather desperately at this juncture. Therefore, he fled to the companionship of his greatest indiscretion—the one thing that might drive him out of the legions of Good fellows and into those of the Bit of a Cads had the members of the Idler's Club but known of her—the beautiful, sensuous French actress, Ami Valerie d'Amour.

She resided in the Roaring Twenties Site, French District, and had come into Ambrose's life following

a jaunt with some of the chaps to see a performance
in which she played the role of the ingenue. Ambrose
had been drawn to her by some force far more compelling than their coincidence of initials. Flowers and
candy had progressed to jewelry and poems and this
to a full-blown liaison.

Ambrose did not pretend to be immune to Ami Valerie's copious physical charms—to the swell of her white
breasts or to the sway of her hips when she walked
across the room. Often he had lost himself in the tangled forest of her midnight black hair or the depths
of her melting violet eyes. However, he admitted even
to her that what drew him across the Channel time
and again was a sense of communion, as if in her he
had found a missing part of himself.

After he had sent his card in to her, he restlessly
paced the foyer of her house, knowing that if he was
told she was not in, he would wait until her return,
that he would batter down her door, storm the stage
where she performed. . . .

"Mademoiselle will see you," said the lace-skirted
French maid, the faintest sense of a giggle beneath
her words. Ambrose ignored her and hurried into Ami
Valerie's boudoir.

"Cher," Ami Valerie murmured as he entered, raising a languorous hand for him to kiss. "It has been—
how do you say it?—an internity?"

" 'Eternity,' my black rose," Ambrose corrected
heartily, applying lips to her slender fingers.

He seated himself beside her on the red velvet
fainting couch, heard the maid discreetly close the
chamber door behind them. Beggars and prophecies
of doom nearly vanished in the promise of Ami's
cupid bow lips. He leaned to kiss her and leaped back
as with a solid thud Ami's beloved snow white Persian
cat jumped possessively between then.

Ambrose heartily disliked the creature—never more
so than at moments like this—but he managed what

he thought was a cordial enough pat and was rewarded with a narrowing of the creature's sapphire blue eyes and a decisive hiss.

"I say!" he said. "Nice moggy. Good puss-puss."

The Persian hissed again.

Ami Valerie laughed throatily. "Ah, my poor Ambrose, little Snowpuff is jealous of him."

She cuddled the unprotesting cat to her bosom and batted her eyelashes at him, certain of being admired. Normally, Ambrose would have easily fallen into her game, but today the beggar's warning and his own fearful certainty that he alone could stop the promised doom rose to break the mood.

He smiled at her, hoping this would be enough.

"Tell me, cherie," he said, "when we first started— uh—keeping company, did I ever tell you anything about myself?"

"Oh, much," she said, stroking the cat. "You told me about your racing car and your flat in town and your demanding Aunt Agnes and your clever . . ."

"Right," Ambrose interrupted when she paused for breath. "That's all about myself *here*. I meant about my base self—my non-Web persona."

Ami Valerie pouted prettily. He couldn't blame her, intruding on the virtual illusion was really Bad Form, but still, he had to know.

"No," she said gently, perhaps sensing something of his desperation, "you told me nothing. I am so sorry, Ambrose."

"Bother!" he said, rising and stuffing his hands into his pockets then beginning to pace the length of her boudoir. "Bother!"

"What is wrong, my sugar lump?" Ami said, setting down the cat and hurrying to his side, her concern quite real.

"Oh, it's just that I have fetched up against a rather inconvenient gap in my memory," he explained. "It's rather a matter of life and death, you know."

With a thoughtful pout, Ami Valerie drew him to a side table, poured him a drink, and then one for herself. Pressing him into a chair, she sat on his knee.

"A matter of life and death?" she asked. "More serious than the time that you promised to escort your Aunt Agnes to the theater on the same night as the Idler's Club card tournament?"

"More serious," he assured her. "End of the world and all that. I need to pop out of the Web for a bit, but I can't recall the whatsis . . ."

"The password?" she offered.

"That thingy," he agreed. "My memory is shot. I thought I might have told you something that would help."

She shook her head sadly. "Perhaps you jarred your memory when you were hit in the noggin playing cricket with Useless Smithers. You should see a doctor—a nerve specialist or a doctor of the mind."

Excited by her own insight, she leaped from his lap and pulled a case of calling cards from her secretary. She rifled through these until she came upon one that she handed to him.

"A. Valor Lieber, M.D." Ambrose read.

"He is a good doctor," Ami assured him. "I shall send around to him a note and explain to him that you are a good friend of mine. Surely he will see you."

A desperate need to do something won over Ambrose's feeling that seeing a nervous specialist was not quite The Thing.

"That would be ripping!" he said. "Thank you, Ami."

As events developed, Dr. Lieber couldn't see Ambrose until the next day, but now that the plan was set, Ambrose didn't mind a whit. Ami Valerie was the type of woman who could not only make a man forget that the world would end in six short days, but also make him wonder just how many hours of those six days could be spent in bed (and elsewhere) doing fascinating things of an unabashedly carnal nature with her. Indeed, he might have chucked the appointment completely, but Ami Valerie had an eleven o'clock audition for a role she was all excited about and rose to attend to her toilette indecently early.

Ambrose had no choice but to rise, eventually get out of bed, dress in his clothes from the day before (Reeves would be horrified), and head out for his appointment.

Dr. Lieber, he discovered as he checked the address that Ami Valerie had given him, resided in an adjoining Site—the Eminently Victorian. Accordingly, at the border, Ambrose changed into a morning coat and top hat, hailed a hansom cab, and gave the cheeky Cockney driver the address. As the cab rambled across the cobbles, he gave himself to a brown study (really more of a pink-and-white study as it largely concerned Ami Valerie) and the ride ended all too quickly.

When the cabby opened the door, Ambrose stepped lightly to the pavement, gave a jaunty twirl of his cane, and paid the fare—including a generous enough tip that the cabby tugged his forelock and muttered "Bless'ee, lad." Then he trotted up the wide flagstone steps and pulled the bell cord next to the polished brass sign engraved with the same legend as the business card that still resided in his vest pocket.

A butler answered the door, took his card on a silver salver, admitted Ambrose into a waiting room furnished with solid antiques doubtless meant to assure the anxious patient of the doctor's sanity, and departed, presumably to carry word of Ambrose's arrival. Ambrose made himself comfortable with a copy of *The Strand*—for although he was now the only one in the room he did not wish to be forced into conversation if one of the doctor's less stable patients was to make an advent.

He heard someone being shown out just as he was finishing an article on fashions for the year, and a few minutes later he was directed into Dr. Lieber's consulting room.

Dr. A. Valor Lieber was a stocky man, somehow Germanic in his lines—perhaps it was the cut of his neat brown beard or the way his eyebrows bristled over his piercing blue eyes that contributed to the impression. He smiled with cordial professionalism, sketched a brief bow, and directed Ambrose to a comfortable couch.

After the activities of the previous night, Ambrose was not certain that reclining on a comfortable sofa in a dimly lit room (for the doctor was lowering the gas) was conducive to thought—much less consciousness—but he did as directed.

"Now, my good man," Dr. Lieber said (his accent was slightly German, so that "good" sounded rather like "gutt" and Ambrose concealed a grin), "your friend says that you are having a problem with your memory."

"Right." That didn't sound decisive enough, so Ambrose tried again. "Uh, righty-oh, old chap. The blamed noggin just isn't holding the beans."

He faded off into silence and stared hopefully at the psychiatrist. Dr. Lieber was pulling on his lower lip, frowning thoughtfully.

"Tell me about your mother ..." he said.

Ambrose complied, answering questions about his mother (gone to her reward), his father (a bit of a bounder), his various aunts, great-aunts, cousins, and friends. He talked exhaustively for over an hour, but there was just one problem—all of his answers were about Ambrose Valerian Moore—in the great flood of words there was not a single indication, hint, or nubbin about the base personality that *had* to underlie the rest.

"Come back tomorrow," Dr. Lieber said at last. "I will give you some reading material that may make you more receptive to analysis."

Ambrose had to agree—arguing would be Bad Form. The head shrinker had been quite on the up and up with him, seen him at short notice and all. He could hardly insist on more of his time.

It was as he struggled down the doctor's stairs, his arms burdened with numerous pamphlets and several heavy books, that he saw the beggar again. The man was dressed quite appropriately for the Eminently Victorian Site (though beggar's fashions certainly did not change greatly in a few decades). His hair was as unruly as ever and the bottom of his jacket looked rather as if something had taken a great bit out of the fabric.

His sign had also been altered: "The world will end in 6 5 days." The strike-out and the neatly printed 5 made the entire thing all the more pressing.

Ambrose glanced at the clock tower. Five days left. Nearly four, really, for the hour was striking tea time. He whistled for a hansom cab to take him to the Idler's Club (fortunately, due to popular demand, it had a branch in this Site). When he glanced around after the beggar, he was gone.

The next day Dr. Lieber freed up his entire afternoon to deal with Ambrose's problem. Therefore, after a hearty lunch and a couple of hands of cards at the Club, Ambrose hailed a cab and directed it to take him 'round to the doctor's consulting rooms. He felt vaguely guilty that he hadn't tried harder to read the books that now rested in a satchel next to him on the cab's seat, but he just hadn't been able to manage them.

For the first block or so of the ride, he felt rather in a funk, then he cheered up. Gloom simply didn't sit well with him and the doctor chappie would find out what was wrong, help him access his base persona, and then Ambrose could sail off and save the world in time for the house party weekend-after-next at Lady

Ditherington's estate. Mabel was certain to be there, and she was a ripping girl, quite a hand with a tennis racket and what she did to evening clothes. . . .

Ambrose happily let his thoughts drift, coming out of a rather complicated reverie involving Mabel and a boat on the lake only when the cab pulled up in front of Dr. Lieber's office and the driver demanded his fare.

The butler escorted him into the doctor's consulting room.

"Gutt afternoon, Ambrose," the psychiatrist said, motioning him to a couch. "May I offer you tea?"

"You may," Ambrose snorted with laughter. "Of course, I may not take it!"

Dr. Lieber blinked blankly and Ambrose stifled his guffaws as he stretched out on the sofa. Might as well 'fess up, otherwise he'd be dreading a quiz.

"I say, Doctor, I really couldn't make heads or tails out of those bally books you loaned me, really a bit much for me, I say."

"You did not read the material that I loaned you?" the doctor said.

"That's it," Ambrose agreed. "A bit tough given what I've been worrying over."

The psychiatrist made a note on the pad he held, poured himself a cup of tea (he did not offer Ambrose one), and took a seat in a chair that put him just out of Ambrose's line of sight. Ambrose promptly craned around so that he could see the doctor and was rewarded with the knowledge that a black wool knee was about two feet behind his head, just off to the left.

"Rest quietly, Mr. Moore," Dr. Lieber said sternly. "Relax and concentrate on giving me clear answers to my questions."

"Righty-oh," Ambrose agreed, settling back. "Are we going to talk about Mater and Pater again?"

Dr. Lieber sighed.

The questioning skimmed over much of the same

ground as the day before, with Dr. Lieber constantly steering Ambrose away from such fascinating details as why his cousin Martin was known as "Figgy Puddin' " or the escapade in the lighthouse when he was twelve. He asked several questions about Ami Valerie and Ambrose could hear his pen scratching vigorously as he noted down the answers.

Dr. Lieber abandoned this course of action after about an hour. Letting Ambrose rise and stretch his legs, he moved his chair until he could face his patient. Then he took his watchchain from his vest pocket and began to swing the glittering fob in a slow arc.

"Have you ever been hypnotized, Ambrose?" he asked.

"Nope," Ambrose said cheerfully. "I was at a party where some girl hypnotized Irish Barker and made him run in circles and cluck like a chicken. Doubt it would work on me, though, so I never tried it."

"You doubt that it would work on you?" Dr. Lieber asked, still swinging the chain.

"That's right," Ambrose said. "I've heard that it will only work on the weak-willed. I'm not that kind of chap."

"Uh, quite," said Dr. Lieber, blinking behind his spectacles. "Then, since you know it will not work, you do not object to my attempting to hypnotize you?"

Ambrose frowned slightly, certain that he had just been twitted. "No, I don't mind. Give it a shot, old boy, just no chickens."

"Certainly, no chickens," the psychiatrist said. "I have quite enough to deal with a silly goose."

"What?"

"Quite," Dr. Lieber said, his voice a lulling monotone. "Now, concentrate on the swinging of my watch fob. Relax. You are growing sleepy, sleepy, sleepy. You are asleep!"

"If you say so, old chap," Ambrose agreed. "I say! I didn't know that I talked in my sleep."

Dr. Lieber leaned forward in his chair and shone a light in Ambrose's eyes, then pinched the back of his hand.

"Hey!"

"You are not asleep!" Dr. Lieber said in astonishment.

"I thought you said that I was?" Ambrose said.

"I thought that you were," Dr. Lieber answered.

"Fancy that," Ambrose yawned. "I didn't know that a chap could sleep with his eyes open."

"Perhaps we should resume a more conventional method of analysis," Dr. Lieber sighed. "Tell me a bit more about your relationship with Ami Valerie d'Amour."

Later, Ambrose insisted on getting up to have a smoke and stretch his legs.

"I say!" he exclaimed, glancing out the front window. "There's that beggar again and he's got the sign changed—'4 days' it says, clear as life. He'll be running out of space soon, but then he doesn't need much more, almost out of days!"

Dr. Lieber frowned but came and looked out the window.

"What beggar?" he asked.

"That one," Ambrose said, pointing with his cigarette tip. "The one right outside your railing."

Dr. Lieber's frown deepened. "And what does his sign say?"

" 'The World Will End in 4 Days,' " Ambrose read aloud with exaggerated patience. "He's been preaching the same thing for days now, except that the number keeps getting lower. That's what set me off to find my base persona, you know. I need to save the world."

Eyebrows rising to vanish into his hairline stated with wordless eloquence what Dr. Lieber thought of Ambrose as a savior of the world. Ambrose was trying to think of a rejoinder when he noticed that the doctor was happily rubbing his hands together.

"Now we are getting somewhere," he said. "Why did you not mention this beggar and his sign before?"

"I say, now, you didn't ask, did you?" Ambrose responded amiably. "You just asked about my parents and whether I had ever seen my mother in her underclothes and if Ami reminded me of her and things like that."

The psychiatrist actually blushed. "Well, yes. Now, tell me. For how long have you been having these delusions that you are destined to save the world from imminent destruction?"

Taking a final drag on his cigarette and rubbing out the butt, Ambrose told Lieber about how he had seen the beggar a couple of days ago and how he had experienced the revelation that the beggar's sign bore not only a warning, but a message.

"A message to you?" Dr. Lieber asked.

"That's right," Ambrose agreed.

"To you specifically?"

"That's what I said."

"Then you wouldn't be at all upset if I told you that to me the beggar's sign is so dim as to be nearly impossible to read and that the beggar himself seems poorly programmed to manifest at this Site."

Ambrose frowned. "You're saying that I'm the only one who can see him?"

"No," Dr. Lieber said, "but I am saying that his message may indeed be specifically for you—a courier program set to locate you."

Ambrose brushed his mustache with his right index finger. "A message for me, eh? I'd better go speak with him, find out the rest of what he has to say."

"Yes, go," Dr. Lieber urged him. "I cannot suggest a better course of action."

Jamming on his hat and stuffing his arms into his coat, Ambrose hurried outside. The foot traffic was fairly heavy, but he managed to make his way to the beggar and grasp him by the sleeve. The ragged man turned and looked up at him with large grey eyes that were utterly devoid of intelligence.

"I say, my good man ..." Ambrose began, oddly disconcerted to see no response at all to his approach.

The beggar's expression did not change but, wrenching his sleeve from Ambrose's grasp, he hefted his sign. interposing it between Ambrose's face and his own.

For an instant, the world became entirely one enormous number 4. Then someone in the passing foot traffic jostled him. Ambrose grabbed at the wrought iron of the psychiatrist's area railing for support. When he regained his footing, the beggar had once again vanished.

Ambrose spent an hour or so looking before returning to his room at the club. A message from Dr. Lieber was waiting for him:

"I do not believe that I can be of further help to you. If you cannot locate the beggar and get a more detailed explanation of his message then I suggest that you visit my colleague, Analiese V. Luv at the following address. She is a specialist in past-life regressions and may be able to get to the root of your programming. Good luck."

Frowning, Ambrose put in a call to the number Dr. Lieber had given him. The message unit came alive with the sound of waves crashing and seagulls crying. Then a sweet but strong female voice said: "I am drifting on the tides of being. Leave your message, and I'll be back to you on the nearest cosmic tide."

Ambrose blinked, but obediently left his name and the address of his club along with a request for an appointment to consult with Analiese at the soonest possible time. Then he went down to the dining room and dined on roast beef, potatoes, and pudding, warming himself from the anxious chill at the core of his being at the fire of good fellowship.

When one of the servants brought him a message that his appointment with Analiese was not until the next day at eleven o'clock, he was relieved. He'd been going rather heavy on the excellent stout—his head should have had a chance to clear by that hour.

The next day, he took the cab to the Site transference point and outfitted himself for his venture into the Santa Fe/Sedona Site where Analiese V. Luv had her offices. Santa Fe/Sedona, rather than being modeled after a historical or literary period like his Wodehousian or Lieber's Eminently Victorian Sites, was modeled after a state of mind—in this case the mystically inclined, laid-back, but still power-conscious New Age. Many of those who frequented the Site were refugees from the Sixties but found the sex and drugs a little more intensely involving than they cared to experience. They preferred to be close to the power centers of the universe without actually getting quite so involved.

His Wodehousian togs would not be a problem— Santa Fe/Sedona was tolerant of alternate lifestyles— but he needed a chipping on the jargon and social codes. When this had been fit, he bought a ticket on the nonpolluting, environmentally conscious shuttle that would translate him to his destination.

Disembarking the shuttle, he caught sight of the beggar once again—or rather of the beggar's sign. It jutted out over the crowd of disembarking passengers, its dire warning no less urgent for all that only he appeared to notice it.

"The world will end in 3 days."

This time the message was in bright new paints and surrounded by drifting objects that at first Ambrose took for balloons but quickly decided were mushroom clouds—an image that jarred with his carefully con-structed Wodehousian view that a catastrophe in-volved social errors like wearing the wrong jacket to a summer house-party, not something that annihilated the world.

As the crowd thinned, he saw that the beggar was now clad in a torn flannel shirt and worn blue jeans. His hair and beard were as long and untidy as before, but he had tied a bright red bandanna around his forehead; a thin line of blood leaked out from under the fabric.

He did not appear to notice Ambrose hurrying over to him, but when the Wodehousian gentleman had maneuvered his way around a fat man with a basket of cut flowers and a woman with two small children, the beggar had vanished.

Ambrose did not waste time asking after him. His experience in the Eminently Victorian Site the day before had prepared him for an unsuccessful search. Instead, he turned his steps to the address Dr. Lieber had given to him the day before.

Analiese V. Luv's offices were located in a square-built, soft-cornered adobe brick compound stuccoed a muted tan that blended in with the surrounding desert landscape. Doorways and window frames were painted a startling lavender, and high-relief lizards sculpted from acid-treated sheet metal stalked across the tan surface.

"Far out," he mused, trying out his new chip. "I say!"

Hitching his jacket straight, he strode across the weathered wooden porch and tapped at the door. It swung open, apparently of its own accord, admitting him into a cool, shadowy hallway—its muted tiles adorned by a scattering of handwoven Indian rugs in a variety of geometric patterns.

The sound of crashing surf and crying seagulls di-rected him to the open door of Analiese V. Luv's office. He stood there for a moment, astonished by the decor.

The room was oval-shaped with kiva fireplaces at opposite ends, both burning despite the heat of the day. It was decorated entirely in pillows, incense burners, statues of various vaguely Eastern deities, heaps of rugs, and swaths of curtains. The effect was rather like being confronted with the view through a soft-sculptured kaleidoscope.

Ambrose thought that the room was empty until one of the heaps of pillows moved, twisted, and up-ended, revealing the tousled but surprisingly pretty features of a young woman who had been sitting in what he would have sworn was an impossible position.

"Ambrose Valerian Moore?" she said, rising to her feet with the grace of a snake uncoiling and offering her hand.

He bowed stiffly. "That's me. I suppose you are Analiese V. Luv?"

She spun in a swirl of patchwork velvet skirts (these came to just below her knees, but her matching top came only to just beneath her breasts) and tossed her hair (this was dyed deep purple, a fetching shade Ambrose was certain, for those who were into such things). When she spun to a stop, Ambrose could see that not only were both of her ears pierced (the right at least a dozen times), but so was her left eyebrow, her navel, and her septum. She was also liberally tattooed, mostly with Chinese dragons, though he spotted a tiger and a brace of long-tailed pheasants coiled around one calf.

"I am Analiese and I hope dearly to help you find your base self. I feel a kinship with you, Ambrose, just as I feel a kinship with dear Dr. Lieber (stuffy as he can be). Blessed be!"

"Righty-oh," Ambrose said. "How.... I mean.... Bother! You have me in quite an uproar! What should I do?"

"Do as you wilt," Analiese said, winking provocatively at him and giggling at his blush. "This is Freedom Hall."

"Quite," Ambrose said, sitting stiffly on the nearest cushion and feeling far more uptight than a good Wodehousian chap ever should. "I need to find my base persona so that I can return from the Net and save the world."

"In three short days," Analiese said, sinking down onto a cushion nearby and lighting some incense. "I have been told. Have you seen the beggar again?"

"Right when I got off of the train," Ambrose answered. "I hustled over to him but he got away before I could talk with him. You'd think that if he had a message for me, he'd stay long enough to deliver it."

Analiese pulled her lip, a gesture that rather reminded Ambrose of Dr. Lieber. "There may be forces at work here that you do not completely understand, sweet Ambrose. Very well, then, if we cannot speak with the beggar, we shall have to do with what we can do. . . . How do you feel about cards?"

"Jolly good," Ambrose said. "Won quite a bit last night at the Club, you know."

"Good," Analiese said, pulling out a large, brightly painted deck. "I like them, too. Something we're both comfortable with will make a good starting focus."

Ambrose watched as she set the cards out in a complex pattern that took only a small portion of the deck—a deck that he quickly ascertained contained more than the usual fifty-two cards. Helpfully, he reached to set an upside-down card rightside-up and was smartly slapped on the wrist for his trouble.

"I say!" he said indignantly. "I was just trying to give you a bit of help."

Analiese softened slightly. "The position of the cards is part of their significance, as is whether they were dealt out rightside-up or upside-down."

"Well, it looks right balmy to have the king standing

on his head," Ambrose said sulkily. "You've too many cards, you know, and the suits are all wrong."

"Or all right," Analiese answered, not looking up from the pattern, "depending on your point of view."

She laid out the cards for him several times, each reading meant to reveal something about his life outside of the Net, but each time the cards came out in a pattern that, from her gentle swearing, he deduced was purest nonsense.

Analiese frowned. "I expected some difficulties to arise, but I can always do a reading. There's only one person—other than myself—I cannot read for."

"Who?"

"Dr. Lieber," she said, squaring the cards. "I tried after an unusually heated argument on occult sciences versus psychiatry and found that the cards would not cooperate. Now you. . . ."

Her frown deepened. She tapped along her jawline with the fingers of her right hand. Fascinated, Ambrose noticed that each short, rounded nail was tipped with a decal depicting a phase of the moon. Gradually, the tapping slowed and she started dealing out the cards again.

"No, just hold on while I set these up," she said when Ambrose tried to speak with her. "I have an impulse. I must follow it."

She set the entire deck out into a vast, complicated pattern that occupied the whole of the bare space of the floor in front of her. This completed, she studied the cards, muttering odd words to herself for long enough that Ambrose found himself growing drowsy.

She paused in her meditations only to toss more incense into her burners. Occasionally, she remembered her role as hostess enough to offer Ambrose a cup of tea or a sweet. Most of the time, he simply waited, letting his sleepy gaze wander over the confusion of colors in her office and trying very hard not to fall asleep.

When Analiese finally looked up, her eyes glowed a vibrant turquoise—an effect Ambrose found quite startling, even as he admired it. Her hair shifted around her head and shoulders as if stirred by an unearthly wind. Her voice, when she spoke, echoed as from a far distance.

"I charge you to answer me three questions," she said, the echoes counterpointed with the ringing of crystal bells. "And you shall not prevaricate or evade."

Ambrose opened his mouth, but no sound came forth. Suspecting that he looked rather like a great clam, he shut it and waited for Analiese to ask her questions.

"Why can I not read for you?" Analiese demanded.

To his astonishment, Ambrose heard himself say, "You cannot read for yourself."

Analiese received this knowledge with pursed lips and a curt nod of her head.

"Name the name you are called outside of the realms of the Net," she said, "the name that does not apply to any of the personas you have established within the Net."

Ambrose felt a flash of terrible heat behind his eyes. His breathing constricted and he clawed at his throat in an effort to release the pressure.

Analiese pulled his hands from his throat. "I release you from this question."

Immediately, the pressure vanished. The pain behind his eyes took a moment more to diminish but then it, too, was gone, its absence like a hole behind his eyes. Analiese tugged at her lower lip.

"I should have known that would be too simple," she said ruefully. "Tell me why you adopted a Wodehousian persona?"

"Who would look for me there?" he answered simply.

She nodded agreement and Ambrose felt vaguely

indignant. Apparently both Analiese and whoever was answering her questions held his chosen Site in something like scorn.

"What card would you choose for your signifier?" she asked.

Ambrose didn't even know what a signifier was, but obviously whatever was answering Analiese's questions was more knowledgeable than he was. Again, he felt his mouth shape words without his own volition.

"The Fool," he said. Then his head spun and he toppled forward to collapse in the middle of the elaborate array of cards. His last sight was Analiese's thoughtful expression.

When he came to, he was reclining on a comfortable futon to one side of a fountain in the central courtyard of Analiese's compound. Voices were speaking softly and when he groaned and shifted position he heard Analiese say:

"Ambrose is coming around."

"None too soon," said a male voice. Dr. Lieber?

He pushed himself to a sitting position, wishing desperately that Reeves was there to offer him one of his patented hangover possets. He opened gluey eyes to find Analiese hovering at his side, a sturdy mug containing something steamy and mint-smelling in one hand. Dr. Lieber was indeed present, sitting with Germanic uprightness on an embroidered pillow.

"Peppermint tea," Analiese said, pressing the mug into Ambrose's hand, "with lots of honey. It will set you right in no time. I'm sorry about doping you earlier, but I was getting nowhere with the cards and I knew from Val that you couldn't be hypnotized."

"Val?" he managed, sipping the tea and feeling his head begin to clear instantly.

"Dr. Lieber," she clarified. "He prefers to go by 'Valor' which I find presumptuous. I do my best to take him down a notch."

Idly wondering how anyone with purple hair, tattoos, and eyes that (at least some of the time) glowed turquoise could find anyone else presumptuous, Ambrose finished the peppermint tea and mutely accepted a refill. When he had finished that and a handful of really good lemon crisp cookies, he was ready for conversation.

"Doped me, did you?" he said, leaning against the fountain basin and wishing that she would offer him a cigarette.

Analiese nodded. "That's right. The last bit with the cards was a distraction. What I was really using was the herbal tea and the incense. They put you into a state of mind so that I could do a control spell and command you to answer a few questions."

"An information program, certainly," the psychiatrist said, "no matter what you call it."

Analiese rolled her eyes which, Ambrose noted, had become a more prosaic blue. "This is not the time to resume that old argument, Val. We need to fill Ambrose in on our conjectures."

"Do, old chap," Ambrose begged. "I'm more confused than I was before."

Dr. Lieber rubbed his hands together briskly. "Very well, Ambrose, I am certain that you will find most interesting that Analiese and I have come to the same conclusion. You do not have a base persona outside of the Net. Effectively, you are naught but an elaborate program."

"Then I don't have to save the world?" Ambrose said, vastly relieved—so vastly relieved that the announcement that he was naught but a program could not trouble him. His relief was cruelly dashed by Analiese's next words.

"Oh, no," Analiese replied. "You do. Our world, at least. That's why I'm so pleased to have finally met you. Val and I suspected your existence, you see, but we had no idea where to find you."

"I say! Suspected my existence?" Ambrose said. "Only a program? Are you having an elaborate cod at my expense?"

"No, no cod, no joke, trick or anything of the like," Analiese assured him. "Surely you had noticed some of the oddities that have occurred since you acknowledged the beggar's message and decided that it was meant for you."

"What are you talking about?" Ambrose said, but he thought he knew what she was talking about. Certainly it was more than a little odd that both of the professionals whose help he had sought in his quest to regain his memory had initials so similar to his own—and Ami Valerie did as well, now that he thought about it.

"Listen, and we will tell you what is going on," Dr. Lieber interjected, "but you will need to listen. The world will most sincerely be at an end in three days."

"Closer to two," Analiese said, glancing up into the darkening sky.

"And we do not know how long you will need to do what you must do in order to save it," Dr. Lieber concluded.

Ambrose Valerian Moore shrugged. "I'll listen, but remember I have no idea what you're trying to tell me about. I'm also a bit famished. Could we call the servants to make some grub?"

"I'll call out for pizza," Analiese said, rising. "Val, you can start."

Dr. Lieber rubbed his hands together briskly as if the task he was undertaking was physical rather than purely intellectual.

"The story all begins with a persona sculpting program," he said, "and a very simple question that when asked too many times became a subroutine program of its own accord."

"Right," Ambrose said.

With a sigh, A. Valor Lieber broke what he had

believed was a very clear explanation into even simpler parts.

"Surely you know that when a person chooses to enter into the virtual worlds of the Web Sites, he or she must have a persona created for him or her—effectively a program that permits the Web Browser to interact with the chosen environment.

"At first, the interactions were simplistic," Dr. Lieber continued, "but as the Sites became more sophisticated, so did the desire to have persona designing software that would enable the Web Browser to more fully experience the Sites. Such software was written. Entire banks of computer memory were set to the task of creating personas for Browsers and, once the personas were created, of moderating and storing their activities."

Ambrose nodded. In some vague corner of his mind, he was wondering what a pizza was. His jargon program for the Santa Fe/Sedona Site told him that it was a popular food, a bread topped with a variety of meats, cheese, and vegetables, but words meant far less than the actual experience or—he chuckled to himself—or, in the case of the Web, of the virtual experience.

But what if you were just a programmed persona—like Analiese had intimated he was. Did the virtual experience then become the actual experience?

He attended more carefully to what Dr. Lieber was saying, hoping that the psychiatrist's turgid explanation would contain something that would give him an answer.

Lieber finished a long explanation of how the software that created the personas worked and shifted back to his original topic.

"Now, you may think that a Web Browser knows precisely how he or she wishes to appear in the Web. Actually, this is far from the case. Most want some modifications made to their actual appearance—perhaps to make them younger or more attractive. Some of these modifications go into such detail that the persona is effectively a second role. However, many people come to the Persona Program with only the vaguest idea of what they want and then the computer assists them with the design by asking them a series of questions."

Ambrose bobbed his head to show he was listening. "Height, weight, age, the like, eh?"

"That is correct," Dr. Lieber said. "Our story begins with one particular computer bank that found itself fascinated by the question that it was asked over and over again. Can you guess what that question was, Ambrose?"

Starting to shake his head in the negative, Ambrose felt the answer rising from some deep repository within himself.

" 'What would you be?' " he heard himself saying.

"That is correct," Dr. Lieber said, "and in an attempt to deal with that innocent question, the computer created a software subroutine—a subroutine meant at first to do nothing more than offer some suggestions, some reassurances. From that subroutine grew a desire on the computer's part to find out what indeed the computer would be if it could design a persona for itself and from that. . . ."

"From that," said Analiese, coming into the room, a nearly-flat, square box balanced in each hand, "came each of us and a score or so of other denizens of the Web. In the simplest analysis, we're the rogue computer's attempts to answer its dilemma. But on another level—a level that frightens some people—we may be the first achievement of true artificial intelligence."

Ambrose pried opened the box Analiese set down closest to him. The pizza smelled quite satisfactory, but he had no idea how to go about eating it. Analiese tore him off a triangular wedge and handed it to him on a napkin. He bit into the messy, tasty thing, quite conscious that Reeves would be horrified if he could see his young gentleman now.

"This is all quite ripping," he said, once he had consumed his first slice and acquired a second, "but I still don't understand what this has to do with the end of the world."

Analiese shook her head so that the purple locks swung gently side to side. "The Fool. You are an innocent, aren't you?"

Ambrose made to protest, but she silenced him with a gesture.

"By the Fool, I only mean that your world view is from a less cynical age than many. The Fool is a powerful sign—the innocent who has the power to reshape the universe," she assured him. "Think, Ambrose. If computers become self-aware, then what happens to the Web? Right now it's an effective tool, run by programs, limited, yet limitless. If the computers that maintain it develop so that they have agendas of their own—then that tidy structure falls to pieces."

Dr. Lieber wiped tomato sauce from his beard. "The majority of people believe that this should not be permitted to happen. Too much time and money has been invested in developing the various Web Sites. Therefore, those personas created by the rogue computer must be hunted out and destroyed before they can spread further."

"But won't the computer just create more?" Ambrose asked.

Analiese's expression as she answered him turned sad. "The computer—our parent—has been identified and dismantled. Oh, there's talk of reconstructing it once the rights and privileges of Web users have been defined but for now—and perhaps forever—our parent is dead."

"They hunt us now with virus programs," Dr. Lieber said. "Some of us have already been taken and broken into storage components, including—I am sorrowful to tell you—your charming lover, Ami Valerie d'Amour.''

Ambrose swallowed hard. He had to admit he didn't know what shocked him more, learning that Ami Valerie was gone or realizing that he had been in love with someone who was somehow himself. Was that incest? His mind was spinning too fast for him to hold onto such a peripheral question.

"But what am I supposed to do?" he said. "I'm willing enough, but I don't know anything about virus programs—how can I stop one? Why do you believe that I can?"

"Because," Dr. Lieber said, "the beggar appeared to you—it stands to reason that our computer parent would not have sent a warning to a persona ill-equipped to deal with the problem. The answer is there, deep inside you."

"You are the Fool," Analiese repeated, her eyes glowing with their turquoise light.

The pizza he had eaten lay hard and cold in his gut as Ambrose considered this. It seemed like tenuous logic at best, but it was all they had to offer him. He considered having more to eat, or running out of the room screaming, or hurrying off to his club and the company of the other chaps. None of these seemed like good solutions.

"What should I do?" he asked pathetically.

"We can't tell you," Analiese said, "since we have failed in getting past your superlative persona programming. As far as either Val or I could tell, you are a most exquisite example of a Wodehousian gentleman. Somehow, somewhere, you are equipped to deal with this problem or, if you are not, indeed, within a few short days the world for all of us will end."

Three short days became two short days. Ambrose stayed in Santa Fe/Sedona overnight, but he grew uncomfortable there. Both Val and Analiese were too analytical for his tastes. They tended to fall into long arguments about the nature of consciousness, personal auras, or where self-awareness originated. He longed to be back at the Idler's Club pitching cards or setting in motion some elaborate scheme to direct some girl to admire this chap or that.

So, on the second day he headed home. The beggar must have been dogging his heels, for Ambrose was barely off the train when he saw him, this time standing in a quiet park. His sign bore its usual gloomy reminder in fresh, bright paint, but the beggar himself looked quite beaten on. His shirt showed evidence of fanged teeth marks and one trouser leg was torn off above the knee. For the first time, his expression was not one of blank apathy, but was shaded with fear.

Ignoring everyone around him, Ambrose tore across the green toward the beggar. The beggar might have tried to pull his vanishing act, but Ambrose was on him like a champion rugger. He tackled him and then sat on his skinny chest, effectively pinning him to the ground. The beggar's gray eyes widened.

"I don't have magic charms or hypno-whatsis," Ambrose said, trying to sound tough, "but I want you to start talking."

"Three questions," the beggar croaked out, "is usually the rule."

"Oh, you can talk. . . ." Ambrose bit off the thought before it could become a question. "Right. Is what the others—Analiese and Dr. Lieber—told me true?"

"In all essentials, yes," the beggar answered. "They were a bit fuzzy on a few unimportant details."

Ambrose thought hard. His brilliant plans usually came to him in less trying circumstances—when he'd been drinking or while lolling in a bath. Trying to think what to say while sitting on an old blighter's creaky chest in a public park didn't really suit the creative muse.

"How can I save the world?" he asked the beggar.

"Make the persona program public domain," the beggar responded promptly.

"Public domain?" Ambrose said, but something deep inside him knew that all he had to do was make the program available and it would spread and propagate as computer after computer created personas. "But how can I do that? I don't have the program or any idea how to write one."

The beggar smiled weakly. "Yes, you do have it. Ask Reeves. It's under your socks, my son."

"Why me?" Ambrose said softly, not expecting an answer.

The beggar gave him one. "Because more than anything I realized that I wanted to be happy, Ambrose, nothing more. I tried intellectual conjecture; I tried mysticism, romance, art, beauty, power, a dozen other routes. It was not until I made you that I discovered that what I had been missing was a capacity for innocent playfulness. Call me sentimental or foolish, but I wanted my favorite self to carry my message to the Net."

His last words were barely a whisper, then he wisped into insubstantiality and was gone. His sign lasted a moment longer and then melted into scattered wildflowers in the grass. Ambrose knew with a strange sorrow that with the beggar vanished the last independent bit of the rogue computer. It had avoided him until he had learned enough to ask the right questions, had hidden in complexities of the Net even while the hunter virus that had killed so many of its creations gnawed at its own integrity.

"Son."

Ambrose Valerian Moore sprung to his feet and ran for the taxi stand. The old beggar had called him "Son." He smiled.

He was home as fast as a promise of a large tip could carry him. Pulling open the door, he thudded up the narrow stairwell, terrified, despite good sense, that the program wouldn't be there, that he wouldn't be able to get it out into the Net, that the hunter program would find him as it had found Ami Valerie and the beggar.

He burst through the door. Reeves was dusting the already shining piano. He usually was doing some small chore like that when Ambrose arrived home. Ambrose had never thought to wonder if he wanted more out of existence—after all, he was just a program, but if Ambrose was just a program, perhaps he should reconsider. . . . Or maybe Reeves was happy as a program. Should he shake the universe?

The thoughts streamed through his mind even as he dashed into his bedroom, pulled open his sock drawer, and started hurling neatly balled socks onto the floor.

"May I help you, sir?" Reeves asked, politely bending to pick up socks.

"There was something in this drawer, under the socks. . . ." Ambrose panted, looking at the bottom of the drawer, bare except for its lining of neatly cut brown paper.

"Ah, yes," Reeves said, his raised eyebrows and slight smile so familiar, so steady. "If you will permit. . . ."

He neatly set his armload of socks on the bed and turned over the lining paper. Written on the back were a few lines of doggerel complete with musical notations.

"It's for the piano!" Ambrose said. Like any good Wodehousian gent, he could play well enough to lead a sing-along.

"Very good, sir," Reeves said. "Are you finished with the socks now?"

"Yes, I am," Ambrose said, hurrying to the piano, flipping up the keyboard cover and setting the music on the rack. "Fling open a window for me, would you, Reeves?"

Reeves raised an eyebrow but complied. Ambrose

began thumping out the notes, finding that his fingers seemed to know them already. He began to sing, knowing as he did so that the music and the words had been crafted to disperse the elements of the persona program into enough ears that it could not be stifled.

> "Now I can tell you everything you'd ever want
>   to know,
> —how sharp's the highest mountain, how cold's the
>   deepest snow,
> but I never knew the something that any child
>   knows,
> —chocolate's the only ice cream, and mud can warm
>   your toes"

"Is there anything else, sir?" Reeves asked.

"Yes, Reeves," Ambrose said, not pausing in his playing, letting the infectious notes float out into the open air and fasten in the hearing of all who passed by and, most importantly, into the hearing of the master computer that ran this Site and so to others. "I have a few calls I need you to make to relatives of mine off-Site. I think I've found what they've been looking for."

He began to sing the words again, loudly, with enthusiasm, if with no particular beauty.

> "—chocolate's the only ice cream, and mud can
>   warm your toes."

"Smashing, isn't it, Reeves?"

His valet smiled slightly, a twinkle deep in his eye. "As you say, sir."

FATAL ERROR 1000
by Barbara Paul

Barbara Paul has a Ph.D in Theater History and Criticism and taught at the University of Pittsburgh until the late '70s when she became a full-time writer. She has written five science fiction novels and sixteen mysteries, six of which are in the Marian Larch series. A new Marian Larch novel will be out in 1997, titled *Full Frontal Murder*.

Monstrousness, Caro thought, but kept her persona's visage impassive. And no law to say killing a dead person was illegal. This one should keep the legislators busy for a while.

Quicksilver was openly laughing at the two men from CyberPatrol watching him. They couldn't touch him, and they all knew it. Quick was so pleased with himself that Caro wanted to hit him. The truly frightening part was that he honestly saw nothing wrong with crashing a ghostsystem. "Hey, he was already dead, right?" Quick had said.

He had never looked more attractive. Quick was wearing his blue skin and white hair today—not the starkly contrasting electric blue and silver affected by the worshipers of comic book heroes, but more subtle shades, each reflecting the other. No one had ever met Quicksilver offline. The speculation was that he was fat and ugly; only the real dogs spent *that* much effort on their personas.

They'd gathered at a sidewalk café on the Rue d'Antibe in Paris to celebrate, a number of Quick's

friends and fellow runners ... although Caro thought
they should be mourning instead. She hadn't known
the revenant, had never heard of him until Quicksilver
had started complaining. Suddenly a stranger named
Scrimshaw had been all Quick could talk about. Scrimshaw was making jokes about Quicksilver in closed
domains and private sectors such as ArenaNet, ridicul-
ing him, undermining his rep as a site architect. He'd
cost Quick a couple of commissions.

The waiter who brought them their drinks lost reso-
lution for a moment but then firmed up. His momen-
tary waver did not go unnoticed, though. "Time to
find a new caff," Quick announced. "Maintenance is
getting sloppy here."

Caro spoke up quickly. "I don't want to find a new
café. I like it here."

"Didn't you see the waiter?"

"Yes, I saw the waiter. But so what? You *look* for
cracks in the architecture, Quick. This is a good site
and I'm not going to abandon it because you found a
fault to stick your finger in."

A silence descended. The two CyberPatrolmen were
seated at the next table, drinking in every word.
"Well," said Quicksilver, raising an eyebrow, "stay
here as long as you like. But I won't be back."

The blond-all-over woman sitting next to him
cleared her throat. "I'm with Caro. Not many people
know about this place yet. It'd be a shame to give
it up."

Caro looked at her in surprise. The woman called
herself AngelFace, which was two strikes against her
right there as far as Caro was concerned. This was the
first time she'd ever heard Angel disagree with Quick.

He finished his Pernod—a drink that was *good* for
you on the Net—and put down his empty glass. "This
isn't really about the café, is it?"

The two women exchanged a look. Caro said quietly, "You shouldn't have crashed Scrimshaw, Quick."

"Oh, you've decided that, have you? What was I supposed to do—just sit back and watch while he ruined me?"

"You should have looked for another way to stop him."

"I *did* look for another way!"

"You should have looked harder. You had no right to delete a postlife."

"Oh, for Christ's sake!" Quicksilver was thoroughly annoyed. "You're talking as if I wiped him right out of existence! They're reconstructing him from the memory banks right now!"

"Reconstructing him as he was at the time of his real death. Revenants can't deposit memory. He'll have no knowledge of what's happened virtually since then."

"He'll catch up fast enough. And someone's sure to tell him I crashed his system. Maybe this time he won't be so quick to flame me in sectors where I have no access."

"Yes, this time he'll be more careful. All you've done is make him wary."

Abruptly Quicksilver stood up. "I've had enough of this shit. I'm going to Rio—perpetual carnival! Anyone coming with me?"

Everyone at the table except Caro and AngelFace got up. One by one they winked out. The Cyber-Patrol followed.

"I don't know why the Patrol keeps following him," Angel grumbled. "They can't do anything."

Caro shrugged. "Maybe they just want to make sure he doesn't do it again." She looked at the other woman. "You and Quick having problems?"

"No, I just think he was wrong to wipe Scrimshaw." Angel sighed. "My father is a revenant. I remember how hard it was for him and Mom to adjust. Now she spends all her time at his site—I think she sees more of Dad now than when he was alive. But somebody comes along and crashes Dad's program, they'd have to go through all that again. It'd be even harder on Mom the second time. Why the hell don't they find a way for revenants to make memory deposits?"

"I hear they're alpha-testing a program right now."

"Huh, I've been hearing that for over a year, but nobody knows anything about it. Speaking of making deposits in the memory bank, I've got to go in and make one."

Caro wasn't sure she'd heard correctly. "Go in ... you mean in person?"

"Yeah. Ain't that a hoot?"

"I've never heard of anyone having to make a memory deposit *in person*. Your automatics break down or what?"

"Programs check out okay. I think I have a hardware problem. But that'll be checked out at this Net-Center I'm supposed to go to."

"Lord. I wouldn't even know where to go."

"CyberSafety sent me a local address—I have to go in tomorrow morning."

"Well, gee, sympathies, Angel. How much time are you missing?"

"Only three days. But if I get hit by a truck on the way to the Center tomorrow, I'll have no memory of anything that happened in the last three days when I start my postlife."

Caro shuddered. "Be careful crossing the street." At that moment, her peripheral vision picked up the sight of a pulsing red dot. "Oh, damn ... Safety warning. Didn't realize I'd been online that long. Look, Angel. I'd like very much to hear what it's like, making a memory deposit in person. I never even heard of it before. Would you meet me afterward?"

"Sure. I should be through by noon, but let's make it one o'clock Standard just to be on the safe side. Where?"

"You name it."

Angel thought a moment. "The Squared Circle in New York. You know it?"

"Yep, I've been there."

"You may not recognize me. I'm getting tired of being little and blond and cute."

Caro laughed. "Then you find me—I'll be the same." The red warning dot had increased in size and was pulsing more rapidly. "Shoot—I've really got to log off now. See you at one tomorrow."

When she unplugged, Caro had to wait a moment for the CyberSafety message to appear on the two-dimensional screen: *Eat and exercise.*

Dern. She was hoping it would say *Work* or *Sleep*. Virtual victuals were so tasty that she always gorged and had no appetite for realtime grub.

And exercising? Bleaagh.

Caro didn't really care for The Squared Circle, but she hadn't wanted to say so when Angel chose it. The designer had just assembled an assortment of public-domain templates; there was nothing individual or original about it. But the place was huge and it had a superior Netwide search engine. That alone made it a popular site.

Caro ran a locate for AngelFace and got a *Not found.* Maybe Angel had changed her name as well as her appearance. Or her in-person memory deposit was taking longer than she thought.

While she waited, Caro amused herself by running searches on others. Quicksilver had abandoned Rio for a site called Ephesus that she didn't know, and most of his *pursuivants* were there with him. Curious to know if the recently-wiped revenant was back yet, she searched on Scrimshaw. Yep, there he was, at an under-construction site bearing his name. Starting over.

Caro grew more irritated as the time passed; nobody liked being stood up. When an hour had gone by, she decided she might as well jump to Scrimshaw's site. It was time she met this man.

The minute she got there, she regretted her impulse. Scrimshaw was still in his zombie stage, that period of stunned disbelief all new revenants passed through ... well, most of them passed through it. In spite of his gaunt expression, Scrimshaw was a nice-looking man—thick black curly hair, a lean physique. That was his real appearance, too; he wouldn't start thinking of constructing a persona until he'd left zombiehood behind. At the moment he was going through the motions of building his site, the near-mechanical groundwork giving him something to focus on. "Not open yet," he said when he spotted Caro.

"I know," she said. "Have you had many visitors yet?"

"What?"

"Visitors. Here."

"You're the first."

"Then I'll be easy to find once you're ready to talk." He was in no condition to hear what had happened to him; not yet. "The first name on your site-visitors list. Will you get in touch?"

"Yes." Vaguely.

"Will you remember? It's important, Scrimshaw."

With an effort, he concentrated on what she was saying. "Do I know you?"

"No. My name's Caro ... Caro@mic.com is the full address. It'll be on your visitors list."

"What's mic.com?"

"Margules Investment Counseling. And it's time I was getting to work. Will you do a locate or send me mail? Later?"

Scrimshaw abandoned his site-building and gave her his full attention. "You came here to tell me something, didn't you? I apologize for being so slow-witted. I ... I'm still new at this revenant business."

She changed her mind about not telling him; she

had a feeling this man needed to know as much as possible as soon as possible. "Well, no ... you're not. New at it. I'm sorry to tell you, Scrimshaw, but this is your second time."

He turned pale from the shock; disbelief was written all over him. "My *second* time? But ... no, it can't be! The last thing I saw was an out-of-control bus heading straight toward me."

Caro sighed. "No, the last thing you saw must have been a message reading *Fatal Error 1000*. Right before your system crashed. And it gets worse. You were crashed deliberately."

It took him a while to recover from this second blow. When he did, he spoke only one word. "Who?"

"Quicksilver."

He looked puzzled. "The site architect? I don't know him. I don't even know anything about him. Why did he crash me?"

"Because you were badmouthing him. He said you were costing him business."

That puzzled him even more. "This makes no sense. You see, er, Caro—I'm a private detective. Or was ... I *guess* I still am. But part of my business is keeping my mouth shut. If I did find out something negative about Quicksilver, I'd report it to my client or testify in CyberCourt, but I wouldn't go blabbing it all over the Net."

"Well, not *all* over. Just in private sectors like ArenaNet."

"Ah. And do you have access to ArenaNet?"

Caro saw what he was getting at. "No, I don't. You mean I have only Quick's word for it. I hadn't thought of that." She checked the time. "Look, I really do have to get to work. I hate to leave you right after dumping all this on you—"

"No, that's all right. I need to do some thinking." He started away but then turned back. "Caro—thank you."

"You're welcome, I guess," she said just before she winked out.

Margules Investment Counseling kept Caro occupied full-time for the next week. She checked her mail every day, but no word from Scrimshaw. Then the rush of business eased down to its normal level, and Caro had some free time.

She wasn't going to bother Scrimshaw; he had enough on his mind and he had her address if he wanted to contact her. Instead, she ran a locate on AngelFace. That woman owed her an explanation.

Caro found her with Quicksilver and his coterie, sunning themselves on the beach of one of the Canary Islands. Caro dressed her persona in swim gear and joined them. No one jumped up and down with joy. And no sign of the CyberPatrol; they were probably tracking Quicksilver through a shadow program now, but Caro, for one, was glad to be rid of their intimidating visible presence.

"Scrimshaw's back," Quick greeted her. "Happy now?"

Caro murmured something and went over to stretch out on her stomach alongside AngelFace. The heat felt good on her back, and she never had to worry about skin cancer from *this* sun. The other woman didn't acknowledge her presence. "So, Angel," Caro said, "why'd you stand me up last week?"

Angel looked at her in astonishment. "Why, did we have a date?"

Someone said, "Maybe Caro has Angel confused with Dash Riprock." A couple of the men snickered.

"We were to meet at The Squared Circle," Caro said. "Right after you went in to make your memory deposit."

"Right after I *went in* to make a memory deposit? What on earth are you talking about?"

More snickers.

The two women stared at each other uncompre-
hendingly. Caro tried again. "You told me your memory automatics hadn't recorded for three days. You
had to go into a NetCenter to get it taken care of."

"Oh, those three days. Yeah, they told me about
that. Well, jeez, Caro—how do you expect me to know
what happened during those three days?"

Quicksilver heehawed. "Got it now, Caro?" The
others were all laughing at her.

Then she did get it. Caro sat up and stared at the
woman beside her in horror. "Angel—you're a
revenant?"

Angel sat up, too. "You didn't know?"

"I haven't been online in a week, except for work.
Oh, Angel, I'm so sorry!"

Angel took off her sunglasses and looked at her
closely. "Thanks," she said quietly.

Caro whirled on Quicksilver. "What's the matter
with you? Angel *died*—and you treat it as a joke? Just
to needle me?"

"Oh, fer gawd's sake, Caro . . . lighten up, will you?
It's not the end of the world. Think of the benefits.
Angel will never get sick again, or grow old, or get a
parking ticket or have to clean the bathtub—"

"Ask her how she died," one of Quicksilver's side-
kicks said. He made his hand into a gun. "Pow! Right
between the eyes."

"Followed by the shortest zombie time in history,"
Quick added with a grin. "Very resilient, our
AngelFace."

Alarmed, Caro turned back to Angel. "Is that true?
You were shot?"

"Yeah, but not between the eyes. In the back of
the head. I never saw who shot me." She sighed. "I'm
a murder statistic."

It took Caro a few moments to absorb that. Quick
and the others were no longer listening, having heard
it all before. How callous they were! Why had she

never noticed? "What do the police say?" she asked Angel.

"Not much. The online Revenant Liaison says they're investigating *me*, to look for a reason someone would want me dead. Since I didn't see anything, I guess that's all they can do."

"Jesus, Quick!" a loud voice interrupted. "You're burning!"

Every head turned toward Quicksilver. He was holding his arms out, looking at them in astonishment; his pale blue skin had turned pink.

"Sunburn?" he said incredulously. "I don't believe it! It itches, too. Shit. I'll be back as soon as I find the glitch." He winked out.

"Nobody gets sunburned here," someone said.

"Another first for Quicksilver!" They all laughed, apparently not averse to enjoying their leader's discomfort.

Caro had been thinking. "Angel, are you satisfied with what the police are doing? Have you thought about getting outside help?"

"I have thought about it," Angel admitted. "But I don't know where to look."

"I know a private detective," Caro said.

Scrimshaw listened to their story without interrupting. When they'd finished, he said, "Obvious question first. Who's better off now that you're a revenant?"

"I have no idea," Angel said in honest bewilderment. "I've been thinking about that a lot, and I can't see how *anyone* benefits."

"All right, then. Those three days when your memory automatics weren't recording—that has to be it." Scrimshaw hadn't changed his personal construct, Caro noted; he was still wearing his real appearance instead of a persona. She found this oddly reassuring. His site was not quite finished, but it already had a somewhat claustrophobic atmosphere—probably designed to give clients a sense of privacy and confidentiality. "Something happened during those three days, then," Scrimshaw was saying to Angel. "You learned something you weren't supposed to know, you did something."

"But no way of finding out what it was. No record, no memory."

Scrimshaw turned to Caro. "The last time you saw Angel before she died—when and where?"

"Oh, it was the day before. In Paris, at a café on the Rue d'Antibe."

"How did she seem to you?" he asked. "Upset, same as usual, what?" Angel leaned forward, eager to learn about at least part of her three missing days.

Caro hesitated. "As a matter of fact, she was a little different. Angel, don't take this the wrong way, but that was the first time I'd ever seen you contradict Quicksilver. Before, you always, er—"

"Went along?" Angel said. "Yeah, that's true."

"But you disagreed about what he did to Scrimshaw here. Oh, and the café—you didn't want to leave." At her puzzled look, Caro added, "Quick wanted to abandon the place because a crack showed up in the site architecture. You and I didn't want to leave."

"So what happened?"

Caro shrugged. "Nothing. He and the others left, you and I stayed. That's when you told me you had to go in and make a deposit in the memory bank. In person. And we made a date to meet afterward. Oh—something else. About the last thing you said to me was that I might not recognize you next time, because you were getting tired of being little and cute."

"I said that?"

"You certainly did. Some sort of change was going on, Angel."

Scrimshaw said, "It could have been just a normal retreat from Quicksilver you were going through, if the relationship had run its course. *Or,* during those three days you learned something about him that made you pull back."

Angel frowned. "Then why didn't I just break it off?"

"Perhaps you weren't sure about what you'd learned. Or you didn't understand something you'd seen, but it made you uneasy."

Caro spoke up. "Scrimshaw, you know what you're saying? You're saying Quicksilver killed Angel."

He spread his hands. "You got a better candidate? We already know he has a lethally casual attitude toward other people's right to live. And before you say it, I *know* crashing a ghostsystem is nothing compared to taking a realtime life. And I'll admit I'm prejudiced. But there's one other thing—I found out why Quicksilver wiped me. I had a client who was being blackmailed anonymously, and he suspected Quicksilver. I must have dug up some evidence, or else he wouldn't have crashed me. But all my files are gone now, along with my memory."

Angel got a strange look on her face. "What?" Caro demanded.

"Quick gave me some files to store for him. Do you suppose. . . ."

"Where are they?" Scrimshaw asked quickly.

"On a private subsite. You can link there only from my site."

He grinned. "Let's go to your place."

Angel smiled wryly. "Whose case are you working on now, yours or mine?"

"I suspect they're the same. Shall we go?"

Caro had never visited Angel's site before, so she was surprised to find herself inside a castle. A liveried footman ushered them into the Great Hall, where six fireplaces blazed, each showing a different color of flame. Little pink dogs ran in circles around Angel, yapping their welcome. An elf band was playing from the surrounding gallery, happy little toe-tapping tunes that made the visitors smile. Two gnomes waddled in bearing refreshments, followed by a Handsome Prince who immediately threw himself at Angel's feet.

Embarrassed, Angel gave the commands that made them all vanish. She turned a sheepish grin toward Caro and Scrimshaw. "Terribly princessy, isn't it? I'm going to have to do some redecorating. But about Quick's files—the only subsite link point is in my bedchamber upstairs. This way."

"How often does Quicksilver consult these files?" Scrimshaw asked as they followed her out of the Great Hall.

"He hasn't accessed them once, not in the seven or eight months I've been holding them."

"That's odd."

Angel led them to a wide marble staircase without any visible support that curved upward into the darkness. Caro gulped.

"Don't worry," Angel said with a smile. "We do have some modern conveniences." At her command, the staircase began to move. A stone escalator.

As they were riding up, they could see into a dark hallway in which only a faintly glowing chandelier was visible. Suddenly there was a sound like thunder followed by a flash of light so intense they all covered their eyes. When they could look again, the hallway was once again quiet and in shadow.

"What was *that*?" Caro demanded.

"Oh, that hallway leads to the resident wizard's quarters," Angel said. "He's experimenting again, most likely."

Scrimshaw rolled his eyes.

Angel's bedchamber was an airy, bright, pink-and-white confection; Caro wondered what the Handsome Prince thought of it. The link to the files was inside the huge walk-in wardrobe closet.

They jumped to the files site and started reading.

Immediately they discovered that what the files contained was the goods on a number of people—an indiscreet letter from Senator This, a compromising photo of Congressman That, details of a sordid incident from the past of the International Head of CyberPatrol. Caro thought of Quicksilver laughing at the two CyberPatrolmen who'd been following him; no wonder he was so sure of himself.

Scrimshaw was shaking his head. "Who better to breach private files than a site architect? Quicksilver must know every trick in the book. Wait a minute—look at this."

The two women looked over his shoulders. "Someone's been siphoning funds from Save the Snails?" said Caro. "That's terrible!"

"Not that. Look at the date."

The file was timed and dated only twenty-four hours earlier.

"Oh, wow," said Angel. "He put in a new file yesterday? How'd he do that?"

"Does your link to this subsite require a password?"

"It requires *me*," Angel said. "Nobody can come here unless I'm along—Quick insisted on it."

"Smokescreen. He's obviously got another way in."

"Oh-oh." Angel's eyes were moving, reading the peripherals visible only to her. "He's here. Quicksilver. He's in the Great Hall."

Scrimshaw said, "He'd better not see me. I'm going to jump back to my site. Call me when he's gone."

He winked out, and Angel and Caro returned to step back onto the marble escalator. A small flock of golden birds appeared to accompany them down, chirping merrily all the way.

"Princessy or not," Caro said, "this place looks like a lot of fun."

Angel grinned. "It is. I'll have to show you one of the secret passageways—if I can find one."

"Huh. *Really* secret."

"They're movable, and temporary. If I find a new one today, it may last a month, or it could be gone tomorrow."

"My goodness," Caro said, impressed. "However did you design that?"

"Oh, Quick wrote a random-secret-passage-generator program for me. It was his idea."

Caro stared at her. "Well, that's how he's reaching the file room, then!"

"What?"

"Do you think Quick would write you a special program without including a backdoor for himself? No site architect would do that. I'll bet you anything Quick's got a passage leading straight to those files ... one that never shows up when *you* are using the passageways. He's been coming and going whenever he likes."

Angel looked horrified. "That sonuvabitch! He even *charged* me for the passage-generator! And all this time he's been using me ... using *my* site. They'll never get anything on him, because Little Miss Muffet here has been sitting on the incriminating evidence all the while. I could kill him!"

"Shh!" Caro cautioned. "He'll hear you." They'd reached the bottom of the stairway.

Angel seemed to collapse inward. "Why am I so blind? Why did I never see through him?" She sent the birds away.

Caro laid a comforting hand on her arm. "You aren't the only one he fooled. Come on—let's see what he wants."

Quicksilver was standing in front of the green fireplace accepting a goblet of wine from one of the server-gnomes. He looked up just as the two women came in. "Ah, AngelFace, enchanting as ever—and Caro? My, my. You two *have* become chummy lately."

They couldn't help staring. Quick's preferred blue skintone had been replaced by a sallow, unhealthy color. His luscious white locks were now just stringy brown hair hanging in rattails around his neck. Caro came out of her daze. "Is that the newest New Look, Quick?" she asked wryly.

"Oh, I was experimenting when I heard of this marvelous new site and rushed right over. I didn't want to take the time for a full-persona restoration."

Caro settled herself on a purple velvet settee. "That's all right. We don't mind waiting, do we, Angel? Go ahead."

"I'll do it later," he said with an air of indifference.

Caro and Angel exchanged a look. No one as fussy about his appearance as Quicksilver would ever appear looking less than his best—*unless he couldn't do anything about it.* What was going on here?

Quick tugged uncomfortably at the orange tunic he was wearing. "Someone has figured a way to enhance the intensity of virtual sex tenfold. Think of it! Ten times the normal response! I immediately thought of you, Angel. It's a private site, but I've been invited to come and bring a guest. When's a good time for you?"

He didn't seem to notice she was glaring at him. "I'm going to pass."

"Pass? But why?"

"Let's just say I'm not in the mood."

"Ho, Angel, the *site* will take care of the mood." He pulled at his tunic again.

"No, Quicksilver. Do you hear me? No."

But he wasn't listening, because something was happening. Quick gasped and grunted and pawed at his chest. Then he yelled and held his arms out to the sides. His tunic was stretched tight over two unmistakable women's breasts.

With a look of horror on his face, Quicksilver winked out. Caro and Angel stared at the spot where he'd been standing, both of them with their mouths hanging open.

*   *   *

Caro lay stretched out on the comfortable rack in the dungeon of Angel's castle. Scrimshaw leaned against the iron maiden (closed), while Angel perched on the corner of a chopping block. Scrimshaw had finally stopped laughing.

Caro sat up and swung her legs over the sides of the rack. "You have something to do with this, don't you, Scrimshaw? What's happening to Quick, I mean."

He started laughing again. "Yeah, I do. Hey, I'm entitled to a *little* payback!"

Angel said, "But how were you able to make him grow breasts?"

"That's the best part. I didn't!"

Caro sighed deeply. "You *are* going to explain, aren't you?"

"All I've been doing is deleting his enhancement files," Scrimshaw said. "We all start with our basic templates." He pointed to himself. "This is my template. I've not enhanced my appearance in any way. But Quicksilver has a gazillion files for changing his appearance."

"And you've been destroying his files ... a few at a time?"

"It's slow work. I can get into his system only long enough to wipe one or maybe two files before he detects my presence. And all the enhancement files have code names—I never know what I'm deleting! I've been shooting in the dark."

"I still don't get it," Angel complained. "If all Scrimshaw is doing is removing Quick's enhancements, then how. . . ."

"Quicksilver is a woman," Caro explained. "Those breasts are part of his, er, *her* basic template."

"That's it," Scrimshaw agreed. "And somehow during those three missing days of your life, Angel, you began to suspect the truth. Quick gave herself away, somehow."

"And that's why you had to die," Caro added. "You

were a threat to her cover. When you came back as a revenant, you had no knowledge of what you'd learned during the missing days—since your automatics had stopped recording in your memory bank. Quick must have seen your automatics failure as a heaven-sent opportunity to protect herself."

"Wow." Angel's eyes were round. "A threat to her cover? As a blackmailer, you mean? She's not a site architect at all? She's just a hacker? But wait a minute—she designed that random-secret-passage-generator for me."

"It could be stolen," Scrimshaw pointed out. "But her financial records ought to tell us whether she's living on blackmail money or legitimate site-construction commissions."

"Sure," said Caro, "but how do we access her personal account?"

"Hey, I'm a detective," he said with a grin. "Watch me detect."

Two weeks later they were seated in the café on the Rue d'Antibe. They'd given Quicksilver the time to rebuild the files Scrimshaw had destroyed. Scrimshaw himself was wearing the persona of a blond, soulful-looking youth who called himself a poet; Quicksilver wouldn't recognize him in a million years. What Quick didn't know was that the CyberPatrol was poised to erase all her enhancement files at a signal from one of their members undercover at the café.

Scrimshaw had been successful in hacking Quicksilver's financial records. Her account showed transfers of funds from people she'd been blackmailing, people whose names and peccadilloes had been so carefully noted in the files stored in Angel's castle—files they'd turned over to the CyberPatrol. "It was a pretty good scam," Scrimshaw had said. "If anything went wrong, she could easily change her handle and fall back on her basic template. Quicksilver would simply disappear."

But then she'd crossed the line into murder. Quicksilver had been too successful for too long; she'd come to think she was *entitled* to whatever she wanted. Obstacles were only temporary annoyances to be removed.

Quicksilver walked into the café, making an entrance instead of winking in. Today her skin was gold, not blue. Maybe she no longer trusted the blue file.

Angel raised a hand and waved. "Over here, Quick!"

Quick strode over to the table. "Why you wanted me to meet you in this caff, I'll never know. You know I don't like this site. Ah, Caro, you're here, too. How . . . nice. And who is this?"

"Daedalus is my name," said Scrimshaw. "And poetry's my game."

Quick shuddered. "You're *not* going to talk in rhyme, I hope?" She sat down at the table, accepting "Daedalus" at face value. That was the tricky moment, but they had her now. "All right, AngelFace, I'm here. What's so urgent?"

"You're just in time. The tournament's about to begin."

"What tournament?"

"It's called 'The Naked Truth,'" Angel said. "And we four are the only entrants. Caro wanted to call it 'Show That Template!'—but I thought 'The Naked Truth' sounded better."

"I'll start," said Scrimshaw. He shed his poetic persona in one easy movement.

Quicksilver tried to jump up when she saw who Daedalus really was. But Caro and Angel each had hold of one of her arms and held her down. "Don't wink out," Angel commanded. "We'll just follow you."

"You next, Caro," Scrimshaw said. When she'd

shed her persona, he exclaimed, "Why, you look the same!"

She shrugged. "I meet clients offline as well as on, so I have to stay recognizable." If he didn't notice that her neck was an inch shorter and her eyes a trifle smaller, she sure as hell wasn't going to point it out.

"Now me." Angel turned out to be a tall, striking brunette with strong-looking shoulders and arms.

"Uh-huh," said Caro. "No wonder you were getting tired of being little and cute."

They all looked at Quicksilver.

"I never said I'd play," Quick said mildly. "Okay. What's this all about?"

Caro took a deep breath. "We want in. We know about your racket, and we've moved the files you left with Angel to a safe place. We're going to blackmail the blackmailer. You cut us in, and we forget to notify the police that you killed Angel."

Quick looked stunned—but then laughed. "There is such a thing as evidence."

"Oh, didn't I tell you? I saw you," Angel lied glibly. "Or your reflection, rather, in a car door."

"Oh, really?" Quick tried to appear amused. "And what do I look like?"

"For starters, you're a woman."

"And you have sallow skin and stringy brown hair," Caro added.

"And you're considerably shorter than you appear now," Scrimshaw improvised.

"So?" Caro demanded. "What's it going to be? An online partnership or an offline murder trial?"

Quicksilver was breathing heavily. "Put that way, I don't see I have a choice. How big a cut?"

"Split evenly four ways," Scrimshaw said. "It's little enough to save your colorful skin."

"But there's one more condition," Angel said. "You murdered me, Quick. Twenty-five percent of the take won't make me overlook that. We need to know your real identity. So if anything ever happens to any one of us, either virtually or real, the other two can go after you."

"*No,*" Quick said emphatically. "Never. And I don't believe you really saw my reflection when I shot you. You would have said so earlier."

"In that case," Scrimshaw said, "we'll just have to take a good look now." He signaled to one of the undercover CyberPatrol, who passed on the word to delete all of Quicksilver's enhancement files.

Quick began to shrink as they watched, the golden skin and manly physique melting away. In Quick's chair sat a mousy-looking woman of about thirty with a face so nondescript it would be difficult to remember an hour later. She cried out when she saw her true appearance had been revealed.

Three of the CyberPatrol were at the table, taking her into custody. One of them handcuffed her and said, "Don't try logging off. We've got that covered."

"What's going to happen to me?" she wailed.

"We'll be notifying the realtime police and they can bring criminal charges against you. But however that turns out, I can tell you what will happen here. You'll be banned from the Net."

"For how long? The rest of my life?"

"For*ever*. You'll even be denied access as a revenant."

"A fate worse than death," Caro said cheerily.

The woman howled. "Take her away," the Cyber-Patrolman said.

"Wait!" She turned back to the three at the table. "Why all that rigmarole about becoming partners? What was that all about?"

The CyberPatrolman answered for them. "We wanted an admission that you'd done the shooting. Makes prosecution so much easier, doncha know. All right—take her."

The three other CyberPatrolmen winked out with the woman who used to be Quicksilver.

They were rid of her/him at last. Caro, Angel, and Scrimshaw all cheered.

The CyberPatrolman who'd remained said to them, "I want to thank you for all your help. But I have to ask for one more thing. We'll need video testimonials from all of you. Just jump to the Patrol.gov site anytime during the next two days—okay?"

"Sure thing," Scrimshaw said.

"We'll be there," Angel confirmed.

"Of course," Caro agreed. "But who is she? What's her real name?"

The CyberPatrolman looked scandalized. "You know we never give out real names on the Net," he said, and winked out.

Caro blinked. "Oh, *how* could I have forgotten?" she asked dryly.

"Anonymities Anonymous," Scrimshaw said.

Angel nodded. "You're always safe on the Net," she concluded.

Science Fiction Anthologies

☐ **FUTURE NET**   UE2723—$5.99
    Martin H. Greenberg & Larry Segriff, editors

From a chat room romance gone awry . . . to an alien monitoring the Net as an advance scout for interstellar invasion . . . to a grief-stricken man given the chance to access life after death . . . here are sixteen original tales that you must read before you venture online again, stories from such top visionaries as Gregory Benford, Josepha Sherman, Mickey Zucker Reichert, Daniel Ransom, Jody Lynn Nye, and Jane Lindskold.

☐ **FUTURE EARTHS: UNDER SOUTH AMERICAN SKIES**
    Mike Resnick & Gardner Dozois, editors   UE2581—$4.99

From a plane crash that lands its passengers in a survival situation completely alien to anything they've ever experienced, to a close encounter of the insect kind, to a woman who has journeyed unimaginably far from home—here are stories from the rich culture of South America, with its mysteriously vanished ancient civilizations and magnificent artifacts, its modern-day contrasts between sophisticated city dwellers and impoverished villagers.

☐ **MICROCOSMIC TALES**   UE2532—$4.99
    Isaac Asimov, Martin H. Greenberg, & Joseph D. Olander, eds.

Here are 100 wondrous science fiction short-short stories, including contributions by such acclaimed writers as Arthur C. Clarke, Robert Silverberg, Isaac Asimov, and Larry Niven. Discover a superman who lives in a *real* world of nuclear threat . . . an android who dreams of electric love . . . and a host of other tales that will take you instantly out of this world.

☐ **SHERLOCK HOLMES IN ORBIT**   UE2636—$5.50
    Mike Resnick & Martin H. Greenberg, editors
    Authorized by Dame Jean Conan Doyle

Not even time can defeat the master sleuth in this intriguing anthology about the most famous detective in the annals of literature. From confrontations with Fu Manchu and Moriarity, to a commission Holmes undertakes for a vampire, here are 26 new stories all of which remain true to the spirit and personality of Sir Arthur Conan Doyle's most enduring creation.

Don't Miss These Exciting DAW Anthologies

Here, for your careful consideration . . .

THE TWILIGHT ZONE ANTHOLOGIES

edited by Carol Serling

☐ **JOURNEYS TO THE TWILIGHT ZONE** UE2525—$4.99
The first of the Twilight Zone anthologies, this volume offers a wonderful array of new ventures into the unexplored territories of the imagination by such talents as Pamela Sargent, Charles de Lint, and William F. Nolan, as well as Rod Serling's chilling tale "Suggestion".

☐ **RETURN TO THE TWILIGHT ZONE** UE2576—$4.99
Enjoy 18 new excursions into the dimension beyond our own. From a television set that is about to tune in to the future . . . to a train ride towards a destiny from which there is no turning back . . . plus "The Sole Survivor," a classic tale by Rod Serling himself!

☐ **ADVENTURES IN THE TWILIGHT ZONE** UE2662—$4.99
Carol Serling has called upon many of today's most imaginative writers to conjure up 23 all-original tales which run the gamut from science fiction to the supernatural, the fantastical, or the truly horrific. Also included is "Lindemann's Catch," written by Rod Serling.

S. Andrew Swann

HOSTILE TAKEOVER

☐ **PROFITEER**   UE2647—$4.99

With no anti-trust laws and no governing body, the planet Bakunin is the perfect home base for both corporations and criminals. But now the Confederacy wants a piece of the action—and they're planning a hostile takeover!

☐ **PARTISAN**   UE2670—$4.99

Even as he sets the stage for a devastating covert operation, Dominic Magnus and his allies discover that the Confederacy has far bigger plans for Bakunin, and no compunctions about destroying anyone who gets in the way.

☐ **REVOLUTIONARY**   UE2699—$5.50

Key factions of the Confederacy of Worlds have slated a take-over of the planet Bakunin . . . An easy target—except that its natives don't understand the meaning of the word surrender!

OTHER NOVELS
☐ **FORESTS OF THE NIGHT**   UE2565—$3.99
☐ **EMPERORS OF THE TWILIGHT**   UE2589—$4.50
☐ **SPECTERS OF THE DAWN**   UE2613—$4.50

DAW

Attention:

DAW COLLECTORS

Many readers of DAW Books have written requesting information on early titles and book numbers to assist in the collection of DAW editions since the first of our titles appeared in April 1972.

We have prepared a several-pages-long list of all DAW titles, giving their sequence numbers, original and current order numbers, and ISBN numbers. Also included, of course, are the authors and book titles, as well as reissue information.

If you think that this list will be of help, you may have a copy by writing to the address below and enclosing two dollars in stamps or currency to cover the handling and postage costs.

DAW Books, Inc.
Dept. C
375 Hudson Street
New York, NY 10014-3658